Stargazer

ALSO BY ANNE HILLERMAN

The Tale Teller

Cave of Bones

Song of the Lion

Rock with Wings

Spider Woman's Daughter

Tony Hillerman's Landscape:
On the Road with Chee and Leaphorn

Gardens of Santa Fe

Santa Fe Flavors:
Best Restaurants and Recipes

Ride the Wind: USA to Africa

Stargazer

A Leaphorn, Chee & Manuelito Novel

Anne Hillerman

HARPER LARGE PRINT

An Imprint of HarperCollinsPublishers

HarperCollins books may be purchased for educational, business, or sales promotional use. For information, please e-mail the Special Markets Department at SPsales@harpercollins.com.

FIRST HARPER LARGE PRINT EDITION

ISBN: 978-0-06-306303-7

Library of Congress Cataloging-in-Publication Data is available upon request.

21 22 23 24 25 LSC 10 9 8 7 6 5 4 3 2 1

In honor of Jerome Montgomery Edwards,
Robbie Gallegos, and James Hanson.
Rest in peace, dear friends. Sweet memories of your
rich and valuable lives brighten my days.

Killers are all around us. They are you and me. They may be in the next room, the next house, or the next neighborhood. It matters not where you live. There is no safe place on earth.

—PSYCHOLOGIST DAVID M. BUSS,
THE MURDERER NEXT DOOR

1

He knew he was a lucky guy. First of all, how many guys loved their jobs, made good money, and could honestly say their work had changed the way people saw the world? He'd recently returned to a part of the planet he loved, a place where the night sky shone with brilliance. He was proud of their fine son, although he had to give his estranged wife and her brother credit for raising him. The woman he'd married twenty years ago remained lovely and engaging, and now that he had moved closer to her, he could recapture her affection. His current girlfriend, a fellow scientist, was just a placeholder.

That night's dinner date began encouragingly, two old friends catching up face-to-face. He sipped a glass of cabernet, but she stayed with sparkling water. She'd asked about his work and listened with attention to the details of his research on black holes and gravity. He offered simplified versions of his latest discovery and a knotty issue with his colleagues. She posed interesting questions and laughed at his jokes. She mentioned how she enjoyed her own work and being close to family again.

Her smile convinced him that he could persuade her to give their relationship another chance.

But as their dinner drew to a close, he began to have doubts. When he reached for the check, she said they should split the bill and didn't want to back down. The heat of her outrage over something he viewed as trivial stirred memories of other fights. She stomped out of the restaurant while he paid. The woman wasn't all sweetness.

He opened the passenger door and she slid in, as lithe and graceful as he remembered, and still angry.

Although they had talked on the phone periodically about their son, he hadn't seen her for years before this evening. He was struck by how she had aged into her beauty. She'd gained attractive womanly curves, which, along with the shimmers of gray in her smooth dark hair, added to her appeal.

His car roared to life and then, good Jaguar that it was, began to purr. As they drove toward her house, the warm air created by the car's heater brought a surprise, a scent that stirred deep, pleasant memories, her enticing fragrance of almonds. He flashed back to when she would ask him to rub her favorite almond lotion on the deliciously soft skin of her back and the way one thing led to another. He remembered all over again why he'd fallen for her. Remembered as if it were yesterday. He reached for her hand, but she pulled away.

He adjusted the rearview mirror to deflect the lights of the vehicle behind him. Out here on the plains of central New Mexico, where everything sat at a distance, he appreciated a smooth ride. Tonight, under the canopy of October stars, he was glad that getting to her place meant a long drive on a lonely road with time for her temper to cool and an abundance of places to pull over and, he hoped, refresh some memories.

She didn't bring up the past and neither did he until they had driven awhile. He was about to present the reasons he deserved another chance when she broke the silence.

"If you hadn't called me to set up our date tonight, I would have called you. We've lived apart for years, gone our separate ways. I'd like to formalize our situation. I want to wrap up the divorce. We need to move forward."

He felt his throat tighten. "I took the job out here partly because I wanted to be with you. You sounded happy when I told you about the opportunity. I hoped we could move forward, too, but together and better than before. Let's give it a try."

"No." Her earrings made a faint tinkling sound as she shook her head. "We had some good times, but it wasn't all wonderful. You know that. That's why we split. We listened when our hearts spoke years ago and we moved on. I'm thrilled for you professionally. It's wonderful that you have this great job. You're a fine man, smart, even handsome for a middle-aged bilagáana." He heard the smile in her voice, but it didn't soften her message.

"I was done with our marriage when I moved out. That hasn't changed. I'm sorry about what happened tonight at the restaurant; I didn't mean to have a tantrum. Remember how angry I used to get? And you'd lose it, too. Let's not fight anymore."

He remembered hitting her, her striking back, the guilt that came with it, the sweet lovemaking when they forgave each other. He pulled onto the road's shoulder. "I was younger then and, well, immature. I'm still crazy about you. I had a good time tonight and you did, too, didn't you? Let's do more of that."

"We can be friends. I'd like that. But I'm moving forward with the divorce."

He felt every ounce of good energy from the evening drain away. "You don't have to worry about my black moods from our old days. I have that depression under control. And you aren't drinking. We'd have a chance this time. Be reasonable. You know our son wants us to get back together. I've always loved you. My life would mean so much more with you in it."

He noticed her shifting in the seat next to him, her motion releasing a hint of perfume into the car's darkness. Was she getting ready to put her hand on his leg? To acquiesce? No, she seemed to be looking for something in her purse.

"New Mexico has no-fault divorce. I filled out the papers and I brought a copy for you."

A sudden tsunami of sadness washed over him, sweeping away his hope and leaving sadness in its place. "Stop it. I don't want a divorce." He raised his voice. "When you agreed to dinner, I thought it meant something."

"It meant a meal shared with a friend. That's all. Can't you understand that?"

"I thought you still loved me. At least I hoped you did."

"No." Her voice grew louder, too. "I haven't been in love with you for a long, long time. You've got a girlfriend. You're a bright guy when it comes to looking at the stars, but not so much when it comes to dealing with people. Why do you always have to be so difficult? We should have divorced years ago."

"You're breaking my heart. Your boyfriend must have put you up to this. You have a boyfriend, don't you?"

"That's none of your stinking business." She spit out the words.

"I know you still care about me. I'm fighting you every step of the way." He clenched the steering wheel until he had his emotions under control. "I could turn your life into a living hell. Don't make me do that." The darkness hid his tears, but he knew she heard the ragged edges of desperation in his voice.

"You're pathetic. I don't have to take your craziness anymore. I'm finished with this and with you."

That was when he remembered the gun.

2

Socorro County Sheriff's Detective Tara Williams picked up the call. The president of the Alamo Navajo school board, Ralph Apacheito, sounded breathless. He got right to the point.

"My son, Raul, found a dead man."

"What?"

"Yeah. Early this morning when he was out on the mesa hunting rabbits. He saw a car and went to check it out. He told me about the body in the front seat."

She'd dealt with Apacheito before when a situation arose where a tribal member got crossways with the county law enforcement. They'd built some rapport. "Is the boy playing a trick on you?"

"No, no joke. He ran home crying and he's still shaking. At times like this, I wish his mother was still alive."

"Did you call the Navajo Police?"

"Yeah. They said to call you because it looks like where Raul saw the car, that's the county's jurisdiction. Anyway, you know Officer Pino is on leave."

The man who ran the Alamo Navajo police operations, Peyton Pino, had broken his leg in a freak accident last month. Calls were routed to the Navajo Police in To'Hajiilee, a town about a ninety-minute drive to the north, farther than Williams's office in Socorro. She had teased Peyton that he should station her friend Bernadette Manuelito down this way. Bernie worked out of the Shiprock district and, Williams heard, had a reputation as a good officer.

"Did Raul tell you what kind of car and where it was parked?"

"Hold on a minute."

When Apacheito came back on the line, he gave her approximate directions and the eight-year-old's description of the vehicle. "I'll get him to show you where it is if you need that."

"I'm on my way. I'm sure I can find the car. How's Raul doing?"

"He's scared that a bad guy will shoot him. I called his teacher and told her what happened. She's coming to help deal with all this."

"Good."

"Stop in for coffee when you're done out there."

"Thanks for the offer. We'll see." If Raul really had found a dead man, she'd have no time for socializing.

Williams headed off. Normally her partner, Bob Rockfeld, would have been on duty, too, but he had the day off. A call like this probably didn't warrant two officers anyway. She had seen death but never dealt with a homicide in the three years she'd spent as a beat officer, nor in this inaugural year of work as a detective.

If the deceased had experienced a natural death—a heart attack, an aneurysm, a diabetic coma came to mind—she wouldn't have a crime to investigate. Ditto if it was a suicide. And if the death was homicide, the car and its occupant might be on Navajo Nation tribal land despite what To'Hajiilee had said. In that case, the FBI would be involved.

But for now, she'd handle it. The dead man was all hers. Maybe her first homicide.

As she drove toward Alamo, Williams found herself remembering the other dead people she'd encountered.

The gray face of an old man who died from a stroke still visited her dreams. Later that month, she'd found a deceased young man in a car with a syringe in his arm. Most recently, she'd dealt with a woman who had killed herself with fumes from her running car parked inside a well-sealed garage.

She followed the directions Ralph had offered and spotted the sleek black sedan at the edge of NM 169, a few miles northwest of the settlement of Magdalena. She pulled in behind it, turned on the light bar, and examined the scene before she stepped outside. The vehicle looked fine—no signs of a collision and no broken windows.

She opened the car door and noticed the morning's coolness. Williams loved October's beauty in central New Mexico, even though it signaled a move from abundance and growth to darker, colder months.

She slipped out of the unit and walked toward the Jaguar. The invigorating early-fall air chilled the tip of her nose and slid into her lungs.

She approached the car slowly, looking for anything unusual. She took pictures of shoe prints around the vehicle, careful not to tread on them. The soles of the shoes had left little circles in the dirt. She assumed the tracks were from Apacheito's son, although they seemed a bit large for an eight-year-old. She wanted to rush to the Jaguar, but she knew what she recorded here would be crucial to the investigation if this death turned out to be a homicide.

The sun's warmth had melted the thin layer of ice on the rear window, leaving it streaky with wetness. She noticed that the driver's side window was open and took pictures at a distance, capturing the frost that covered the other windows and the windshield. Watching where she stepped, she moved close enough to peer into the car through the open window.

The man's body lay sprawled, angled toward the passenger seat, a gun near his lap, his seat belt still fastened. She saw no signs of a struggle, and the closed glove box and fancy watch on the dead man's wrist argued against robbery. She guessed that the dude had taken his own life. She didn't recognize him.

Williams photographed everything, then stepped away, settled herself, and carefully returned to her unit. She called the station to arrange for transport of the body to the Office of the Medical Investigator in Albuquerque for an autopsy, routine in an unattended death like this, and requested an officer to help protect the scene until the body could be removed. She rattled off the vehicle's license plate number for an ownership check. As she prepared to go back to the death car with the evidence kit, her cell phone rang. It was Bob.

"I just got a call to come out there to give you a hand. I reminded them that this is my day off, so Taylor's on the way. Do you really need my help?"

"No. Unless you wanna bring me some coffee. I'll be here awhile. Looks like a suicide. Someone shot in the head out toward Alamo. How's Honey feeling this morning?"

"Hard to say. The antibiotic may have calmed down the infection, but I can tell my girl is still in pain. She drank some water. Ate a little, but she's not out of the woods yet."

His tone carried more worry than the words themselves.

"I'm sorry. I was hoping she'd be better by now."

"Me, too. So, this is your first death as a detective, right?"

"Right."

"Is the victim anyone we've dealt with before?"

"I didn't recognize him. He's in a black Jaguar with leather inside. New Mexico plates. I don't know about you, but I'm not familiar with anyone who has a car this fancy."

"Did he use a gun?"

"Yeah, but it's not too messy."

Officer Bernadette Manuelito had finally finished her paperwork and was looking forward to leaving for her home by the San Juan River, sacred Sá bito', the place she shared with Sergeant Jim Chee, her husband and temporary boss. Then the call came.

"Bernie, it's Leon Kelsey."

"Hey there, Spaghetti Legs. I haven't seen you for ages."

"I know. I need your help. I'm worried about Maya."

Bernie had been friends and roommates with Leon's sister, Maya, briefly in college. Leon's protectiveness of his sister and easygoing nature made them friends, too. Leon shared Bernie's passion for plants. When she and Maya lived together, Bernie was the one who watered the potted mums and orchids he gave Maya for special occasions.

"What's going on?"

"That's what I want to know. My sister was supposed to meet her boy and me at my house this morning, but she never showed up, never called. Junior and I have tried reaching her all day. I left messages. No answer. It's just not like her."

"You know how phone service can be out there." She thought of saying, *As bad as those shaky attempts at track that gave you your nickname,* but she heard the strain in his voice, the tone words take when bad news weighs them down.

"It's more than that, Bernie. Since she stopped drinking, she's never late anymore, and if she thinks she could be, she always lets me know. I'm concerned that she had an accident on the road up here. Have you heard anything?"

"No. And that's good." Alamo, where Maya lived and worked, was an island of Navajo culture, Diné families separated from the rest of the Navajo Nation by distance, non-Navajo land holdings, and Interstate 40. It took a drive of several hours to get from that central New Mexico town to Shiprock, where Leon lived. "Tell me what Maya's up to these days."

"She teaches third grade at the Alamo Community School and has a house out there. She comes here some weekends and for longer during the summer when the kids don't need her."

"Does she live by herself?"

"That's right. Junior has been here with me, but he's thinking of moving in with his mom and going to school out there at Tech. He missed the fall semester, so maybe after Christmas."

"Tech? What's that?"

"New Mexico Institute of Mining and Technology. You know, in Socorro."

"I've heard it has a good reputation in science." She pulled out a pad and made some notes as she spoke. "Did you and Maya have an argument?"

"No. We get along great. I love my little sister."

"Let me see what I can find out. Do you know what she drove?"

"A green Dodge Caravan with a big dent in the back bumper and a sticker that says 'Save the Grand Canyon—No to Escalade.'"

"What's her birthday?"

Bernie jotted it down.

"I'll let you know if I learn anything. And call me if you hear from her, OK?"

"You'll probably hear me shouting hurray from wherever you are. Thanks, Short Stuff."

No one had called her by that nickname for years. She thought about reassuring Leon that things would be OK, but she'd been a cop long enough to know that might not be the case. When reliable people slipped into the ozone, it wasn't necessarily a matter for the police. Sometimes they simply didn't want to make contact with whoever was trying to reach them. Sometimes a medical incident or a mental health issue landed them in the hospital. Sometimes—and she had seen this too often with former drinkers—they fell off the wagon, embarrassed themselves, and ended up arrested. In worst-case scenarios, the missing person had become a crime victim.

Bernie remembered Maya as one of those girls who liked everyone and whom everyone seemed to like. Maya volunteered to stay after the meeting and put up the chairs, offered the stressed waitress a compliment, greeted strangers with a smile, didn't mind sharing class notes or giving you a ride. A genuinely good person, Bernie thought, as long as she stayed away from the bottle. When she drank, she made bad decisions that hurt the people she loved. Leon had rescued his little sister, scolded and cajoled her, and given her a shoulder to lean on. She hoped for Leon's sake, as well as Maya's and Junior's, that nothing bad had happened.

Bernie called the New Mexico State Police and learned that there had been no major traffic accidents in the last forty-eight hours involving a green van. She contacted the Navajo Police Alamo substation next, introduced herself to the dispatcher who answered the phone, and explained the situation.

"We haven't had any calls from Alamo in the last few days. You know their guy, Officer Pino, has been out, so we're covering that area from here in To'Hajiilee."

To'Hajiilee. Another Navajo island, a community on the other side of Mount Taylor, separated from the rest of the Navajo Nation. The dispatcher said, "We'll be glad when Pino gets back or when headquarters finds somebody to help him out there. He's been a one-man show for a while, and that's a lotta territory."

"Can someone do a safety check on a woman who seems to be missing?"

The dispatcher took a few moments to answer. "Well, there's a retired cop who helps out a little. I'll ask him. What's the address?"

"Gosh, I don't know. I'll ask her brother to call you with it."

"Why doesn't he take care of it himself?" Bernie heard the irritation. "That's how families used to operate. Why doesn't he call one of her neighbors?"

"Thanks for your ideas." Disappointed, Bernie ended the call.

She wondered if Spaghetti Legs had thought of contacting the neighbors, or if he knew who Maya's neighbors were. If her little sister Darleen didn't show up at Mama's as expected, she could check with the elderly gentleman Darleen worked for and with Darleen's friend who'd persuaded her to move to Chinle. But neighbors? No, she didn't know them, and Mama almost certainly didn't either.

She called the Socorro County Sheriff's Department to check on accidents in their jurisdiction, which adjoined the Alamo reservation, and left a message. She called the Socorro County Detention Center and after a few transfers got the answer to her question.

"No Maya Kelsey on the incarceration list." The man on the phone gave her the number for Socorro General Hospital. "Good luck finding her."

Bernie called Leon and told him what she'd discovered. "This is good news. She's not in jail, not in the hospital, and hasn't been in an accident serious enough to involve the police."

"So, where is she—abducted by Star People? I'm worried. I checked with our relatives and no one has talked to her."

"When was the last time you spoke to Maya?"

"A couple days ago when we made the plan to go out to see our auntie. She sounded fine, told me about some stuff happening at school, and said she'd leave early so we could have a nice long visit. What if her car broke down and her phone is dead?"

"Try to relax about this. Your little sister is an adult, she's got a right to radio silence for a while. Don't worry, OK? I promise to let you know if I hear something."

"Don't worry? What if it was your sister, Short Stuff?"

Ah yes, Leon knew that her sister Darleen had certainly created some family drama. Bernie worried about that one every chance she got. "If it was my sister, I'd drive out to look for her."

She ended the call, finished her notes, and was standing to leave when Sandra, the station's receptionist and dispatcher, and a friend, buzzed her.

"Someone from Socorro County Sheriff's Department on the line for you, returning your call. Are you looking for a new job?"

"Nope. I'd miss you lunatics too much."

She picked up the phone at her desk.

"Hey, Manuelito, it's Tara Williams. Long time no see."

"Tara . . . ?"

"Oh yeah, you knew me as Mansfield. I'm Williams now. It's a long story. I'll tell you over a beer. Oh, that's right, a Coke for you."

Bernie smiled. "I'm cutting back, switching to iced tea."

Just as the Navajo Nation, despite being larger than New England, was a small world, so was the community of law enforcement in New Mexico. She and Tara had met at classes at the state's Law Enforcement Academy. "Hey, girlfriend, I didn't know you were with Socorro County."

"Going on eighteen months. I just made detective. What can I do you out of?"

"There's a woman with family here who may be missing. She teaches at Alamo Community School. Her brother expected her this morning, but she didn't show up and she's not answering her phone."

"So, I'm assuming he knows her well enough to rule out all the logical reasons and you followed up and got nowhere."

"Right." Bernie detailed the dead-end phone calls.

"What's the name?"

"Maya Kelsey."

"Say again."

Bernie did, and gave her Maya's birth date and Leon's description of the vehicle she was driving.

"That's interesting. I came across that name earlier this morning. I got a call about an abandoned car with a dead guy inside. I found evidence that the victim knew someone named Maya Kelsey. What can you tell me about her?"

Bernie thought about how to answer the question. "Maya and I went to high school together and were roommates in college for a while. She grew up in Shiprock like me, but now she's teaching on the Alamo Navajo reservation. Her son and brother worried when she didn't call or show up today as she'd promised. They say it's not like her." She took a breath. "Who is the dead guy?"

"The driver's license in his wallet says Steve Jones."

"*Steve Jones?*" A common name, Bernie reminded herself. Don't assume anything.

"Don't tell me. You knew him, too."

"I might have. I met a man by that name in college. He dated Maya and they got married. Last I heard, *that* Steve Jones was working in Hawaii."

"Well, *this* Steve Jones drove a Jaguar with New Mexico plates and his name on the registration. He was in his early forties. The car had a sticker from Tech, so maybe he was on the staff or faculty there. Sound like the guy you knew?"

"Maybe. Years ago, he worked as a grad student teaching assistant at the University of New Mexico. How did he die?"

"Looks like suicide, a single shot to the head. No signs of a struggle and no one stole his watch, his wallet, or his fancy ride."

"How did you get the call?"

"A kid out hunting saw the car, got curious, and peeked inside. Then ran home, told Dad, and the father called us."

"Do you think the kid saw—"

Williams interrupted. "No. The guy died last night. The boy came across the car early this morning."

"Too bad."

"Yeah. His dad said that the kid was really shaken. Let me know if you learn anything more about Maya Kelsey, OK? I'd like to talk to her."

"What did you find linking her to Jones?"

"Divorce papers." Tara paused. "So, in answer to your question, I haven't come across Maya Kelsey in the flesh, but I'm curious about her. Call me back in a day or two if this gal hasn't shown up and we'll see what we can do." Williams rattled off her cell number. "So, Bernie, is the Navajo PD still treating you OK?"

"Yes, except for the paperwork, but that gives me something to complain about. How's life with you?"

"Good. I love this new job. I'm the chief investigator on the Jones case." She laughed. "Chief and only. I thought I'd miss being on patrol, but hey, this suits me better."

After the call, Bernie pictured the Steve Jones she recalled from college, a bright, quiet white man. Maya met him in her astronomy class. She remembered the first time her roommate called from Jones's apartment to say she wouldn't be back at the dorm that night. Before the end of the semester, Maya had moved in with Jones. Next semester, Jones landed a job at one of the observatories on Hawaii's Mauna Kea. Maya invited her friends to fly in for the wedding, but Hawaii was too far and too expensive.

Then, after the birth of their son, something happened, something Maya never shared with her. She and Jones split. Maya and her son returned to the Navajo Nation. She went back to school for a teaching certificate while Leon and her extended family helped raise Junior. Leon stepped in as 'shidá'í, the little father. Bernie's good opinion of the man had grown as she watched him with the baby.

Sergeant Jim Chee, for the time being substation supervisor, walked up to the desk, disturbing her reverie. "I thought you were going home."

"I was. I am."

"You looked puzzled. Did you just talk to Darleen?"

Bernie smiled. Darleen was working in Chinle and, as far as Bernie and Mama knew, behaving herself. "No trouble with my sister this time. Leon Kelsey's sister, Maya, didn't show up for a family event. And I just learned her ex-husband's body was found out by Alamo."

"That's an odd coincidence. You know her, right?"

Bernie nodded. "I hope she's OK."

"What happened to the dead guy?"

"The detective working the case said he was shot in the head."

"Nothing exciting like that in my world today. Just the rising tide of bureaucracy trying to drown me.

The captain called and things are moving so slowly in Window Rock and he may be gone until next week." Window Rock, the capital city of the Navajo Nation, was home base for the tribal council and president, and the assembly spot for other tribal entities including the Law and Order Committee, which set policy for the police department. "He didn't sound as cranky as usual for when he's away from home."

Bernie nodded. "Speaking of home, my shift was over an hour ago. I'll see you there."

"Get some rest, Sweetheart. I'll be leaving soon. Officer Sam asked me to write him a recommendation, and I want to get that done before I go."

"There's a rumor floating around that he applied for a job with the Albuquerque police department."

"It's true."

"Can't Captain Largo do that when he gets back?"

"I mentioned it to him and he passed it to me. Helping Officer Sam move on will improve morale around here. I don't mind."

"But what can you say?"

"Well, that's why I haven't done it yet."

Bernie drove home in her aged Toyota, picturing Sam working in the big city of Albuquerque. She was glad that she and Chee didn't have to do that. Living in the shadow of Ship Rock, Tsé Bit'a'í, the Rock with

Wings that had carried the People to safety, was where she belonged. And from their trailer home by the San Juan River she could be at her mother's place in less than an hour. She wanted to stay on the Navajo Nation and work with the people who shared her heritage. Wilson Sam could have the big city.

She switched to Steve Jones and Maya. Their heated romance had transformed her friendship with Maya into a more distant relationship. They kept in touch sporadically after Maya and Steve moved to Hawaii, and she remembered sending a small silver bracelet for Junior, a traditional gift, after she received a card with a photo of the parents and their new baby.

When Maya and her son returned to Navajoland, she tried to rekindle the closeness they'd had in college. But after an embarrassing incident in which Maya climbed into the back seat of a stranger's car, refused to leave, and then fell asleep, Bernie told her friend she didn't want to be with her when she was drinking. Maya took offense and the relationship cooled.

What had happened to her old friend now?

Bernie drove home, parked, and turned off the engine. She climbed out of the car and listened for a moment to the sweet low murmur of the San Juan River, S bito', one of the sacred Navajo waterways in a place where all water was a blessing. She heard the solemn hoot of an owl, and it brought her thoughts back to the dead one. Jones hadn't seemed like the sort of guy to kill himself. But people changed, and some changes weren't for the better.

She waited for Chee until exhaustion overtook her. She put her book aside and turned out the light next to the bed. She'd fallen into a light sleep when she felt his warm and irresistible presence beside her. She woke with a smile. Sometimes there was no need for talking.

Afterwards, she enjoyed the rhythm of his deep breathing and reviewed all the things she had to be grateful for, including the fact that, on this night, no emergency had called either of them back to work.

3

October, Ghaaji' on the traditional calendar, brought cooler nights and the first snows to the higher mountains of the Navajo Nation. Sandra had made the coffee, especially welcome on a cool morning, and the smell tickled Bernie's brain to life. She took her cup into Captain Largo's office, where Chee had again set up camp, to discover what assignments he had for her. It was Sunday, her last shift on patrol before she switched from serving as Officer Bernadette Manuelito to focus more closely on her role as Mama's eldest daughter and Darleen's big sister. With Chee working more OT until Largo returned, she'd reassigned time they would have spent together to her mother, with positive and not-so-positive results.

Chee smiled at her. "Good morning, Officer. I've got a warrant for you to serve out by Red Mesa. Failure to appear."

"Sure thing, Sergeant. Anything else while I'm over that way?"

"Not at the moment. Old Mrs. Toadachene lives in the area. If you can't locate the guy, she'll know where to look for him."

"I remember her. I might not be back until tomorrow if I stop at her place. The lady likes to talk."

She climbed into her unit with a sandwich, a water bottle, some baggies for seeds in case she saw unusual wildflowers in bloom, and a book in her backpack. Off to find Mr. Melvin Shorty and haul him to jail.

Serving warrants could be simple or complicated. The encounter called for caution and a bit of compassion. Sometimes, the person had honestly forgotten about the missed court date or whatever else had caused the judge to want him or her arrested. Sometimes he—most of the warrants were for men—knew he should have gone to court and that afterwards he could end up in jail, and therefore wanted to avoid the process. When she went to serve a warrant, sometimes she arrived at the address, found the person there, and arrested him while he was still shocked. Other times, the Navajo green-and-white pulled up and the suspect fled. Sometimes, a wife or mother answered the door and said the man she sought was not there, even though they both knew it was a lie.

She hoped Mr. Shorty would go with her peacefully.

Bernie had been driving about half an hour, heading west on a reasonably smooth dirt road, when she came across a herd of cattle grazing as they strolled along what would have been the shoulder if the road had had a shoulder. She slowed as she passed them and considered how best to deal with the situation. A pickup truck approached and she turned on her emergency lights. She stopped at an angle so that her unit partly blocked the road.

The young man in the truck looked surprised, a normal reaction at both the sight of a police car and the realization—even today—that a woman cop had climbed out from behind the wheel.

"Be careful," Bernie said. "There's a bunch of cattle along the shoulder here."

"Where?"

"Just up the road. Are they yours?"

"No, ma'am. I wish."

"Do you know who owns them?"

"They say she died. The woman who lived down there." He moved his lips to the left, toward the compound with a manufactured house, a traditional hogan in the rounded female shape, and some unoccupied corrals.

"OK. Drive safely and watch out for those animals."

She radioed the station and told Sandra about the loose cattle, giving the approximate location and telling her to ask Chee to call the livestock officers about the situation. As if he didn't have enough to do.

Bernie bounced along in her unit, looking for the pile of tires that indicated a road that led to the place where she hoped to find and arrest Mr. Shorty for failure to respond to a court date for his third DWI. She parked next to a pickup and heard the buzz of a chain saw. Before she shut off her engine, three dogs came up to her car, barking ferociously. The noise from the saw stopped, and a deep male voice called the animals away.

The man who approached had sawdust in his short-cropped black hair. She noticed the tattoo of a running horse on his bicep. His sweat made the sawdust stick to the skin on his arms beneath the sleeves of a well-worn T-shirt.

With DWI warrants, she often found the person she'd come to arrest intoxicated. From the way he walked toward her, Mr. Shorty didn't seem drunk, a mark in favor of anyone using a chain saw.

Bernie climbed out of the car as he approached. "Yá'át'ééh."

"Yá'át'ééh, Officer."

She introduced herself, first with her clans, then where she lived, and finally her job as a police officer.

The man reciprocated and, to her relief, identified himself as Melvin Shorty.

Bernie got to the point. "Mr. Shorty, I'm here with a warrant to arrest you for not going to court for your DWI hearing."

"When was that?" Shorty looked surprised.

Bernie told him.

"I remember now. The truck broke down." He moved his chin toward a pickup partly filled with large logs. "My friend said he'd help me fix it, but then his daughter got sick."

The tailgate hung open. Bernie noticed an axe, a huge flat-topped stump that served as the chopping block, and a pile of split wood. The air held the pungent smell of fresh pine sap.

"Mr. Shorty, the courts don't care about excuses. You've got to go to jail now."

He put his hands in the pockets of his overalls. "Call me Mel. Officer Bernadette Manuelito, my wife made some pumpkin pancakes before she left for her job, and there are three of them left. They sure are good. Could you use one?"

She shook her head. "We need to leave for Shiprock."

"What's the hurry? You sound like a white person." Melvin chuckled. "I told my friend I would give him some wood to repay for working on the truck. You know, the nights are cooler up here now and we'll have snow next. I need to keep my family warm. Especially if I'm in jail."

Many homes on the Navajo Nation still lacked electricity despite the recent growth of solar power. Coal and wood-burning stoves provided winter's warmth. She and Chee had used their woodstove twice that week.

"You should have thought of that when you decided to ignore the court date." Shorty's problem wasn't hers, but she understood his situation. "Your friend will have to make another plan. You're going to jail."

Shorty turned his palms toward the sky. "You know, I wasn't that drunk and I didn't hurt anybody."

"It's out of my hands, sir. You'll have to talk to the judge about all this. You should stop drinking."

"I did stop drinking. Six months. But when my buddy's wife left him, he came over and he brought a bottle and a six-pack. I felt sorry for the guy. One beer wouldn't hurt me, but we drank all of them and the bottle, too." Melvin shook his head. "I shoulda let him walk home, but he was so wasted I didn't think he'd make it."

Melvin Shorty looked at the load of wood in his truck. "Can you at least give me a few minutes to unload this so my brother can drive the truck tomorrow? We shouldn't have packed it so full, but they are good logs and we sure can use them."

"Can't your brother do it?"

"He could, but it's hard for him. He only has one arm."

Before she could answer, Shorty tugged at a log on the top of the pile, grunting as he pulled it to the edge of the truck bed, jumping aside when it fell to the ground.

"That looked heavy."

"Yeah. Some of these are still green, full of juice."

He rolled the big log to the side of the pile, and went for another.

"Hold on. I'll help you. Then we go."

She got an old jacket from the trunk of her unit and some gloves. They worked companionably in silence. It felt good to move outside under the brilliant blue cloudless sky, to fill her lungs with the sweet fresh air of the Chuska Mountains. There were only a few logs left when she felt her cell phone vibrate. It was Sandra.

"Hey, Bernie. No luck with the cattle. The livestock folks won't get there until maybe tomorrow at the soonest. They asked if you could follow up, maybe figure out who they belong to and get the owner to solve the problem."

"Seriously? They can't deal with those animals any quicker? Someone could die out here."

"It's not my fault. Chill."

"Did you tell the sergeant?"

"Not yet. He's been on the phone all morning."

"Give me the livestock number. I'll take care of it."

She took off her work gloves to type the information in her phone.

Shorty looked up from his perch atop the load of wood. "I heard you mention cattle. Were you talking about the steers roaming along the road?"

"That's right."

"They say that after the man who lived there went to the old folks' home—you know, that place the Little Sisters of the Poor run out by Gallup—his daughter took over. I heard she was supposed to move the livestock."

"Do you recall her name?"

"I always called her Mrs. Redskins because she wore that Redskins cap her grandson gave her. The family name is Nez."

"OK. Thanks." Nez, she thought. The Smith of Navajoland.

"I heard a steer got killed by a truck already, and they say someone is having a sing next weekend. You don't want meat to go to waste."

A sing, a ceremony to restore physical, psychological, and spiritual health to the person being cured, meant many mouths to feed. Friends and relatives came from all over to support this powerful healing as the hataḷii used chants, prayers, and sandpainting. The unfortunate animal would be put to good use.

She watched Shorty finish unloading the logs. "We've got to go, Mel. Come on."

"Can I leave a note for my wife?" He motioned toward the house with his chin.

"Quickly. I'm coming with you."

Shorty brushed the sawdust off his clothes and bent at the waist to shake his hair. The dogs, sensing a change in activity, came up to him and Bernie, got ignored, and went back to a spot in the autumn sun. Bernie took off her jacket and brushed it clean, avoiding the sap on a sleeve. She shoved the work gloves into a pocket.

The house smelled of woodsmoke. A single mattress sat on the living room floor, neatly covered with a superhero quilt and, on top of that, a beautiful Teec Nos Pos rug. Beyond it, she noticed a bedroom. Melvin stood at the kitchen counter and took a while writing.

She watched him remove a cell phone, a wallet, and a handful of change from his pants. He took his driver's license from the wallet and put it back in his pocket. He slipped a turquoise-and-silver ring from the middle finger on his left hand. The skin below it was pale. He kept on his wedding ring.

"OK. I'm ready." He folded the note he had written in half. "You wanna see it?"

"Sure." Bernie read: "Honey, I forgot about a warrant and a lady officer arrested me and now I have to go to jail in Shiprock and I'm sorry about all this. I did the best I could with the wood. I don't know how long this will take and if it gets too cold at night you and the boys should sleep together in our bed and use all the blankets. I love them and you, too."

She handed it back and he put his wallet on top of it. "You know, Officer, when those bigwigs in Washington get sentenced to prison, they get time to get their act together. It's a shame Navajo doesn't do that. My wife and the boys would appreciate it if I could split a little more wood to keep them warm until I get back."

"Melvin, if you hadn't ignored the court date, I wouldn't be here. And if you hadn't been drinking in the first place, your story would be different."

"I know. It's on me."

Bernie had some discretion as the arresting officer and she decided to use it.

"I'm going to give you a break. If you promise you'll stay here, you can keep working on the firewood until I return from dealing with the cattle."

He looked surprised. "I'll be right out there when you get back, I promise."

"If you are not, you will be in more trouble than you can possibly imagine. Understand?"

He nodded. "Thank you. Do what you need to, and be careful out there."

Afterwards, she wondered why she trusted him.

4

Joe Leaphorn, retired Navajo Police lieutenant turned private investigator and consultant, looked forward to lunch with a former cop and ancient codger like himself, Jerry Hancock. Hancock, who had become a friend over the years, suggested an Italian restaurant on the north side of Gallup. They both liked the food, and if they timed it right, the place would be quiet. Hancock mentioned that he had a proposition for him. The fact that he'd offered to buy lunch suggested that the proposition included asking for a favor.

As he drove toward the restaurant, Leaphorn thought about his friend and housemate, Louisa Bourbonette, and the trip she was urging him to take. After years of solitary life as a widower, he'd invited the outspoken anthropology professor to use the guest room of his Window Rock home as her base as she traveled throughout the Four Corners researching Native American origin stories. He discovered how much he enjoyed her sharp mind and independent spirit. He asked her to marry him. She said she didn't want to ruin a good relationship. He'd made peace with that decision and she had become his housemate. Still, the invitation to fly to Washington, DC, with her left him uneasy.

Louisa had been invited to speak at a conference, and she wanted to spend some time sightseeing in the nation's capital and then go to Mount Vernon and Monticello. He told her he'd consider it. He had never seen those famous old presidential homes and had heard that Washington's National Museum of the American Indian and International Spy Museum deserved a visit. More than that, he liked Louisa's company; he'd missed her regular presence ever since she'd gone back to teaching.

After he graduated from the intensive speech therapy that helped him regain most of his skill in English—following a gunshot to the brain that nearly killed him—Louisa had returned to her faculty position at Northern Arizona University. He felt fine except for random aches and pains that came with age. His problem with saying yes to Louisa's invitation stemmed from the fact that people who lived in Window Rock had to take a plane to Washington, DC, unless they made time for a very long drive. Flying terrified him.

Louisa mentioned that the conference organizers would pay a small honorarium and cover their hotel, her flights and meals. He said he would check his work schedule. She'd brought up the trip again recently in an email:

I need to book our plane tickets. When can you let me know?

I'll tell you soon. He remembered typing it with confidence. I've got some pending contracts and I need to make sure I can get away.

When is soon?

He suggested a day when she'd be home from NAU and they could talk face-to-face.

Now, the day had trotted up and he still didn't know what to say. He dreaded the idea of flying anywhere, even with his longtime housemate. How could he reject her invitation without seeming to reject her?

Leaphorn pulled his truck into one of the restaurant's empty parking slots, grabbed his laptop, and went inside. He spotted someone sitting alone at a table, rounder and a bit older than the Hancock he remembered. But the grin was the same.

"Howdy. Glad you could make it." Hancock rose to his feet. "You're looking good, Lieutenant. I mean, good for an old coot."

Leaphorn eased himself into the chair across from his friend. "Tanks. Still some troubles wid English."

"That's OK. I'll do most of the talking."

Hancock was a straight shooter, an old Indian Country hand who had grown up with Hopi and Navajo buddies in Keams Canyon, the son of a Mormon woman and a father who, Hancock joked, was half Spanish, half Apache, and half salesman. Leaphorn noticed when they'd worked together that Hancock had some of the salesman in him, too. The man put people at ease and won their cooperation.

They ordered drinks, looked at the menu, and spent a few minutes getting used to each other's company again. Hancock mentioned that his wife had undergone surgery and follow-up treatment for cancer. "The treatment saved her. We'll have our fortieth anniversary next year. Christina wants to go on a cruise to celebrate putting up with me for that long. Just the two of us sharing a boat with enough strangers to fill a basketball arena—romantic, huh?"

Leaphorn sipped his coffee, thinking that even though it involved a potentially lethal plane flight, a trip to Washington, DC, was better than a week on a boat.

"So, how's things with you and that professor?"

"Fine. She doin' a lot more teachin'. She wants me ta go wid her to Washingdon. I'm thinkin' 'bout it."

Hancock laughed. "I don't know, Joe. It seems like a big step. You guys have only been living together in the same house for how many years? Two of my dogs died of old age while you've been close friends, or whatever you call it."

The waitress arrived with Hancock's second beer and news that food would be there shortly.

After she left, he grew more serious. "I've been working on a task force with a national committee of law enforcement folks along with people who run domestic violence prevention programs. We're trying to come up with ideas to better coordinate efforts on the growing problem of missing, exploited, and murdered indigenous women. You've seen the statistics. Native women account for more than their share of the cases."

Leaphorn knew of the problem, as did everyone with a beating heart in Indian Country.

"We're trying to get a handle on the availability of resources on the Navajo Nation and with the Hopi,

Zuni, and other Pueblos, Utes, Paiutes, maybe the Apache groups, too. We want to figure out what tribes need to combat this and how to give Indian nations more authority and resources to investigate and prosecute these incidents."

"Dat's a good way ta spend your retirement. Hol' on." Leaphorn opened his laptop and typed: We Navajos set up our Strengthening Families Program to provide and coordinate crisis intervention services in this area, working with federal, state, and nonprofit agencies as well as other tribes. A lot of challenges here, lots of work to do.

Hancock sipped his beer as he read. "I figured you kept an eye on this. It's not a new problem, but it's getting worse. By the way, your English sounds fine, Joe. Last time we talked you were struggling."

"'Peech therapy, an' Louisa's help." After the gunshot damaged his brain, Louisa had encouraged him to keep speaking English even when he much preferred to stay quiet.

"You mean the lady nagged you?"

Leaphorn smiled. "Maybe. She's a good frien'. I'm glad I can get back ta work."

"Any interesting cases?"

He nodded and typed. I tracked down an important donation for the Navajo Museum and figured out how a young woman died. Leaphorn thought about the ancient weaving he'd investigated and how it led to murder. "How 'bout you?"

"I put work aside, except for the task force, until Christina gets better. I'm doing what she used to do, you know, shopping, laundry, cleaning. I'm a pretty good cook now. I can make a spaghetti sauce so good you'd think it came from a jar."

Hancock took a long swallow of his beer and put the glass down. "Getting back to the task force. My term is up, and with what Christina and I have been through, I want to focus on good times with her, you know. I'd like someone from this part of the world to replace me. That would be you."

"Wud's involved?"

"You'll need to go to a few meetings, join in some brainstorming. We're looking for someone to research the way the system handles, or doesn't handle, repeat offenders."

"I'm not one for meetings des days. I'm not sure I'm da right person for dis."

"Sure, you are. You were dealing with cases like this as a cop and a PI before the problem got much attention. I remember a case that involved a woman who worked for public health or something and vanished out on the reservation. You recall that one?"

"I do." He had discovered the young woman's body.

"If you go back to your case files, I'm sure you'll find dozens of incidents where you helped women who'd been abused. Take a look in your files. You probably saved more lives than you know."

Praise made Leaphorn uneasy. "My frien', you're actin' like an old . . ." He couldn't think of the word.

"An old geezer?" Hancock chuckled. "I am an old geezer."

The server headed toward them, and the fragrance of garlic, oregano, onion, and tomatoes interrupted Hancock's train of thought and relieved Leaphorn's embarrassment. Leaphorn's pizza, a concoction called a New Mexico Roadrunner, combined green chile, pepperoni, and sausage. It tasted as good as it looked, and reminded Leaphorn that he had skipped breakfast. He ate two delightful slices.

Hancock pushed a piece of garlic bread into a puddle of pasta sauce on his plate.

"This wasn't domestic violence, but what about the woman kidnapped by that whacked-out Red Power activist who robbed a bank and got away with the cash. I think he also kidnapped some Boy Scouts. You found them all in a cave, remember that? And you did it without the help of Facebook. You didn't even have a dang cell phone."

Although he hadn't thought of that case for decades, Leaphorn recalled it vividly now.

"Didn't the crazy dude have a son who was a minister or something?"

"Da killer's twin brudder was a priest and his grand-dad a hataɬii." He knew Hancock understood the term for a medicine man, a healer.

Leaphorn remembered hiking for miles over the rugged sandstone in the heat of summer to track the terrorists, nearly getting incinerated in a fire meant to kill him, and retreating from the snarling determination of the leader's huge, vicious dog. He'd taken a bullet in the leg, and could still recall his sweet relief when he'd heard the whirring beat of the rescue helicopter.

And while he decided whether to have one more slice of pizza, Hancock carried the conversation with amusing stories of his wife's adventures dealing with the complicated, confusing, and contradictory world of medicine. He came back to his request about the task force as they said their goodbyes.

"I'll email some information. Just think about it. OK?"

Leaphorn agreed. As he walked to his truck, he noticed a small young woman putting a poster on the utility pole next to his truck. The wind blew it out of her hand, and it landed at his feet. The flyer had a photo of a young Navajo woman with beautiful long hair and a brilliant smile. Beneath it was the woman's name, the word "MISSING" in large black capital letters, and a phone number. Next to the number and inside a heart, someone had written, "We love you."

He handed it to her and spoke in Navajo. "The woman in the picture looks like you."

"She's my sister. People always tell me we look alike but she's a little older and her hair is longer. Or it was."

"What happened?"

"We don't know. It's been two months. We worry every day." The woman sighed, and Leaphorn guessed that she'd told the story too often.

"Are you from here?" she asked.

"No, Window Rock."

"Please take a poster with you."

He put it in his truck. He thought about the woman and the problem of missing women on the Navajo Nation, throughout Indian Country. He'd been to enough meetings to last a lifetime, but maybe there was something else he could do to help.

5

Bernie bounced the few miles back to the house she'd noticed from the main road, hoping to find Mrs. Nez or someone who could deal with the livestock. The herd was behaving, lying in the shadow of a clump of junipers a few yards off the road. She parked beside an old piñon tree and waited, her eyes on the house. No dogs barked or rushed out of hiding. No one opened the front door. The place looked deserted.

She walked to the home and up a couple of wide wooden steps. She knocked on the front door, noticing the debris on the porch and that someone had draped the windows with what looked like bedsheets. Their glass reflected the blue sky and her own image. She knocked harder. "Hello in there. Anyone home?"

She waited, listening for the telltale footsteps of a person approaching, but heard only the cry of blue jays harvesting the piñon nuts. She rapped on the wooden door again.

"I'm a police officer." She offered her name. "Cattle are roaming loose on the road, and they say they belong here. You need to take care of this before a driver or one of your animals gets killed."

A sound came from inside the building, a thud like a lamp or table or something heavy falling to the floor. She pressed her ear against the door and heard a muffled moan.

"Everything all right in there?"

She heard the moan again, still faint but a bit louder.

"I'm coming in."

Bernie took a breath, put her right hand on her weapon, and used her left to turn the doorknob, surprised to find it unlocked. She paused for a tense moment, then stepped through the open doorway into the house, her weapon extended.

The room smelled of old food and stale cigarette smoke with a touch of sewage. Sunlight from the open door created a bright rectangle on the brown carpet. That, and the diffused light filtering in through the sheets, allowed her to do a quick scan of the room, searching for the source of the sounds. She saw a small kitchen and a hallway, its darkness broken by soft illumination seeping in at two points, possibly from bedroom windows. She studied the front room, noticing the clutter of takeout meal containers, plastic bottles, and beer cans. She repeated her name, her voice amplified by the adrenaline. "Is there someone here?"

She heard the moaning again and followed the noise with her eyes, focusing on the left side of the room. She saw an overturned wooden chair and then the gagged woman bound to it. The woman's struggle made the chair move against the carpet, causing the thudding sound. Bernie recognized pure terror in the wide-open brown eyes. She signaled the woman to be still, pressing the index finger of her left hand to her lips. The woman complied.

Bernie yelled, "If anyone is in here, show yourself. I'm an armed police officer. Come out. Now."

Silence. Energized by fear and duty, she knew what she had to do next.

She examined the front room for a few seconds more, observing the disorder, all her senses sharpened. No more humans, bound or free, came to her attention. She walked cautiously into the kitchen, saw nothing threatening, and proceeded to search the rest of the house. In the front bedroom she found dresser drawers emptied on the floor, closet doors open, the bed stripped of sheets and blankets and the mattress on its edge, slumping against the wall. She stepped over the clutter to examine the stinking bathroom. No one lurked behind the door or cowered in the shower stall.

In the next and final room, she discovered the same disarray, but whoever created the chaos had left the bed intact and piled with women's clothing. She noticed lacy panties and a pink T-shirt. As she moved past the bed to the closet, she saw a doll facedown on the rumpled bedspread. She stopped and stared at it, aware on a deep level that something was wrong. Not a doll. She pulled the baby toward her, even though she already knew she'd come too late.

The dead infant wore a blue one-piece outfit decorated with dancing elephants. She sat on the bed and cradled the cold stiff little body for a moment, looking at the tiny face and the shock of fine dark hair.

Adults left behind chindiis, restless spirits that caused trouble, but that wasn't true of a tiny one like this. She saw no obvious signs of trauma. Perhaps the baby had suffocated from lying on his tummy. She placed the small one down gently on the bed in the same position as she had found him, wondering if someone had held this baby so he didn't die alone and if he belonged to the woman in the other room. She allowed a moment for her emotions to settle, and felt anger replace shock, horror, and sadness.

She had been careful from the moment she opened the front door, but now she moved with extra caution, knowing the importance of not compromising any evidence that could solve the sad mystery of that dead child.

She returned to the bound woman, for the first time noticing the chill of the unheated rooms. The woman looked to be in her late twenties. She wore jeans and a short-sleeve T-shirt. Her skin had a grayish cast.

"My name is Bernie." She squatted next to her. "You're safe now. I'm going to remove your gag first."

The woman nodded in agreement. Her left eye was swollen shut, the face below it red with the start of a bruise. Her nose looked freshly broken. Bernie noticed flecks of something like soot on her cheeks, the residue of mascara.

The gag had pulled the skin taut above her jaw, and strands of hair had been caught with the fabric. Bernie cut through the cloth and felt it begin to go slack. She heard the woman gulp a breath as the gag fell away. She stretched her jaw, opening and closing her mouth. A small gold ring pierced her upper lip, the skin around it inflamed with infection.

"Wah . . . wah . . . water."

"I'll get you a sip in a minute. Stay still." Bernie stood and used her cell phone to reach the Shiprock station. She opened the conversation with the code for a dead person, requested an ambulance for the woman, and gave the location, with a caveat to watch for the cattle on the road.

"Got it. I'll tell the sergeant. Be careful."

She left the front door open as she raced to her unit. She activated the blue-and-red light bar, slid on her jacket, and grabbed an emergency blanket, gloves, and a water bottle from the trunk.

The woman remained exactly where Bernie had left her. She slipped on the gloves, unscrewed the cap, and held the water bottle to the woman's trembling lips. She noticed the victim had lost some teeth. Because she was tied to the chair and lying on her side, she couldn't drink without the water running down her cheek. She slurped greedily and resisted when Bernie pulled it away, leaning toward the bottle like lambs Bernie had fed.

"You can have more if what I gave you stays down. I'm going to free your ankles now. Try to relax. Then we'll talk." The woman closed her good eye, and Bernie noticed the tears.

She adjusted her position, scooting to the base of the fallen chair to work on the rope, more aware now of the stench of urine from the woman's jeans and the carpet. She cut carefully, avoiding the skin of the swollen ankles, noticing the chipped bright silver paint on her toenails. The rope had left blood-red ligature marks on both ankles. The woman was thin, but her bare feet had become so engorged Bernie couldn't see the outlines of the bones.

The woman moaned as she struggled to straighten her knees.

"Take it easy. Give your body time to adjust."

The woman ignored her, whimpering as she struggled to inch her legs outward.

"What's your name?"

"Do my hands. Hands!" The woman exhaled the word in English with fierce urgency.

"I'm getting to them. What's your name?"

Bernie repeated the question in Navajo.

The good eye closed, and Bernie saw the tears again. The area where the gag had been was chapped and raw.

"I'm here to help you. Talk to me."

The eye opened. "Bee." Her voice was a hoarse whisper.

"Your name is Bee?"

The woman moved her head up and down ever so slightly. Then the grunting sound came again, and the woman went rigid. Bernie raised her head off the floor just before the woman began to vomit. She had nothing to throw up except the water.

When the heaving stopped, Bernie went to work on the rope that bound the woman's wrists to the back of the fallen chair. Like her feet, both hands had swollen from the tight stricture. The fingernails were ragged, but traces of bright red polish remained.

Bernie's own hands were cold, but the hands she worked to free felt colder. She saw bruises on both fore-arms and the painful angle of dislocation at the right elbow. As she cut through the nylon rope, she looked at Bee's injured wrists, wondering how long the woman had been bound.

"Huh." The woman tried to push herself to sitting with her good arm, winced, and rolled onto her back. Bernie sat cross-legged next to her.

"Bee, why were you tied up?"

The woman didn't respond.

"Do you have a baby?"

She uttered a swear word and then "No."

"Do you know about an infant in this house?"

The woman struggled again to sit up. Bernie put a hand on her back for support, feeling bones and cold skin through the thin shirt. The woman pulled away, moaned, and sank down on her back.

Bernie suspected that someone had broken Bee's ribs.

"Why did they beat you?"

"Water." Her voice sounded as scratchy as an old record.

"In a minute. Stay still to keep the nausea down. I found a dead baby in the back room. Is he yours?"

"No. No."

"Why is he here?"

Instead of talking, the woman began to heave again.

Bernie heard the sound of a vehicle turning onto the dirt road and felt her heart rate increase. She sprang to the window, her hand on her weapon, and cautiously pushed aside the sheet that served as a drape. A big gray SUV approached the house. She drew her gun and watched as the driver parked and stepped out.

A moment later she recognized the man—Agent Berke, Federal Bureau of Investigation, Farmington, New Mexico, office. She holstered her gun. She opened the door and stepped onto the porch.

"Hey, Manuelito. What's up?"

"There's an injured woman who was bound and gagged in the front room and a dead baby in the back. No bad guys on the scene." She briefed him, offering what she'd observed with no speculation. "She told me her name is Bee. Other than that, she's hardly spoken."

"There's an ambulance behind me. They had to stop for the cows. I could scoot around them thanks to four-wheel drive. When I got the call that Navajo Police were on the scene, I should have known you'd be here. You and I seem to go together like flies on a cow pie. Did you mess with anything in there?"

She resented the question. If anything, he was the one with the black spot on his record. On a case they'd both worked, she'd had to call him out for his shoddy treatment of a young woman accused of a crime. The fact that she, a female Navajo cop, took charge and defused a volatile situation embarrassed him in front of his colleagues. Berke had resented her ever since. His attitude consistently made it clear that he was a big shot and he considered her nothing more than a lowly tribal employee.

"Everything is as I found it, except I untied the woman and she threw up. I gave her some water; you'll see the bottle. Why are you here, Agent?"

He strolled past her into the house without a word. Bernie watched as he spent a moment studying the scene in the living room and taking photos, then ambling toward the kitchen.

Bee lay on her back, staring at the ceiling. Bernie knelt down to gently place the blanket around her, watching Berke disappear to the rear of the house. In a few moments he was back and stood towering over them.

"Manuelito, I know you picked up that dead kid. Did you put the body down just exactly like you found it?"

"Of course."

"You probably see yourself as a big hero here, Officer, but you would have saved us all a lot of trouble if you'd gone back to keeping the cows off the road. You know, let nature take its course."

"You mean let her die?" Anger ignited her. She stood. "What's wrong with you, Berke? Why would you say that?"

Instead of responding he bent forward and waved his index finger at Bee's battered face. "I know you, honey, at least by reputation."

Bernie cringed at the rudeness. Her grandmother and mother—who taught her never to point with her hand—would have been horrified.

Berke's voice grew deeper. "Bee, huh? No way. You're Gabriela Hernandez, right? You finally went too far, didn't you, doll. Who did you double-cross?"

The woman kept her good eye closed and lay still.

Berke chuckled. "Manuelito, you ought to consider working for the Bureau. You have a way of getting in our business."

"I guess I'm guilty if you're criticizing me for saving her life. I found this scene. Where were you? Having coffee?" The words came out in fury.

Her anger rolled off him. "This girl's been on our radar for a while. I never expected to run into her in a dump like this. Not to find her alive here, anyway." He turned toward the woman. "Remind me. You speak English, right?"

Bee, or Gabriela, didn't react to the question.

Bernie had assumed that the woman was Navajo, spoke English, and had understood what she'd asked. But Bee might be Nakai, a new immigrant from Mexico or a Hispanic from the area who'd somehow gotten involved in major trouble. She could learn something even from a jerk. But language and ethnicity didn't matter as much as decency. No one deserved to be treated so badly.

In the distance, Bernie heard the wail of the ambulance. Bee looked toward the sound and tightened her lips. Bernie sensed the fear, or maybe it was confusion.

"Our Evidence Response Team will be here soon. Manuelito, you can get back to whatever you should have been doing."

"I'll stay awhile longer."

"Suit yourself." Berke went to meet the ambulance, and Bernie felt her phone vibrate. She pulled it out.

Chee. They had a knack for calling each other at awkward times. She'd get back to him. Through the open door she saw Berke pull the team leader aside. The second medic hurried toward the house, and she realized she knew him. Before he checked Bee, he spoke softly to Bernie.

"What's the story?"

"I found her about an hour ago tied to that chair. I noticed the abrasions on her wrists and ankles. Her left elbow could be dislocated. She winced when I put my hand on her back and when she tried to sit up, so maybe some broken ribs. I gave her a sip of water and she vomited. Her skin felt cold, so I covered her with the blanket."

"Do you know her name?"

"She told me Bee. The FBI man called her Gabriela."

"Thanks. Ahéhee'."

Despite some initial resistance, Bee allowed the medic to take her vital signs. His partner came in, and they gently loaded her onto a gurney and wheeled her to the waiting vehicle.

The attendant Bernie knew came back to the house.

"I heard there was a child . . ."

"A baby. That's why I waited." Bernie sighed. "From the clothes, I think it's a boy. You can't help him."

He paused. "Is it Bee's child?"

"She told me no."

"Where is he?"

"In the back bedroom. On the bed."

He studied his hands, rubbing his wedding ring. "I dread these calls. They give me nightmares. How are you doing?"

She looked at the floor. "Fine, I guess. We both knew situations like this came with the job."

"Hang tough."

"You, too."

Bernie left the house, noticing Berke in his SUV, the phone to his ear. Bee lay on the gurney, now with a bit more color in her face. No matter who she was or what her life had been, no one should be beaten, gagged, bound, and left for dead.

Bernie leaned toward her. "You're in good hands. These guys will take care of you now." She watched the ambulance leave, and as she climbed into her unit, she saw the federal crime scene investigation team pull into the driveway.

Deep in thought, she drove back to Melvin Shorty's place. She was angry. Berke's attitude grated on her almost as much as the injustice and evil of the situation she had accidentally discovered. Whoever did what they did to Bee—no matter what she had been involved in that led to this moment—should be held responsible. She pictured the little one, and her anger intensified. She wished Agent Johnson had responded to the call. They held each other in mutual respect.

She almost missed the tower of tires that marked the winding dirt road to Melvin Shorty's house. She drove closer, windows open, but didn't hear the drone of the chain saw or the whack of Shorty's axe splitting logs. Raucous cries of jays feasting on piñon nuts filled the air. When she reached Shorty's home, she saw the large, neat pile of split wood and then the empty spot where the pickup had been parked. Her heart sank. She held a sliver of hope that Shorty's brother had come for the truck and that she would find the man she needed to arrest inside the building.

She hopped out of the unit.

"Shorty. Melvin Shorty." She banged on the door. "Officer Manuelito here. Let's go."

He didn't respond. He'd locked the front door. Peering in the front window, she saw that the truck keys, note, ring, and wallet he'd left on the kitchen counter were gone. She trotted around the house, calling for him without success.

After a few more minutes of pointless searching, she headed back to the station, simmering with rage and disappointment at Melvin Shorty for conning her and at herself for the serious misjudgment. She'd had him and she let him go. She considered ways to explain her failure to serve the warrant to Chee. She could say she went to Shorty's address and the man wasn't there. She had searched for him with no luck. It happened frequently on warrant assignments, and it was the truth. Just not the whole truth.

She came to the intersection that led to the house where she'd found Bee and turned toward it, compelled by too many unanswered questions and in no hurry to explain her failure to the man she loved.

Berke's car was gone, but as she'd anticipated, the FBI Evidence Response Team remained at work.

She walked inside and introduced herself to the first team member she encountered. "I'm the officer who found the woman and the baby. I was serving a warrant down the road and saw that you were here. How's it going?"

"Special Agent Jeff Parker. I'd shake hands, but you don't want what's on the outside of this glove."

"Did you learn anything about the baby?"

"I don't think so, but it's hard to know what might be relevant. So far, we haven't found anything to tie the child to something or someone involved here. Gabriela is the obvious connection, but it looks like three or four different people also hung out here."

"She denied the baby was hers."

He nodded in acknowledgment. "I understand someone hurt her pretty good."

"She's suffered a lot of damage, and that's just what I could see. It makes me furious."

"Berke and Johnson seem to have a solid idea of who else was involved. It seems like a complicated mix of drugs and sex trafficking. I'm not privy to the details, but Berke has worked this case for a while now. I know he'd like to see someone in custody." Parker squinted at her. "I've heard of you, Manuelito. You were the one who found that body off the jogging trail, right?"

"Guess I'm on a roll here."

"Agent Johnson speaks highly of you."

The comment caught her by surprise.

Parker rubbed his chin and looked toward his team. "Nice to meet you. I better get to work."

The steers had moved back onto the road, and Bernie stopped to cowgirl them to safety. She called the livestock people and left another message, harsher than the first, fueled by residual anger at herself, Shorty, Berke, whoever hurt Bee, and this miserable excuse for a day. When she was in range, she radioed the station for Chee. Sandra told her he had left for lunch. "Want me to tell him something for you?"

"Does he know about the dead baby?"

"Yeah. We're all upset that someone would do that."

"Tell him I couldn't find Shorty to serve the warrant, and I'm on my way in."

She dialed Mama next, putting the call on speaker. They usually talked right after Bernie had gone for a run and said morning prayers. But when she'd phoned that morning, something on television had stolen her mother's full attention. Mama said she'd call back, but she hadn't.

Without her younger daughter Darleen's steady company, Mama had grown more forgetful. Because Darleen was working—and figuring out what came next for her life—Bernie talked to Mama at least once a day. Sometimes they chatted for a minute or two. Sometimes Mama relayed big news of the neighborhood, and sometimes Bernie did most of the talking.

As she waited for Mama to answer, she thought about her friends who had lost their mothers to death or from physical, psychological, or emotional distance. Maya's mom had died when she was in high school, and Bernie remembered how the tragedy had strengthened the bond between Maya and her brother, Leon. Even though Mama got on her nerves at times, Bernie felt blessed to have her.

"Daughter, what happened? Why didn't you call me earlier?"

"I did call. You were watching TV." There was no point in telling Mama she'd promised to call back and forgotten. "I had to leave on assignment and things got complicated."

"I have some news, my daughter. It's about that old man who used to live here. You know the one in Chinle now."

Bernie understood that she meant Mr. Natachi. Mama adhered to the tradition of not using a person's name unless absolutely required.

"When my neighbor took me to the grocery, we heard that man feels very much better. They said your sister had taken good care of him and that he might come back to Toadlena for a visit in the next few weeks."

Word traveled fast on the reservation.

"Have you talked to Sister?"

"Yes. She's turning into a good woman."

Mama had long been critical of her younger daughter. Bernie smiled to hear those sweet words.

"Have you seen the new baby?"

Bernie pushed the disturbing image of the dead infant from her mind. She knew Mama meant her clan brother Officer Bigman's child. "Not yet. I'm sure he's special."

In the background, she heard Sandra on the radio, asking for her. "I hope you have a good day, Mama. I'm calling from the police car and I have to go."

"I worry about you, my daughter, out there with bad people. Talk to me tomorrow."

"I will."

Sandra sounded busy. "Two things. A Socorro County Sheriff's Department detective, Williams, wants you. Her number is on your desk unless you need it now."

"Thanks. I have it."

"And a woman walked in. She says she knows you and has to tell you something important."

"What's her name?"

"Maya Kelsey. Chee's dealing with her."

Maya. Bernie smiled. Maya was alive and Leon need not have worried. She hoped nothing major had brought her old friend to the station.

She called Detective Tara Williams and left her cell phone number as well as the station number. She gave the cell number out stingily, but a sister in law enforcement made the cut.

Bernie focused on the road, wondering if she needed to say more to Chee about the botched warrant, and thinking about the dead baby. If the child's relatives lived in the area, someone knew something about him.

Sandra greeted her with a frown. "The sergeant wants to talk to you. He's in the captain's office. I'm warning you—he's not happy."

"Is Maya Kelsey still here?"

"Yes indeed. She's waiting in one of the interview rooms."

As she walked down the hall, she pictured Chee scowling at the computer, wishing he could deal with crime instead of bureaucracy. Until she learned the cause of his grumpiness, she'd save the story of the warrant and limit her complaints about the FBI.

The door was open to the captain's office, and Jim Chee motioned her to the empty chair across the desk. "I've got news. You're not going to like this."

6

C hee ran a hand through his short-cropped hair. Bernie saw the exhaustion in his eyes.

"I'll get right to the point. Maya Kelsey came in asking for you but settling for me. She says she's responsible for the death of Steve Jones."

"You're serious?"

He nodded.

"What happened?"

"She says she shot him. I read her the Miranda rights and she signed the waiver. She officially confessed to murder and then stopped talking." Chee gave the news a moment to sink in. "Sandra mentioned that you had a call from a detective in Socorro. Is she handling the investigation?"

"That's right. Tara Williams. I know her from the Law Enforcement Academy. I contacted her after Leon called to say Maya was missing. Detective Williams told me they found papers tied to Maya in that man's car." Bernie and Chee tried to avoid saying the names of the dead as much as possible. Addressing those who had died by name could summon their chindiis.

Chee stood. "OK. Maya's waiting. Let's get this over with."

"Is she upset?"

"Not at all. Calm as a rattlesnake watching for a mouse to come out of the rocks."

Bernie hadn't seen her former roommate for at least a year, maybe longer than that. Instead of the vibrant person she remembered, the woman in the interview room sat with slumped shoulders in a faded, threadbare flannel shirt. Maya's thick dark hair had partially slipped out of her ponytail. She glanced up as the officers entered, then stared at the tabletop without a sign that she and Bernie used to be friends.

"Yá'át'ééh."

Maya didn't return her greeting. The words translated roughly to "All is good" and, clearly, that was not the case today. Her former roommate looked exhausted.

Chee opened the conversation. "Maya, you told me that you wanted to talk with Bernie present. I read you your rights, and you signed the form agreeing to speak to us, remember?"

She nodded. When she looked up, Bernie saw the worry in her dark eyes. "Like I told the sergeant, I'm the reason that man is dead." Maya's voice had a steely yet serene quality to it. "I want to get this over with."

Bernie sat a bit straighter. "Is this what you need to talk to me about?"

"Partly. I want Junior to have my vehicle. That's why I came here rather than turning myself in to the Alamo police. It's the green van outside there, and he knows where the extra keys are. Will you do that?"

Bernie said, "Wait a minute. You said you killed someone. Walk me through it."

The woman looked up. "Will you tell Junior about the van?"

"Of course."

"And you'll let Leon know I'm in jail so he won't worry."

"Yes." Although, Bernie thought, hearing a person you care about is in jail created worries of its own.

"And that I love them both."

Bernie nodded.

"OK. I killed Steve Jones and I'm ready to go to jail. That's all I have to tell you."

Bernie shook her head. "It doesn't work like that. When I asked you why you left your husband years ago, you told me you'd just grown apart, that you'd always love your son's dad. And years later you decide to murder him? Come on."

"People change." Maya focused on the tabletop. Bernie noticed a tear sliding down her cheek.

She leaned toward the woman and spoke gently. "My old friend, you need to explain. Did he threaten you?"

Maya wiped away the tear.

"Were you defending yourself?"

She spread her hands on the tabletop and silently studied her fingernails.

"Your brother called me earlier, worried because you didn't show up for a family event. You are lucky to have someone who cares about you and Junior that much. I can't believe you'd throw all that away. Was it an accident? Were you defending yourself?"

"Wait." Chee sounded gruff as he took charge. He straightened stiffly in his seat. "Maya Kelsey, do you have anything else to say to Officer Manuelito?"

Maya kept her eyes lowered and her thoughts to herself.

Chee stood. "We'll be back in a minute."

Bernie followed him. He closed the door and they walked to the hall.

"We need to pass this whole thing up the line." He spoke softly. "She's confessing to a murder that's not even in our jurisdiction."

Bernie leaned against the wall. "You're right. From what Williams told me, the car with the body was outside the Alamo reservation. That's why it's her case. But something's screwy about this. What's your take?"

"Maya came in here to confess and she's sticking to it. We can't put words in her mouth. You can't coach her."

"Was I?"

Chee frowned. "Officer, you're lucky there wasn't a lawyer in there."

"I know that woman. Something's wrong."

"I think that about most murders."

Bernie glanced toward the closed door of the interview room. "Well, think about this. We have an unsolicited confession without any excuse, motivation, or justification for the murder. She must be lying. The Maya I lived with was kind, thoughtful, funny, smart."

"That was years ago, Sweetheart." Chee spoke more loudly now. "Like she said, people change. I'll finish dealing with Maya. Call Detective Williams and give her the update."

"But . . ." She swallowed her argument. "Yes, sir."

She started to leave.

"Bernie?" She turned toward him. "Don't make this personal, Officer. We have to do our jobs."

"I'll let you know what Williams says, Sergeant." She spun on her heel and walked away.

Chee gathered his composure and went back to talk to Maya.

"Where's Bernie?"

"Officer Manuelito had a call to make. So, let's talk about the murder. Why did you do it?"

Maya brought her shoulders toward her ears and down again.

"I don't want to talk about it. I don't have anything else to say."

Chee pushed his chair back. "I'll write up your confession and you can sign it. We'll keep you in jail here until they can come for you from Socorro."

That done, he went to Captain Largo's office to sort out the problem of excessive overtime under his temporary leadership and review his handling of the interview and Bernie's reaction. He hadn't meant to make her mad, but he had to do his job. And, he told himself, she'd get over it. She always did. The Navajo Nation had picked a busy time to call the captain, but he dreaded administrative and supervisory work no matter when it came.

Bernie called Williams's cell number and told her about Maya's confession.

"From missing person to murderer?" Tara made a clicking noise with her tongue. "Why did she do it?"

"She wouldn't say."

"Self-defense?"

"I didn't see any signs of physical violence."

"What can you tell me about her?"

Bernie explained their old connection. "When we lived together, she never said anything negative about anybody, not even Jones after they split. But that was years ago."

"The dead man still listed Maya Kelsey as his emergency contact on a card in his wallet. Any kids?"

"Yes. They have a son together."

"Former partners with a son? That sounds like some unresolved business. Jones tools around in a Jaguar, and she's scraping by as a single mother on a New Mexico teacher's salary out in the middle of nowhere. Let's say she bumps into him at a gas station, and he's driving that fancy car. She remembers every stinking thing he did that he shouldn't have done— each insult, all the criticism, you know? Maybe they argued over custody or child support."

"You're jumping to the wrong conclusions. The son just graduated from high school. Maya's brother, Leon, mentioned that she loves teaching and living at Alamo. Making a lot of money never mattered to her. She wanted to get back home, closer to family. And, you know a lot of us think that what people call the middle of nowhere is actually somewhere special."

Williams laughed. "Chill, girlfriend. I love it here, too. You and I know all about doing something we enjoy instead of making more money. That's why we're cops, right? I was just trying out a scenario on you."

"Sorry. This is your case. The idea that a woman I shared a dorm room with confessed to killing a guy doesn't sit well. Did you find the weapon?"

"The gun? Yeah, in the car next to Jones. But I agree. Something is out of whack here."

"What's bugging you?"

"Parts of the crime scene look like suicide, and I'd almost convinced myself that's what happened. With the confession, I need to rethink it. Why would someone bother to make it look like Jones killed himself and then confess? Usually, a heavy dose of guilt combined with fear of being caught, that's what prompts a confession. How did she act when you interviewed her?"

Bernie thought of how to answer. "Resigned, cool, withdrawn but not nervous."

"You said she's a friend, or used to be. Did she ask for special treatment?"

Bernie explained about the van and the call to Leon, her next order of business. "Why don't you drive out and pick her up? It would be great to see you."

"I can't." Williams's tone changed. "I just realized we've got a problem. The deputy who does transports went to Texas with an inmate. Do you have someone in Shiprock who could bring her down?"

"I'll check."

"Hey, why don't you do it? You know this gal. Talk to your supervisor about it. I'm serious. You could help me with the case."

"I'd like that."

Ten minutes later, Bernie knocked on the door of Chee's temporary office. When he motioned her in and closed the door, she expected him to say he was sorry for the way he'd treated her.

He didn't. "If you've come to apologize, you don't have to. I know you're emotionally involved in Maya's case. It's OK."

"Apologize for what, Sergeant? For speaking my mind? For trying to help a friend?" If anyone needed to say, *Sorry for being a jerk*, it was Chee. "I'm here because, as you ordered, I talked to Detective Williams." She gave him the details with professional detachment, swallowing the irritation she felt at his condescending manner. "Socorro SO doesn't have anyone to do the transport. I volunteer to drive Maya to jail down there."

Chee looked at her.

"I've got the next two days off, Sergeant. I'd like to spend them helping Williams resolve the case."

"You really want to do this? You've already put in almost a full day, tried to serve a warrant, found a woman and a dead baby, dealt with roaming cattle. The drive takes about four and a half hours."

Yeah, she thought, a day with nothing to show for it except sap on my jacket, a close look at human cruelty, a quick lesson in how people you trust can disappoint you, and now friction with the man I love.

"Sergeant, I know how far it is. I believe Maya will open up to me on the trip, tell me what motivated her." When they lived together, frank conversation flowed easily between them.

She could see Chee thinking.

"Is it because you're angry at me?"

She hesitated. "Yes, sir, partly. As my boss, you've got a right to call me out, to disagree with what I did. As my husband, you stepped way, way out of line."

He started to say something, and fell silent.

"Sergeant, you have no reason to deny my request. You'll have to pay someone overtime and I have as much right to that as any officer here. More, actually, because of my connection to the prisoner."

"Bernie, I . . ." He sucked in a breath and gave her that look that normally melted her heart. "OK then. The department will pay for you to transport Maya Kelsey and spend the night in Socorro. Be careful. I know you think you know the woman, but neither of us pegged her for a murderer."

Bernie took a step back. "I'm always careful, sir. Something bad happened to lead Maya to this. I have to find the truth she's not telling us."

"Something bad? She killed a man. That's about as bad as it gets."

"Don't you wonder what provoked her? What turns a schoolteacher into a murderer?" Bernie paused. "I guess not."

She left the office before he could answer and called Leon as she had promised.

He answered on the first ring. "Did you find her?"

"Yes."

"Thank goodness. Is she in the hospital?" He didn't give her time to respond. "If that guy she was married to hurt her—"

"Calm down, Spaghetti Legs. Maya's here at the police station." She hesitated a moment. "Your sister asked me to tell you that she confessed to murdering Steve Jones."

"What? No, she couldn't kill anybody. This is crazy."

"She also asked me to tell Junior to come and get her van." Bernie took a breath. "And you'll need to let him know that his dad is dead and his mom is going to jail."

"Was Maya drunk?"

"No. Well, not today when I saw her."

"Bernie, listen. Whatever happened, she didn't do it. She couldn't have. You know that. Can I talk to her?"

"Not right now."

Before he could argue or ask questions for which she did not have an answer, Bernie ended the call.

She went home to pack the things she'd need to spend the night. When she returned to the station an hour later, Sandra motioned to a white plastic bag.

"Sergeant Chee told me you were driving to Socorro and asked me to get the dinner he ordered for you and the prisoner. There aren't many places to stop between here and there. Especially with someone in handcuffs."

Chee's effort to feed her and Maya softened her heart.

"The sergeant has a box for you, too. It's in his office."

"What's in the box?"

Sandra shrugged. "You better talk to him about that."

She rapped on the open door and entered. "I'm about to leave. Thanks for the food. Sandra said something about a box."

"That's right. Leon Kelsey brought it in when he came to see Maya. It's full of little models—some project he did for Maya's class. He planned to give it to her to take to school." Chee paused. "I told him he couldn't see his sister and that I'd ask you if you could bring the box to Socorro. That's up to you. He said he'd arrange for someone from the school to pick it up when you called. He wrote a note to go with it." Chee handed it to her.

She noticed the envelope had been opened. "You read this?"

"I did. I inspected the box, too. I had to be sure he wasn't plotting anything. He kept saying we'd made a mistake."

She read the note. Directed to the school principal, it explained that the models were imaginative fabrications of the Hero Twins and some of the monsters they killed in the quest to make the world safe for humanity. Leon had designed the figures to go with a lesson for the third grade on Navajo culture. He made no reference to his sister or her situation.

She handed the note back to Chee. "I'll take the box."

Chee put the note inside and secured the lid. "I'll miss you."

"Yeah. You, too."

"You don't sound convincing, Officer. Be safe out there."

She didn't respond. She would miss the husband she loved, but not Sergeant Chee as her boss.

Bernie stowed the box in the trunk and carefully placed the bag of food on the front seat, noticing that Chee and Sandra had even provided a fresh cup of hot coffee. She shackled Maya using the wide leather belt to secure the handcuffs with a chain at her waist, putting her prisoner in the back seat behind the protective bulletproof partition. She reminded her that the Miranda rights waiver still applied. They headed south on 491 toward Gallup. She should have told Chee she loved him before she left. But had he said *I love you* to her?

After only twenty minutes, she heard deep breathing and then an occasional snoring sound. She adjusted the mirror and saw Maya asleep, her head angled toward the window.

In light of the day's chaos, she welcomed the long drive. She passed the rocky dark volcanic remnants along highway US 491. Bennett Peak, Ford Butte, and Table Mesa rose to the sky, conspicuous landmarks and, according to some, places witches and skin-walkers frequented. The Chuska range, Níłtsá Dził, or Rainy Mountain, rose in the west and stretched north-northwest across the Arizona–New Mexico state line. The mountain's beauty in the soft October light made her heart sing.

She cruised through Gallup, hitting green lights and merging onto Interstate 40. She passed the tribe's Fire Rock Casino, the eerily quiet bunkers of Fort Wingate, and the red sandstone cliffs that marked the edge of the Colorado Plateau. The road climbed, and vegetation changed from the hardy shrubs of the high desert to piñon pines and juniper trees that enjoyed higher elevation. Traffic flowed well, and she felt the tense muscles in her neck relax.

She noticed the few buildings that comprised New Mexico's town of Continental Divide. Nearby was the geologic Continental Divide, the line of summits in the Rocky Mountains that separates the Atlantic and Pacific Ocean watersheds. She tried to imagine the thousands of streams joining to create the Grand Canyon's mighty Colorado River and finally emptying into the Pacific Ocean. And the other streams rushing toward the Rio Grande, the Gulf of Mexico, and the Atlantic.

She thought about Maya's unexplained move to the dark side, to murder. Maya was sober today when she made her confession. But in her experience as a cop, Bernie had observed that most bad behavior came from poor decisions that often started with alcohol. Maybe alcohol had sparked her old roommate's move to murder, and embarrassment about falling off the wagon explained the silence.

Drugs. Alcohol. Poverty. Violence. The seeds of the problem were planted long before she or Maya or anyone of their generation took a breath. The heritage of historical trauma loomed large over all Native people. For the Diné, Hwéeldi, or the Long Walk, epitomized the cruel efforts of mainstream society to turn Indians into white people. The forced march from their homeland to the prison camp at Bosque Redondo and the devastating loss of elders and infants during those years of captivity and dislocation still rippled through the Navajo world. When the People returned to their sacred land, they faced more hardship. The boarding school movement sent children to institutions that forcibly prohibited them from speaking the Navajo language and returning home for ceremonies.

How did people learn to be parents if they grew up without the example and guidance of loving relatives?

It was a testimony to the enduring strength and wisdom of the Navajo culture that so much of their traditions remained vibrant and resilient. They were as much a part of this landscape as the mountains and rivers.

She heard Maya shifting in the seat behind her. "Hey back there. How are you doing?"

"Fine. It felt good to finally sleep."

"When did we see each other last?"

"When my grandfather died. You paid your respects."

"That was also the last time I saw your son. We didn't get to talk much."

"Speaking of kids, do you think of starting a family?"

"I'm not ready. What was life like for you and Junior way out there in Hawaii?"

"Lonely. I missed my family and my friends. My husband worked all the time. When Junior arrived, I felt even more isolated. I stopped drinking when I got pregnant, but I started again after Junior arrived. I couldn't take it out there. This is where we belong. My son and I wouldn't have survived without Leon. I owe him so much."

"How's your sobriety coming?"

"Three years and counting. When I'm tempted, I remember that time I embarrassed you. You asked me if I wanted to drink or to have you as a friend. I said friendship, but I kept drinking."

"I don't remember your husband as a drinker. Was he?"

"Oh, not really. He'd have a glass of wine at dinner once in a while."

"I remember you and Jones from college days, how crazy you were about each other."

Maya sighed. "I love that man, but I was too young to make a commitment."

"Did he hurt you?"

"We hurt each other. I . . . I . . . I don't want to talk about him."

"I don't understand why you killed him if you still love him. Why did you shoot him?"

"I'm glad you don't understand." Maya fell quiet, but she didn't deny loving the man she'd killed.

Bernie watched the sunlight fade as Tsoodził, sacred Turquoise Mountain, appeared on the horizon to touch the clear sky. Mount Taylor, as the maps identified it, marked the southern boundary of Dinétah, the land the Holy People gave the Navajo. First Man covered it with a turquoise blanket, decorated the slopes with dark mists and female rain, and anchored it to the earth with a stone knife thrust through the sacred mountain from top to bottom.

The mountain rose northwest of Grants, a good place to stop. Bernie's eyes felt heavy. She'd been up since before dawn and had at least another two hours or so before they reached Socorro.

"I'm going to pull over in Grants for more coffee, and then stop so we can eat. Do you want something to drink?"

"A Pepsi would be good. And I have to use the bathroom."

Bernie took a convenient exit and cruised through the drive-up, where the girl at the window gave her the drinks for free despite her protests. She pulled onto I-40 East again and a few minutes later took the off ramp that led to the entrance of El Malpais visitor center. The building had clean restrooms and picnic tables outside. She checked to make sure Maya was secure, locked the unit, and went inside to inform the staff that she was transporting a prisoner who had to use the toilet.

Happy that the center had no other visitors, she opened the unit's rear door for Maya and escorted her to the ladies' room.

"I'm removing the handcuffs, but the stall door stays open."

"You're watching me?"

"That's right."

"You're kidding."

"You better get used to it. There's no privacy in prison."

That done, they went outside, and Bernie got the food Sandra provided. They sat across from each other at the table. Maya sipped her soda and Bernie tried the coffee—hot and weak. Sandra had provided a roast beef sandwich, a bag of chips, and a cookie for each of them. She took the one that was meat and bread and gave the container with the sandwich that had lettuce and tomato a shove across the picnic table. "This is for you."

Maya shook her head. "What's going to happen to me when we get to Socorro?"

"A bunch of paperwork. Then they'll put you in a cell. The detective handling the case will want to talk to you in the morning. You'll have to wait for your initial court appearance and a preliminary hearing. After that, it's up to the judge. Because you confessed to murder, I figure you'll have to stay in jail until the trial." Bail might be an option, but she didn't say that.

"Do you think I'll get the death penalty?"

"New Mexico abolished it years ago, and the Navajo Nation doesn't believe in it. In terms of your sentence, your motive for killing the man will make a difference."

"I shot him because he needed to die." Maya said it without adding any drama.

"You could say that about a lot of people, but you didn't kill them."

"Not yet anyway."

Bernie laughed despite herself. "When did you learn to use a gun?"

"A long time ago. Steve taught me in Hawaii. He said it might come in handy in case I had to defend myself."

"And did you?"

Maya left the question unanswered.

"When you came back to the Navajo Nation with little Junior, I admired the way you picked up the pieces, went to school, got your teaching creds, reinvented yourself. You seemed philosophical about the split in those days. What happened to make you shoot him?"

Maya studied the bag with her sandwich and then reclosed it.

"What did he do to you?"

"Bernie, stop. I don't want to talk about it. I need to think."

"Think? Did you think about the impact his death would have on your son?"

"Shut up." The flare of anger in Maya's voice surprised her. "Leave Junior out of this. I got married too young, had a kid, made a lot of bad choices. You don't have to understand. Let's go. Get this over with."

Maya rose from the table and tossed what was left of her drink onto the lava, the ice cubes bouncing like little diamonds against the dark rock.

"Sit down. Chill. I'm finishing my meal. You should reconsider that sandwich. You won't have a chance to eat again until morning."

Maya glared at her, and then sat.

"Detective Williams will have a lot to ask you. A temper tantrum won't work with her either."

"You don't . . ." They heard a whoosh of air from the muscular motion of big wings. The red-tailed hawk, atsáeelchii, settled in the tree across the parking lot, its back toward them as it peered into the lava field. After a few moments it flew on, soaring over the black rock where edible creatures hid. The bird, revered as a fast and efficient predator, rarely makes a mistake as it swoops down on its prey. Bernie watched, remembering that like the hawk itself, she needed to pay attention to small things as well as the big picture. Small things, for instance, like Chee remembering to order a sandwich without the garnish she always removed.

She loaded and resecured her prisoner, clicked on her own seat belt, and swung back on I-40. At exit 126 she gladly left the interstate highway traffic and pulled onto NM 6, heading to Los Lunas, where she would catch I-25 south for the final sixty miles or so to Socorro.

Unlike the interstate, NM 6 didn't carry much traffic. She noticed the bright front light on an occasional locomotive rolling along on tracks that paralleled the paved two-lane road. The trains stretched into the distance for a mile or more, a parade of container cars on their way to markets.

The empty highway gave her space to think, and she relived the confrontation with her husband. If the captain had spoken to her the way Chee had about Maya's interrogation, she would have let it roll by, perhaps even acknowledged that she'd been out of line. But how could Chee, her equal partner, her lover, her beloved, also be her boss? What would happen if the rumor circulating around the station came true and the captain retired? What if her husband headed the department? Today's conflict signaled that the transition would be hard for both of them.

It might be time to reconsider applying to be a detective. She had dismissed the idea earlier because the job involved travel, time away from Chee and Mama, but she'd prefer that to risking her marriage.

A voice from the back seat intruded on her thoughts. "How much longer?"

"About an hour. When did Junior's dad come back to New Mexico? Last I heard, he was still at the observatory in Hawaii."

"He got a good job out here late last year. It made me happy because it gave him a chance to spend time with our son."

"And for you two to try to rekindle something. Or was he seeing someone else?"

Maya didn't respond right away and when she spoke Bernie heard the cold logic in her voice.

"What if he wanted to get back together and I didn't? What if I wanted a divorce and he didn't? Imagine that we fought and I got mad and shot him?

"Or what if he tried to hurt me? What if the whole thing was an accident? Does it matter? He's still dead. I'm on my way to jail. What happened is between us, OK?" Maya's voice rose for emphasis, like a teacher bringing home a point or a frustrated parent. "Got it? Bernie, give it a rest."

And Maya fell silent.

As she drove, Bernie's thoughts circled back to the hawk she'd seen earlier that night, and to the concept of predator and prey. Lieutenant Leaphorn had told her that he once encountered a villain who viewed a select percentage of humanity as predators—men and a scattering of women destined to dominate. Everyone else was their prey, born to be dominated. That paradigm led to crime, including murder, with no remorse. Maya's cool demeanor, and, from what Williams suspected, the foresight to plan a murder to look like suicide, could be the marks of a predator. But the dead man, a successful scientist, seemed unlikely prey. And Bernie remembered Maya's tears from the first conversation.

The scenario didn't fit the Maya she had known. Something was wrong and it bothered her.

7

When they reached the Socorro County Detention Center, Tara Williams met them. She gave Bernie a grin. "It's great to see you."

"You, too."

"Thanks for driving her here."

Bernie watched her prisoner disappear down the hall in the company of a guard. She exhaled with a huge sense of relief.

"Did Maya say anything important on the trip?"

"Not really. She said she and Jones had some difficulties when they lived in Hawaii, but that was years ago. I noticed her crying when I brought up his death."

"Maybe she's just feeling sorry for herself, thinking of the time in prison ahead of her." Williams pushed a strand of hair behind her ear. "Let's get a pizza. You look like you've had a long day and I'm hungry. And if you don't feel like making that drive home, I've got a spare bed."

"I just had a sandwich, but yes to the pizza."

Williams laughed. "Pizza means pepperoni, right? I remember watching you remove the olives and green peppers and making a neat little pile of them."

While Williams went to change clothes, Bernie called the Shiprock station to tell them she'd arrived safely. Wilson Sam answered and said that Chee had finally left for dinner. "I wasn't surprised that the sergeant gave you the job of driving the suspect to Socorro. How much overtime will that be? Enough for a new battery in your Toyota, Manuelito? Some of the rest of us could have used the money. I thought you were more of a team player."

"I don't have to defend myself. But just to make it clear: I know the suspect and I wanted the opportunity to talk to her, to move the case along."

His laughter sounded bitter. "Right. No one else, like me for instance, could have a conversation with a person under arrest. You guys better watch yourselves."

"What do you mean?"

"Oh, nothing."

"Are you threatening me?"

"It wouldn't be smart to do that, would it?"

Bernie hung up, angry again. Chee didn't like being the one in charge, but he handled the job well. He did not play favorites, despite what the rookie thought. She was about to slip the phone in her pocket when it rang. She looked at the screen and answered the call. "Mama? Is everything OK?"

"Daughter, I have a bad feeling about you."

Bernie breathed a sigh of relief. "Everything's fine, Mama. I'm with a friend and we're just about to have a pizza."

"I pictured you outside under the moon with fear in your heart and Ma'ii singing. I needed to make sure you are safe tonight."

Mama's concern made her smile. "I'm fine. A little tired, that's all. I haven't heard any coyotes tonight. I've been traveling for work and I'm in Socorro." Before the question came, she told Mama that she'd had to transport a person for questioning, and then, to derail the discussion, she focused on the beauty of the ride.

"How is Cheeseburger tonight?" Mama and Darleen gave her husband that nickname when they were dating. It stuck.

"He's fine."

"That's good, my daughter. I have news about your sister. She's coming to visit next weekend."

Darleen had a job as a part-time assistant to old Mr. Natachi, and even though Mama and Darleen's relationship was well peppered with disagreement, Mama missed her younger daughter desperately.

"Darleen has been doing some art at the senior center there. You know, helping the elderlies make drawings, jewelry, things like that."

Mama talked on and Bernie listened, glad that her mother sounded happy and coherent. Mama didn't repeat herself once.

Bernie saw Williams striding down the hall toward her, swinging a beaded fob so the keys on the end clinked together like out-of-tune chimes. "I have to go now, Mama. I'll see you on Saturday."

"Saturday?"

"Yes, when my sister is there."

"That's right. You can come with us to pick apples at Mr. Youngman's place. They say the trees are full this year. Bring Cheeseburger, too."

"That sounds like fun. Gotta run."

The restaurant Williams selected was busy with couples, parents and sleepy-looking youngsters, and several groups of twenty-somethings with pitchers of beer on the table along with their pizzas. In uniform, Bernie drew some looks of concern from the beer drinkers as she and Tara headed to a table.

They caught up on personal news until the arrival of the pizza, half pepperoni and half what the menu called "veggie paradise," interrupted their conversation. The familiar spicy aroma of crust, cheese, meat, and spices made Bernie's mouth water. Williams added red pepper flakes and extra cheese to her slices. Bernie's had more than the usual amount of pepperoni. She thought about Chee. If he were there, she'd offer him some pepperoni. One of love's mysteries, she thought, was that she could miss him and still be annoyed.

They ate in companionable silence for a few minutes. The laughter of a child in the background made Bernie wonder what had happened to Bee, and if anyone knew anything yet about the dead infant.

"Tara, have you ever dealt with an unidentified body?"

"Yeah. A couple of them. One we tracked through fingerprints because he was an Iraq War veteran. I never could identify the other. Are you involved with something like that?"

"Indirectly. I found a dead baby in a house with a woman who had been left there to die. She vehemently denied knowing anything about it. The FBI has the case now, but I can't seem to shake off what I saw."

"Dead kids get to me even when they aren't my cases. And abused women, too. Makes me wonder about Maya Kelsey. Do you think that was her motivation?"

"The Maya I knew wouldn't put up with anyone slapping her around. But she wasn't a killer."

Williams sipped her beer and put the glass down. "Why would she admit to killing Jones if she didn't do it? It's not like anyone forced her, right?"

Bernie nodded. "She walked in to confess. I wonder if Maya didn't actually pull the trigger, but thinks she said or did something that provoked him to take his own life? You said you initially assumed he'd killed himself. Maybe he did."

"Maybe, but some things about the scene don't jibe."

"Like what?"

"It was cool last night. Why was the driver's window rolled down? Why hadn't Jones removed his seat belt? Why not kill yourself at home?" Williams tapped her fingernails on the tabletop. "Maya made this easy. One dead guy and one person who confesses to shooting him. Let's go with it."

Bernie lined up the pizza crusts on her plate as she spoke. "Maya and Jones have been separated for years. Maybe he did things when they were married that made her want to kill him, but why wait all this time?"

Williams raised her hands, palms toward Bernie. "Let's think about this objectively. The perpetrator needs means, motive, and opportunity. Opportunity? The guy came here to Socorro County, where Maya lives. Means? His own gun in the car with him. Motive? That's TBD. But two out of three?" She turned her beer glass around so the brewery's logo faced her. "I'd appreciate it if you could hang around awhile tomorrow, examine photos of the crime scene, read the report, and tell me what you think. My partner took some time off, and I could use some help with this."

"I'd like that. You'll have to check with the captain, I mean with Sergeant Chee. Captain Largo got called to Window Rock."

"Your sexy husband is filling in as your supervisor? Get out."

"Yeah, it's awkward that everyone knows I'm sleeping with the boss."

Williams laughed. "So, stay at my place tonight and come down to the station with me tomorrow."

Bernie gave Chee's cell number to Williams, hoping he'd be home after his long day. But he answered at the office. The detective made the request and nodded at Bernie.

"He wants to talk to you." She handed Bernie the phone.

"Hello?"

"Hey, beautiful. I'm glad you got down there OK."
Chee sounded tired. "Did Maya say anything interesting?"

"Nothing earthshaking. A few hints, like learning how to use a gun to protect herself. I'm disappointed that I couldn't get her to talk about what happened."

"Don't be hard on yourself. If she wouldn't respond to you, I think she's a lost cause. Don't worry about it."

"I just can't see that woman as a killer."

Chee chuckled. "That's what everyone says when their quiet neighbor gets arrested for storing corpses in his shed."

She laughed. She didn't want to be angry anymore.

"Give Williams the help she needs in the morning. I'm glad you aren't driving back tonight. I worry about you. And, yes, I'd say the same to Bigman, or anyone else who'd worked as many hours today. Sleep well, Sweetheart. And don't rush back. I'll give you the night shift."

"No, you won't, Sergeant. I'm off the next two days, remember?"

"You're pretty sharp for someone who worked a twenty-hour shift. I need to run. Good night."

"Good night." She waited for him to say *I love you* first, but he hung up instead.

Williams lived in a tidy stucco home in an older subdivision. Her second bedroom served as home gym and guest quarters. The exercise equipment looked like someone actually put it to work.

"There's an extra blanket in the closet if you need it. And shampoo and whatever for guests in the front bathroom."

"Thanks."

"Make yourself at home. I have to step out for a while. I'll see you in the morning."

"Great."

"It's good to have you here, my friend."

Bernie used the treadmill, which blocked the closet, as a place to drape her uniform and unload what she needed from her duffel. She put her gun on the bedside table.

She fell asleep before she had time to wonder if she would have trouble dozing off in a strange house and a single bed. But the sound of the front door opening pulled her instantly awake. She sat at the edge of the bed and reached for her gun, listening intently.

"Tara?"

"It's me. Sorry to wake you."

She recognized the sound of more than one set of footsteps headed down the hall. The carpet muffled most of the noise, but she heard the squeak of a shoe and some whispering as her friend and the companion walked to the bedroom. Bernie put her gun down, stretched out beneath the covers, and placed the extra pillow over her head as soundproofing.

She awoke before first light, dressed, and left the house quietly to run, watch the sunrise, and sing her morning prayers. When she came inside, she heard water running in the shower and saw Williams's "Help yourself" note along with a mug and a basket of energy bars. The coffee smelled wonderful. She took her mug to the porch and enjoyed the cool morning. Strange, she thought, not to hear the music of the San Juan. *Socorro*, the name the early settlers gave the town, means help or aid or assistance in Spanish. She wondered if there would be help for Maya or only punishment. She thought about Chee starting his day and about Bee and the baby.

"I see you found the coffee." Williams interrupted her reverie. "I remembered that you like it black, but if I'm wrong, there's milk in the refrigerator."

"Black is perfect."

"I'm not much of a breakfast eater, but I have cereal if you want some."

"Don't worry about me. I appreciate your hospitality."

"It comes with a price. After what you told me about Maya, I think we'll have to tag-team the interview to get her to say something we can use in court. After you look at the photos and the crime scene report, I'd appreciate it if you'd sit in with me."

"I had zero luck getting her to open up yesterday."

Williams sipped her coffee. "Bob—the other detective and my partner, Bob Rockfeld—he called this morning to tell me his Honey is really sick. He's taking another day off. If you don't want to join in the interview, that's your choice, but if you can help, I'd be grateful."

"What kind of staffing does your department have?" Bernie knew outsiders weren't always welcome.

Williams had been watching the sky brighten but turned her glance toward Bernie. "Oh, probably like yours. Too few of us doing too many things. And even though the Alamo Navajo reservation is in the county's jurisdiction, we have no Navajo-speaking officers. If someone needs to go to Alamo to ask questions, you'd get a lot further than this white girl."

"So, you think I'll need to go to Alamo?"

"We'll figure it out after we talk to Maya. I'm curious to see if a night in jail encouraged her to take back her confession. Or maybe she'll tell us why she did it."

At the police station, Williams introduced Bernie to her colleagues and then motioned her to a chair. She brought the computer to life and clicked on a case number. Bernie opened the file and started with the photos.

She saw a black sedan at various angles and shoe prints around the vehicle, difficult to discern on the hard, dry earth. The photographs had captured what looked like little circles on one shoe sole. She saw places where the dried grass next to the vehicle was flattened, as though someone had been standing on it. Maybe Jones had climbed out to relieve himself, she thought. She'd ask Tara what kind of shoes he wore.

Bernie studied the inside of the car, noticing the mess caused by the shooting. She saw the gun and the divorce papers Tara had mentioned, and a cell phone charger but no phone. She assumed it was in Jones's pocket, but she'd ask about that, too.

Finally, she clicked on pictures of the victim himself.

The entrance wound left a dark circle on the left side of Steve Jones's head, and the bullet's exit had splattered blood, bone, and brain matter inside the car. She looked at the man from different angles, noticing the gun next to the body. Nothing here indicated murder. Jones seemed to have died at peace with the world.

She began reading the report. The information matched what Williams had told her and supplied more details. The boy who discovered the car, Raul Apacheito, said he had touched nothing. After looking in the open driver's window, he raced home.

Bernie glanced away from the report. The image of the dead man must have burned itself into the child's brain. Raul would remember that morning for the rest of his life.

Williams wrote that she found a Rolex watch on the dead man's wrist and a wallet with three twenty-dollar bills, four credit cards, and a license belonging to Steve Jones in his pants pocket. Her inventory of what else she discovered in the car showed nothing unusual except the lack of a cell phone. Interesting, if it was a robbery, that the thief would take only his phone. She catalogued divorce papers involving Steve Jones and Maya Kelsey, noted the date on the forms and the fact that only Maya had signed them.

If it were her case, and if Maya hadn't confessed, Bernie might have closed the file as soon as OMI, New Mexico's Office of the Medical Examiner, verified that the cause of death was the wound to the head and that it came at an angle that could have been self-inflicted. But she would have wondered about the open window on a night cool enough for frost. And did the shoe prints in the photo match those of the boy who found the car? Or were they Maya's? She'd want to know if the victim had been fighting depression and spoken of suicide. Was he dealing with a problem at work, or a health crisis?

Williams returned. "Maya's on the way. What do you think so far?"

"Based on the photos and your report, I would have concluded that Jones died of a gunshot wound to the head inflicted without a struggle. I gather he didn't leave a goodbye note."

"Not in the car. I looked." Williams cleared her throat. "I just checked on the fingerprints. Jones's, of course, and Maya Kelsey's, and a third set that doesn't seem to be in the system.

"You forgot to tell me that your friend had been arrested before. DWI. Twice."

"I didn't know about the DWIs."

"We also found a copy of a restraining order Jones had filed in Hawaii against his wife. He charged her with physical and emotional abuse."

"Jones filed it on Maya, not the other way around?"

"That's right. The order was from fifteen years ago, a single incident. And before you ask, I found no reports that she had filed against him."

"Interesting. According to what her brother told me, the abuse went both ways." Bernie gave herself a moment to process the information. "What about Jones's cell phone? I didn't see it on your inventory."

"His phone wasn't in the car or in his pocket."

As if on cue, the phone on the desk rang.

"Detective Williams." She listened, then reached for a pen. "And who am I speaking with?"

Bernie watched her make a note.

"Yes, Steve Jones's body was discovered Saturday morning." She jotted something down. "Did you know him well?"

Williams listened. "Hold on a minute please, Dr. Mwangi. I'm putting you on speaker so Officer Manuelito can hear, too." She motioned to Bernie and pushed the speaker button. "Go ahead."

"Steve always gets to work early, so I worried when he didn't show up this morning. Then I called his house, got no answer. Called his cell. Nothing. You're sure it's him?"

"Yes. We're looking into what happened"

Dr. Mwangi's voice wobbled. "I know he was depressed, but I can't believe . . ." She stifled a sob. "There's a bunch of awards and certificates in his office. On the desktop he has, uh—*had* a couple little photographs of himself with a young man, I think his son. I'm sure someone in his family might like that stuff now. Especially now because . . ." Her voice trailed off. "Where was he when he died?"

Williams jumped in. "We can't talk about it. His death is under investigation. I'll ask Officer Manuelito to come out today and talk to you."

"I'm glad."

"Knowing more about him will help us figure out exactly what happened."

Bernie said, "I can contact his son and give him those items you mentioned. I'll come for them as soon as I'm done here. Where did he work?"

"Here at the VLA."

"The VA?"

"No, no. You're not from here, are you? The VLA. Karl G. Jansky Very Large Array radio telescope facility. I'm talking about his office here." Dr. Mwangi gave her directions and told her approximately how long the drive would take. "He killed himself, didn't he?"

"I can't discuss it."

As soon as they hung up, Williams said, "Did you hear what she thinks about suicide?"

Bernie nodded. "I'll go after we've interviewed Maya, before I head home. It's sort of on the way."

"Thanks." Williams gestured toward the door. "Maya's waiting for us. Let's do this."

Instead of the jeans and shirt she'd worn yesterday, Maya had on an orange jumpsuit. She looked up when they entered and then lowered her gaze to the tabletop. She'd seemed tired in the car; now, Bernie thought, she was the poster image for exhaustion.

Williams introduced herself, read Maya's Miranda rights, and obtained the waiver.

"Based on your preliminary confession, you've been arrested on an open count of murder. Officer Manuelito and I want to find out what happened. Would you like some coffee or water before we get started?"

Maya shook her head. "Just do it."

"I understand you teach at the Alamo Community School. How long have you been there?"

Maya sighed. "Three years. Ask me about Steve and why he's dead. Bernie already tried chatting me up."

"Tell us what happened that night with Steve Jones. Go through the evening he died step by step. Begin with why you were in the car with him."

Maya caught Bernie's eye and then turned to Williams. "I was in the car because we went on a date. Afterward, he pulled off the road. I shot him. That's all I have to say."

"We need more details."

"OK. Here are two details. He's dead and I've confessed to killing him."

Williams stood and raised her voice. "Look, I don't know you. I don't care one way or the other what happens to you, but it's my job to understand why Mr. Jones died in that car."

"Like I said, he's dead because I shot him."

Williams gave Bernie a look that said, *Your turn.*

"Maya, let's start over with something easy. Why were those divorce papers in the car the night Jones died?"

"I brought them, that's why." Maya sat a bit straighter. "Remember that Junior gets my van. Tell my brother not to forget about those models. Can I talk to him?"

Bernie deferred to Williams, who answered, "You're asking about talking to your brother, right?"

"No, my son."

"How old is he?"

"He'll be nineteen in November."

"If he wants to see you, that's allowed. They have the form he'll need to fill out at the jail."

Williams leaned in toward Maya. "I answered a question for you, so now it's your turn. Why did you kill that man?"

"He deserved it. That's all I have to say."

"It is in your best interests to give us the details of the murder. The way the courts see it, there are several kinds of homicide. When a judge passes sentence, your punishment could range from life in prison with no parole to only eighteen months behind bars. Your motivation for the murder will play a huge factor in how the case against you proceeds."

Maya lowered her head as though she were considering this.

"We're offering you a chance to explain yourself. We know that crime never happens in a vacuum. One action leads to another." Williams turned to Bernie. "Officer Manuelito, do you have anything to add?"

"I know you loved that man once, and he loved you, but I bet things weren't always easy. I can picture the scene where he started calling you names. Maybe getting physically abusive. You mentioned during the ride down here that you argued and Detective Williams found divorce papers in the car. Did you argue about that?"

"I don't remember."

She took a new approach. "Maybe Jones accused you of being a bad mother, or criticized Leon for how he helped raise your son."

Maya sat straighter. "Leave Leon out of this. This has nothing to do with him. My brother did as much as he could to be a good 'shidá'í. Don't you dare accuse him. I'm done here. Take me back to my cell."

Williams shook her head. "I'm in charge. The interview ends when I say so." She asked a few more questions, but Maya stayed silent.

8

J oe Leaphorn noticed the message light blinking on his landline. He played a little *Who called?* guessing game with himself before he picked up the voicemail. His housemate, Louisa, planned to head back to Window Rock and always called before she left the Northern Arizona University campus. Perhaps she'd finished early.

More likely the message came from his longtime buddy Captain Howard Largo, in town for police meetings about budget, new procedures, training, and the state of law enforcement on the sprawling Navajo reservation and in border communities. He'd left an invitation for the captain earlier, asking him to come by for coffee when today's session finished.

Leaphorn punched in the retrieve-message code, expecting Largo's deep voice explaining why he couldn't make it. Instead, he heard a woman, and it wasn't Louisa: *"Hello. I'm looking for a Navajo police-man, John Leapfrog. If this is the right number, I'd really appreciate a call. My name is Ginger Simons and Officer Leapfrog saved my life."* She left a phone number and hung up.

Leaphorn shook his head. If he'd answered, he could have told her Officer John Leapfrog wasn't at this number. You'd think the scammers would at least figure out who they were calling. Clever, though, adding the *saved my life* twist. Most cops he knew had saved someone's life, sometimes by something as routine as arresting a drunken driver.

The phone rang as he thought about that, and he answered. Largo dispensed with formalities, and as usual, they spoke in Navajo. "I didn't know you knew how to make coffee."

"I've got the recipe right here. It says to start with building a fire to warm the water."

"I'll be there after I turn in some forms so I get paid for this exercise in bureaucracy."

Leaphorn and Largo's camaraderie had been formed by shared frustration, shared loss, and shared triumphs. Their history as friends and colleagues, he knew, outdistanced what they had to look forward to. He put that notion aside, set up a pot of coffee, and got two mugs from the cupboard along with sugar for his friend.

He remembered with a touch of nostalgia how these department meetings worked. After the formal session came the time for kibitzing, catching up on things more personal than professional. He didn't miss the agendas, but he had enjoyed the companionship.

He heard the Navajo Police unit pulling into the driveway. He opened the door before Largo could knock. He noticed his friend's shoulders sloped a bit more than when he'd seen him in the summer.

The captain put a brown paper bag on the kitchen table. "These came from the meeting. The waitress knows me, so she packed them up."

Leaphorn poured the coffee and grabbed some napkins. Largo ripped the bag open, and the yeasty fragrance of the pastries, slightly abused but still tempting, floated into the room. One had pockets of red jelly at both ends. The two others were finished with something bright yellow. Thick lines of sweet white frosting decorated them all. Louisa would have been horrified.

Largo motioned to the treats. "You first."

"Which is better?"

"Oh, they're both good. Take the raspberry so I won't have to decide."

Leaphorn did as suggested. "How was the meeting?"

"The usual. We spend too much time talking about things that don't matter, and the important stuff comes up when we're all ready to leave." He paused. "Every time I'm there in the Navajo Inn, I think about the day you got shot. I'm glad you're a tough old bird."

They sat in companionable silence for a bit. Largo finished his pastry and broke the remaining Danish in half. "Did you hear the news? I'm thinking about retiring. I've put in plenty of time, and long, slow days like this make me wanna call it quits. And there seem to be more of them lately."

His friend had mentioned retirement before. Leaphorn had decided long ago that retirement was overrated. Largo wasn't married, lived alone, and, like Leaphorn, had no children. His job was his mistress, his reason for getting up in the morning.

"So, too many meetings? That's the reason you'd leave the department?"

Largo nodded. "That and the fact that I'm getting older."

"You could delegate the meetings to somebody. You've been getting older since the day you were born. You'll still be a senior citizen whether you're a policeman or not. It's nothing we can fix."

"Maybe I'll take the route you did and become a consultant. You working on anything interesting?"

"I've been offered an undercover job at a casino shadowing an employee they think might be stealing from them. And our tribal government wants me to help with background checks." Leaphorn sipped his coffee. "And besides that, another old cop asked me to serve on a task force to help to reduce violence against women. He reminded me of that case where a woman was kidnapped along with those Boy Scouts. You remember that one?"

"Weren't there some sandpaintings involved in that mess?"

Leaphorn nodded. "They were in a different part of the cave from where the hostages were held. Did you hear what happened to those things?"

"I know we had a hatałii go out there, but I never found out what came of it." Largo added sugar to his coffee. "So, do I have this right? You're OK with retirement as long as you're working."

Leaphorn smiled. "I like a challenge to keep my brain active but I appreciate the flexibility. I can take a nap or go somewhere on vacation with Louisa if I feel like it."

Largo grinned. "Vacation? When have you done that?"

"Well, I'm thinking about it. Louisa has a chance to go to Washington, DC, and the group that invited her is paying her expenses. She wants me to go."

"How is Louisa?"

"Oh, as feisty as ever. I worry about her driving to Flagstaff to teach, but she loves the job. So, are you seriously considering hanging it up?"

"I am. Every time my back aches. Every time an officer gets hurt on my watch. Every time I have to study up on new regulations. Every time I get to defend the budget for the Shiprock district and beg for more money. And especially when there's a horrific case like the little girl who was abducted and killed. Retirement means not worrying each time the phone rings."

Leaphorn remembered the little girl case as if it had happened yesterday. She was walking home from school with her brother when a stranger offered them a ride. He let the boy go, then raped and killed the sister. The man confessed and went to prison, but the loss and unease hung in the air like a bad smell. Leaphorn, and probably everyone else on the Navajo Nation, had become more aware of and incensed by the number of women and girls who were victimized.

Largo reached for a napkin. "If I wasn't working, I could spend time with my sister's kids, read, fix things around the house, maybe buy some cattle. I want to drive to California and visit friends from my days in the Marines. I'd like to get an old motorcycle and cherry it up. But then I think, what will I do when that's finished? I can't see myself picking up a job at Walmart."

"You could be a consultant, go to work for one of the television shows about cops. Keep them straight. That would be a full-time job."

Largo grunted. "I've always been a cop. It's in my DNA, you know? I tell myself I'm too old for this life, but it's really, well, it's who I am. Who would I be without it?"

"That's the question I wish I'd figured out before I gave notice. Life as a civilian would have been easier if I'd had a plan." After Emma's death he couldn't focus on work; retirement seemed the logical step. Friends, contacts from the courts, and, eventually, Navajo Nation law enforcement began asking him for help with tough cases. They paid for brainstorming or research. What he'd initially done as a favor morphed into a part-time business. For Leaphorn, leaving things to chance had worked, but he never recommended it.

"By a plan, you mean more than drinking coffee with another old coot?"

"Yeah, but friends matter to me more than they used to. Maybe because it's harder to make new ones and the old ones are passing on. Take my advice and generate some ideas for how you'll spend your time. Think of something you'd like to do as an elder that makes a difference."

"Like that task force?" Largo sighed. "There's another thing that keeps me coming to the station. I want to know that the Shiprock operation will be in good hands when I decide to pull the plug on work."

Leaphorn waited for his friend to mention Jim Chee as his logical successor, but Largo changed the subject.

"Bernie Manuelito asked me what she'd have to do to join the criminal investigation unit. I told her to apply. She's already a good detective by instinct. Some training and she'll be a whiz."

"Is she going to go for it?"

"I don't know. I'd hate to lose her." Largo folded his paper napkin into a neat rectangle. "You're right about that planning stuff. If I got bored enough, I figure I could get a job at one of those call centers, using my skills at badgering suspects to persuade people to get a new credit card."

"Speaking of unwanted calls, I got a message from someone looking for Officer John Leapfrog. She said this Leapfrog guy had saved her life."

Largo chuckled. "That's a new one. What did she try to sell you?"

"I don't know what the scam was. But she left her name and an 800 number. More sophisticated than the average con."

"Maybe she's legit. What was the name?"

"Ginger Simons."

"I remember when you helped rescue some college professor collecting witchcraft stories. Seems like there was a missing bilagáana woman involved. Do you recall that?"

"Vaguely." Leaphorn stared at the ceiling. "Her name was Ellen. Ellen Leon. Not Ginger."

The captain hoisted himself from the kitchen chair. "Time to hit the road. I appreciate the coffee. You know, if I got a message like that, I'd call back out of curiosity and for some attaboys. You can hang up when she asks for your bank account number."

Leaphorn washed his friend's cup and discarded the pastry bag. He poured himself more coffee and noticed the pad where he had written "Ginger Simons" and the phone number. Maybe he should return the call. It would be entertaining if nothing else.

He turned on the computer and typed Ginger Simons into the search bar. The instant response directed him to dozens of people with that name or something similar on Facebook and LinkedIn, websites to search public records, and more. He scanned links to botanical information about gingerroot and gingersnaps. He noticed Ginger as a nickname for redheads and women named Virginia.

Frustrated, he typed in the 800 number. The results came back with the name of an international nonprofit foundation, Closely Watched. Then Giddi strolled in, reminding him noisily that she hadn't been fed. He left the computer, and she followed him like a shadow to the kitchen.

He dished some wet food for the cat, her expected afternoon treat, and freed his cell phone from the charger, noticing a text from Bernie. Her question was complicated, so he texted back asking that she call him. He thought about Jim Chee. Why hadn't Largo mentioned the sergeant as a logical successor? Chee had worked in Shiprock for years, knew the ropes. He was due a promotion. What trouble had Chee cooked up now?

9

The drive from Socorro to the VLA was the sort of journey Bernie loved. Open spaces framed by the blue bulk of the Magdalena Mountains without traffic to distract from the view. The morning light gave the grass a golden glow as it shimmered in the autumn breeze. She slowed when she reached the town of Magdalena, a small, picturesque settlement that had seen its heyday decades ago, she thought, if it ever had a heyday. She pulled off at a coffee shop with a turquoise bear on its sign. The proprietor greeted her warmly.

"What kind of coffee for you today?"

"A small cup of regular, no room for cream. How much farther till the VLA?"

"Maybe twenty minutes, depending on how fast you go. You'll start to see the discs pretty soon." He poured her coffee as he spoke. "You know much about this place?"

"No, sir."

"Magdalena was a big deal in its time. It got the name Trails End because the cowboys loaded the herds onto the railroad here to ship them out for beef. Mining was huge, too."

"I noticed a bunch of art galleries."

"Right. Our galleries draw some visitors, but we get more than our share of astrotourists. Bet you never heard of that."

"You're right. Who are they?"

"Folks who come to see VLA and for our Enchanted Skies Star Party. This area has some of the best star-gazing anywhere. The altitude, dry air, and the fact that we're away from city lights. All that draws those people with their telescopes."

"That's an advantage to living in t'áá dzígaidi. You know, the middle of nowhere."

The man smiled at her. "You've got it."

Bernie took the to-go cup back to her unit. If she was a detective, she wondered, would she miss the diversity of patrol work? She checked her phone for messages as she sipped her coffee. Chee hadn't called. She knew he had too much work, but still felt the cold disappointment.

She headed toward the VLA and after a few miles spotted the disc-shaped telescopes. They rose from the arid remoteness, offering their concave faces to a cloudless sky. They reminded her of the equipment used for satellite TV, except on a grander scale. As she drew closer, she noticed that the devices were mounted on train tracks. The convergence with the area's history as rail center for cowboys made her smile.

She followed the sign to the parking area, locked her unit, and headed to the closest building, the visitor center. The entrance took her directly into a small gift shop. The young woman behind the counter looked up from her book. "May I help you?"

She gave the woman her name. "I'm here to see Kathy Mwangi."

"Oh, Dr. Mwangi. Just a moment, please, while I page her." She handed Bernie an information card. "Here are the guidelines for guests. You'll need to turn off your cell phone and any other Wi-Fi or Bluetooth devices. Those signals interfere with our sensitive equipment."

Bernie complied.

A few moments later a tall, slim, dark-skinned woman with a runner's body came through the door.

"Hi, I'm Dr. Katrina K. Mwangi. Call me Kathy. You made good time. The items for Steve's family are in his office. Come this way, please."

They walked outside and moved down a concrete sidewalk to a second building a bit closer to the giant telescopes.

The scientist's long-legged stride in her purple athletic shoes challenged Bernie to keep up.

"Kathy, are you a runner?"

"Yes. I'm training for the Duke City Marathon. You know about it? It's in Albuquerque."

"I've heard of it."

"Do you run, Officer?"

"Call me Bernie. I run for fun and to stay in shape. It helps clear my head. But I haven't done a marathon."

"After a day of brain work, I crave something physical. My ancestors came from Kenya, where running is a tradition. Even though I was born in Chicago, I guess I'm carrying it on."

"Running is big with many of us Navajos. We Diné run to honor our relatives, too, or at least some of us still do."

When they arrived at the second building, Kathy opened the door with a key card.

Beyond the small front alcove Bernie noticed a stairway, an elevator, and what looked like at least one office. "What kind of research are the scientists out here involved in?"

"We do radio astronomy. Most people have never heard of it, but it's a major branch of observational astronomy. Sensitive telescopes like those outside the building can reveal otherwise hidden characteristics of the universe by detecting radio waves. Then, with the help of our supercomputer, we analyze their data to learn about things such as glowing remains of exploded stars, the birth of the planets, what lies at the hearts of galaxies, black holes, pulsars, or even the final ticks of a dying star."

"That's amazing. Where does the radio come in?"

"Those telescopes you saw out there listen for radio waves, lower-frequency transmissions or, I guess you could say, energy waves more subtle than the human eyes discern. It's energy not detectable with the optical telescopes most people are familiar with. We transform the radio waves into images to make it easier to understand them."

"Have there been any big discoveries out here?"

Kathy nodded. "These telescopes found ice on the planet Mercury and a supermassive black hole at the center of the Milky Way galaxy."

The Milky Way, Łees'áán yílzhódí. Bernie smiled as the old name came to her. The Navajo term translated to "cake that is dragged along." It conjured an image of the cosmic star cloud as a trail that would be created by pushing a cake through the sky, leaving a path of tasty crumbs behind as it moved among the celestial bodies. She had marveled at the starry cloud as a girl sleeping outside in the summer. The swath of twinkling light against the dark night still delighted her.

Kathy took her key card in hand and tapped the door to unlock it. "Steve Jones worked in here."

The security surprised Bernie. "What kind of research did Jones do? Was it something secret?

"I'm not sure of the details because his work was outside my field. But in general, he and his team were helping us understand why the universe is expanding. They were investigating a large cosmic blast. Imagine that a black hole at the center of the explosion pulled in cosmic material to form a rapidly rotating disc. The disc radiates prolific amounts of energy and propels superfast jets of matter from its poles. But what else is happening? What's the rest of the story? That's what Dr. Jones wanted to discover."

Kathy smiled. "You look puzzled. Can you take a few minutes to watch a video Dr. Jones and his team made? It explains his project better than I could."

"I'd like that."

Kathy pushed the door open. "I liked Steve. What happened to him?"

"I can't discuss the details."

"Sorry."

They entered a windowless room. Dim light radiated from the computer monitors. Three men and a woman, all wearing headphones, sat at workstations. They looked up when Bernie entered. The men went back to work, but the woman stood and came toward them. She looked to be in her late thirties. Her most striking feature was her blonde hair stylishly cropped asymmetrically, chin-length on the right and longer on the left. She wore a white blouse with a blue sweater, dark jeans, and flat-soled shoes that looked comfortable, attractive, and expensive. She reminded Bernie of a tough professor she'd had at the University of New Mexico.

"Hello, Officer. I'm Dr. Joy Peterson. Are you here because of Steve's death?"

"I'm Bernadette Manuelito. I'm assisting with the investigation."

"We're all devastated. Such a loss to everyone here and to science." Peterson sighed. "But not a huge surprise. We all noticed how depressed he'd been lately. I assume it was suicide. Dr. Jones was a fine man and a smart researcher."

Bernie's curiosity clicked into action. "Did he mention suicide?"

Dr. Peterson nodded. "I'd be glad to talk to you about him, but I'm in the middle of something right now. If you can wait a couple hours, I'll be free then." Peterson reached into the pocket of her designer jeans, extracted a silver case, and gave Bernie a card. "I'm surprised the police are involved in Steve's passing."

"Any unattended death gets our attention."

"I understand Dr. Mwangi has set some of Dr. Jones's things aside for his son."

"Yes, that's why I'm here."

"Steve kept a small notebook with his thoughts from a project he and I worked on together. I looked through the items Kathy has for you and didn't see it. If you come across it, I need it for my work."

"I understand."

As Peterson returned to her computer, Kathy steered Bernie toward a large monitor. "Dr. Jones used this computer to build the presentation. I can't believe . . ." Her voice cracked. She turned away, tapped the keyboard, and the screen came to life with pinpoints of light and small swirls of bright color against a deep blackness. The stunning images resembled nothing Bernie had ever seen before.

Kathy clicked on something and the image changed. "He often spoke to schools and civic groups about why science matters, and what we can learn from the stars.

That's the reason he developed this presentation. He wanted to share his curiosity about gravity and a force that we view as its opposite."

"The opposite? What's that?"

"The name we've given it is dark energy."

"Sounds menacing."

Kathy smiled. "I figure Dark Energy would be a good name for a racehorse."

She clicked on the program, invited Bernie to sit, offered her headphones, then stood beside her as they watched the pictures from deep space. The approach, while basic enough that a nonscientist could understand it, offered a smart introduction to a world Bernie found intriguingly unfamiliar.

"Can you replay some of it? I would like to see the opening again."

"Hold on." Kathy looked for the mouse. "I get thrown off at Steve's computers because he's, I mean he *was*, left-handed."

Kathy found the mouse and made the adjustment.

"I see Steven Jones, PhD, here in the credits. Who are the others?"

"The colleagues who collaborated with him. The two names in biggest type were the lead scientists on his team, Dr. Peterson and Dr. Bellinger. The rest of us were technical support and advisors—you know, worker bees. He could have given us more credit, but that wasn't Dr. Jones's style."

"Is your name there?"

She tapped the screen. "Yeah, in the small print. Dr. Katrina K. Mwangi."

"How did Jones get along with the rest of the staff?" In mainstream society, professional jealousy could provide a strong motive for murder. She had never known a killing like that among Navajos.

"I respected him for his brilliant mind. And I was taught to never speak ill of the dead."

Bernie heard her uneasiness. "What was he like as a person?"

Kathy pressed her lower lip between her teeth. "I don't know how to answer that. We rarely interacted unless it involved our work, and I never saw him socialize with the other researchers except for Dr. Peterson. He was quiet, totally passionate about his research. Never missed a day."

One of the men glanced in their direction. Kathy lowered her voice. "I was surprised to find the photos I mentioned. He never talked about a family."

"So, tell me about Jones and Peterson."

Kathy shifted her weight from heel to toe; then she stood still.

"I have a conference call in a few minutes. Let's go upstairs to Steve's office. I want to give you the pictures and awards."

The second-floor space opened onto a dramatic view of the radio telescopes, the broad plain on which the engineers had erected them years ago, and the mountains that framed the scene. From this perspective, Bernie noticed, the Very Large Array resembled huge white metal flowers or giant saucers filled with sunlight. The discs lined up in a Y on their specially configured metal tracks.

Kathy introduced the woman who worked at the computer consoles and then pointed out the large room to the right. "That's WIDAR, the computer I was talking about. State of the art."

"It's huge."

"And so fast it can perform sixteen quadrillion operations every second."

"I can't even picture a number that large. Why do you call it Whydar?"

"It an acronym. The initials stand for Wideband Interferometric Digital Architecture."

"Wouldn't it be more convenient to have all this in Albuquerque or Los Alamos where they do so much scientific research? Why is it out here?"

"We get that question a lot. The telescopes live here because both people and humidity can interfere with the signal reception and we don't have much of either. This place is ideal."

Jones's office window framed the mountain vista. He had two more computers, and a bookcase packed with bound manuscripts, books, and notebooks, all neatly arranged. Bernie saw nothing personal to offer an insight into the dead man. A cardboard box on which Kathy had written "Steve Jones Family" sat on the desktop.

Bernie took in the view. "I gathered you had something to say back there that you didn't want to share with a roomful of people."

"You asked how Dr. Jones interacted with the rest of us. As I mentioned, he was polite, professional, focused on his work. He and Dr. Peterson, the woman who introduced herself to you, were more than scientific colleagues. In a place as small as this, we're like family, and you know families gossip." Kathy walked to the window. "And then things changed. I noticed less friendly behavior, as though they'd had a disagreement. That's what I was thinking about when I mentioned that Dr. Jones seemed more withdrawn, troubled."

"Did you hear him talk about suicide?"

Kathy shook her head. "Not to me, but like I said, we never discussed much except work. He went through a phase a few weeks ago where he seemed especially quiet and, well, sad. I asked him about it, and he said that he'd hit a snag in his research and that his team was bickering. Then, last week he seemed to perk up. I assumed whatever bugged him had passed."

"Did he say what the work problem was?"

"No. You ought to talk to Dr. Peterson and Dr. Bellinger, their colleague in Hawaii, about that."

Bernie tried again. "Why did you say Jones seemed happier last week?"

Kathy smiled. "Well, I noticed that he had a nice haircut. I was teasing him, and he told me he did it because he had a date with a dear friend. He even winked at me."

"Did he tell you who?"

"No."

"Did Dr. Jones have enemies?"

She shrugged. "Ask Dr. Peterson. She knows, I mean *knew*, him best. If there's nothing else, I need to prepare for my call."

"Before you go, could you open the box for me?"

Kathy raised her eyebrows but took scissors from the desktop and sliced through the tape. She started to leave.

"Please stay until I've unloaded these things and done an inventory."

"I made a list. You'll see it there on the top."

Bernie removed the folded piece of white paper. The inventory numbered and described each of eighteen items. She took out the first picture, a framed photo of a man beside an antique telescope. He looked like the person she remembered from years ago. "I assume this is Steve Jones?"

"That's him."

Jones had aged well, grown more handsome and distinguished-looking. Bernie noticed the watch on his wrist, a similar timepiece to the one in Detective Williams's crime scene photo.

She placed the other items on the desktop. The inventory matched, as she'd expected, and the notebook Dr. Peterson had inquired about wasn't there. She signed the inventory sheet at the bottom, had Kathy sign and date it, and put it back in the box. She gave Kathy a business card.

"Thanks for your assistance. After the shock wears off, you might think of something else that could be helpful in the investigation. Please call me, or the Socorro Sheriff's Office."

"I will." Kathy put the card in her pocket. "I miss Steve. Thanks for seeing that his family gets this."

Bernie began to repack the collection, snapping a photo of each item for the record.

A pair of photographs framed together captured her attention. In the picture on the right, Junior and Jones stood in front of a small rock overhang. Junior gazed up toward the inside of the shallow setback. Jones looked relaxed and happy. The second photo showed a rock face decorated with four-sided black stars, what archaeologists call a star ceiling.

Bernie studied the image. This was a place of power, a shelter where ancient ancestors honored the benevolent Black Star People. They decorated the roof of the cave with a single star or sometimes clusters of stars painted or stamped. She had heard that they placed the stars on the highest ceilings by using stencil-tipped arrows dipped in pigmentation and shot with a bow from the ground.

She had seen star ceilings at Tsegi in deep rock shelters. The Canyon de Chelly elder who led her and Chee to those places explained that these centuries-old depictions of stars had links to healing ceremonies. Quite simply, he said, the celestial pictographs left by the ancient ones literally possessed star power.

Afterwards, Chee had explained that the shelters with their star ceilings were also places of protection. She put the photo in with the rest, hoping that the picture would ease Junior's grief and give him a buffer from despair in his period of mourning.

Needing to reseal the box, she opened the top desk drawer looking for tape. She found it, along with Post-its, paper clips, pens and markers, and a handwritten list of phone numbers. She glanced at the list, noticing Maya Kelsey's name, and snapped a photo of it before closing the drawer.

She said goodbye to the woman on computer duty with the million-dollar view and made her way back to the visitor center, where she spoke again to the receptionist. "I'd like to talk to Dr. Joy Peterson. Can you let her know?"

"Sorry, but I can't disturb her. All the scientists are tied up on a conference call. Shall I give her a message for you?"

"No thanks." She knew she or Detective Williams would follow up if necessary.

"Come back and take a tour. This place is totally cool. If you have kids, they'll love it."

Outside, the day reminded her of why she loved October. Warm sun, clear blue sky, crisp air—and technically, at least, it was her day off. After she'd driven a few miles, she turned on her cell phone, called Williams, and gave her a summary of what she'd learned. "I have the box of awards and photos for his family, and I briefly met a scientist who worked closely with Jones here. Both that woman and Kathy mentioned Jones's depression, although Kathy said his mood had lightened recently."

"Anything special about what's in the box?"

"Not that I saw. I documented the contents, just in case something might be relevant to the investigation. I'll send you the images and my report when I get back to Shiprock, but you've heard the highlights, such as they are."

"I'll let you know when I get something from OMI." Williams cleared her throat. "I have a friend who works there. I'll check with her to see where Jones's case is on their to-do list. Maybe she can nudge things along. Thanks for your help."

"I wish we'd gotten Maya to open up. I'd feel better about her confession if I knew what motivated the shooting."

"Yeah, me, too. We did our best. Safe travels. Tell your new boss to be good to you."

She needed to call Chee and begin to resolve their misunderstanding. She ought to check in with Darleen, too. But for now she limited her focus on the beauty of the drive. She felt herself smile. It made her happy to be heading home.

10

Jim Chee awoke alone that morning for the first day in a long time. He pulled the arm that had reached out to give Bernie a squeeze back from the coolness of her side of the bed, returning it to the warm territory closer to his torso. He closed his eyes. Usually he looked forward to going to work. But not lately. Today, he'd face soul-numbing bureaucracy, finding himself toe-to-toe again with administrative problems that threatened to sap his spirits more than the crimes and human weaknesses he dealt with as a cop on the beat.

After five minutes, he padded to the kitchen to start the coffee—half as much as usual this morning—and to check out the day's beginning from the kitchen window. He heard the drumbeat of a downy woodpecker in the cottonwood and the low, smooth call of the doves. Migration time. Much to be grateful for.

Ghaaji', the start of the Navajo calendar, had long been his favorite month. He loved October's cool nights and the gentle way the days warmed, the changing light, the flutter of gold in the stately trees along the San Juan River, the start of thicker coats on the cattle. This year, because of the captain's absence, he had reluctantly turned down several opportunities to work under the big sky, including an invitation to help his clan brother in Monument Valley build some new corrals. Instead of cruising in his unit and enjoying the scenery as he answered calls, he found himself at the station sitting behind a computer.

He never realized how much interference Captain Largo ran for his officers. He wondered what would happen when the man finally retired. Although the captain hadn't spoken of it to him directly—Largo kept his personal life far removed from police business—the man had reached the age and level of experience where doing something else might look increasingly attractive.

Chee's thoughts roamed from there to the question of encouraging Bernie to become a sergeant and therefore the logical go-to person next time Largo had to leave someone in charge. But when they'd talked about her going for a promotion, she mentioned that working as a detective, joining the criminal investigation unit, sounded more appealing. He saw the sparkle in her beautiful eyes as she said it. Then she told him that she'd worry about Mama because the job could involve extensive travel, and that she'd miss him on those days and nights away from home. And finally, she said, she'd have to give up the chance to help fix problems immediately, the opportunity she had daily as a regular cop.

He could see both sides of the issue. He knew she loved the challenge of solving a mystery, thinking about a situation and the best way to find and ultimately arrest the bad guys. Becoming a detective would offer her the mental stimulation she craved.

On the other hand, Bernie liked dealing with people who needed help at the moment. Leaving patrol would deprive her of that. And he enjoyed her presence, her wit, her sweet company, and a new position would mean less time together. She'd only been gone for one evening and he already missed her.

He trusted her to make the right decision for herself, her mother, and their marriage. As he sipped his coffee, he realized, again, how deeply he loved her and how fortunate he was to have such a fine woman in his life.

Chee had just climbed out of the shower when his phone rang. He grabbed a towel, hoping it was Bernie, and grimaced when he saw that the call came from the station.

Wilson Sam was on the line. "Bad news, Sergeant. I have a heads-up for you."

"Yá'át'ééh. Officer, when you call someone, especially this early, give them a respectful acknowledgment before you get to business." Chee wondered how Sam had failed to learn the basic politeness that not only shaped most Navajo-to-Navajo relationships but eased human interaction everywhere.

"Yes, sir. Yá'át'ééh."

"So, what's up?"

"Well, you know that woman Manuelito found, the one all tied up? She managed to get herself out of the hospital early this morning and she's on the run. The FBI called and they need us to help find her, to make it a priority. Agent Johnson's office sent a photo and description. You know how she never tells us anything? I chatted her up. Agent Johnson let on to me that this gal isn't our average victim."

As Bernie had described things to him, he'd assumed that Bee's situation resulted from sex trafficking, or maybe that the woman had found herself on the wrong side of gang activity or a botched drug deal.

Sam paused, hoping, Chee knew, that his sergeant would acknowledge the rookie's accomplishment.

"Why is this so urgent?" He figured someone at the FBI was deeply embarrassed, but the woman on the loose didn't seem to pose much danger to others.

"Ah, Agent Johnson didn't tell me. But she sounded angry about the way Manuelito handled things out there."

"Angry? Why? Johnson wasn't even there."

"Well, ah . . ."

Chee felt his stomach tighten. "What did she say about Bernie?"

"So here's how it unpacked. Agent Johnson wanted to leave a message for Captain Largo about the gal who ran from the hospital, but I informed her that the captain was in a meeting and you were in charge. She said she couldn't talk to you about whatever it was because it concerned your wife."

Chee took a breath. "Anything else happening this morning?"

"Oh yeah. The cattle Officer Manuelito couldn't deal with yesterday moved back to the road. Someone called to say he and his kids almost hit one. The dude yelled at me. He wants us to take care of it."

"Call the livestock folks again. Tell them about the man, and stay on it until they agree to send someone to deal with this. Then call Angry Man back to give him the name and number of the livestock person you talked to."

As he dressed, Chee thought about the woman Bernie called Bee leaving the hospital and the news that the FBI wanted help finding her. He recalled Bernie telling him that the woman was dirty, hungry, and dehydrated when the ambulance took her. She had a dislocated elbow and perhaps some broken ribs. He could understand why the FBI hadn't considered her a serious flight risk in that condition. Someone must have assumed she'd feel safe, taken care of, in the hospital. Grateful, even.

But he had seen behavior similar to Bee's before, impulse motivated by terror. Whatever she feared mattered more than temporary comfort. In addition to her physical damage, Bee must have suffered deep emotional and psychological trauma as she waited to die in the abandoned house. Those injuries took longer to heal. Sometimes they just scabbed over until the next crisis.

Chee stopped on the way to his truck and stood in the sun, shaking off Bee's gloomy story, grateful for a moment of peace. The river's laughter had grown quieter as fall advanced, and now its liquid music whispered. He watched the water shimmer. The monolith of Ship Rock rose against the cloudless blue sky, solid and unchanging. A perfect reminder, he thought, of his people's resilience and their firm place in this blessed world.

His cell phone buzzed as he walked to his truck. He hoped it was Bernie. It wasn't.

"Sergeant Chee?"

"Sandra?"

"It's me. Listen, I'm sorry, but I can't make it in today." Sandra was the main dispatcher. Reliable was her middle name.

"Is everything OK?"

"Not exactly. I can't talk about it, Sergeant."

He heard the upset. "Take care of yourself and stay in touch. Let me know if I can help."

She hung up without another word.

Sandra not only did a fine job at dispatch, she also made sure the morning crew had fresh coffee. Her level disposition helped keep the station on course. Now, he'd have to scramble to find a temporary replacement. He knew Captain Largo used someone else for her shifts when Sandra went on vacation, an older woman, Mrs. Slim. He couldn't recall her first name but assumed the captain had her contact information in an obvious place. In the meantime, the rookie could handle the phones and radio, and try making the coffee, too.

He called Sam from the car to catch him before he left at the end of his shift and got the reaction he expected.

"You're kidding. I've been on duty forever already."

"Excuse me?"

"Yes, sir."

At the station, Chee got some coffee (Sam made it too weak, but at least he made it), sat at the captain's desk, and brought the computer to life. If there were fires to put out, he'd deal with that before searching for Mrs. Slim. He found an announcement for training in analyzing criminal behavior and several notes about the new class of graduates from the reopened Navajo Police Academy. He was proud of the way his station managed with the staff they had, but another officer or two would be great. Competition to hire the newbies would be intense because their training dealt with the specific challenges that confronted law enforcement in the Navajo Nation. He marked the email as IMPORTANT and added a note to the captain: Can we get some of these folks assigned to us?

He'd started to look for Mrs. Slim's phone number when Officer Sam buzzed him.

"Sergeant, there's a call for Manuelito from the livestock office."

"Can you handle it?"

"Well, it seems like Manuelito complained about the problem yesterday and the gal on the phone is breathing fire back at us."

Chee sighed. "Forward her to me in the captain's office."

He picked up the call, explained that Bernie was off and he was the person in charge.

"I'm Stephanie Dawson. I heard that Officer Manuelito was hot under the collar about some cattle on the road and that you had another call this morning about a near accident. I wanted her to know that the situation is on our radar."

"Tell me what that means."

"We finally tracked down the family who lives, or used to live, out there. I reached a daughter, Mella Atcitty, in Farmington. Her parents, Mr. and Mrs. Arthur Nez, had lived on that ranch for fifty years, always keeping the place in good shape. Mrs. Nez died, and shortly after Mr. Nez had a fall, fractured a hip, and got moved to an old folks' home."

Dawson paused, but Chee knew that she wasn't done with the story. She didn't seem upset. Leave it to the rookie to get things wrong.

"One of the nephews agreed to care for the livestock, but he hasn't done the job. Mella gave me his phone number, but no one answered and there was no way to leave a message. I called the daughter back and explained the problem. By law, we have to allow the family another few days to take care of the hazard before we confiscate the animals."

Chee understood. "I appreciate your call and the limitations you face. I'm concerned that someone could get hurt out there, especially at night. Those steers hang out along the road."

"I know. We're lucky that there's not much evening traffic. We're working to get this resolved as soon as possible. I'd appreciate anything you can do to help with this, Sergeant."

Chee asked for the phone number for Mella Atcitty and for the unanswered cell number of the negligent nephew caretaker.

"We'll work on it from this end, too. Animal abuse incidents like this bother me. You have an old man who cared for the land and the animals, who probably worked hard all his life, and then the next generation who doesn't seem to respect that. It's sad."

"The world is changing, but there are still more good people than otherwise. Like your Officer Manuelito. She went out of her way to try to fix this. When you see her, tell her we appreciate it."

He'd let his coffee get cold, and that gave him an excuse to leave the desk. The rookie frowned as he walked past.

Chee stopped. "Something wrong, Officer?"

Sam studied a turquoise ring on the center finger of his left hand. "Sir, I'd like to go out to where those animals got loose and secure them. I've had a lot of experience with cattle. And then I could serve that warrant that Manuelito screwed up."

Chee clenched his jaw. "Officer Manuelito did what she could. The guy wasn't there."

"Yes, sir."

"Are you tired, Officer?"

"No, sir. My last shift was slow, you know? I got some sleep."

Chee thought about that. "Tell you what. Find me the name and phone number of the lady who substitutes for Sandra, Mrs. Slim. I'll call and ask her to come in today. If she can work, then you can go out there."

"Thanks, sir. You know, I might be even better with animals than I am with people."

Chee believed him.

Then, to Chee's happy relief, the morning got better. Sam discovered the information for Mrs. Teresa Tsosie Slim. Mrs. Slim answered the phone. Yes, she could come in. She had no other plans and could return to work tomorrow if necessary. She would pack a lunch for herself and be there within the hour. She made it in twenty minutes.

Chee had almost finished the required paperwork for Mrs. Slim as an emergency temporary employee and was thinking about lunch himself when she buzzed him. "It's Officer Bigman, sir."

"Put him through."

Bigman sounded tense. "Sergeant, I've got a lead on the woman the FBI wants."

"Go ahead."

"Mario Arnold, you know, the pastor at Living Waters, said a woman came into the church office asking for money. She wouldn't tell them her name. When he said no, she asked him to call Officer Manuelito—she called her Officer Bernie—and told him Bernie had saved her life. The pastor promised to call the police station and persuaded the woman to let him take her to the shelter. I'm at the Tsé Bit'a'í shelter now."

Bigman took a breath. "Because Bernie's off, I took the call. I haven't gone inside yet to talk to her."

"Did the pastor give you a description?"

He had, and Bigman relayed the details. "He said she was in bad shape physically and really nervous."

"You're right. This could be the person the Feds are looking for. Stay at the shelter with the woman until they can pick her up."

"Yes, sir. What about Bernie?"

"She's on her way back from Alamo today."

Chee called the Farmington office of the FBI. Because it was early, he expected to leave a message, but Agent Sage Johnson answered. She sounded as though she'd been at work for hours.

"Chee here. I have a lead for you on a person who could be the woman Manuelito discovered yesterday."

"Go ahead."

He told her what Bigman had said. "I asked him to stay with her until you guys arrive."

"Thanks. That'll be me. Where are they?"

Chee gave her the address. "Also, I have some information about the people who own the house where Bernie found that woman." Chee offered Johnson the names and numbers from the livestock bureau.

"That matches what we discovered, but I didn't have that cell number. Thanks."

"Why wasn't Bee under guard?" The question escaped before he'd thought of a less confrontational way to put it.

"Actually, she had a guard. We're looking into what happened." Chee heard the edge in the agent's voice.

"And before you ask, we don't know anything more about the baby except that it, I mean he, had been dead about twenty-four hours. We believe he belonged to the woman Manuelito found."

"Bernie said Bee denied being the mother. What about a DNA test to make sure? And who's the dad?"

"Agent Berke is handling that. Anything else?"

"Officer Sam told me you wanted to talk to the captain about Officer Manuelito."

"When will Captain Largo be back?"

"Maybe tomorrow. Maybe the end of the week. In the meantime, I'm the guy in charge here. Can I do anything for you?"

"Yes. You can tell Wilson Sam I said to keep his mouth shut. And . . ." She hesitated. "And you don't need to worry about Manuelito."

But, as things turned out, he did.

11

Bernadette Manuelito was ready to go home.

After some time behind the wheel, she noticed less tension in her neck and that her shoulders had relaxed too. She was about an hour out of Los Lunas on the shortcut to I-40 West and had not seen another vehicle for the past twenty minutes. The day had improved.

Why, she wondered, did the drive home usually seem faster than the drive out? Tomorrow, her other day off, she looked forward to going for a long run, visiting with Mama, fixing a nice dinner for herself and Chee, and maybe finding time for some romance.

Because she was too far away for the radio, she phoned the Shiprock station. A voice that wasn't Sandra's answered and told her Sergeant Chee was in a

meeting. She would let him know that Officer Manuelito was headed back to Shiprock.

"Who am I speaking to?"

"It's Mrs. Slim, Bernie. I'm filling in for Sandra
today."

"Hi." She hadn't seen Mrs. Slim at the station for
quite a while. "Is Sandra all right?"

"As far as I know."

"OK then. Thank you." She wanted more details
but didn't push for them over the phone. "I'll see you
at the station."

She thought about Sandra, who had seemed perfectly healthy, and gave Chee credit for finding Mrs.
Slim and arranging for her to come in and work. Then
she circled back to Maya.

As a cop, she had dealt with several suicides and even
a murder disguised as such. In that case, the caller told
her he'd found his girlfriend dead: she'd killed herself.
The woman had been depressed, he said, and used a
kitchen knife to end her life while he was outside working on his car. But a knife was not the suicide weapon
of choice, especially for a woman, and the six wounds
through her clothing made the incident extra suspicious.
The boyfriend confessed on the way to the station.

If she could choose to work a homicide or a suicide,
she'd pick a homicide, hands down. Suicides left her

with a residue of grief; homicides stirred her anger and created an opportunity to find the killer, to do what she could to restore hózhó, a sense of peace, harmony, beauty, and balance. Murders led to involvement with the FBI, an enjoyable experience if she had the opportunity to work with Agent Johnson. Not so good if Agent Berke got the assignment.

She shook her head and focused on the scenery. Laguna and Acoma Pueblos owned this open, mountain-rimmed land, each Pueblo government claiming different sections and so far leaving it mostly undeveloped. She caught a glimpse of a plant she hadn't noticed before blooming at the edge of the road. Time for a break anyway—and this was theoretically her day off. She pulled onto the shoulder, grabbed her backpack, and locked the unit. It felt good to stretch, to move under her own power, to breathe the clean fall air. She bent down to look at the plant and realized it was a white version of the purple asters she saw everywhere. She gathered some seeds in a ziplock bag to try cultivating back in Shiprock, being careful to leave plenty for nature's rejuvenation.

Bernie walked along the shoulder, hoping to see animal tracks or perhaps find the intricate skeleton of a tiny rodent. She noticed rabbit pellets and the elongated triangles of deer tracks in the soft earth. The tracks reminded her of the photos of footprints around the dead man's car. Now that Maya was in custody, Williams could verify that Maya owned sneakers with the interesting circles on the soles. Had the detective looked at Raul Apacheito's shoes? She hadn't seen mention of it in the report. If the concerned father went to the crime scene to verify his son's discovery before he called the sheriff's office, the prints could be his. Another question for Williams.

She heard the rumble of a train, the sound adding its acoustic layer to the noise from the interstate. The freight cars snaked along beneath a sky as blue as a white man's eye. An assembly of towering early-fall clouds added to the scene. She took her phone out for some photos to share with Chee and Mama and noticed that she had missed several calls: one from the Shiprock station, one from Detective Williams, and two from a New Mexico number she didn't recognize. She'd check later when she could call back if necessary; there was no service here in the backcountry.

She snapped the photos, then trotted to her unit to resume the drive. She enjoyed another half hour of quiet before she felt her phone vibrate. She hoped it was Chee, but the caller ID said Maya Kelsey. Odd. She clicked on the speaker.

"Maya?"

"Officer, it's Junior Jones, you know, Maya's son. She pays for my phone."

"Hey, Junior. What's up?"

"I need to talk to you."

"OK. I'm listening."

"Ah, it's tough to do it on the phone. Can I see you?"

"Sure. I'm off tomorrow, but come down to the station the next day."

"Oh." She heard the disappointment. "Is there any way we can meet today?"

"What do you need to talk about?"

"It's complicated. It's about my mom. She's still not answering her phone, and she never showed up here at all. I'm really worried. I even called Dad—he lives down there, you know. I wanted to ask him to check her house, but he didn't call me back either. Something's not right."

Bernie felt the punch of deep cold sorrow in the center of her gut. Leon had not told Junior that his father was dead and Maya was in jail. By default, the job now fell to her. But not over the phone.

She knew the house. "I'll stop by tonight before I go home." She gave him an approximate time. "Will you be there all evening?"

"Yes. Come when you can. I know you're busy."

Eventually, Tsoodził appeared on the horizon, a solid, welcome landmark. *Hold steady*, it seemed to tell her. *The dark clouds will pass.*

She merged onto I-40 near Grants and then pulled off at a truck stop for coffee. Her phone buzzed again as she entered the building, reminding her of the unchecked messages. She looked and saw that the call came from Darleen.

"Hey there, my sister."

"Hi. How's crime-solving today?"

"It's OK." She stopped. "Actually, it's been tough this week, and I still have to tell a young man his dad is dead. I'm glad to hear your voice. How's things with you?"

"Fine. Mr. Natachi's strength is returning, and I like working with the elderlies at the senior center. The jobs don't leave me much time to draw, but I'll live. You know what? I miss Mama. We talk on the phone, but it's not the same. Wanna talk about your day?"

Bernie thought about what part of the confusion she could best share with her sister. "An old friend confessed to killing her husband. I'm having trouble believing she did it, and she won't offer an explanation. And my husband took charge at the station because the captain's out. It's complicated."

"So you're working for the Cheeseburger? Good luck with that. Mama told me you're coming this weekend. We can catch up on everything then."

"Right. I'll be there unless something comes up with this case. I'm glad Mama remembered. When we talked this morning, she sounded confused."

"I know you visit, but, well, it's not the same as someone staying there. Hold on." She could hear Mr. Natachi's deep voice, Darleen saying something, and then Mr. Natachi again. Then her sister was back. "What time will you get to Mama's?"

"Oh, I don't know. If I don't have a shift, I'll come early to help her cook. How about you?"

"I'll leave here after work on Friday."

Bernie considered mentioning her concerns about Darleen working all week and then driving to Mama's house alone in the dark in a car that had issues. She didn't. "Call me when you leave Chinle, OK?"

Darleen laughed. "You worry too much, Sister. Catch you later."

And you think caution *is a dirty word*, she thought, but she just said goodbye.

She used the rest of her time in the car to listen to her messages.

Detective Williams called to thank her for her help and said she looked forward to Bernie's report on the VLA meeting to help wrap things up.

The next message came from Chee. She played it twice. "Sweetheart, I'm sorry for being so tough on you in the interview with Maya. I, I never meant to hurt you. I love you more than I can say." Then his voice lightened. "And I never, ever, ever want to be your boss again. Be safe out there."

At the Shiprock police station she said hello to Mrs. Slim and rapped on Captain Largo's door. Chee opened it, the phone at his ear, and gave her a smile and the *just a minute* sign. She went to her desk and began to type up some notes on her visit to the VLA for Williams. After that she would give Junior the sad news and the box from his dad. And then she could dream of a shower, dinner, and some private time with the busy sergeant. But a phone call changed that.

"Officer Bigman is on the line for you."

"Thanks."

"Have you talked to the sergeant?" She heard the tension in her clan brother's tone.

"Not yet. He was on the phone when I got in."

"Well, I'm at the women's shelter with Bee, you know, that one you found. She says she has to talk to you."

"I thought she was in the hospital. Berke told me that she was officially the FBI's problem."

Bigman lowered his voice and gave her the update. "This gal is skittish. I can tell I'm making her nervous, and I'm afraid she's going to bolt. She's really strung out and she keeps saying that you're the only one who can help her."

"I just got back from Alamo. I'll be there as soon as I check in with the sergeant."

She walked past Largo's office and saw Chee still on the phone, frowning now. She asked Mrs. Slim to let him know she was off to the domestic violence shelter to give Officer Bigman some backup.

The Shiprock shelter had room for a dozen women, some of whom arrived with only the clothes on their backs and fear in their hearts. Some came with children. Bernie had been here many times and, unfortunately, always found the place busy.

Although it might not have seemed so at first glance, the shelter's location provided security and privacy for its guests. Hidden in plain sight in a commercial building surrounded by businesses that probably had no idea of the nurturing dispensed behind the closed doors, the shelter survived. The buzz of cars made it easy for those who worked here to remain anonymous. No one would think twice if a law enforcement vehicle pulled up. Bernie knew the director and staff by first names.

Inside, the place looked inviting, a refuge of hope and new beginnings for people who arrived in a fog of sadness, confusion, and terror. The transition from victim to victim-no-more to survivor offered a profound challenge, and everyone who worked here did more than expected to help the women heal.

The director, Rheta Morgan, met her at the door. Bernie read bad news in the woman's face.

"Bee's gone. We tried to keep her. She asked to use the bathroom, and then enough time had gone by and she didn't come back. I don't know how she got out the window with her bad arm." Morgan sighed. "We can't force people to stay here."

"Did she steal a car?"

Rheta looked out the open door to the parking lot. A baby wailed in the background.

"Not from us. All the staff vehicles are there."

"Where's Officer Bigman?" Bernie had noticed his Navajo Police unit as she'd parked.

"He raced out to look for her as soon as we realized what happened."

With Bee on foot, Bernie thought, it made sense for Bigman to search that way.

"Officer, you understand, I'm sure, that our residents have mixed experiences with you cops. Officer Bigman talked to Bee, but I could tell that he made her uneasy. I wish you'd come sooner."

"How long ago did she take off?"

"Ten minutes more or less."

"If Bee comes back, do whatever you can think of to get her to stay. Tell her I really want to talk to her."

Rheta nodded. "I didn't mean to criticize you, Bernie, or Officer Bigman. I know you guys do your best."

"Don't worry about it."

Bernie jogged back to her unit and called Bigman's cell phone.

He answered, breathing hard. "I guess you heard."

"Where are you?"

"Near the Giant gas station across from the bridge. She didn't eat at the shelter, so she's probably looking for food and a ride somewhere. I'll check the convenience stores out this way."

Bernie knew the station was north of the shelter. "I'll drive south and then west. I hope we can find her while it's still light."

She cruised along 491 and Bluff Road for about half an hour and didn't see Bee. She asked the owner of a white Jeep with a flat tire if he'd noticed a woman walking along the road or hitchhiking, and got a no. She knocked on a few doors, heard the same response. She checked back with both Bigman and the shelter but they had no good news. Then she called the police station and asked for Chee. He picked up quickly.

"Sergeant, Bee took off and Bigman and I had no luck finding her. I've got one more stop to make." She explained about Junior and the box from the VLA. "Then I'm done unless you have another job for me."

"Stop at the station to see me before you head home. I mean, please?"

She smiled at his voice. "I will. I got your message. I love you, too."

She pulled up to the well-kept house Junior Jones shared with Leon, noticing the inside lights through the front window. She heard something skittering in dry grass. Mice, she thought, or maybe even a pack rat looking to feast on whatever it could find before winter set in. The stars had begun to poke through against the purple-gray of the early-evening sky.

Junior opened the front door and stood waiting for her.

"Yá'át'ééh. Nice to see you, Junior. It's been a while."

"Yá'át'ééh." Junior shoved his hands in his pockets and then took them out again.

"Mind if I come in?"

"Oh, sure. Sorry. Can I get you some water or something?" His voice was tight and strained. "I don't know if I should treat you like a lady or like a police officer."

He stepped into the house and she followed. He moved a plate with some chicken bones, stacking it on top of a bowl with grapes that were attracting the season's last fruit flies. "Sorry about the mess. I should have cleaned it up. My 'shidá'í doesn't like me to leave dishes around, but I can't seem to focus on anything until I know about Mom."

"Let's sit."

As Junior plopped himself on the couch, Bernie took the chair across from him. He was younger than Darleen, at almost nineteen still more boy than adult.

He started talking. "So, Mom wanted all of us to drive out to help my shimásání and get piñon nuts. We had a plan, see, but Mom didn't show up or text or anything. It's like she just blew us off and disappeared. I know Leon called you to help find her. Do you know what's going on?"

"Yes. Your mother is in jail in Socorro."

"No way." He stared at her with eyes wide open. "You're kidding."

She let her silence make the argument.

"It was a DWI, right?" Junior bolted off the couch and started to pace. "She's been so good for so long.

My 'shidá'í and I have to raise bail money and get her out."

Bernie took a deep breath. "Not drunken driving. Sit down, please."

Junior sat.

"She's in jail because she confessed to killing your father."

She saw the color drain from his face. "My dad? He's dead?"

She shook her head once. "I'm so sorry."

Junior stared at her, openmouthed, and slumped back into the sofa. "Dad's dead?"

"A boy found his body in a car near the Alamo reservation. Your mom came into the Shiprock police station and confessed to the murder."

"I don't understand."

She shook her head. "I don't either. I'm sad to give you such terrible news."

In general, Bernie knew, the younger you were when a loved one died, the harder the loss. The death of one family member at the hands of another came packed with complications and pain, even when the death was an accident, no one's fault. In the case of murder, the emotional fallout was more extreme.

Junior buried his face in his hands and they sat together. After a while, he broke the silence and she saw the disbelief and sorrow. "Does my 'shidá'í know about my dad?"

"Yes."

"Why didn't he tell me? Well, I've hardly seen him. He's been busy because a lot of the guys he works with are on vacation. I can't understand any of this. What did Mom say about it?" He shook his head. "No. No."

As Junior spoke, she saw the reflection of headlights through the window and heard a vehicle pull up. Leon let himself into the house, carrying a galvanized bucket filled with red apples. He took off his black Stetson.

"Hey, Bernie. I hope Junior . . ." He stopped talking when he saw the young man's expression. "What's wrong?"

Junior stared at the floor. Leon put the bucket and his hat on the kitchen counter and sat next to his nephew.

Bernie scowled at him. "I just told Junior that his father is dead and that Maya confessed to the murder. I thought you would have delivered that news."

"I didn't tell him because she couldn't have done that. I've known Maya her whole life. There's a huge mistake, a big problem here."

When Junior looked up Bernie noticed the tears pooling in his eyes. "Dad's dead?"

Leon nodded. "I'm sorry. I just didn't have the words to tell you." Junior took a breath, then stumbled outside to sit on the dark porch.

Leon looked as shaken as the son of his heart. "Steve Jones had had some hard times. Are you certain he didn't kill himself?"

"The death is under investigation, but I heard your sister said she did it."

"Can I talk to Maya?"

"You'll have to check with the detention center." The anger she'd held for Leon and the deep heartbreak she'd felt for Junior gave way to a numb sadness. "Why do you think Jones committed suicide?"

He ticked it off on his fingers. "The jerk never got over Maya leaving him and blamed her for his depression. He had a gun. And Jones wouldn't care how offing himself would devastate his boy. He saved his love for his work." Leon motioned toward the porch with his chin. "That one lit up when he learned Jones had come back to New Mexico. He thought they might finally have a real father-son relationship. But I knew that wasn't in the cards." He took a deep breath. "My little sister confessed to murder?"

"She said it several times."

"What happens now?"

"Detective Williams is investigating the case. She needs to know what led to the crime. Maya hasn't been open about that."

"You told me Maya confessed. What did she say?"

"Basically, that Jones deserved to die."

"That's it?"

Bernie nodded.

Leon exhaled. "Tell me how to contact Detective Williams."

He punched the phone number Bernie gave him into his phone.

As she left the house, she saw Junior sitting outside alone, the lenses of his glasses catching the light from Tł'éé'honaa'éí, the October moon. She said good night, but he didn't respond. As she drove away, she remembered that the box of his father's awards, the treasures she'd intended to give him, were still in her trunk. They'd wait until the next visit.

As promised, she stopped at the police station.

The last time she'd encountered Mrs. Slim, Sandra's substitute, the woman had had short hair. Now she wore it smoothly pulled into a braid, a beautiful mixture of gray and raven black.

"Yá'át'ééh."

"Yá'át'ééh." Mrs. Slim lowered her voice to a whisper. "Sandra called, and she told me to tell you not to worry about her. She said she'll talk to you when she can." She turned away toward something on the desktop and swallowed, her chin quivering but her upset kept at bay.

"Mrs. Slim, I remember when you worked here before. Thanks for coming in."

The woman nodded in acknowledgment. "The sergeant wants to see you. You'll find him in the captain's office."

Bernie walked away, thinking about Mrs. Slim's unshed tears and Sandra's unexpected absence. She'd call her friend as soon as she had time.

She found Chee waiting for her, not on the phone. Not on the computer. He closed the door, wrapped her in his arms, and held her close. He smelled warm and tired and irresistible.

"I'll be home as soon as I can. I missed you."

She pushed back a bit to study his face. "We need to talk."

"How about tomorrow?"

"I'd like that. But remember, it's my day off so I can sleep in. How about you?"

He shook his head. "I have to be here early."

She drove home to the dark house, and made some tea Mrs. Darkwater had recommended to help her relax. It would be good to talk to Chee tomorrow, she decided, when she wasn't so tired.

She went to bed alone, lying still between the cool sheets, thinking that she would need to add a blanket in the next few weeks. She dreamed she stood outside watching the stars, focusing on Átsé Ets'ózí, First Slender One, also known as Orion, the warrior moving across the sky. Then, with the logic of dreams, she found herself indoors looking at the same constellation on a computer monitor at the VLA. Kathy stood next to her and enlarged the stellar image. Bernie realized that the warrior had Chee's face. He pulled the bow with strong arms to fire off an arrow that turned into a comet, soaring away with a stream of light and fire behind it. Kathy said . . .

She awoke with a start when she heard the front door open. Then the reassuring sound of Chee's footsteps headed toward the bedroom.

"Hey there." He spoke in a husky whisper.

"Hey yourself."

"Sorry to wake you."

"I don't think so. Hurry up and get in here. I've been dreaming about you."

12

J im Chee left for work before first light, slipping away so quietly she hardly stirred from her deep sleep. Now Bernie had returned from her run, showered, and was sitting down to breakfast when the house phone rang. She'd already called Mama.

"Officer, this is Mrs. Slim. The sergeant wanted me to tell you we got a report of a woman shoplifting at Bashas' and that it sounds like someone named Bee. The security guard has her. He told me to ask you to go over there as soon as you can. And he's sorry about your day off."

"Thank you. I'm on my way."

She slipped into her uniform, picked up her unit at the station, and parked in front of the grocery store.

The lot was empty except for employee vehicles and a few early shoppers.

Bernie said hello to the store manager, a slim man in his late thirties whom she'd met on earlier shoplifting calls. He thanked her for coming and escorted her to the rear of the building. He pushed the numbers on the keypad to open the door to a small, windowless office. The monitor displayed a grid of video transmissions from the security cameras that kept an electronic eye on the shoppers.

A hefty young woman in a T-shirt and jeans sat in one chair, and Bee occupied the other across from her. The guard stood when Bernie and the manager entered. Bee stayed seated, chin down. Bernie couldn't see her eyes.

The manager nodded to his worker. "Officer Manuelito, this is one of our loss prevention specialists, Tessie Nieto. Would you please tell the officer what happened?"

Tessie pointed to Bee with a quick nod of her chin. "I followed this woman out of the store because I noticed her shoving a package of hot dogs into her pocket, all shifty-like. When I told her who I was—you know, security—she tried to run, but I took ahold of her jacket. Then she started yelling at me not to touch her, grabbed for my hair, and kicked me hard. I wrapped my arms around her—you know, like you do with a kid having a tantrum. Then she started crying and kinda went limp, and I brought her back here."

Tessie's voice had risen as she told the story, and now she spoke loudly. "I didn't do that damage to her. I swear I didn't. Somebody else hurt her."

The manager looked concerned. "What damage?"

"You know, her face and the bruises on her arms. Somebody's been beatin' on her pretty good."

The manager seemed to notice Bee's black eye and swollen lip for the first time. "You said she kicked you. How badly are you hurt, Tessie?"

"That don't hurt much. My leg's OK. She didn't break the skin or nothin'. I'll just have a bruise for a while."

Bernie noticed blood on the guard's arm. "What happened there?"

Tessie glanced at the scratch marks. "I didn't see that. It musta been when she was trying to get away."

The manager looked at the wound. "I'll get the first aid kit. Come to the break room when you've finished talking with Officer Manuelito and we'll deal with that injury."

On his way out, the man glared at Bee. "If I see you in this store again, I'm assuming that you're here to steal from us. You are banned for life. We have a zero-tolerance policy for shoplifting."

Bee sat motionless, her head down, her face partly concealed by her long dark hair. Her hands were bound behind her back and fastened to the chair.

Bernie looked at the security worker. "What did she take?"

"I put it in that bag over there."

Bernie reached for the paper sack. It held an un-opened bottle of extra-strength Tylenol, a large carton of orange juice, a jar of almonds, a bag of M&M's, chips, a package of beef jerky, and an open package of hot dogs.

"Is this all of it?"

"No, Officer. There was the rest of the hot dogs. She'd started to eat them outside and she dropped most of them when I caught up to her. I guess that's still out there. Should I have saved 'em?"

"No. This is plenty. You had your hands full."

Tessie nodded. "I felt bad, you know, when I saw her eating those hot dogs right out of the package. I've been hungry myself."

"You did the right thing. Now she can get some help."

Bernie squatted down in front of Bee. The woman had looked bad before, but now she looked worse. The bruises on her neck had developed a deep purple hue.

Her nose had puffed up to at least double its size, and she sucked in her breath through her mouth.

"Bee, listen to me. They could have helped you at the shelter, given you a meal, a shower, clean clothes. You made a very, very bad choice."

Tessie cleared her throat. "Officer, you don't have to use a code or nothin' to get out. Just push that button there and wait a little and the door opens."

"Thanks for your help. Go take care of your arm."

The young woman moved with surprising grace for someone her size. The door closed silently behind her.

"It's just us here now, Bee. What did you want to tell me?"

The blackened eye opened, a small slit between the lids surrounded by swollen, dark flesh.

"Nothing." She added a swear word. "I asked for you to come to the shelter. You sent that man instead."

"I was out of town on another case. Officer Bigman has lots of experience helping women who've been hurt. He's a good guy. I drove to the shelter to find you when I got back to Shiprock because they said you needed to tell me something. But you'd run off."

Bee's voice shook with emotion. "Don't give me that. You're a stupid liar, like all the damn cops."

Bernie felt her anger rise like dust when the wind strikes it. "We can talk now. Or I can take you right to jail for assaulting that woman and stealing."

Bee spit. Bernie dodged the saliva except for the spray that landed on her boot. She stood, took a breath, cut the plastic zip tie Tessie had used to secure the shoplifter to the chair. Bee rubbed her wrists.

"Stand up and put your hands back behind your back."

Bee gave her a desperate look. "Let me go. We can make it seem like I hit you and got away. Your sweet ass won't be on the line."

"Stand up."

"Why should I?"

"Bee, get out of the chair."

"Make me."

Bernie gripped the woman's thin forearm and pulled against Bee's resistance to force her to rise. She moaned, and Bernie remembered the dislocated elbow, then remembered that it was the other arm.

"You're just like all the other stinkin' pigs. You witch. You don't care about me and you didn't care about the baby either, did you?"

"I didn't mean to hurt you. Shut. Up. Now."

As Bernie handcuffed her, Bee screamed another obscenity.

They went down a hallway to the parking lot and into the patrol car, Bee yelling about police brutality the whole way. Bernie knew she had nothing to gain by responding, but her frustration rose by the minute. She radioed the station to let them know she had Bee in custody. Bee wet her pants in the back seat of the unit, and by the time Bernie delivered the woman to jail to await the FBI, she was glad to be rid of her. She went to the captain's office to check in with Chee.

The sergeant sat scowling at the computer screen. She knocked on the door frame to get his attention.

His face lit up. "Come on in."

She sat across from him, noticing the fatigue in his shoulders. "How much longer until Captain Largo comes back?"

"Excellent question. He told me he's had enough meetings to last a lifetime." Chee studied his hands. "The new police chief had a man-to-man with him about retirement. He asked the captain to set a date."

"No. He can't retire." But as she said it, she realized that Captain Largo had been in charge on the day she began her service as a green rookie. Back then, Lieutenant Leaphorn still wore a uniform and set the standard for many of them as the smartest person working on the Navajo police force.

"That's what I told him, too. I can't wait to leave this paperwork jungle." Chee rolled his neck from side to side. "I wanted you to know that the rookie tried to serve that warrant and couldn't find Shorty either, the same trouble as you. Officer Sam went to the place where someone said Shorty had been selling wood, but the man never showed."

"There was something I didn't tell you about the warrant. I screwed up. I—"

Chee held up his hands, palms toward her. "Stop. I don't wanna hear it. Sweetheart, I mean, Officer, forget about it. Whatever happened, it's history now. Let it be."

"Are you wearing your boss hat? Or is that my husband talking?"

"Both. You'll always be perfect in my eyes."

She couldn't help smiling at him.

"So what happened with Bee?"

"I brought her in. She's here, locked up."

"Good. Agent Johnson told me she would come to fetch her. Did that woman open up to you?"

"Only to spit on my boot."

Chee chuckled. "Who knew that was what she had in mind when she asked to see you."

"She objected to that fact that I didn't get to the shelter before she ran away. Evidently Bigman didn't live up to her high expectations of law enforcement."

The phone rang, but Chee ignored it. "For a person who could have been dead without you, she has quite the attitude."

Bernie nodded. "I can't help thinking that there's someone out there who is worried about that woman. I'd like to let her relatives know that she's safe. I don't want her to be another statistic. She's someone's sister, someone's daughter, maybe someone's wife."

Chee nodded. "Maybe even someone's mother. We can't forget about the baby. Did she mention anything about him?"

"Only that I didn't care about the little guy. Sergeant, this was my day off, but let's count it as an on-duty day."

"That's good because, well, Window Rock wants us to stay involved with that Alamo murder case since Officer Pino can't work yet. Because Maya is Diné, the chief told the captain to make sure we've got her back." The phone rang again, and Chee glared at it until it finally went quiet. "We means you. Because you've been down there and you know the detective in charge, Window Rock thinks you have a handle on who's who at Alamo."

She didn't, but she let the comment stand. "Why not let Detective Williams handle this? I know she's competent."

Chee nodded. "She's wise, too. She had her sheriff make an official request for your help. Specifically, to sit in on a follow-up interview with Maya tomorrow and to talk to a Navajo man Williams thinks may be involved in the homicide. And to offer advice and assistance as required."

Maya had an accomplice? The idea stirred her curiosity.

"Wait. Even though I'm Navajo, you know I'm a stranger out there. Nobody opens up to someone they've just met, especially about bad stuff like murder. Even Maya, who knows me, wouldn't tell me anything in her own defense."

The phone began to ring again and Chee spoke over it. "But a stranger as charming as you will have a better chance at getting some cooperation out there than a bilagáana. Right?"

Bernie didn't feel charming. The statement irritated her. Why hadn't he said *smart*? Or *experienced*?

Chee leaned back in the chair. "You mentioned that nobody likes to open up to strangers. Well, what about the suspects we interview who spill their guts? And what about white people in therapy? They pay someone who isn't a friend or relative to listen to them complain. And then they get to complain about how much it costs."

Her relatives had survived desperate times by focusing on a positive future, not rehashing their troubles. That vision of walking in beautiful balance, and an ingrained sense of humor like Chee's, kept a person upright.

"So, back to your assignment." Chee frowned at the phone and the ringing stopped. "Head on out to Socorro again and work with Williams. You can help her figure out why the guy is dead. See if you can get Maya to talk about whatever led up to the shooting."

"You and I tried that already. We failed."

He shrugged. "Just give it your best. And get back here as soon as you can." He glanced at her feet and grinned. "Maybe you should leave those boots at home in case the Feds need some DNA from Bee."

"Sure thing. Tell Berke to shine them up for me too, OK?" She understood that, with Bee in custody, a clean sample to match her DNA to the baby's would not be a problem.

Chee, with his boss hat on now, hadn't asked if she wanted the assignment but simply told her it was her job. Fair enough, she thought. It reminded her of their early days together, when she was a rookie. Back then he gave the orders, and they tried to ignore the mutual attraction they felt for each other.

"Sergeant, I'd like a couple hours to check on Mama before I make that drive again."

"Go ahead. Give her a big hello from me. I'll let Window Rock know you've got this, and you can call Williams when you're on your way. Everyone's happy."

"You don't look happy."

He gave her a lopsided little half smile. "I don't like this boss stuff. And I don't like the idea that Window Rock could push the captain into retirement. Maybe he's not up on all the new technology, but he knows everybody—the bad guys, the kooks, the grand-mothers raising the grandchildren, the complainers, the potential troublemakers, the drunks, the meth heads, and the addicts trying to get clean. The people who work hard to make life better. I respect the man."

"Me, too. There aren't many like him."

"None." The phone began to ring again. Chee frowned and reached for it.

Back at her desk, Bernie finished the report on Bee and left it for Chee to pass to the Feds. Shoplifting was a Navajo Nation crime, but whatever had led to the FBI's involvement would take precedence. She thought again of the dead baby; he was also the FBI's problem, but someone knew something. Eventually, a person would come forward. In the meantime, she faced another long drive.

She went home and repacked her duffel with a clean uniform, toiletries, her running shoes, and some casual clothes. She noticed the blinking message light on the landline and ignored it. Darleen always called her cell number. If it was Mama, she'd be there soon to talk about whatever was on her mind. Most likely, someone wanted to give her a better rate on insurance or tell her she'd won a trip to Las Vegas.

She drove toward the Chuskas, the blue range rising along the New Mexico–Arizona border, the mountains where her grandmothers once grazed their sheep. She was lucky to have grown up in Toadlena with this scenery as her backyard. The few Navajo ranchers and herders who followed the old ways here shared the land with mule deer, elk, black bears, mountain lions, bobcats, and coyotes. At lower elevation, prairie dogs thrived. This time of year, domestic livestock left the mountains to the wild creatures.

It was a gorgeous October morning, one of those instances when she wanted time to stand still. Would the golden light, the pleasant warmth, the hint of a breeze to make the leaves dance seem so remarkable if they lasted longer than a few precious days? Ghaaji', a time of transition. Was the season's beauty intended to inspire humans to embrace their own life changes? She thought about her situation. If she applied to be a detective and got the job, she wouldn't be working for her husband. But she'd have to spend more hours on the road and away from Shiprock, which meant less time with Chee and Mama. She weighed the issue, came to no conclusion, and pushed the consideration to the back of her mind.

She noticed Mrs. Darkwater's car in front of her mother's home and parked her unit beside it. Mrs. Darkwater, Mama's neighbor and friend, often picked up groceries or whatever else Mama needed. Sometimes the two senior ladies went together to Farmington on shopping adventures.

Knowing the Darkwater dog might have come with its owner, Bernie sat a moment, waiting to be barked at. But the yard remained dog-free. She heard the television—on loud, as usual—as she walked to Mama's front door. The ladies sat together on the couch. She knocked, then entered.

"Mama, Mrs. Darkwater. It's Bernie."

"Come here." Mrs. Darkwater didn't turn around. "So, you got my message."

"No, I didn't." She turned to Mrs. Darkwater with a question in her eyes.

"Sit down, honey, next to your shima."

Mama looked pale. Bernie took her hand. It felt cool against her own. "Mama? What's wrong?" When Mama didn't respond, she said it again, a bit louder, in Navajo.

"Don't shout at me. My daughter, why aren't you at work?"

Mrs. Darkwater joined the conversation. "This one and I were at the senior center for lunch, but we didn't eat because she told me she needed to come home. She said she felt dizzy. I called from there because I thought you should know."

"I told her not to call you. She doesn't listen." Her mother's voice sounded like an angry burst of wind.

"Mama, she did the right thing. You could be having a heart attack or something. Do you have any pain?"

"I'm better already. How are you, daughter?"

"I'm fine."

"You look tired."

Mama's eyes stayed closed as Bernie put her hand on her mother's forehead. She felt no fever.

"Mrs. Darkwater, do you have one of those devices that takes your blood pressure?"

The neighbor nodded.

"Could you bring it?"

Mrs. Darkwater hurried off.

"Mama, did you eat breakfast today?"

"I had my coffee. They have cookies at the senior center. Sometimes doughnuts and those give-you-energy bars."

"Did you have some?"

"What about you? You look too thin."

She knew Mama's avoidance of the answer was the same as *No, and don't bother me.* "Did you have dinner last night?"

"Don't make a fuss over a little spell." Mama sat a bit straighter. "You must be hungry. Have some of that soup in the refrigerator and crackers. Put some peanut butter on them. That's good for you."

Bernie sighed. "I'll warm the soup if you'll eat some with me."

"You eat. Keep up your strength."

"Have you been drinking water today?"

"A little."

"Did you take your pills?"

"Stop. Enough of this. Go fix the soup."

Bernie put the pot on the stove, hoping the aroma would stir Mama's appetite, and improve her mood. She heard the door open.

"My blood pressure machine is on the table. It's a nice one. Just push the start button; it runs on batteries." She spoke as she walked to the kitchen. "I'll take care of this. You be with your mother."

Bernie put the cuff around Mama's upper arm and tightened it, noticing that her mother seemed to have lost muscle. She watched the numbers rise and then fall and stabilize.

"Your blood pressure looks good, Mama."

"You worry too much." Mama closed her eyes. "Daughter, aren't you tired?"

"Let's have a bite of soup and then we'll rest. Mrs. Darkwater has it ready for us."

"This is a good time to take a rest. You two eat." Mama struggled to rise from the couch; Bernie took her arm and helped her stand. She seemed as light as a pillowcase filled with feathers.

When Bernie came back from Mama's bedroom, she found Mrs. Darkwater in the kitchen, looking out the window at her police car. "Do you expect your sister this weekend?"

"That's what Mama said and Darleen confirmed it."

Mrs. Darkwater dished out two bowls of soup and turned off the heat under the pot. Bernie carried them to the table.

"Will you come back when your sister is here?"

"I hope I can. I'm working a case down on the Alamo reservation. I'm driving there when I leave."

"Way over there with the Turtles?"

Turtles was an old, unflattering nickname for the Alamo people, a term that some said related to the return from captivity at Bosque Redondo and the fact that the Alamo band did not walk all the way back to Big Navajo. The stories said these Navajo were slow, like turtles, and carried their homes with them. Bernie had read that, attracted by the flowing spring and protective isolation of the area, the Alamo people smartly made a good home for themselves and intermarried with Apache families who also found the area attractive.

Other stories held that some Navajos hunted by Kit Carson in Canyon de Chelly escaped through a side canyon and fled south to the Alamo area to avoid the Long Walk. Or that families hearing of the impending roundup hid among the Zuni and then made their home at Alamo. Another version described a brave group of Navajos who escaped from the holding camp at Fort Wingate and fled to Alamo, settling here before the Long Walk.

"The case involves a woman from Shiprock. Will you call my cell if Mama needs me?"

Mrs. Darkwater nodded. She pointed toward the bedroom with her lips. "I'll check on that one later and make sure she eats. You have a long trip. You better go."

Before she left, Bernie went to the hall to say goodbye to Mama and found her asleep. She checked the pill box and found that her mother had taken her medicine. She wrote a quick note, a reiteration of her schedule in case her mother forgot, along with advice to eat and rest. She signed it with a heart and left it on Mama's beside table.

When she opened the front door, she saw Mrs. Darkwater's dog on Mama's porch. Its dark eyes studied her. She took a deep breath, told herself there was no reason to be frightened, and began to walk slowly toward her unit. She heard Mrs. Darkwater behind her, speaking to the animal as if it were a child. The dog remained on the porch. Bernie felt the tension drain away as soon as she started the engine.

She sent a text to Darleen with an update on Mama, and radioed the station with the news that she was on the way to her new assignment. Mrs. Slim had something for her. "A man named Junior Kelsey just came in. He said he needs to talk to you and it's important. I told him you were out, but he said he'd wait."

"So, he's still there?"

"That's right."

"Please put me through to him."

Junior sounded younger than in real life. He spoke fast. "So, I came in because, well, I got this thing from my dad."

"What kind of thing?"

"Umm. A letter."

"What does it say?"

"It says he killed himself." Bernie felt instantly relieved—her friend did not murder the man—and yet confused. Why had she confessed to the crime?

"When did you get it?"

"Yesterday. I picked up the mail after you left. It's spooky, like getting a message from the grave."

"Sergeant Chee ought to be at the station. He's up to speed on the situation with your mother. Show the letter to him."

"But . . . I wanted to talk to you."

"Chee can help you. This is important, Junior. You did the right thing to bring the letter to the police. Talk to Chee."

"When will you be back?"

"I don't know. Talk to Chee. Promise?"

"OK."

Speaking with Junior reminded her of yesterday's visit and the undelivered box of photos and certificates for him in her trunk. And that memory reminded her of the other box. The models Leon had created for the third grade remained in her trunk. She'd drop them off this afternoon, she told herself. She'd make a detour to the Alamo school before she went to Socorro.

Bernie reached Detective Williams on her cell phone and told her she was on her way back to Socorro.

"Great." The background noise made it hard to hear Williams. "We can wrap this up. I just learned that Maya's prints are in the car. She tested negative for gunshot residue, but too much time may have passed before we did the test. Or maybe she wore gloves. Hold on."

Bernie heard Williams yelling something, then she was back. "Jones tested positive for residue, but not as strongly as he should have if he'd pulled the trigger. That supports the fake-suicide theory. I picture the two of them quarreling in the car. His gun is there. He might have threatened her, so she shoots him and then transfers the gun and residue from her gloves to his hand. But it's all speculation without her side of the story."

"Here's a new wrinkle in the case. Maya's son says he got a suicide letter from his dad."

"Say that again." The background commotion now sounded like an escalating argument in progress.

Bernie repeated the information. "I haven't seen the letter, but I talked to Junior about it a few minutes ago. He's at the Shiprock station. I told him to talk to Chee."

"Why did he ask for you?"

She explained her visit with Junior. "Leon said Jones was prone to depression. Besides swearing that Maya couldn't kill anyone, he hinted that she might still have feelings for Jones."

"Homicidal feelings? I need a copy of the letter." The noise on Williams's end of the conversation continued to increase. "What happened to the woman you found and the dead-baby case?"

"No news on the baby. With the woman, it looks like one of those situations where I thought I could make a difference and jumped to conclusions without a safety net. I tried to help her and got spit on and cussed at."

"I've been there. No wonder you sound like you could wrestle a bear and come out on top." Williams laughed. "I gotta deal with something here. We'll talk soon. Glad you're coming."

Bernie slowed until she could pass a pickup pulling a horse trailer, then looked out onto clear highway. If Steve Jones committed suicide, he'd test positive for residue, which he did. Maya's prints on the gun and in the car could be explained, and the lack of gunshot residue spoke to her innocence.

That brought Bernie back to where she'd been last time she drove to Socorro. If Maya didn't kill Jones, what motivated the big lie? The case grew more confused and her frustration more palpable with each new development.

13

Leaphorn picked up the call.

"Hello, Lieutenant. It's Bernie. I'm heading toward Window Rock and was wondering if we could talk. I mean face-to-face, not over the phone." She spoke in Navajo. "No emergency, but if you've got a minute, I'd appreciate it."

"I'm available." Bernie sounded tired, Leaphorn thought. Or maybe stressed. "Come by the house."

"Twenty minutes?"

"Sounds good. I'll start the coffee."

When she arrived, Leaphorn noticed the dark circles under her eyes.

They sat at the kitchen table. Giddi padded in and jumped onto an empty chair as if invited to join the conversation.

After politely asking for news of Louisa, Bernie got to the point.

"Sir, how can you tell for sure if someone is lying to you?"

"Well, if it's Chee, just stare at him a minute and he'll confess everything and offer to take you out to dinner."

She laughed. "No, I meant a suspect."

"Well, *for sure* that is hard. A skilled liar can fool just about anybody. But in general, I look for fidgeting, talking too fast, or too many pauses. Some try to distract you by focusing on small details they know are true but don't really matter so you'll go along with the big lie. Or they try to convince you they are not lying by telling the truth about something you have not asked. Some are so good, they believe their own story and even pass polygraphs. Those are harder to smoke out."

As Bernie listened, she thought of what Maya had told her about the divorce papers in Jones's car. Did she offer this a small true detail to distract from the big lie?

Leaphorn brought the coffeepot to the table and filled their cups. "It sounds like you think you're dealing with a liar, but you don't know for sure."

She put both hands around her cup and sighed. "Do you have time for the details?"

"All the time you need."

She told him about young Raul and the corpse, Maya's confession, and the suicide letter that the dead man's son just received. "I'm headed to Socorro now for another session with Maya. I ought to find some joy in having a murder case resolve itself so quickly. But I don't."

Leaphorn made sure Bernie had finished. "Maya fell short of your expectations with that confession, so you assume she's lying."

Bernie smiled. "I wouldn't have put it that way, but that's partly correct. I'd believe her if I understood the motivation. She mentioned something about an argument over divorce, but the woman I knew would have negotiated that issue, not taken such drastic action."

"Did Chee ever mention Hastiin Archie Pinto?"

"No, sir, I don't think so."

Leaphorn told her how Pinto worked as a translator for a bilagáana researcher. During a trip to the reservation, someone killed the white guy. Pinto seemed like a harmless old drunk, but he confessed to the murder. Chee didn't believe it and tried every which way to distance Pinto from the crime. It turned out to be a complicated case, but Pinto was involved in the death.

"Chee assumed Pinto lied when he said he did it and wasted a lot of time spinning his wheels because he couldn't picture such a mild old soul killing anyone. As Chee's commanding officer, I told him to put aside his emotions and focus on the facts. I tried to get him to think like a detective. I offer you that same advice. Don't let friendship get in the way of the facts. But don't hesitate to use what you know about the suspect to lead you to a deeper investigation."

"Sir, that's good advice." Bernie sipped her coffee. "I've been meaning to ask you something. Should I apply to be a detective?"

The question caught Leaphorn by surprise. "You already are a detective. You just don't have the title, and you still get patrol-duty pay. To move to investigations, you have to ask yourself a big question. Do you want the exposure to . . ." He stopped, then said the word in English: "Bureaucracy?"

Bernie gazed out the window. She still looked tired, he thought, but a bit more energy showed in her face.

"How bad was the official BS for you, sir?"

"Tolerable, for the most part. I concentrated on my job. I ruffled some feathers, caught some flak, but it came with the territory. And I think our Navajo operation is better than most." Those incidents had been few, but recalling them still bothered him. "I loved the work, so I took the rest in stride." Back then, he had his dear wife, Emma, who knew what to say if he came home frazzled, angry, ready to give up. And when to say nothing.

"What does Chee think about it?" Emma had encouraged him to make the change from patrol and worried less after he'd done it.

"I don't know." He watched her give Giddi a rub under the chin as she collected her thoughts. "He says whatever I decide is cool with him. When I ask for advice, he stresses that it's my decision and he just wants me to be happy. I can't believe he really wouldn't mind if I was away from home more as an investigator. I don't get it."

"You are overthinking it. Take him at his word. He wants you to be happy. Would the change do that?"

"I'm happy now. I love the variety of patrol work. But I'd enjoy the mental challenge of chasing down a case and finding the evidence to hold the bad guys accountable. I handed a case over to the FBI yesterday that I would love to see through to the end."

She stopped and swallowed, pushing down the anger and sadness. "I found a woman someone had beaten and left to die in an abandoned house. I found a dead baby lying facedown, alone in another room. I can't get that scene—the woman, the little one—out of my mind. I keep remembering the stench, how cold the place was, how light that infant boy felt in my arms. I'd like to be the person to find out who did this and then bring them to justice."

He nodded and poured them each a little more coffee.

They sat quietly a moment.

"Sir, I've been doing all the talking. What projects have your attention these days?"

He summarized. "And an old friend invited me to join a task force and help come up with some solutions to the problem of missing and exploited Native women. Not just Diné, but nationwide." He sipped his coffee. "Who is leading the investigation into the situation you found?"

"Berke was the agent who took charge while I was there, but you'll have to ask Chee. He's been in touch with the FBI." Bernie rose. "You've given me a lot of your time, sir. I need to head on to Alamo. It sounds like an honor for you to be part of that task force."

"An honor and a responsibility. I haven't said yes yet."

"Any final advice about liars?"

"One way to get to the heart of what you think is a lie is to move from the *what* to the *why* of it. Understand?"

She nodded.

He thought for a minute, then said, "Ask Chee about Archie Pinto. That's a great example of how assumptions get in the way of reality."

And then Officer Manuelito was gone.

Leaphorn poured the last of the coffee into his mug.

He went into his office and wasted about half an hour checking his email and doing a search for the foundation that the mysterious Ginger Simons headed. It looked legitimate, a national group that offered counseling and support to refugee women and children. He was considering an afternoon nap when the phone rang.

"What are you up to, Joe?"

He resisted the old joke of five foot something and told Louisa a little about Bernie's visit.

"She'd make a fine detective. If she brings it up with me, I'll encourage her."

He switched to his lunch with Hancock and told her about the invitation to join the task force and that he was considering it, although he dreaded the idea of meetings. "As I was leavin', a woman came to put up a poster about her sister. Anoder missin' woman."

"I remember a white family who adopted Navajo siblings years ago. I never heard if the kids tried to locate their birth mom or her people. I wonder what happened to them."

"If dey came back to Navajo to find dare clans, every family I know would welcome dem. We call dem Lost Birds." In a way, he thought, those adopted kids were refugees, too. Like the international children Ginger's foundation worked with. The Lost Birds had been displaced from their natural homes and culture because of some tragic event.

"Lost Birds. That's sweet. It makes me think that those children would migrate home if only they knew the way."

Louisa continued the conversation. "That task force your friend mentioned might be interesting, but don't get overextended. You are supposed to be retired, you know, and you're just now back to feeling well enough to be doing investigations. I'd like to see you relax more, enjoy yourself, take a vacation with me."

He let the statement stand. Work gave him pleasure, and he looked forward to the challenge of each new case. Relaxing wasn't his strong suit.

"I have one last student to talk with and then I'll be on the road. I should make it back before dark."

"Giddi and I waitin' for you. Drive safely." Louisa drove too slowly for his taste. She considered the speed limit a line that should never be approached too closely.

"See you shortly. When I get home, we need to chat about the Washington trip."

"See ya soon."

Talking to the most important woman in his life had a good effect. When he went back to his computer, he found an email about his pending casino contract. His services would be needed for several weeks and his fee was acceptable. They'd like him to start the first of next month but he knew he could finagle a delay to allow him to go to Washington. Or he could use the contract as an excuse to avoid the airport. He wrote back that he would check his schedule to suggest a start date.

As long as he was at the computer, he did a search on violence against Native women and found several links to sites with law enforcement data on the scope of the problem. He'd followed the topic but not closely. The situation had continued to worsen. The stories made him worry all the more about Louisa. He was glad she'd be home soon.

Leaphorn checked the time, then went to the kitchen and turned on the oven. When the temperature signal beeped, he inserted the frozen lasagna. If he'd timed it right, it would be about half done when Louisa walked through the door, giving them time to say their hellos. She could relax with a cup of her special tea before they had dinner.

As he set the table, he thought about Washington.

His last trip there had involved tracking down the identity of a body dumped from a train car, culminating with an explosion at one of the Smithsonian museums. He remembered the rain and the gray days, the crowds and how deeply he wanted to get home. He knew he could use the sour aftertaste from that experience as an excuse to say no. But he wanted to go with her. If only they could drive to her meeting.

He heard his cell phone ringing in the office and went back to get it, recognized the number as Jim Chee's.

Chee spoke in Navajo and got to the point quickly. "Sir, I'm calling about three things. A woman phoned here wanting to reach you, although she said she was looking for Officer Leapfrog. I asked if she meant Leaphorn, and when she said yes I told her that you had retired from the department. Her name is Ginger Simons."

"Did she say why she was calling?"

"Sort of. When I asked, she mentioned that you had saved her life and she had some unfinished business with you." Chee laughed. "She sounded like one of those white women who's used to getting what she wants. She told me to give you her name and phone number. Not asked. Told."

"Never mind. I have it. She called here, too. What else?"

"I've got a job for you if you're interested. Bernie encountered a woman who she thinks may have been a victim of sexual exploitation. In the same house, she found the body of an infant, a male child. The woman is now in federal custody and denies any knowledge of the infant." He heard Chee take a breath. "The FBI will get the results eventually, but they have other cases in the pipeline. I'm really jammed up. I was hoping you'd have time to figure out who the child belonged to."

"Are you hiring me to investigate this?"

"I'm hoping you'll do it as a favor for Bernie. I know she'd follow up herself, but she's working a possible homicide."

"Where was the body found?"

Chee gave him the location of the house. "The gentleman who had lived there moved into the home run by those Catholic nuns in Gallup. A relative was supposed to be caring for the cattle."

"Supposed to be?"

"Yeah. The animals had strayed out to the road. That's why Bernie checked on the place, and found the dead baby and the woman." Chee gave him the name and number of the alleged caretaker and contact information for the old man's daughter. "The captive woman told Bernie her name was Bee. The FBI knows her as Gabriela Hernandez."

"I'll see what I can find out."

"When can you work on it?"

Leaphorn appreciated the question, which moved the request from a favor to a job.

"Probably this afternoon. If it takes too much time, I'll bill you."

"That's fine." He noticed that Chee didn't hesitate. He gave him credit for that, too.

"What's the third reason you called, Sergeant?"

"Have you heard that Captain Largo might be retiring?"

"Have you?"

"Well, yes, actually. It might just be a rumor. I know you keep your hand in down there at headquarters, so I wanted to check with you. Is it true?"

"Why don't you ask the captain? Whatever he and I talk about is none of your business."

The phone went silent.

"Anything else on your mind, Chee?"

"No, sir." Leaphorn heard the irritation in Chee's voice. "Have a good evening."

"You, too." But Chee had hung up.

Since he was already sitting at his desk, Leaphorn turned on the computer and sent Hancock a note that he'd enjoyed the lunch and reminding him to send the information about the task force. He wondered why Hancock hadn't approached someone still active in law enforcement, someone like Largo. If Largo decided to retire, his connections would be fresher, and serving on the task force could give him a meaningful transition from cop to civilian.

He thought about Ginger Simons again and how Chee had described her as a woman accustomed to getting what she wanted. The depiction stirred a faint memory of something unpleasant. He closed his eyes and focused on it. Instead of a face, he pictured a blue Corvette. Then he heard the back door open.

Louisa was home.

14

If he hadn't faced a backlog of unanswered messages from people with complaints, as well as too many emails about payroll, and if he hadn't just listened to a bad-tempered message from Agent Berke about Officer Manuelito, Sergeant Jim Chee would have been more polite. Instead, he got to the point with Junior Jones while they stood in the front lobby. "You wanted to show me a letter, is that right?"

"Yes, sir. Here it is, and the envelope, too. I put it back inside." The young man looked nervous, but no surprise there. Most civilians were nervous—either that or angry—when they showed up at the police station.

Chee studied the envelope Junior extended toward him, noting the lack of return address and the blurred postmark on the stamp. He thought it looked suspicious.

"My father sent it. You know who he is, right? And you know he's dead? Officer Bernie told me to talk to you about this."

Chee felt his heart soften. "I know. I'm so sorry he died. Come on. We'll find a better place to talk."

They headed to the captain's office, Chee in the lead. He motioned his visitor to a chair.

"Would you please take the letter out and set it here on the desktop so I can read it. I don't want to touch it."

Junior raised an eyebrow but complied, slowly unfolding the sheet of paper and laying it flat before turning it toward Chee.

Dear Junior,

I wanted you to know that I took my own life because of many factors. No one is to blame, especially not you or your mother. In my life, I did a lot of things I'm not proud of, but I am proud of you, my son. Don't ruin yourself with drugs and drinking. Don't let sorrow take a hold of you. I want you to know that this act has nothing to do with you or anyone else except myself. I'm all twisted up inside. It was time to go. I love you, son, and I will miss you. Be good to your mother.

Your father,
Steve Jones

Chee felt Junior's eyes watching him as he reread the letter.

"How did you get this?"

"Like I told Officer Manuelito, I just found it with my mail."

"Did you ever hear your father mention suicide?"

"No, sir, never, not at all. Can my mom get out of jail? From what this says, Cosmo killed himself. Mom didn't do it."

"Cosmo?"

"That's what I call, I mean *called* him." Junior smiled weakly. "Mom always teased him, about how his first love was the stars, that he was a cosmo nut, like the Russian cosmonauts, you know? Next thing you know he was Cosmo. He called me Sherm."

"Sherm?"

"Yeah, that's short for Sherman. When I was little, after my folks split, and Dad came to see me or I'd go to see him, we'd watch those old cartoons with a talking dog. The dog was a professor same as my dad and even wore glasses kind of like Cosmo's. The dog had an adopted kid named Sherman. The kid was cool. We'd joke around, and he'd call me Sherman and then Sherm."

Junior sighed. "Maybe, when someone decides to take his own life, his brain doesn't work right. Cosmo never called me Junior—always, always son or Sherm. You know how a lot of us Diné have our secret name, our special family name that no one hardly uses except at certain times? Well, Sherm and Cosmo were like that. Our secret names just for each other." He tapped the edge of the letter. "Do you think this is how the brain gets when someone . . . before they do it?"

"I don't know. Besides not calling you Sherm, is there anything else odd about this letter?"

Junior looked at the ceiling for a moment. "Well, yeah . . . the whole thing is crazy. Cosmo never sent me a letter. Never ever in my whole life. He would shoot off an email with an article he thought I'd like, usually something about space and maybe a link to a new discovery. And if he was gonna be around, he'd text me and we'd try to have lunch."

"When did you see him last?"

"A couple of weeks ago."

"What happened then?"

"Cosmo seemed happy. He told me he finally figured out a problem at work. And he said he had told Joy, this lady who was flirting with him, to back off. He mentioned again that he was glad to be back in New Mexico so we—him and me—could spend more time together and so he could make peace with my mom. He talked to me about going to college at New Mexico

Tech, where he taught. Not nagging or like that, but telling me he thought I'd enjoy studying there. He said there were grants I could get and that he'd help me with that financial stuff."

Junior shook his head. "And now he's dead. It's so bad and strange. I used to think I didn't need Cosmo as a dad because Leon, my 'shidá'í, took care of me and Mom. He told her to forget about my dad. But, you know, even though they weren't together anymore, my parents still cared for each other."

Chee noticed that the young man spoke more and more rapidly, the words pushing their way out. "I could have seen him a few days ago, but I blew it. The place where he works had a tour and then a chance to look at the night sky at the observatory on the campus at Tech. He wanted me to go, but my 'shidá'í had already planned a camping trip. I thought I could do it later, you know? And now there is no later." Chee felt the sadness, familiar but different with each death. "Why would Cosmo kill himself? The whole thing doesn't seem possible. It's just not right."

He noticed tears glistening in Junior's dark eyes and looked away. They sat quietly. Even the phone respected the silence.

Chee focused on the letter. "I need to show this to the detective handling your dad's case."

"When can I have it back?"

"I'm not sure. I'll make you a copy."

"Mom can get out of jail, right? Cosmo killed himself, so his death wasn't murder."

"That's what the letter says. As I mentioned, the case is still under investigation. The detective and her team are working to figure out what happened."

Using gloves to handle the document, Chee scanned the letter and envelope for Detective Williams, with a copy to Window Rock and another for Junior. He secured the original. After Junior left, he called Bernie's cell and prepared to leave a message, but she answered.

"Hi. Where are you now?"

"I just passed Fire Rock Casino and Church Rock, and Fort Wingate with those awful bunkers. Do you remember that case we worked with Lieutenant Leaphorn, the woman who died trapped out there?"

"Yeah, I do." They had solved the mystery, but the missing woman died long before they discovered her.

"I'd be farther along, but I stopped to see the Lieutenant. He's been invited to serve on some task force that's investigating what happens to women who disappear. I think of the problem as new, and I guess the scope of it is. But seeing those bunkers reminds me that it's been with us a long time." She slowed down as the truck in front of her pulled out to pass another semi, both going less than the speed limit.

"I'm sure some of our own female relatives were kidnapped and sold as workers and slaves to other tribes and the Spanish who came out this way." He took a breath and changed the subject. "I called because I talked to Junior and examined the suicide letter. He didn't come right out with it, but he said enough to make me suspect that he thinks it's a fake. The postmark doesn't look right. There are lots of red flags here."

"You're kidding."

Chee explained Sherman and Cosmo and the rest. "I sent it to Williams. Take a look when you get down there."

"Williams can compare the handwriting and the signature."

"The whole message, including the signature, was typed. Maya must have known she wasn't a good forger." Chee made a sound that could have been half a laugh. "I guess she had second thoughts about the fake suicide idea because she didn't even allow time for Junior to find the letter before she gave herself up."

"So, you think Maya wrote it?"

"Absolutely, until a better idea comes my way. She thought she could exonerate herself, then changed her mind and confessed."

"So, let's say the letter is fake. What if Junior wrote it himself to try to get his mom out of jail?"

"If he wrote it, either he would have used the right names, or he wouldn't have pointed out the inconsistency. The letter clearly shocked him, and it fits the staged suicide. You wanna bet her fingerprints are on it and the gun?"

"You're right about the gun." Her voice had an edge. "They found Maya's prints along with Jones's. But there's a third set. Unidentified."

"Why are you so touchy?"

"Touchy?" She started to deny it, but what was the point? "Maybe because Maya was my roommate. Maybe because she's a bad liar. Maybe because I want to see real justice done here." She swallowed. "When Largo gets back, you should take some time off. These past few weeks have made you the touchy one."

"Me? You're the one who wants to argue. You've been wound tight ever since you found the dead baby and failed with the warrant. Give yourself a break. And give me one, too."

She thought about defending herself, but she realized Chee was right. She hated fighting with him. And now he pulled the rank card. She stayed silent.

"Bernie, if I'm grumpy, part of it is because I had to deal with the fallout from your exchange with Berke the Jerk over the Bee case. He left a message beating on you."

She felt a knot growing in her stomach. "What I did out there was right, and you know it. I'd do it again. I'd never ask you to run interference for me. I'm going to talk to Agent Johnson about that loser."

"I've been a policeman a long time. I can deal with Berke and whatever else comes my way. Don't let him get to you, Officer. That's an order."

She exhaled and ended the call with a quick "Catch you later." She squeezed the steering wheel and told herself to calm down, commanded that inner scream full of heat and hurt to shut up. She consciously relaxed the muscles in her jaw. Tried to focus on the hum of tires on the asphalt, the congruity of the dash of white stripes in the center of her side of the road and the overarching blue beauty of the broad sky. She invited this stark land of sunbaked earth, ancient rocks, and tough plants to soothe her.

When she pulled off the highway for gas at Sky City Casino, she called Williams, ready to talk about the letter.

"Hey, Bernie. We got some bad news. The medical investigator is backed up and probably won't get to the Jones autopsy for a few days."

"That's inconvenient and unusual. They're usually quick with deaths like this."

"On the plus side, we found a receipt in Jones's wallet for a charge from a Socorro restaurant, Big River Brew Pub, the night he died. Amazingly, the place has working surveillance cameras. Their tape shows Jones and a woman who looks like Maya leaving together about nine p.m. It appears that they had some sort of argument in the parking lot. You can watch it when you get here."

"Does it show her getting in the car with him?"

"Yep. And before you ask, she did so willingly." Williams paused for a couple of beats. "Meanwhile, we got an anonymous phone call about the case. The caller said he knew Jones, and that Jones and another scientist were at each other's throats over someone stealing someone's research. It made me curious. You know, another motive for murder."

"That's interesting, but I'm always wary of anonymous calls. Did you get Junior's letter?"

"Yeah. You know, Jones was a PhD scientist who lived at the computer. Why send a typed letter through the post office?" Williams made a clicking sound with her tongue. "It looks like someone besides you wants me to believe the suicide theory. My hunch is that Maya wrote that thing."

"Chee believes that, too, as part of her abandoned plan to get away with murder. I'd like to read it."

"Of course. I hope you can get Maya to explain herself next time we talk to her."

"I like the we part in that. I haven't had much luck."

"I'll arrange the interview for later tomorrow morning, and you can look at surveillance footage from the restaurant and read the letter before that. You're staying with me, right?"

"If that's an invitation, you bet."

"I'm glad you'll be here." She heard the smile in Williams's voice. "I'll pick up something easy for dinner. It's been a long day." Williams gave her a code to open the garage door if Bernie arrived at the house first.

She pulled over at a convenience store in Los Lunas and went inside for a Coke and a couple spare ones for Williams's refrigerator. She thought about calling Chee, felt a clutch of anxiety and residual anger, and decided against it. Maybe he'd call her.

15

L ouisa had returned from Flagstaff talkative as usual, laden with groceries. She summarized the latest challenge educational bureaucracy had placed at her threshold while she unpacked the trove of vegetables and the bottles of that special greenish juice she enjoyed. Leaphorn listened to her monologue, trying to keep the players and the petty incidents straight in his head, knowing what came next.

She washed her hands and dried them on a kitchen towel. "So, Joe, what do you think I should do?"

"Let it sit. You're smart. You'll find da answer. You been in dese situation a'fore."

She laughed. "Don't remind me. Thanks for the attagirl, but I could use some specifics."

"Hol' on." His laptop was on the kitchen table and he typed out a note.

I bet you've worked with someone who has dealt with these issues, successfully or otherwise. In either case, that person could give you practical advice. I'm willing to listen and offer an opinion, but I'm out of my depth here. Check your mental rolodex and make some phone calls.

Louisa laughed again. "I haven't heard the word *rolodex* for ages. There's an app for that now. I hope you realize that thinking out loud helps me figure out what to do, even when you just listen."

The timer chimed and Leaphorn turned off the oven. Removing the lasagna, he inhaled the warm spicy aroma of tomato sauce, meat, cheese, and oregano. His mouth started to water as he set the dish on a hot pad on the table.

Louisa had made a salad to go with the lasagna. She gave it a toss and joined him at the table. "I've been doing all the talking. What's new with you?"

"Did I tell you abow Captain Largo?"

"No. How's he doing?"

He outlined the highlights of their visit, leaving out the pastries.

When he was done, she let out a long breath. "I'm glad you encouraged him to make a plan instead of jumping in to retirement. That makes change easier. Speaking of that, I'm working on a plan for our time in Washington. If you're coming, you'll have to tell me what you'd like to see."

He nodded because the idea made perfect sense. He felt the tension in his jaw rise at the thought of the trip, so he served himself some salad and passed the bowl to her.

Even after long experience, Leaphorn still never knew what to expect when Louisa took to the kitchen. Many of her healthy concoctions left him craving what he called *real food*, but he liked the salad. In addition to fresh spinach, she'd added onions, red and green peppers, tomatoes, and something white, crisp, and slightly sweet he hadn't tried before. He speared a piece on his fork and extended it toward her. "What's dis?"

"Jicama. It has a lot of fiber and vitamin C."

He could say he liked it without fibbing.

Louisa brought up the trip again. "So, I need to book the flights for the conference. Have you decided about Washington?"

"Na yet."

"Joe, you told me about your first—and last—trip there. I can understand why you're hesitating. But this won't be like that. That was work, and this will be a vacation."

"Na very good at takin' bacations."

She sipped her water. "You and I aren't getting any younger. There are places I'd like to see now, while I can move without hurting, and while I have my wits about me. I'd enjoy traveling even more if you can share it. But I'm going to Washington to give my talk at the conference and take a little vacation, with or without you."

"I tell you soon."

"Promise?"

He nodded. "Les na talk 'bout dis anymore."

They finished dinner in companionable silence. When she cooked, he did dishes. Tonight, they had shared the duties, but Louisa looked tired.

"I got da cleanup tonight."

"Thanks." Louisa retreated to the living room and her favorite chair.

When he'd finished, he noticed that she had fallen asleep with both a book and Giddi on her lap. The return to teaching and the drive to and from Flagstaff twice a week took a toll on her, but she never complained. She had the age and years of experience to retire, too, but as far as he knew, she had never considered it. She teased him about failing retirement when he stayed up late and rose early, enthralled by a new case.

Before it got too late, he went to his office to call the man who was responsible for the property where Bernie had found the dead baby. As he'd expected, no one answered, but he left a message explaining that he was a private investigator with a question or two. He stressed that the man wasn't in trouble and how appreciative he would be for a returned phone call. He left his cell number only.

That done, he clicked on the television with the sound turned low. It was almost time for the evening news.

"Hey there." Louisa's voice was soft with the remnants of sleep. "I thought you had to make a phone call."

"I did. I lef a message."

Before going to bed, they always watched the news together and questioned the weather forecast. Even though Window Rock was in Arizona, the Navajo Nation's capital city received what they called *local* news from Albuquerque's television stations. Most of the stories concerned fresh crime and ongoing investigations, which, as a veteran cop, he found riveting. The reporters ignored the Navajo Nation unless there was an election, a pandemic, an environmental disaster, a winning high school sports team, or perhaps a Sasquatch sighting up in the Lukachukai Mountains.

As Louisa pushed herself upright, Giddi stretched and gracefully pounced to the floor. "That time already? I'll make some tea. Would you like some? It's good for you."

She always said that, and they always ended the day with a cup of the foul-smelling herbal blend she concocted herself. As bad as it tasted, Leaphorn had noticed that it led to solid sleep. He'd grown used to the flavor the way a person with a skunk under the porch grows accustomed to the stench.

"Do you fix dis tea when you spend da night in Flag?"

"Well, no. I made some when I first started staying with Helen. She wouldn't even try it. She told me she didn't like the aroma. Can you believe that? It's one thing I look forward to when I'm home."

"Did you say id was good for her?"

"Indeed I did. I even told her you liked it."

When Louisa came back with the steaming cups, the weatherman on KOB was gesturing first at California and then toward the north end of Arizona and New Mexico. Leaphorn turned up the volume.

"A strong storm front will be moving in rapidly from the Pacific in the next few days. It could bring rain to the Four Corners and maybe even the first snow of the season." He moved his hand toward the Mexico side of the map. "And this plume of moisture from the Gulf might join it, creating precipitation for the rest of the state later in the week."

Louisa shook her head. "You know, Flag gets the news from Phoenix. According to what I saw, this storm was only a bit of rain. I think we could say forecasting the weather is like predicting human behavior, always full of surprises and mistakes."

He nodded. "Weather is interestin' because id always changes. Like people."

They finished their tea and he took the cups to the kitchen. He noticed the olive oil she'd used for the salad dressing. "Did you get da oil change in your car?" He left the maintenance of her vehicle to Louisa. It wasn't her strong suit.

"Thanks for reminding me. I'll do that. And remember, you're taking the truck in for a tune-up."

He nodded in acknowledgment.

She made a clicking noise with her tongue. "I hope the weather guy is wrong. I don't like to drive in the snow, or even when it's raining. The swish of the wipers bothers me, and then there's all those people going too fast, spraying road muck all over."

Before he recovered from the head wound, he'd had to leave the driving to Louisa. In retrospect, he believed that helped him get well more quickly. On each trip, he turned the challenge of keeping his mouth shut into motivation to grow strong enough to be his own chauffeur.

He heard his cell phone ring from the office. If it was Bernie, she could wait. Anyone else ought to know better than to call so late.

They watched a story about the closing day of Albuquerque's International Balloon Fiesta. The reporter interviewed a redheaded college student surrounded by a forest of giant, colorful hot air balloons. The young woman had qualified for her balloon pilot's license a few weeks ago. The tall balloon behind her had a picture of the state of Wisconsin.

Something about the interview made him think of the old Boy Scout case again. Wisconsin? Were the kids from Wisconsin?

Louisa said good night and went to her bedroom before the sports coverage came on, Giddi following close behind. The cat slept with him when Louisa was gone, but clearly preferred female company.

Leaphorn checked his phone before he went to bed and saw that the call he ignored had come from Hancock. He listened to the message.

"I can never remember what time it is in Window Rock. Are you Navajo Nation guys on Arizona time or in October with the rest of us on daylight savings? Anyway, I called to tell you I might have to leave the task force sooner than expected. Christina and I just got some bad news. Her cancer is back, and we're heading down to the University of New Mexico Cancer Center in Albuquerque for, you know, whatever they can do. I'm sending you the agenda for the next meeting and some more information in an email. Say yes, my friend. Or at least call me back and argue. Thanks."

He erased Hancock's voicemail and went to bed.

Leaphorn had always prided himself on his sharp memory, and his inability to make the connection between the Wisconsin balloon and the Boy Scout case bothered him. If he couldn't remember by morning, he decided, he would read through the old file.

He picked up the guidebook to Washington, DC, that lay on his bedside table, hoping something he read would offset his ambiguity about the trip.

Instead it put him to sleep.

16

The streetlamps had flickered on by the time Bernie drove up to Williams's house. Although the detective had given her the code to open the garage door and a second set of numbers to silence the alarm, she didn't do that. Instead, she climbed out of the unit and stood a moment. Then she locked the car and started to walk. She always thought better when she moved.

It was warmer by a few degrees here in central New Mexico than in Shiprock, and the air held some moisture. She noticed the lack of dust and the juicy smell of someone's dinner—a roasting chicken—dancing in the night air. Dinner would be welcome.

She'd had longer and tougher days of driving, but her eyes felt heavy, her back tight, her spirit exhausted. It wasn't the 280-mile trip, she realized. The harsh words she and the man she loved had exchanged left her drained and saddened. Recalling the conversation raised her temperature. How dare he order her to cheer up? Even as a joke.

She walked faster.

By the time she got back to Tara Williams's place, her anger had cooled, but she'd reached no conclusion on how to deal with Chee. She removed her bag from the trunk and took it to the front door. The house glowed with welcome light.

"Hi, Bernie. I saw your unit out there. Did you forget the codes?"

"No. I wanted to stretch my legs after all that time in the car."

"I hope you're hungry." Williams didn't wait for an answer. She had set the table with cloth napkins and a plate at each place. "I'm starved. Let's eat and then we can plan how we'll approach Maya tomorrow."

Bernie washed her hands and sat at the place where Tara had put a glass with ice and Coke. "Thanks for dinner. I want to talk to you about something else, too. Something personal. Well, personal and professional."

"Chee, huh? Eat first, my dear. Food is a good thing. The brain likes it."

There were two white boxes in the center of the table, one with a check mark on the lid. Williams reached for a plastic bag and unloaded chopsticks wrapped in red paper, orange-colored liquid in a small round container, little packets of soy sauce and hot mustard, and even fortune cookies. She handed Bernie the box with the check mark. "I hope you like it."

Bernie watched as her friend opened her own box. Ah, just as she feared. Vegetables floating in a brownish sauce probably named for a mysterious place in China. Tara unwrapped a set of chopsticks and lifted up a bite-sized white cube from the sauce. Mama always told her never to complain when someone offered you a meal but to be grateful for something to eat. OK then, she could do this, she told herself as she studied her box.

"I remembered how you are about chopsticks. You could use your fingers, but here, just in case." Williams handed Bernie a little package with a plastic knife, spoon, fork, and an extra napkin.

Bernie lifted the lid and prepared for the worst, but the delicious aroma of roasted meat greeted her. The tray held small meaty ribs arranged on a pile of fluffy white rice. No odd green things. No mystery sauce.

Williams chuckled. "Don't look so surprised."

Later, Bernie mentioned her argument with Chee. Williams listened intently without interrupting.

"You wanna know what I think?"

"I do."

"The man is under a lot of stress. That doesn't excuse how he acted, but give him some space. And you told me about that dead baby. Give yourself a break, too." Williams smiled. "I'm a fine one to give advice. You've already been married longer than I made it."

They said good night, and Bernie read awhile before turning out the light. Putting her feelings into words had helped her sort through them. Stress, as Tara suggested, made Chee irritable. She knew he was exhausted and doing his best. She loved him even though she didn't *like* him at the moment. Maybe becoming a detective would help their marriage. She took some deep breaths and fell asleep.

17

Although he was awake, Leaphorn had decided to allow himself a few moments of laziness before he left the warmth of his bed. Louisa's footsteps in the hall and a knock on his bedroom door changed that.

"Joe, you've got a call. Your friend Hancock. I told him I'd give you a message, but he says he really needs to talk to you."

"I be right dare." He put on a bathrobe and his slippers. He noticed only darkness through the eastern windows as he headed into the kitchen. He glanced at the clock on the way to the telephone: 6:15.

"Hancock?"

"I hated to get you out of bed, old man, but this couldn't wait. My wife had a heart attack last night. I'm here with her in intensive care."

"Sorry to hear dat."

"It's tough. They don't know . . . Anyway, that task force I mentioned to you is meeting next week and I was hoping to send you the information I promised, but, well . . ."

Leaphorn exhaled. "Don't worry 'bout dat now. Jus' focus on your wife." For a brief moment he remembered the days he'd spent in the hospital with Emma. If he'd known it was their last time together, he would have left all those calls from the station unanswered. On the other hand, work gave him the illusion that in the face of chaos, he still controlled a tiny sliver of his life.

"I didn't want you to think I'd forgotten or whatever, you know? This effort to make a difference is really important and you'd . . . Hold on a minute."

Leaphorn heard the mumble of conversation, including Hancock's telling someone he understood.

"Joe, I've got to focus on stuff here. If you can help, fine. If this is too big a favor, I get it. No harm, no foul." And Hancock ended the call.

Leaphorn put the phone on its base and padded back to his bedroom, reviewing the conversation as he showered and dressed. By the time he returned to the kitchen, Louisa sat reading the newspaper.

She frowned. "At least from your end, that didn't sound like a happy call."

He poured himself some coffee, then reached for his laptop and typed:

Jerry Hancock's wife had a heart attack and they're at the hospital. He wanted me to know that he might have to leave that task force sooner than expected and said he would email me some information so I could decide what to do about that. I encouraged him to focus on his wife for now.

"Good advice. I saw your light on last night. Did you sleep well?"

"Sorta. I had a bad dream." He had woken in the middle of the night after a nightmare about the vicious killer who had hidden the kidnapped Boy Scouts in a cave. In the dream, he saw the redheaded girl with the Wisconsin balloon and a priest saying Mass for their sorry souls.

"How 'bout you?"

"No dreams I can remember. It's so good to curl up in my own bed."

He ate some of the oatmeal she'd made and served him. It tasted as consistently bland as always and was, as she often stressed, good for him. But the nightmare had depressed his appetite.

He wondered if Bernie would relive her experience with the bound woman and the abandoned baby in her sleep. He hoped not. His dream seemed to urge him to find the Boy Scout file.

Louisa sipped the coffee. "I forgot to ask if you'd talked to Jim or Bernie lately."

"Chee called yestaday. He said some woman wants ta talk ta me 'bout savin' her life."

"That's interesting."

He shook his head. "Wait."

He typed: I don't have a clue who this is. Her name isn't familiar at all. And she asked for John Leapfrog. The phone number she left links to a foundation.

Louisa put her cup down on the table. "Aren't you curious? I mean, it seems like you would want to know what happened to a person who is alive now because of you."

He shrugged off the question. "I dink id's a scam."

"Don't be too cynical. I've had a few former students seek me out. To be honest, some of them were people I'd forgotten, the ones I thought wouldn't make it through college. I was touched that they came to thank me for encouraging them. They'd done well and they thought I deserved some of the credit."

He anticipated the punch line.

"Maybe this gal just wants to thank you. What harm can a phone call do? If she's a scammer, hang up. Or report her to someone."

He shook his head.

Louisa laughed. "Joe, you're a detective. If that woman is part of some criminal undertaking, who better than you to deal with it?"

He laughed, too. "I'll dink about id after breakfast."

He typed something:

Before you bring it up, I'll let you know about Washington today. I heard from one pending client and I still need to find out from the others.

She read it and then looked at him. "I don't understand why this is so hard for you."

He shrugged. "It's not about bein' wid you."

She took a few moments to respond. "That's sure what it looks like. If you're interested, I need to know soon so I can book the flights. All I'm asking from you, really, is the courtesy of a yes or no. Just so we're clear on this, I have to go to the conference."

He heard the suppressed frustration in her voice.

"I'm not asking for a kidney, for goodness' sakes, just a yes or no answer. I don't understand why you keep procrastinating."

"I know ya doan. I gid it. I'll let ya know."

After breakfast, he poured himself more coffee and went back to his office. The unease caused by the nightmare lingered, so he decided to look for the Boy Scout file before he did anything else. Then, of course, the phone rang.

"Sir, it's Chee. Have you made any progress on the dead-baby situation?"

"Not yet. I'll get back to you on that."

"Thanks. The sooner, the better."

Leaphorn smiled as he ended the call. Jim Chee had sounded like a boss. While it was on his mind, he called the nephew again and left his message in English as well as Navajo. Then he called the nursing home where the old man who owned the house now lived. To his surprise, the woman who answered transferred him to another woman, the old man's daughter who'd come to visit. Even more encouraging, she spoke Navajo. Leaphorn explained the situation.

"Oh, gosh, that's so sad about the baby. My father has lost most of his words, and his memory. I'm sorry he won't be able to help you."

"Were any of your relatives expecting a baby or caring for a newborn?"

"No babies that I know of. Give me your name again, sir."

Leaphorn complied and added his phone number. "Get back to me if you learn anything, please."

"I will."

After that, rather than think about the old case, he made a call to Agent Sage Johnson and found her in the office.

"Joe Leaphorn. I've heard of you."

"When we find out what happened out there, we hope to press charges against the perpetrators for the death of the baby, depending on cause of death in the OMI report. And for the assault and exploitation of the woman Officer Manuelito found. Agent Berke is handling the case. At this point, that's all I can tell you."

"Did da baby belong to da woman dare?"

"Berke thinks so. We're hoping the DNA test leads to the father. We believe he might have been involved in what happened."

The answer didn't satisfy Leaphorn. "Did Berke ask for da child's maternal DNA?"

She paused. "I'll check on that. Tell me again why this matters to you."

He explained that he'd been hired to try to help identify the child in case he was related to a Navajo family in the area. The discovery of an abandoned little one didn't sit right with any of them.

Johnson said, "Appreciate your help. Keep me in the loop if you find out anything."

Then he emailed a resource at OMI to request the cause of death and the results of the baby's DNA test. His contact answered quickly. The child had died from brain injuries compounded by malnourishment and dehydration. The DNA results weren't available yet. The FBI had provided a list of possible fathers whose genetic information would be in the system based on previous cases.

Leaphorn responded with a thank-you and a new request. "Can you verify the mother's DNA, too?" Then he stood and stretched, and gave Giddi a pat. The cat moved to her favorite chair and watched him open a drawer in his old file cabinet. Time to think about the Boy Scout case.

When the department went digital right before he retired, he asked to keep the files on some of his more interesting cases rather than designating them for the shredder. Here they sat.

Leaphorn valued records. He had stored the files by year, and he remembered roughly when he had handled the case. After about ten minutes, he found what he needed. He placed it in the center of his desktop. First a sip of coffee, and then he'd see why Ginger Simons reminded him of this ancient case and what, if anything, the dream girl with the balloon had to do with it.

He closed his eyes and tried to recall as much as he could about the incident. He pictured a cave. He remembered the killer and his crew of cronies. Then he saw a priest with a Navajo face who had also been captured. The name came to him. Father Tso. Benjamin Tso. In cinematic detail he relived the exact moment when Tso, who had managed to free himself, stepped in front of a bullet meant for cop Joe Leaphorn. The priest had a look of peace on his face as he moved forward to his death, a human shield to protect Leaphorn's own chest.

He opened his eyes and shook off the memory. Giddi stared at him.

Father Tso died with honor, an unrecognized hero. Tso's sacrifice enabled Leaphorn to rescue the other hostages. He replayed the scene with the terrified little boys, their leader, and, he recalled, a very disagreeable woman. A redhead like the girl with the balloon.

Leaphorn reached for the file folder. He read his notes, starting with the mysterious murder of Benjamin Tso's grandfather. He'd become involved by accident, and his role began because of the aggressive and obnoxious woman. He found her name: Theodora Adams, a person he'd hoped to never see again. He remembered the blue-eyed redhead vividly now, and with a sour taste in his mouth.

The young woman had driven herself west in a new blue Corvette Stingray that, although beautiful, lacked the necessary clearance for the dirt tracks that served as backcountry roads. She asked Leaphorn for a ride, and when he explained that department rules didn't allow hitchhikers, she offered to pay him. That bribe, he recollected, said a lot about how she made her way in the world. When he continued to refuse, she took it as a challenge. She hid in the back seat of his vehicle and, finally, after a string of half-truths, told him why she had come.

Her daddy, a physician, sent her to Europe to have some fun. In Rome she encountered Benjamin Tso. Leaphorn imagined the attraction. Father Tso, exotically handsome compared to the non-Natives she'd grown up with, posed a challenge—his vow of celibacy made him totally unavailable. She tracked him from Italy, where he tried to end the relationship, all the way to the remote Navajo Nation. Tso had come to quietly mourn his grandfather and, Leaphorn believed, escape from this woman who wanted the priest to continue to be her lover. Even as a much younger man, Leaphorn knew enough about love to recognize its absence in the woman's ruthless obsession.

He finished the main file and found a second, thinner folder with "Theodora Adams" printed on it. Inside, he'd saved a single sheet, a missing person report filed by Dr. Winthrop Adams of McLean, Virginia, concerning his adult daughter, whom he believed might be somewhere on the Navajo Nation. The report listed the gentleman's address and phone number.

Leaphorn jotted down the relevant information. The report was ancient, of course, but it gave him a place to start. He typed Theodora Adams into the search bar. He found a science fiction writer who looked nothing like the woman he remembered, several links to African American women of that name, and obituaries for ladies much older than Adams would be. He added the words *kidnapping*, and even *Boy Scouts*, and then wasted considerable time with interesting trivia that led him no closer to his goal. He found no connection between this woman and Ginger Simons.

Giddi left her chair and came over to rub against his leg. "You're right." He reached down to pet her. "Time to do something else."

He typed in Dr. Winthrop Adams McLean, Virginia and had more success. Dr. Adams's obituary listed Theodora Adams as his only child. The notice didn't give her hometown. He realized that he had to call in reinforcements: his smart friend Carla, who worked at the Window Rock police headquarters, spoke fluent computer and had helped him search for information before. If she'd come to work today, perhaps she'd have a few extra minutes to spend on this little problem.

The office door creaked open, intruding on his thoughts. Louisa came in and sat next to the window. "I'm going to my exercise program and then meeting Genny for lunch, and then taking these books back to the library. Do you need me to pick up anything for you while I'm out?"

"No tanks."

Giddi, who had been perched on the windowsill, moved to Louisa's lap. "If you decide to make the Washington trip, we'll have to get someone to take care of the cat."

"Dat's righ."

"You know, there's medicine people can take for anxiety. That might help with your fear of traveling."

He tried to focus on the file he'd been reading, hoping she would drop the subject and head out to her fitness class.

"You like being in charge, Joe Leaphorn. Is it because this trip is connected to my job and it's my idea? Is that why you're hesitating?"

"No, na ad all."

"You're retired. You work for yourself. I think . . ."
She stopped.

He typed a message on his computer and motioned
her over. When Louisa stood, Giddi bounded gracefully
onto the floor. She read the message over his shoulder.

I'm not afraid of traveling. You know I like road trips
and the flexibility of being able to stop when and
where we want. I'm figuring things out. Please don't
keep nagging me.

"Okay, but make up your mind. If you decide not to
come, I'll ask someone else. Maybe Helen."
He typed:

I told you there are some pending assignments I have
to consider in terms of the time commitments. I'm
still waiting to hear from one client and figure things
out. Don't take it personally.

Louisa left. From the pain in her face, he could tell
she didn't understand.

Giddi moved to the warm spot in the empty chair.

Helen, he remembered, also taught at NAU. Louisa
stayed with her when she didn't feel like driving the

long way back to Window Rock. He'd joined the two for dinner in Flagstaff once or twice and felt totally out of place. If Helen was available, Louisa wouldn't have to travel alone.

And, he knew, his absence would make additional absences, additional time not spent together, easier for Louisa until, perhaps, his friend moved out of his life. Even his delay in deciding had caused tension.

Louisa was right; he worked for himself and set his own schedule. That wasn't the issue. The jobs merely offered a convenient tool to buy him time to face his fear. No reason not to accept them with the arrangement that he'd start work in a few weeks, after the trip. No reason except that going to Washington meant getting on a plane.

He joined Giddi in watching out the window as a few dark-eyed juncos and house finches enjoyed a free meal at the seed feeder. When the phone rang, he answered out of long-standing habit without checking the caller ID.

"Hey, Joe. It's Helen. Louisa there?"

"No. Do you hab her cell number?"

"I tried that first. Can you ask her to call me? I really need to talk to her."

"Sure." Something in Helen's voice kicked in his cop training. "Everythin' OK?"

"Actually, no. My daughter's having some issues. Louisa always gives me good advice."

He barely knew the woman, but it didn't matter. She talked on.

"She sounds really depressed. I need to go out there and spend time with my girl, but that throws everyone's schedule here at the university into chaos. I've got some vacation time saved up, but I didn't think I'd have to use it for something like this."

"What's da trouble?"

"She had a bad car accident. She was driving and her fiancé was in the front seat. It wasn't her fault. She wasn't badly hurt, but the man she planned to marry died in the wreck. She hadn't even told me she was dating anyone."

"Dat's too bad. I'm sorry." And he meant it, both for the lost lover and the damaged relationship.

"Don't forget to tell Louisa I called. She always has good advice."

He jotted "Call Helen" on a slip of paper and placed it on the counter near the cookie jar. He dished up some leftover lasagna for lunch, and as he waited for the microwave to warm it he realized that Helen's daughter had made his life more complicated. She wouldn't go to Washington for a vacation with her daughter in need of mothering. The travel ball had bounced back into his court. Louisa deserved his answer.

He ate, then picked up the phone. Carla had come to work, and of course she'd be glad to help him with something and could probably work on what it was that afternoon.

"Thanks. I hope it won't take much of your time. I'll stop by."

He could have given her the information over the phone, of course, but getting out of the house might clear his brain and help with the Washington dilemma.

Before he left for the station, he did another online search. He typed fear of flying into the Google bar and then scrolled through the lists of studies on the psychology of the condition and drugs for anxiety until he found something that captured his interest. He closed the door to his office and clicked on the video. The introduction talked about the value of deep breathing and positive thinking. He frowned, but he didn't turn it off.

18

Leaphorn realized that Louisa had forgotten the books she wanted to return and took them with him since the library was on the way to the police station. He put the books on the seat next to him, moving the poster of the missing woman he'd been given in Gallup. But before he started his truck, he noticed someone parked across the street in the shadow of a Siberian elm. The car was hard to miss. The gray passenger door stood out from the deep green of the rest of the vehicle. The rear taillight was covered with thick plastic, and the front end looked like someone had backed a truck into it.

He drove past, wondering who had parked there and why. The car looked empty, but when he checked the rearview mirror a few minutes later, it was behind his pickup, headed the same direction. A person with a white ball cap sat at the wheel.

Leaphorn pulled over, and the car behind him did the same. He waited. The other driver waited, too, and Leaphorn felt his irritation rising. He always carried a gun, and in a situation like this, he was thankful for its reassurance. As he opened his truck door, the suspicious car pulled onto the road and drove ahead. He caught a better glimpse of the driver, a short man wearing sunglasses.

He slammed the door shut and continued toward the police station. By the time he had backed into a parking spot with a visitor sign, he had calmed down from greatly annoyed to moderately disturbed.

When he had first retired, Leaphorn still felt at home at the headquarters. Now, many people he'd worked with had also retired or moved on. Even the building had been remodeled. Coming here today made him feel older.

He smiled to see Carla at work at her desk.

"Lieutenant Leaphorn! And you aren't using your cane today." She spoke in Navajo.

"Yá'át'ééh. This man is getting stronger. I'm glad I caught you."

"I just got back from a week's vacation, so now I seem to have more to do than ever. You remember how that goes."

He didn't. He never took off more than a day or two at a time when he served on the force. He loved his job.

When Carla removed the glasses she used to see her computer screen, he noticed a trace of green eyeshadow. "I'm always glad to help you. What can I do for you today, sir?"

"I received a phone call from a person who says I saved her life, but the name isn't ringing a bell with me. I'm wondering if this is just a clever scam." He gave her a piece of paper on which he had written "Ginger Simons" and the phone number. He'd also written "Closely Watched Foundation" and that number, too, and the website.

Carla set it on her desk. "Sir, do you think this woman is in danger?"

He understood the reason for the question. If he said yes, Carla could work on the project as part of her job. "Well, I don't know for sure, but she could be. A woman named Theodora Adams was one of several people kidnapped on a case I handled. I wonder if she is connected to that woman."

"Kidnapped? Wow. That sounds official to me. What happened?"

"Oh, it's complicated and it happened a while ago."

"Come on, Lieutenant, tell me more." Carla smiled at him. "It might help me find her."

"Well, in addition to Miss Adams, the situation involved a troop of Boy Scouts and their leader, and a Catholic priest. The priest's brother, a deranged guy, and some associates stirred up a bunch of trouble."

"Like a cult or something?" Carla stared at him for a second, then remembered her manners and looked away. "I bet a whole bunch of officers—a SWAT team—worked with you on that case."

"No, but after I got the hostages out of the cave, then some rescuers helped us."

"It was just you! How many bad guys were out there, sir?"

He thought about it. "Four. I just did my job."

"That's something." She studied the desktop. "I'll do my best to find information on this woman for you, Lieutenant. I'll call you. I'll have it by this afternoon."

He liked the fact that she seemed so sure she'd come up with something.

"Sir, would you tell me the whole story someday? I mean, from start to finish, with all the details about everything?"

Her eagerness embarrassed him. He didn't like being thought of as a hero. He changed the subject. "Could you do me another favor?"

"I hope so."

Leaphorn gave her the name of the task force. "They're looking for new members. A friend asked me to consider it, and I'd like you to find a little background on the group to help me decide. Would you do that?"

She nodded. "Missing women. That's a big problem. You know, a family just came in concerned about their daughter. She's been gone about two months, but she'd taken off before, so they didn't worry at first."

"How do you know this?"

"Oh, I heard them in the lobby before they went in to file a report. They left some flyers. Here." She showed him a bright pink paper, and he remembered it from his lunch with Hancock.

"Sir, do you have time for a question?"

"Go ahead."

"I'm thinking of applying to the Navajo Police Academy. I enjoy this job, but I'd like to move to the next step. But I'm not sure I've got what it takes. I mean, when that family was here, worried about their sister, their daughter. It broke my heart. How did you deal with all the bad stuff you have to handle?"

He said the first thought that came to him. "You focus on the good things. On the people you can help. You do the best you can, and you realize that's all you can do."

Carla put her glasses back on. "Which of your assignments should I work on first?"

"Theodora Adams."

As he was headed to his truck, someone called his name. Through the open window of the patrol car, he saw Officer Brodrick Manygoats.

"Yá'át'ééh, Lieutenant. Are you coming back to work with us?"

"Not me. Not today anyway." Leaphorn responded in Navajo.

Officer Manygoats followed. "I've been chatting with your old buddy Jim Chee a lot this week. He's filling in for Captain Largo in Shiprock. I hear the captain's thinking of retiring." Manygoats turned the statement into a question with the tone of his voice.

"Well, he's a good man and he's put in more than enough time. Who'd you hear it from?"

"Oh, you know . . . rumors are thicker than flies at a rodeo. I couldn't blame Largo if he left, but it's hard to picture the district without him. He was there when the road was two lanes and we called it the Devil's Highway."

"He was there when Ship Rock landed and our relatives climbed off and started planning for the first Navajo Fair."

The officer chuckled. "I'll tell Largo you said that."

"I know it's true because I was there, too."

Carla's interest in the kidnapping had brightened his day. Revisiting the case reminded him of what he liked about police work—and of how much younger he was then.

Louisa's library books on the front seat of the truck reminded him of his next stop. The Navajo Nation Library shared a large modern building with the Navajo Nation Museum, offices, and meeting rooms. He spent a lot of time there, using the brains and resources of the staff to help his research.

The archivist greeted him. "Hey, my friend. I want to show you some treasures we just received. I know you love maps. Come take a look at these."

During his work as a detective, Leaphorn used a map with pushpins of different colors to help him track his cases. When he retired, he left it in his office—a decision he'd regretted ever since.

They walked into the archivist's work space, where several large topographical maps were spread out on a table. The collection he saw spanned the Navajo Nation and beyond. He took a long look at the Four Corners, where New Mexico, Colorado, Arizona, and Utah meet. He studied Cameron and the area near Tuba City, Canyon de Chelly, and Kayenta. He spent some time with the map of Lake Powell. Somewhere in that harsh landscape was the cave where he'd stumbled across the sand paintings Largo had mentioned. "What treasures. Where did these come from?"

"Someone donated them to the Placitas Community Library in New Mexico. They already had a set in their collection, so they contacted us."

"Could I take a picture of this one?"

"I'll send you a digital copy. You enjoy that country?"

Leaphorn hesitated, remembering how he'd almost died there. "It's beautiful."

Looking at the terrain where he had stalked the killer stirred muscle memory of the exhaustion, his injuries, and, he realized, the exhilaration of the physical and mental challenge of the case. He wondered if rising Lake Powell had washed away the sand paintings. Someone should document them, he thought. He knew the medicine men had created the images with painstaking care in case a disaster befell the Diné. The cave held its own sacred library.

He left the maps, returned the books, and walked outside. He noticed the suspicious green car again, parked a few spaces down from where he'd left his truck. The driver's door opened; a slim leg in a cowboy boot emerged. Remembering the woman in the sedan who had nearly killed him with a gunshot a few years ago, he felt his adrenaline rise. He froze in place and put his hand on his gun.

"Stop right there." Leaphorn yelled at the person in Navajo.

"Lieutenant Leaphorn?" He could barely hear the quivering voice.

"Speak up. Who are you?"

"I'm Carla's sister's son. Jonathan."

"Carla?" It took him a moment to put it together. "The lady who works at the police headquarters?"

"Yes, sir. She's my auntie."

"Jonathan, why were you parked outside my house? And why are you following me?"

"I, I can explain." The young man had a silver earring shaped like a long feather in the ear that wasn't covered by his hair. It moved as he spoke.

"Go ahead. Louder."

"I didn't mean to make you mad. I just wanted to talk."

"This isn't the way to do that. You could have gotten yourself shot. Do you have sawdust where your brain should be?"

"I, uhm, yeah. I'm sorry." The young man's confidence evaporated as quickly as virga from a summer storm.

A king-sized van drove up and pulled into the spot next to Leaphorn's truck. Jonathan stared at it.

Leaphorn softened his voice. "Talk about what?"

"Uh. I wanna . . . Could we go somewhere, like, more private?"

"No."

"Sir, it's kind of sensitive. My auntie—"

The van's passenger window opened, and a woman started talking to Leaphorn. Yelling actually. "Hey, is that the museum over there?"

"Yes," Leaphorn answered.

"You speak English?"

"When I hab to."

The woman looked startled and stopped shouting. "Is there a restaurant in there?" She pointed to the museum with her index finger.

"No."

While she spoke, the van's side door slid open and a girl in white jeans stepped out, followed by a younger boy. "Mom, I told you. We should have stopped at Mc-Donald's. You guys never listen to me . . ."

Jonathan spoke. "You'll find a good restaurant across the street and down a couple blocks at the hotel."

A man said, "As long as we're here, we should take a look inside the museum. It wouldn't hurt you two to learn something."

"Mommy, I'm hungry," the boy whined.

The woman took the younger child's hand and they started toward the building. The girl glanced briefly at Leaphorn and then focused on Jonathan. "Are you guys Indians?"

Leaphorn nodded.

"Navajo," Jonathan said. "How about you?"

The girl looked surprised. "No, I'm from Sacramento."

"Well, welcome to Dinétah, the home of the Navajo."

"Does Navajo mean Indian?"

"Yes. Well, actually it means 'the people.'"

"I never met an Indian before. Do you have a horse?"

"No, just that old car over there."

"Maybe your granddad will buy you one. I like your earring."

"Thanks. The restaurant is right over there. You can go after the museum. They serve all afternoon."

The father said, "Come on, sweetie. It's chilly out here."

"Thanks for talking to me." She gave them both a shy smile. Jonathan smiled back.

Leaphorn watched the girl walk off with her father. Maybe curious children held the hope for the world. He turned to Jonathan and spoke in Navajo. "Is there a problem with your aunt?"

"Oh no, sir. She's fine. She's happy. But, well . . . it's kind of complicated. It's about changing her job, and since she talks about you all the time, I thought you might be able to, you know . . ." Jonathan lost his words.

"Are you concerned about Carla wanting to become a policewoman?"

Jonathan looked surprised. "Not me. She's so cool and tough, I'm excited for her. But some of our relatives worry, and they asked me to try to talk her out of it. I just want her to be happy, and she wants to be a cop. I thought maybe you could, well, maybe tell me how to get them to back off."

"Your relatives are right to be worried. Police work can be dangerous."

Jonathan's face fell. "I'm sorry I . . ."

"I'm not finished." Leaphorn held up a hand, palm toward the young man. "Carla knows what she's doing. She observes police work from the inside every day. She's smart and good with people. Tell your relatives to leave the decision to her."

"Ahéhee', I will." The young man practically ran back to the car.

When he got home, Leaphorn took the poster from Gallup in with him. He wondered if this was the woman

Bernie had mentioned in the case of the dead baby. He took a picture of it with his phone and texted the image to her with a note. It might be nothing, but perhaps it would help the worried family find their missing loved one.

19

After her morning prayers, a run, coffee, and an energy bar, Bernie called Mama. They chatted briefly. Mama sounded strong and healthy.

Bernie drove to the Socorro police station to review the video, take a look at the letter Junior received, and prepare to get Maya to supply some answers. As she eased her unit into a parking spot, she heard the rumble of a pickup and watched it cruise toward the front of the building. A slim Navajo stepped out of the passenger door. She recognized Junior Jones immediately. He had his dad's strong chin and Maya's good looks. He disappeared through the entrance, and the classic old black pickup proceeded to park in the empty space in front of her patrol car.

As she walked toward the truck, the driver lowered his window. "Yá'át'ééh, Officer. I thought you worked in Shiprock."

"Yá'át'ééh, Leon. Nice wheels."

"A 1977 Silverado. It runs real good. I just got it this week."

"Congratulations." She mentioned Maya's van parked at the Shiprock station for Junior.

"Never mind that. Maya will be outta here, and she'll need her wheels."

"Are you going in to see your sister?"

"No. The boy went to talk to whoever runs the place about when Maya can get out of jail."

"I heard about the suicide letter."

The corners of Leon's mouth turned up ever so slightly. "Finally the jerk does something decent, apologizes for killing himself and makes it clear my sister is innocent. When Junior told me, I knew we had to drive over here so Maya can come home."

"That letter must have been a shock."

"Not really. Maya didn't do it. She's too soft-hearted. And that dude had lotsa problems."

"I meant the idea of getting a letter from a dead man."

Leon turned off the engine. "It was a surprise. I'm glad Jones wrote it. I think it made Junior feel better about the whole stinking mess."

"Why would your sister lie about shooting someone?"

He shrugged. "Beats me. Did she tell you about the time he broke her tooth?" Leon squeezed his hands into fists as he talked. "She said it was an accident, but she had bruises that time, too. I know it all came from him. If she had killed him then, I wouldn't have blamed her. But murder isn't in her personality."

"She didn't mention the abuse. Your sister hasn't been very talkative."

"When will she get out of jail?"

"Hard to say. You'll have to ask Junior what he finds out." Bernie pushed a strand of hair away from her face. "Tell him hey for me."

Inside the station, Bernie didn't see Williams or Junior Jones. She settled in at the detective's desk to watch the surveillance footage of Maya at the restaurant. The detective had downloaded the crucial part of the tape, and Bernie saw Maya and a taller white man approach the cashier's station. She noticed the man, whom she recognized as Jones from the photos she'd seen, offer the bill and his credit card to the woman at the register. Maya pushed forward and attempted to hand the woman some cash, but Jones extended his arm to block her.

Bernie watched Maya's jaw jut forward and her body tighten. She seemed to be yelling. Jones stepped away and raised his hands in the classic *I surrender* position. Maya moved toward him, still yelling. The cashier said something, and then Maya froze for a moment, fists clenched. She shoved the cash into her pocket and stomped out of the restaurant.

Bernie backed up the tape, watched that scene again, wishing there were sound. Clearly, they were arguing over the bill, but Maya's anger seemed stronger than that.

She allowed the video to advance and saw Maya standing outside the restaurant in the glow of Big River Brew Pub's neon sign. She reached into her purse, pulled out a phone, tapped it, studied it, tapped again, and replaced it just as Jones came through the doors. He said something to Maya, but she didn't respond. He stood a moment, then walked toward the parking lot. He stopped and looked back at her and spoke again.

A car passed by, blocking the camera's view of Jones, and then the lens caught him again. Bernie couldn't read his lips, but whatever he said persuaded Maya to walk toward him. He opened the passenger door and she climbed into the Jaguar. Jones drove toward the exit and waited for traffic to clear. Bernie watched as a pickup and an SUV came up behind the Jaguar, also waiting to drive away. Jones led the parade as all three vehicles turned left out of the parking lot.

She viewed the confrontation again, focusing on Maya's body language. Whatever the disagreement concerned, it remained unsettled when she got into the car. The tape wasn't proof she killed him, but it pointed to the opportunity. And whatever the argument centered on might have provided a motive.

Next, Bernie read the letter Junior received. Then she called the Lieutenant's cell phone in case Louisa was home and sleeping. They got the preliminaries out of the way quickly.

"Do you have a minute for a question, sir?"

"I do. What's on your mind?"

"Sir, we talked about liars, but did you ever deal with false confessions?"

"Yes, a few times. Speak up. I'm at Jason's garage, waiting for my truck to get serviced."

She heard the whine of spinning power tools in the background. "Do you know what was behind those phony confessions?"

"Usually, the guy didn't want to answer any more questions. He told us what he thought we wanted to hear to buy some relief. Some interrogators were so, ah, let's say persuasive, they could convince a rooster he'd laid an egg."

"Did you ever know someone to confess to a crime without prompting? You know, walk into the station and say, *Arrest me. I did it?*"

"Not personally, no, but I've read about that. Usually it's high-profile cases where a guy thinks saying he's guilty will make him famous. It happened with the Black Dahlia murder, for instance. Maybe you've read about that. It was one of the examples I studied when I was learning to be a cop."

"There's no fame attached to this case, sir."

"In my experience, most of the time when people voluntarily said they did it, they did it. The confessions weren't false. The perpetrator got tired of living with guilt and the fear that someday he'd be found out. You know, always looking over his shoulder for the flashing lights or expecting that knock on the door. Hold on."

He was back in a moment or two. "Looks like my truck is ready. Anything else?"

"No, sir." She didn't like his answer. "Thanks for your help."

Out in the station's hallway, she noticed Junior and Detective Williams. They were talking, and neither looked happy. She walked toward them.

"Hey, you two. What's up?"

"Mom has to stay in jail because the case is still under investigation, whatever that means. It isn't fair." He had some papers in his hand. "And I have to answer a stupid questionnaire before I can even talk to her."

"It's routine. We're not picking on you." Williams's voice was gentle. "Bernie, I'm helping Mr. Jones find his way out. I'll be right back."

Junior flinched. "Don't call me Mr. Jones. That was my dad. The one who killed himself, remember?"

Bernie put her hand lightly on Tara's arm. "I'll show him out. I want to talk to his uncle for a minute—he's waiting in the parking lot."

The morning sun had made its way over the building and reflected off the windshield of Leon's truck. Junior opened the door.

"What happened in there, son? Should I wait for Maya?"

Junior shook his head. "No. The officer said she has to stay in jail. She asked me a lot of questions about Mom." His Adam's apple rose and sank as he swallowed. "I gave her the letter, but she already had a copy. What he wrote didn't matter to that detective."

Then Leon noticed Bernie. "The letter Junior got said Jones killed himself and specifically said Maya wasn't to blame. I don't get it. Should I go in there and talk to that detective? This isn't right."

"No, Leon, there's nothing you can do. Maya confessed to murder. The detective has to follow the rules." As she said it, Bernie felt her heart sink. She'd hoped the letter would set Maya free, too, but she agreed that it left many unanswered questions.

She watched Junior climb into the truck. "I'm sorry about your mom, about your father, about everything that's happened. It's a lot to deal with, I know—"

Leon cut her off. "I'm his father, his 'shidá'í, not that white guy. This is our private business."

She gave Leon a hard stare. "It's not private anymore. You called me, remember, when Maya didn't show up at your place and asked for my help." She softened her tone. "I'm working this case now because your sister confessed to murder."

"Maya didn't do it. That letter tells the truth about her and about Jones's suicide." His voice rang with frustration. "You've seen how the system treats Indians. You're one of us. Don't let that happen to Maya. She's all twisted up inside over this."

"If she didn't do it, she has to take back her confession and explain a lot of things. Until Maya decides to cooperate, my hands are tied."

Leon started the engine as Junior put on his seat belt. When the young man looked up, Bernie saw the unshed tears. "If you can, tell Mom I want to visit her. I'm gonna fill out that dumb form."

"I'll tell her you love her, too. OK?"

He managed a quivering smile before the truck moved away.

Williams was waiting with coffee for both of them. "Did you read the letter?"

"Twice."

"What do you think?"

Bernie mentioned Chee's conversation with Junior about the names he and Jones used. "Sherm or son should be here, not the name his father never used. That's suspicious. And Jones was a scientist. He wouldn't write so disjointedly. If he did decide to kill himself, he must have been under some emotional distress, but that doesn't explain the randomness of the ideas here."

"We agree that it's probably phony. Actually, the distress comes before you make the decision. After that, a kind of weird calmness settles in."

"Really?" Bernie picked up her coffee.

"Yes. Deciding to go through with it is the hardest part."

"And you know this how?"

Instead of an answer, Williams posed a question. "If Jones didn't write that, who did?"

"I don't know."

"What's your best guess? I say someone with a reason to make anyone looking at Steve Jones's death believe he killed himself."

Bernie considered that bothersome question, and the one that followed: If Maya faked the letter to make the murder seem like suicide, why confess?

Williams sat at the computer. "Did you watch the tape from the restaurant?"

"I did. It's clear that Maya is furious that Jones won't let her help pay for dinner and that Jones is trying to placate her. I could tell she was still fuming when she got in the car with him."

"Too bad we couldn't hear the argument. I wonder if it concerned more than just splitting the check."

"We'll ask her about that."

Williams nodded. "While you were outside with Junior, I got the call from OMI. They finished the autopsy."

"Really?"

"They got to it quicker than I thought they would."

"So? Come on, tell me what they found."

"We won't get a copy for a while, but I cajoled a staffer into talking. The bullet that killed Jones entered his skull from the left side and the angle was down. Those two factors make suicide or an accidental self-inflicted wound unlikely. But the autopsy found no scratches, bruises, or other damage to the body consistent with defensive action."

Bernie felt her spirits sag. Suicide topped her wish list for Jones's cause of death.

Williams continued, "He suffered no other wounds except the single gunshot to the head, fired at close range. The gun didn't contact the skin."

"Would there be contact in a suicide?"

"It depends. Usually, but not always."

Bernie felt the start of a headache at her temple. "If someone shot him, why didn't he fight back?"

"I don't know the answer to that. Drugs? We'll have to wait for the toxicology report. From what I saw on the tape, he didn't seem drunk when he left the restaurant."

"The left side of his head would be the side of the open window, right?"

Tara looked at the ceiling for a split second. "Right. When I first saw the car and the body, I assumed Jones lowered the window so he'd have more room to raise his arm for the gunshot."

"Instead, it looks like Jones lowered the window for someone who came to shoot him? Why?"

Tara shook her head. "What I know for sure is that we have a suspect in custody who has confessed, a video that shows her arguing with the victim, and her prints on the gun."

Bernie pictured the car parked on the dark road, an argument, Maya storming out of the Jaguar and then coming back for a last word. Jones, of course, lowers the window. Bang. "How did Maya get the gun?"

"That's another thing we'll ask her this afternoon." Williams drained the last of her coffee. "I'm optimistic that we can wrap this case up with that interview."

"This afternoon?" Bernie frowned. "Not any sooner?"

"No. Before we talk to her, we need to interview someone else. I'd like you to take a look at a report Officer Taylor wrote up last week about a possible person of interest I'm bringing in for questioning."

"Chee mentioned this to me. Who is it?"

"A man who says he's Maya Kelsey's boyfriend."

"How did *he* get on the radar?"

"Something happened before Jones's death that might be connected to the case. We received a call from the principal at the Alamo school about a fight in the parking lot. She couldn't reach the Navajo Police and she thought someone could get hurt. When Officer Taylor arrived, he expected to give some kids a lecture, but this man, Chavez, had a bloody nose and a bad attitude. The other guy was gone."

"Don't tell me. The other guy was Steve Jones."

"You got it."

Williams clicked the computer and called up a file. "Here's Taylor's report. Chavez coaches football out there and asked if we could talk when he'd finished practice. I'd like you here for that interview."

Bernie nodded. "This could be a good new lead."

"Don't get too excited. He's got an ironclad alibi. He was coaching a game the night Jones got shot. Hundreds of witnesses saw him on the field, urging the Cougars to victory." Williams stood so Bernie could sit at the computer. "When you're done here, I'd like you to make another trip to the VLA. A scientist out there, a Dr. Peterson, mentioned that she had some information for us on tension between Jones and a coworker. It's probably nothing but I want to make sure we've got all the bases covered."

"Peterson? I met her when I was out there but we didn't have a chance to talk. Can we handle this over the phone?"

"She said she needs to show us something that involves classified material that couldn't leave the building. She said it concerns Jones's research."

If the material was relevant, they could subpoena the documents. "I'll talk to her. I don't mind going out there. That star stuff fascinates me."

Williams left, and Bernie read Officer Taylor's report on the Alamo confrontation.

Coach Chavez saw a man talking to Maya Kelsey, a teacher he described as his girlfriend, in the hallway outside her classroom. The man kissed Kelsey when he left. Chavez confronted her, but she refused to tell him what was going on. Chavez followed the man outside to the parking lot and told him to leave Kelsey alone. The man identified himself as Kelsey's husband. (The school principal confirmed that the man's name was Steve Jones.) Chavez called Jones a liar. Jones told him to talk to Kelsey and called him a fool. More words were exchanged. Chavez told Jones to stay away from his girlfriend or he'd "beat his ass." Jones took a swing at Chavez, connecting with the man's nose. Chavez grabbed Jones by the shirt as he turned to walk away and Jones punched him again. A parking lot fight ensued.

The report noted that Jones had driven off by the time Taylor arrived and that Chavez was working with the football team. The officer talked to two witnesses who had heard the men swearing at each other and seen the fight. Officer Taylor wrote that he "was unable to locate either Maya Kelsey or Steve Jones for an interview." Chavez declined to press charges. Taylor wrote that he told the coach to "cool off and behave himself."

Bernie closed the file and called Joy Peterson to let her know she'd be there soon. She headed to the parking lot. She had a lot to consider on her drive to the VLA.

After signing in as required, Bernie learned from the receptionist that Peterson had been delayed. "She asked me to tell you to look around at the exhibits and watch the movie while you wait. She said all this will give you some background into what she wants to talk to you about."

When she'd first stopped at the VLA visitor center, Bernie hadn't had time to look at the stunning photos of space and the informational posters about the wide range of research that involved the VLA telescopes. She appreciated the opportunity today. The information might come in handy during the interview. A few minutes before the movie began, she headed into the theater. She took a seat in the middle of the empty third row, joining a handful of other viewers.

For the next twenty minutes or so, she listened to the voice of Jodie Foster explain the VLA's history and the work the scientists engaged in. She learned that the Y-shape arrangement of the multiple antennas enhanced their function. The size and shape of the array enabled the telescopes to zoom in for more detail or zoom out to see a greater swath of deep space. To get a complete understanding of a distant planet, astronomers studied the light from as many wavelengths as possible, including ranges invisible to the human eye, such as the cosmic radio waves the telescopes pick up. The facility had been at the center of pioneering scientific research for decades, beginning with its first observations in 1976, and was famous for its work concerning black holes.

When the movie ended, she left the cozy theater, slightly overwhelmed. Dr. Joy Peterson waited for her just outside the door, and she introduced herself a second time. "We met before, briefly, when you came to pick up those things for Junior."

"That's right." Bernie was surprised that Dr. Peterson knew the name of Jones's son.

The scientist smiled. "I'm sure you deal with a lot of people as a police officer. I didn't expect you to remember me. What I'd like you to see is on a computer in the next building. I think it could be relevant to Dr. Jones's death."

"Thanks, Dr. Peterson. I appreciate it. And of course I remember you."

"Please call me Joy."

Bernie followed her outside into the sunlight and then into the neighboring building. They climbed the stairs to a small office. Joy opened the door and motioned Bernie to enter. "Here's why I called."

On the computer monitor, Bernie saw a brilliant golden circle with a dark blue interior surrounded by deep blackness. The image resembled modern art. "What's that? It's amazing."

"You're looking at a black hole in the center of the giant galaxy M87." The photo stayed on the screen while Peterson typed. "The image also marks a stunning achievement in astronomical inquiry, technology, and persistence. The picture is the work of a woman in a field where women are still a minority. I'm sure you can relate to that."

"Did you take it?"

"No, but I know the photographer."

"Until I saw the movie at the visitor center, I imagined a black hole as a colossal sucking vortex of emptiness. This image is beautiful."

"You're right about the colossal part, but we don't have to worry about Earth being consumed by the black hole at the center of *our* universe, at least not anytime soon. You could visualize everything in the sky as part of an ongoing struggle between dark and light. Or a dance, perhaps, with both partners wanting to lead." Peterson laughed. "That kind of describes my friendship with Dr. Jones, too."

"How long had you known Jones?"

"We met when he came for his research earlier this year. He was doing important work, the kind that crossed borders and laid a path for scientists of the future. I loved being part of his team." Peterson sucked in a breath. "It's hard to believe he's gone."

Bernie looked at the image on the computer monitor again. "You mentioned that you had some information about Dr. Jones that might be linked to his death. Let's talk about that."

"I've been thinking about this ever since I heard he was dead. Someone said that Dr. Jones killed himself and, sadly, that makes sense. I looked back at my notes about the project we were doing together, wondering if something we'd been struggling with upset him to the point of suicide and I'd missed the signs. Kathy mentioned that his death is under investigation. I believe he took his own life, but if not, well, he did have an enemy."

"Go on. I'm listening."

"Before I do, I need to put Steve's work in context for you. One of the things that drove his research was his curiosity about neutron stars. Have you heard of them?"

"Yes, but I'm vague on the details."

"Most people are. A neutron star is the collapsed core of a giant star that died in a fiery explosion, what you'd call a supernova. When their cores collapse, the protons and electrons essentially melt into each other to form neutrons. We call them neutron stars because that's what's left because of the pressure. They are among the heaviest items in space. Can you imagine something so dense that on Earth, one teaspoonful would weigh a billion tons? And the gravity on a neutron star is two billion times stronger than gravity here."

Peterson elaborated, gesturing with her hands to underline her points. Bernie listened, waiting for the chance to return to the issue of Jones's death. "In addition to that research, Dr. Jones and I were involved in developing a program to use the VLA telescopes to search for events or structures that could indicate the presence of life beyond Earth. Have you heard of the SETI Institute?"

"Yes. Those are the scientists who want to find aliens on other planets, right?"

"Well, we don't use the word *alien*. The study will look for things like laser beams, indications of constructed satellites, or atmospheric chemicals that could have been produced by industry. With the SETI Institute, we will conduct a powerful, wide-area survey of space, and data we collect will be analyzed to see if it reveals signs of life beyond our home planet."

"Wow."

"Wow is right. Those telescopes you saw when you drove up and our computers will help answer the long-standing question of what other intelligent beings might share the universe. The VLA gives researchers the opportunity to search farther than ever before."

"Do you think there is life out there besides us?"

"Well, the candidate pool of relevant planets numbers in the billions. It seems more likely than not. I'll tell you why."

Joy continued in a monologue with no mention of Jones. Bernie's initial characterization of Joy Peterson as a frustrated college teacher had been on the money. Mama taught her not to interrupt, and that precept even extended to overly talkative white people. She admired Joy's passion for her field of science, and found what she was saying fascinating, but how, if at all, did neutron stars and intelligent life in distant solar systems relate to the investigation?

Joy reached into her pocket for a tissue, and Bernie grabbed the opportunity to return the discussion to the business of human death.

"I have an interview soon back in Socorro. I'll ask if I need more on the specifics of Jones's research. What did you want to show me?"

Joy frowned. "OK. Sit here." She motioned Bernie to a seat in front of the computer with the photo of the black hole. She tapped the mouse, and a screen saver with a photo of a large white cat with a rhinestone collar came up.

"That's my spectacular Fur Boy. I spoil him, but he deserves it." Joy tapped again and Bernie saw an email screen. "These are excerpts from early exchanges between Steve Jones and a second colleague. Their collaboration on the neutron star project began the year before Dr. Jones got the grant to come to the VLA. Don't worry about the details of the science we're talking about, just focus on the pleasant, relaxed tone of our early exchanges."

"So, is this the man you think might be involved in Jones's death?"

"Perhaps. His name is Giovanni Bellinger. He and Steve had worked together on a similar project at an observatory in Hawaii." Joy leaned closer and moved the mouse to some messages near the end. "You'll see here that Giovanni begins accusing Steve of stealing his research. Dr. Jones refutes this, first politely and then things grew angry between them."

"Was the claim true?"

"I can't say for certain because the material they held in dispute was an area outside my field of expertise. However, knowing Steve, I doubt that he would have done anything underhanded. The integrity of his research was above reproach."

Bernie read a few more exchanges and looked up from the monitor. "Dr. Bellinger threatens legal action here. Something serious must have been at stake. What was it?"

"Credit for the discoveries. Professional recognition, and maybe awards, grants, advancement, teaching positions. Many of those come with money, but I think the prestige of being a pioneer in the field motivated their disagreements."

Joy scrolled through the file. "Here, in this last exchange, Giovanni again says he'll sue Steve." She tapped another file. "Steve fires back that Giovanni is better at calling people names than he is at science and tells the guy to get back to work and quit whining."

Bernie read the screen. "I need a copy of these threats."

Dr. Peterson frowned. "The science involved in the discussion is privileged. We can't release this without a court order."

"Besides these emails, did Giovanni make any other threats?"

"I'm not sure, but probably. He and Steve spoke on the phone a couple of times that I'm aware of. I could hear Steve shouting, telling Giovanni to back off, calling him a jerk and a fraud and challenging him to produce proof of plagiarism or shut up. I'm sure Giovanni said rude things in response."

"Do you have a phone number for Giovanni Bellinger?"

"No." When she shook her head, her wedge of shoulder-length hair moved like a golden curtain. "Dr. Jones did all the communication. I believe he only included Giovanni on the team as a professional courtesy since they worked in the same field and knew each other from a previous project. I'm sorry his good-guy effort blew up in his face."

Bernie realized that Giovanni's number and any texts they had exchanged would be on Jones's missing phone. While she hadn't expected a smoking gun, the emails seemed to come down to a battle of egos. She saw no reason to get a subpoena for the information but memorized a few key phrases and Giovanni's email address.

"Are disputes like this common among astronomers?"

"Not at all. The whole incident was bizarre. I know the accusation that our groundbreaking discoveries had merely been a riff on Giovanni's work bothered Steve. The idea that he might need to hire a lawyer to clear his name and that the two had once been friends added to Steve's depression. Like I said, I believe Steve killed himself, but the situation with Giovanni contributed to that unfortunate decision. Or maybe Giovanni hired someone to kill him—and make it look like suicide."

Bernie filed away that idea. "Did Dr. Bellinger ever threaten you?"

"No, thank goodness."

"You mentioned that Giovanni worked in Hawaii. Is he here at the VLA now?" Bernie needed his side of the story.

Joy shook her head again. "Last I heard he was at Mauna Kea."

"What else should I know about Dr. Jones?"

"Well, in addition to his son, a nice young man, he had an ex-wife named Maya something, who lives in Alamo. There may have been an issue with her."

"Why do you say that?"

Joy shifted slightly away from Bernie. "All I know is what Steve told me. He thought she was still in love with him."

"I gather that you and Jones were more than professional colleagues." Bernie said it as a simple statement. "You were closer than just coworkers, right?"

"We were. He even introduced me to his son. If one of them told Maya about me, I imagine she went through the roof." She stopped suddenly. "Oh my God. What if it wasn't suicide? What if she shot him rather than, you know, lose him to me?" Joy's eyes opened a little wider and then she looked away. "I know he loved me. I broke it off last week."

"Why?"

"I found him attractive, enjoyed his company, but office romance? No thanks. He didn't take it well. That's another reason suicide wouldn't surprise me."

Joy looked at the ceiling for a moment. "Steve kept some emails Maya sent him in case, you know, in case things got nasty between them and he needed proof that she'd threatened him."

"Did she?"

"Steve thought so."

Bernie hid her surprise at another piece of evidence pointing to Maya as a person with a motive in Steve Jones's death. "I'd like to see those messages."

"Hold on. I can find them."

Joy clicked on a computer icon and a folder came up. "Here they are. Junior told me his mother had confessed to the murder. Is that true?"

"I can't comment on that."

"But you aren't denying it. I still think Steve took his own life, but these emails give murder some credence."

As she reviewed the computer file, Bernie's heart sank. Jones and Maya had exchanged some sharp words about Junior's future, about Leon's role in the boy's life, about where they wanted their son to go to college, about whether he should enroll right after high school or work for a year. Even though the messages were terse, Jones's vocabulary and use of language differed substantially from that of the suicide letter. Clearly, the man who had written the emails was not the man who composed the suicide note.

"I'd like these."

"Of course." Joy disappeared and returned a few minutes later with printed sheets in a folder. "Anything else, Officer?"

"Do you remember seeing Steve Jones with some injuries last week?"

"I do. The big dummy told me he went hiking, stepped on some loose rocks, and had a tumble. Lucky he didn't break anything." She shook her head. "I told him he looked like he'd lost a fight."

"Did he mention a man named Chavez?" Chavez was a common New Mexico name, but she'd seen his first name in the police report. "Bronson Chavez."

"No. Never. Why?"

"Just curious. Thank you for your time. Did you want to tell me anything else?"

"Oh, just that if I'd known how deeply he'd fallen into depression, I would have talked him into getting help."

The contrast between the tight indoor space of the office and the vastness of the San Agustin Plains where the great telescopes did their work lifted her spirits. Bernie stood a moment, took a deep breath of the dry air, and looked at the huge white saucer-shaped telescopes. When she first noticed them, they'd all stood at an easterly angle. Now the dishes sat almost horizontally, open to the sky like giant birdbaths. The splendor of nature and the beauty of human ingenuity came together.

She called Williams with the highlights of the Peterson interview. "I don't think the dispute with the other scientist amounts to much, although Peterson suggested the guy could have hired a hit man."

Williams chuckled. "Scientists hiring hit men? If Maya falls through as the number one suspect, I guess we'll have to check that. Anything else?"

"A couple interesting things. Peterson showed me some angry emails between Maya and Jones. I've got copies. Maya doesn't threaten to kill him, but I could feel the animosity. And the Peterson-and-Jones relationship extended outside the office, but Peterson didn't know if Maya realized she and Jones were dating."

"That's interesting."

"I thought so. Peterson said Jones never mentioned Bronson Chavez, and when she asked why he looked like he'd been in a fight, he lied to her."

"Why lie?"

"I assume because he hadn't told his girlfriend that his wife still held some attraction for him. I'm heading back now, but do you recall the mile marker closest to where the kid found the car with the body?"

"Just a second." Williams checked and told her the number. "It's near the southern edge of the Alamo reservation, the Magdalena side."

"Thanks. I want to see how much of a walk it would have been for Maya to get herself home if she actually killed the guy. What shoes was she wearing?"

"Let me think. They looked like low heels—you know, like something I'd wear on a date. Not that that's gonna happen."

"Really?"

"Yeah . . . except for Bob, all the guys I know are weird or in jail. And Bob's idea of a good time is mucking out the barn together."

"You mentioned that he had a family emergency. How's it going?"

"Poor Honey. Bob's off again today, too."

Bernie drove north on the paved, two-lane NM 169 toward the Alamo reservation. The road edged the mountains and had enough ups and downs to require her attention. She noticed the sheep, cattle, and several small herds of horses. The sight of wood chopped and piled for winter led her back to Melvin Shorty. She hoped Chee had found someone to successfully serve the warrant. And, she wondered, had the FBI solved the mystery of the dead baby?

The lightness of that cold little body in her arms; it stayed with her like a recurring bad dream.

She began tracking the green mileposts every five miles and pulled off at the place Williams had directed and parked. She easily spotted the disturbance on the road's shoulder. This was where the boy had discovered Jones's car and where it sat until finally the tow truck had come. Why had Steve and Maya stopped here? Did he pull over because their argument had escalated? Or did they want to make up after their quarrel?

She recalled the unusual shoe prints Williams had photographed when she arrived, prints now eradicated by the towing service. They were shoes—not Maya's dressed-up footwear as shown on the video. They seemed too large to belong to the child who found the car. Did Jones leave the car before he died? She thought of Giovanni Bellinger, the disgruntled scientist. Could the prints be his—or his hit man's? If Maya had shot him through the open window, where were her foot-prints?

Bernie looked closely at the surrounding landscape. A breeze stirred the yellowed grass along the edge of the highway and made her wish she had worn the jacket stowed in the trunk. No houses were in sight, no neighbors to hear a gunshot. She'd find out where Maya lived, but it must be miles from here, a long hike in heels on a dark October night. Perhaps Bronson Chavez, the man who called himself Maya's boyfriend, had somehow provided Maya's transportation after Jones's death.

She opened her trunk to find the jacket and saw the box of models she'd agreed to take to the school, as well as the things for Junior. She'd go to the school now and also clock the distance to Maya's house. She climbed into her unit with a head full of unanswered questions.

The scenic drive to the town of Alamo led to a complex of newish buildings. Bernie pulled up to a large convenience store and parked. She had noticed the sign for the school just up the road, but first, she wanted to stretch and savor her first and probably only Coke of the day. She'd kept her promise to herself to cut back on sugary drinks; she'd seen too many friends and relatives struggle with diabetes.

A gray-haired woman with glasses watched as she entered. "May I help you, Officer?"

Bernie walked to the counter and introduced herself.

"Well, hello. I'm Tanya Rodriguez, the boss here, at your service. What can I do for you?"

"Can you tell me where to find the Cokes?"

"We keep the cold ones in the back. You'll see the regulars on the aisle next to the window. If you want a fountain drink in a cup with ice, we've got a little restaurant there." The woman pointed with her chin. "Are you here to help Sergeant Pino?"

"No, I'm taking something up to the school for a friend."

"Did you hear about the dead guy?"

"Yes." News spread in small towns. Especially, she thought, news of something terrible.

Rodriguez nodded. "People are all upset, you know. We're not feeling safe, wondering who did it and why and why out here of all places. I heard that the man in the car was the husband of one of our teachers." Rodriguez's lips tightened. "That woman stops here for the mail, but she didn't come in today. I don't like that. Maybe she's deceased, too."

"I know the lady you're talking about. She's OK."

"If he was her husband, she knows the dead man's secrets. You police ought to talk to her about that."

Rodriguez indicated the soft drink cooler with a twitch of her lips. "The Cokes on the bottom shelf are the coldest."

20

The modern Alamo Community School, with its east-facing entrance and ramada for gatherings, looked like something out of a wonderful design magazine. Bernie grabbed Leon's box from the trunk and walked down the entrance hall to an open door labeled "Office." She saw a middle-aged Navajo woman seated at a large desk and two children standing nearby—a boy with a short haircut, faded jeans, and a plaid shirt and a taller girl in a red sweater with a worried look on her face.

The children backed away toward the other side of the room when she entered. The woman stared at her with wide eyes and bolted to standing. "Officer! What's wrong?"

"Nothing's wrong." Bernie smiled to neutralize the terror that filled the space. She spoke softly and slowly. "There's nothing to worry about."

She turned to the children. "You kids are safe. Everyone at the school . . . everyone is safe. Don't worry. I'm here to drop off something. That's all. There's no problem."

"Thank God." The woman's voice still sounded tight and strained. "These days, when a cop walks in, we all think the worst. Not about you. I mean . . ." The woman grimaced.

"I know. I'm Officer Bernadette Manuelito." She glanced at the boy and girl again. "How are you two doing this morning?"

The children stared at the floor, either too shy to respond or still shaken by her presence. The woman lowered herself back into the chair, her silver-and-turquoise earrings swaying slightly. "Mrs. Heather Guerro, principal and chief problem solver at your service. Call me Heather."

"Pleased to meet you. I have something to deliver from a volunteer and I wanted to chat with you a moment." As long as she was there, she thought, she'd get Heather's take on Maya Kelsey.

"Officer Manuelito, if you don't mind, I'll finish with these young ones so they can get to their lessons. Then I'm all yours. I'm glad you came. I'd like to talk to you about something, too."

While Heather helped the children, Bernie studied

the front office. The Alamo school seemed like the heart of the community; she noticed announcements for fundraisers and yard sales and a photo of a lost Chihuahua. Student artwork and awards for the classes and their teachers hung on the walls. Sports trophies and medals on broad red, white, and blue ribbons gleamed from a display case.

Bernie's phone vibrated, and she saw that it was her mother. She picked up the box and walked into the hallway to take the call. Before she answered, she flashed through the bullet points of their last conversation and found no abandoned promises or anything to be concerned about.

"Daughter, where are you?"

"Oh, I'm working. I'm visiting a school."

"You were taking me for groceries. I've been waiting."

Bernie's heart fell. "That's not until Saturday."

"What day is this?"

Bernie told her.

"Are you sure?"

"Mama, if there's something that you need, maybe your neighbor lady can help."

As Bernie waited for her mother to respond, she watched Heather write something on a yellow slip of paper and give it to the boy. He rushed out of the office but lingered in the hallway, his shining eyes studying

Bernie's uniform and then focusing on her duty belt and her gun.

Bernie acknowledged him with a nod of her head. "Buddy, I hope you work hard today."

He gave her a solemn nod back and then ran down the hall.

Mama said, "What did you say?"

"I was talking to a little boy, one of the students here. I am waiting to meet with the principal."

"Is a crazy person with a gun there?"

"No, no. All is well today." As she said it, she hoped it was true.

"It's strange that the children have to go to school on Saturday. So, why did you call me, my daughter?"

Bernie sucked in her breath. "Oh, just to hear your sweet voice and make sure you are safe. Did you sleep well?"

"I greeted the dawn with my song and corn pollen, so beauty and good order surround me. I miss you, my daughter. Why don't you ever come to visit me? Our neighbor's son is coming and that little grandson, too. You should see him." Her mother went on.

Bernie watched Heather tap in a number on a phone and give it to the little girl. The youngster shifted from one foot to the other as she talked. Bernie read the relief in her face and her slim body. The child returned the phone and walked quickly out of the office. She kept her eyes low as she bounced past.

"Mama, I have to hang up now. We will talk again soon."

She made a mental note to call Darleen and make sure her sister still planned to come home from Chinle that weekend. Darleen had lived with Mama until recently and could assess her sharpness as well as or even better than Bernie. When Mama hadn't rested well, or forgot to eat, she grew confused. She had bypassed the question about sleep, so insomnia could be the reason for her fogginess.

Bernie put the phone in her pocket and tried to squeeze her concern about Mama in with it as she returned to the principal's office.

Heather rose and shut the door. "The kids and staff will come back later if the door is closed. No one interrupts unless it's an emergency. I'm sorry you had to wait."

"I wanted to make sure I gave you this box. Inside is a note and some handmade models of the Navajo Hero Twins. They go with a Navajo cultural unit for the third grade—Maya Kelsey's class. Her brother asked me to drop them off." Bernie set the box on Heather's desk.

Heather studied it a moment, then turned her gaze to Bernie. "Maya. Dear Maya. I knew something terrible had happened when she didn't show up to teach—or even call. And she didn't answer when I tried to reach her. It's so unlike her to not communicate. I'm sick with worry. That's really why you're here, isn't it?" She didn't give Bernie time to answer. "What's going on? Where is she?"

Bernie had expected the questions. "Maya's OK. She's in Socorro, assisting with a case under investigation. I can't say more than that."

Heather didn't seem to hear. "When I came in, everyone was buzzing about little Raul Apacheito, the boy who found the car with the body. And now you're telling me that something's up with Maya, Raul's teacher."

Of course the boy would go to the Alamo school, Bernie realized. And of course he and his father would talk about what they'd seen and the news would spread like a virus.

Heather toyed with an earring. "Last week, Maya sat right where you are. We did her evaluation, and she stressed how much she loved the job, the kids, our school, and how happy she was to work here. She mentioned that her ex-husband, Steve Jones, was doing research at the VLA on black holes or something like that. She said she'd be seeing him over the weekend and could ask him if he'd come out and talk to the students about the planets."

The mention of an evaluation raised a red flag. "Have you had any trouble with Maya?"

"No. Not a bit. She's wonderful. So devoted to the kids. She goes far beyond what's expected." Heather shifted in her seat. "Maya is my friend besides being my employee. Is she in trouble?"

Bernie ignored the question. "Do you remember what else she said about Steve Jones?"

"She told me he'd invited her to dinner and that she hoped he wouldn't give her grief again about the divorce. She was dating again and her brother, Leon, had been pushing her to make their split official." Heather took a breath. "I don't think Leon ever cared for Junior's dad. He acts like a father to her *and* to her son. I know Maya loves Leon, but I think he makes her crazy, too."

"Did Maya seem anxious about seeing Jones?"

"No, she was happy. A little nervous because she needed to talk to him about the divorce stuff. She liked her ex."

Heather stopped talking. Bernie waited for what else she had to say. The silence felt comfortable.

Heather said, "If you know Maya, you know she has had a drinking problem. She told me that's why she lost her other job. She's several years sober, but I wonder if seeing Steve again challenged her sobriety. Was she arrested for drunk driving?"

"I can't talk about it except to tell you what I've already said. Maya isn't hurt, and she's safe."

"She's in jail, isn't she?" Heather shook her head. "If you can, let her know I'm thinking of her. We all are."

Bernie's first stop after that was the convenience store for another conversation with Tanya Rodriguez.

After some cordialities and a bottle of water for the road, Bernie got to the point. "Ma'am, can you tell me how to find Maya Kelsey's house?"

"Is this police business?"

"Yes."

"Alrighty then." Mrs. Rodriguez cleared her throat. "Drive out that way." She indicated a road. "Then, after about three miles, you'll see a truck on blocks. Turn left, and I think it's the second road after the truck, but look for that fence there. Keep going and then you'll see some buildings on the left. You know, a house, a shed, a hogan. Go up the hill and turn by the old windmill." The directions continued. When she'd finished, Bernie repeated them back to her.

Mrs. Rodriguez nodded. "That sounds about right."

Bernie checked at the substation, just in case things had changed for Officer Pino. But the door was locked, with a sign that explained that To'Hajiilee was handling the calls and listed that phone number.

Half an hour and at least one wrong turn later, Bernie realized the subtle difference between "about right" and "right." She returned to the cluster of buildings she had passed and parked outside a neatly kept home with a metal roof. She saw no vehicles, but the warning barks of a muscular black dog and a smaller brown one told her someone might be home.

A slender Navajo woman opened the door and took a few quick steps toward the police unit, speaking as she approached. "Oh no. Did something happen at the ranch?"

Bernie lowered the window a few inches. "Call off the dogs."

"They won't hurt you." But the woman yelled over the barking and the animals retreated toward the porch. "Is Frank OK? My husband, Frank Toledo. Did something happen?"

"I'm not here about him. But isn't he a police officer?"

Bernie saw the woman relax a few degrees.

"Well, not anymore. He's working cattle out past Magdalena, but I still worry. And with that dead man the boy found in the car . . ." Her voice trailed off.

She swallowed. "If you are here because of that, I don't know anything except what I've heard."

"I just need directions and to talk to you a minute about someone you might know who lives out here. Would it be all right if I came in?"

"Oh, sure."

Keeping an eye on the dogs, Bernie followed the woman inside to a small front room and introduced herself with her clans.

The woman gave her clans on her mother's side in Navajo, then switched to English. "I'm Kristen. My father and his family are Chiricahua Apache. Have a seat." She motioned to one end of a couch covered with an Eyedazzler rug, a style of Navajo weaving especially popular in Alamo. "Like I said, I don't know much about the dead man except that the boy who found him was really scared, told his daddy, and then a lady sheriff came and talked to the Apacheitos about it."

"Did you hear anything else?"

Kristen hesitated. "Just gossip."

Bernie waited, but Kristen didn't elaborate. "I'm looking for Maya Kelsey's house. Do you know where it is?"

"Yes. Maya's my neighbor. Her house is up the hill from me."

Bernie realized she didn't have to drive to Maya's place to check the miles. She'd already driven far enough to reassure herself that Maya didn't walk home from the place Jones died. "Did you see Maya on Friday?"

Kristen hesitated. "I saw her drive home after school. I called to ask if she'd like to join Frank and me for dinner and to watch a movie or something. But she said she had a date. She wouldn't tell me who, so I knew it wasn't Coach."

"Who's Coach?"

"Bronson Chavez. Nice guy except when he gets hot under the collar. He runs the football team."

"Did you see Maya leave?"

"Not exactly. But I noticed a car, a fancy black one, drive up the road toward her house and then come back about fifteen minutes later. I guess the guy driving was her date. Nobody else lives up that way."

"Did you see any other vehicles?"

Kristen learned forward. "Well, somebody went up her road about ten thirty, and then maybe half an hour later it came down again."

"The same car?"

Kristen raised her shoulder ever so slightly. "I just saw the lights. Why are you asking me all this? Did something happen to Maya?" Bernie heard worry in the woman's voice.

"Maya's OK."

"Why all these questions? Something's wrong."

"She's involved with a case that's under investigation. That's all I can say." Bernie opened her hands, palms up. "When you talked to her about coming for dinner, did she tell you anything else about her date?"

Kristen wrinkled her brow. "Yes. She said she would be glad to get it over with."

Bernie thought about that. "Anything else?"

"She asked me not to mention it to Coach."

Bernie reached into her pocket for a business card. "If something else comes to you, please call me."

"I will. Do you know when Maya will be home?"

"No."

"Well, if you see her, tell her I'll keep an eye on her house."

She drove away from Kristen's place and pulled onto the shoulder to make a few notes and check her phone. She saw that she had two missed calls, one from Chee and one from Williams. And at the moment, she had no phone service.

21

Bronson Chavez, a stout man probably in his mid-forties, tapped the toes of his right foot on the floor and crossed and uncrossed his arms, appropriately twitchy as he waited for the interview to begin. Williams motioned Bernie to one of the seats across from him while she stood. As they'd discussed, Williams would take the lead with Bernie tossing in her own questions as appropriate. If the man started to hesitate or froze up, Bernie would step in as the good cop to ease his anxiety and get him talking.

"Thank you for coming in, Mr. Chavez. As you may know, we are investigating a death out by the Alamo reservation." Williams had a folder, which she placed on the table in front of her empty chair. "That's what we want to talk to you about."

Chavez shrugged. "I don't know anything about that except some rumors. The kids at school said Raul, Ralph Apacheito's son, found a dead man in a car."

"Do you know who the man was?"

"I heard he was a bilagáana who worked at the VLA. A scientist. They said the car was real nice."

Williams nodded. "A scientist, that's right. His name is Steve Jones."

Bernie noticed that Chavez didn't react to the name.

Williams turned the empty chair around, straddled it, and sat. "Steve Jones? Ring a bell?"

"No. Wait. A musician or something like that, right?"

"He was the man you got in a fight with a few days ago. Remember?"

Chavez pressed his lips into a thin line. "That guy. I didn't know his name. He kissed my girlfriend. We had words. He threw a punch at me."

"I heard he whooped you good."

"Who told you that?" The man leaned forward. "You ought to know what happened. I explained it all to the policeman who showed up out there."

"I've read the report." Williams tapped the folder. "But tell me in your own words."

Chavez looked at Bernie for the first time. "Well, I saw the dude with Maya. We had words. He went outside, and I followed, yelling at him to leave my girl alone, stay away from her or he'd get what was coming to him. He threw a lucky punch."

Chavez raised his right hand to the black-and-blue splotch near his jawline.

"What happened next?"

"What do you think? I hit back. I don't wanna talk about this. I made a fool of myself. It's over."

Williams gave Bernie a *go ahead* look.

"Mr. Chavez, we aren't accusing you of anything. We just need to know your side of the story." Bernie spoke softly in a tone she used with Darleen when trouble arose.

"OK. The dude punched me. I punched back. Then, nothing much."

"But something, right?"

"Well, not for him. He drove away in his fancy car. Officer Taylor came out and gave me a lecture. I had already cleaned up and started the warm-ups and drills. Some of the players asked why my nose was swelling. I thought the principal might put me on probation or something, but that hasn't happened yet. That's it."

"Had you met Steve Jones before?"

"Never."

Williams jumped in. "So, let me see if I've got it." She spread her hands on the tabletop. "Some guy kisses your girlfriend and bloodies your nose. He drives away before Officer Taylor gets there, leaves you to take the heat. And that's the end of it?"

Chavez shrugged and stared at the table.

"Didn't that make you angry?"

"Sure it did."

"Didn't you want revenge?"

Chavez ignored her.

Williams glanced at Bernie, who picked up the interrogation.

"Mr. Chavez, if I had a boyfriend like you and he saw me kissing someone else, I would hope that he cared enough about me to at least ask what was going on. Did you do that?"

"I tried to." His voice sparked with anger. "Maya had already left school by then. I called her, but she wouldn't answer the phone. I drove to her house. She wasn't there. I went in to wait for her, you know, to get this settled."

The man stopped talking. Bernie waited. Williams raised her eyebrows, but Bernie let the silence do its work.

"I went in, like I said, and, well, I found out that Maya wasn't who I thought she was. I had some of my stuff there for when I'd spend the night. I gathered that up and took off."

"What do you mean, she wasn't who you thought she was?"

"She lied to me."

"It sounds like you saw something at Maya's house that made you think she hadn't told you the truth. What was it?"

"Flowers. She had a fancy bouquet on her table. You know, from a florist." He shook his head. "It wasn't her birthday or anything like that. That's when I knew she'd been cheating."

"I don't understand."

He shook his head. "It's something that the guy who kissed her woulda done."

"Did you ask Maya about it?"

He shook his head and folded his large hands on the table. Bernie saw the swelling at his knuckles. "Why do you care about this anyway? It's personal."

Williams took charge. "We need your help. We're wondering if your fight had anything to do with what happened to Jones later."

"You're kidding. When I said I'd kill the jerk, I was just, you know, venting. I wasn't anywhere near that car. I've never been in trouble."

Williams leaned toward him. "So, you threatened to kill Mr. Jones?"

Chavez sat back in the hard chair. "No, well, not really. I was really pissed. I didn't mean it."

"And you *have* been in trouble. I checked your record and discovered you have been arrested before."

"All that was back when I was partying hard." Chavez looked down at the table again. "I made restitution to the people I screwed over. I had a healing ceremony. I got this good job working with the kids. I met Maya. Life has been good. Smooth until now."

Williams moved away from the table and stood with her back against the wall. "Let me make sure I've got this straight. A stranger embarrasses you at school. You believe he's having an affair with someone you love. You exchange a few punches, he drives off, and then you let it go. Is that right?"

"You got it."

"No. I think you're still angry. You head over to your girlfriend's house to find out what's up, and instead of working things out, you see a fancy bouquet that you assume came from him. Now you're really angry. Right so far?"

"Yeah, but—"

Williams didn't let him continue. "So Friday night you're working, right?"

Chavez laughed. "Coaching the mighty Cougars to their big win over the Magdalena Steers. Twenty-one to fourteen. The stands were packed. Lot of witnesses."

Bernie injected herself. "The game ends. Then what?"

"I went to Dave my assistant coach's house for a beer, and we relaxed awhile, relived the kids' glory. Then I went home and called my brother in California and told him about it because he follows our team. You can check with those dudes if you need to. Even if I'd wanted to kill that guy—and I didn't—I couldn't have done it on Friday."

They let a few beats pass while Williams glanced at her folder, then closed it.

"Any more questions, Manuelito?"

"That's all for now."

Chavez cleared his throat. "Where is Maya? I didn't see her at school today. A sub had her class."

Williams answered. "She is in custody."

"For what?"

"I can't talk about that."

"Does she know he's dead?"

"She does."

Chavez turned to Bernie. "Tell Maya I'm sorry that guy died. If she loved him, that must hurt."

"I'll tell her." Bernie stood. "Thank you for your cooperation."

Bernie and Williams followed Chavez out and went to the break room. Bernie told herself she deserved a Coke, but settled for a bottle of cold water. Williams asked the question on both their minds. "What do you think of Chavez?"

"He seems like a decent guy. I believe he told the truth. I listened for something that said he and Maya might have been in on the murder together. I didn't hear it. How about you?"

"I agree. He seemed appropriately regretful about the fight." Tara put the folder on her desk. "Do you need to follow up on anything from the VLA?"

"Yes. I'd like to talk to Dr. Bellinger, the scientist I mentioned who accused Jones of stealing his work. Joy Peterson showed me an explosive email exchange between them. She also showed me a photo of a black hole. Right now, I feel like that's what we've slid into."

Williams laughed. "Let's get something to eat and strategize before we talk to Maya again."

"I'll meet you somewhere. I need to make a phone call."

"You're calling your boss and begging to be given a saner case?"

Bernie smiled. "Sort of. I'm calling my mom."

Mama's confusion from the interrupted call at the Alamo school bothered her. She wanted to make sure her mother was OK.

Mama answered on the second ring. "Daughter, you never come to see me. That makes me angry. I think you are too busy to care for your family."

The comment caught her off guard. She had spent time with her mother just yesterday. Mama had not been well then. That might explain the holes in her memory.

"How are you feeling, Mama? I've been thinking about you ever since your bad spell yesterday."

Her mother's voice turned icy. "I'm perfectly fine. I can't talk now. Mrs. Bigman just drove up. She wants to show me the baby and to take us to the senior center. I wouldn't be around a baby if there was anything wrong. The little ones get sick. You should know that."

Bernie let the comment slide. "Have you heard from Sister?"

"That one calls me every day. I help her know what to do with Mr. Natachi. She's working hard." It was a welcome change to hear Mama say something positive about her sister. "But you? You forget about your mother. You never come to see me."

"I haven't forgotten you, Shima. Yesterday . . ."

She stopped talking when she heard Mama put the phone down. After a few moments, Mama came back. "I'm leaving now, but I have something to say. I am disappointed in you, my daughter. I thought you would be living the Navajo way. You act like a white person." And with that, Mama hung up.

She called Chee before she had a chance to feel sorry for herself.

Mrs. Slim transferred her call, meaning Sandra hadn't returned to work.

"Hello, Sweetheart. How's it going?"

She gave him an update on the case. "Williams and I will talk to Maya again this afternoon."

"You've been busy out there. When you come home, I'll leave Bigman in charge and fix us a great dinner. It will be wonderful to see you." His voice lifted some of her gloom, but then he said, "Have you talked to your mother?"

"Yes. Mama doesn't think I'm so wonderful these days." Bernie summarized without repeating the hurtful words.

"Maybe she woke up on the wrong side of the bed."

"She told me my sister is practically an angel."

"The sister I know?" Chee laughed. "Well, I think *you're* an angel."

She heard his office phone ring. "Any news on when the captain will be back?"

"No. Don't worry about your mother and don't let the Maya case discourage you. Get that mess with her sorted out so we can celebrate."

Another order, she thought.

Chee kept talking. "And, ah, I *was* grumpy on the phone yesterday. You were right about that. Gotta go."

Maybe Chee was right. Maybe her mother didn't mean it. Maybe she was having a bad day. But the sharp words stayed with her, like a cactus spine embedded in the soft side of her shoe.

She headed off to meet Williams for food and strategy.

22

True to his word, the archivist sent the digital copy of the map. Before he opened it, Leaphorn looked for information from Carla. Nothing yet.

But he did have a response on the job from the tribe's Office of Background Investigations. They'd like the work done ASAP so they could proceed with hiring the candidates in question. They would send the information he needed to begin, such as an applicant's social security number, in a secure file immediately after he signed the contract. Leaphorn took care of that electronically, and within half an hour he had what he needed to start the assignment. If he focused, he could finish before they left for Washington. And, he reminded himself, if he decided not to make the trip, it offered a solid excuse.

After forty minutes at the computer he stood, stretched, and was getting ready to resume when the phone rang. It was Chee.

"I'm calling to apologize. I was out of line asking about Largo's plans. You're right. It's his business."

"Forget it. I'm glad you called. I was at the library, and I saw an old map that reminded me of something I discovered years ago, something important to traditional Navajos." He stopped, considering what to say next and knowing that Chee wouldn't interrupt his thoughts. "Maybe important to Diné heritage in general. Anyway, it would be good to discuss it with you."

"You have my attention, sir."

"I mean face-to-face."

"Once Captain Largo returns, I can meet you in Window Rock. I have some time off coming up."

He heard the eagerness in Chee's voice. "I'd like that."

Leaphorn suggested a date and Chee agreed. "Sir, is this business?"

"Not officially. It concerns your avocation, your training as a hatałii."

The phone went silent for a moment. "Well, thank you. I look forward to that."

Then Leaphorn refocused on the background checks. He found everything he needed to give the first candidate a clear report. The work absorbed him so much that he hadn't realized Louisa was home until she rapped on the door frame.

"The mail's here. A couple things for you besides the regular junk." She handed it to him.

"Thanks. I'll letcha know about Washingdon later."

"You . . ." Louisa left the comment unfinished. She headed back down the hall.

He finished the phrase for her. *You need to make a decision.* Maybe even, *You aren't being fair to me.*

Joe Leaphorn prided himself on his decisiveness, on pushing obstacles aside to do what he needed to do. He'd faced a mountain of hard decisions, but none like this. Saying yes meant finally wrestling with a deep, long-standing fear. If he said no, he would disappoint a person for whom he cared deeply.

He glanced at his mail and discovered a check. Enough to pay for his share of the trip with money left over. A sign, he thought, of what he had to do.

He went back to the computer to wrap up his task and noticed a new email from Carla. Her subject line read: "About T. Adams." He clicked it open.

Lieutenant, I think I found the woman you are
searching for. I have attached her address and phone
numbers and also a little biography I came across
online. I discovered information on her nonprofit
business and included that, too. Because she made
reference to a trip out here on one of the blogs
for the foundation, I believe this is the woman you
wanted. I found marriage documents to explain
the Symons name. By the way, Theodora now calls
herself Ginger.

The information you asked for about that missing
women task force is also attached. They look like a
good group.

Please let me know how I can be of further help.

He sent off a thank-you email, then opened the attachments and scanned the information.

Theodora Adams and Ginger Symons—he noted
the *y*—were the same person. Adams became Symons
through marriage and shortly thereafter legally changed
her first name to Ginger.

Carla listed the woman's employer as the Closely
Watched Foundation and her position as president.
She included Ginger's most recent home address and
the foundation address, both somewhere in Maryland.
She even gave him a magazine article on the foundation's

efforts to help refugee children and their displaced mothers.

He thought about Theodora Adams, a.k.a. Ginger Symons, for a few minutes. Then he went to find Louisa.

"I got some news I was waitin' for."

"About the contracts?"

"No. Somethin' else. You 'member da woman who called for Officer Leapfrog?"

"Yes indeed. Did you solve the mystery?"

He explained how Carla had helped.

"So, are you going to call her?"

He shrugged. "I neber liked her."

Louisa put the book she had been reading aside. "Some people get better with age. Maybe she's not the same disagreeable woman."

He sat next to her, thinking. Had the kidnapping changed Theodora from an arrogant self-absorbed young woman into something less offensive? Or had the fact that she had survived because of her boyfriend and Leaphorn reinforced her sense of privilege? And why, so many years after the cave, had she called him?

Louisa reached for his hand. "I think I'm more curious about this than you are. What if I make the call as your assistant and find out what she wants? If the woman sounds sane and isn't a scammer, I'll ask for her email and you can communicate that way. If she asks, I'll mention you were injured and have some trouble speaking."

Leaphorn felt a wave of relief.

"Dat's great. Tanks. I been dreading this, but you're right. I wanna know da end of da story."

They went to his office, Giddi following, and he invited Louisa to read Carla's note while he sat in the cat's chair, watching her reaction.

"Great information. Shall I call Ginger now?"

He nodded.

Louisa put the phone on speaker and placed the call. After five rings a mechanical voice repeated the number and asked her to leave a message at the beep.

She looked at Leaphorn.

"Go ahead. Leab my name and da house number and my email."

She did, suggesting that Ginger email first. "If she calls back when I'm here, I'll talk to her."

"Tanks." She'd done more than he had asked, willingly and with grace.

Louisa started toward the door.

"Wait a sec. I need ta tell you somethin'. I'm going to Washingdon wif you. I mean, if you'll still hab me after all dat procrastination."

She wrapped her arms around him and held him close for a few seconds.

"I'll make the reservation now." And she trotted off, Giddi following like a shadow.

Besides the darkness labeled *fear of flying*, he had two issues left to resolve: Hancock's invitation to join the task force and Chee's assignment about the dead baby.

23

Detective Williams texted a change in plans, suggesting she and Bernie meet at the station and drive to the restaurant together. Bernie was studying the view from the break room when a tall, unshaven man entered and went directly to the coffee maker.

"Manuelito, you enjoying it down here?" He looked exhausted.

Bernie shrugged. "I'd like it better if I could see more progress in the case. I don't think we've been introduced, have we?"

He inserted a pod, positioned his cup, pushed the button, then turned toward her. "Bob Rockfeld, Tara Williams's partner. She's talked about you so much I feel like I know you. But Tara hasn't said much about the investigation, so I guess there's not much to say."

"She told me about Honey. How is she today?"

He shrugged. "Still running a fever this morning. She won't eat, but at least she's had some water. The doctor says the antibiotics ought to kick in within the next few hours. I told Tara if Honey doesn't pull through, I'll need another day off. We ought to know more by this evening."

"Good luck." It was all she could think of to say. If a relative of hers died, she'd want more than a single day away from work. Mourning must not be Rockfeld's strong suit.

She heard a squeak as he walked to the refrigerator. She watched him grab three little creamers. "You want something?"

"Any regular Cokes in there?"

"I'll check."

"Oh wait. How about some sparkling water?"

He walked toward her with a can, and she heard the squeak again. "I'm sorry this investigation got dumped on you, but Tara says you've been great. If you're looking to make a change, she'd lobby for you to work with us." He opened two creamers and stirred them into his coffee. "I was up with Honey all night. I just stole away for a minute to take care of a few things here that couldn't wait."

He took a sip of his coffee, added the third creamer, and sealed the cup with a white plastic lid. "Nice to meet you. Say hi to Tara."

Bernie sat at Williams's computer and worked up notes about her conversation with Dr. Joy Peterson. She listed what she knew and her speculation concerning the death of Steve Jones. Then she listed the case's nagging questions:

Who had a motive to kill Steve Jones?
Beside Maya, who had the opportunity?
Does the fake suicide evidence point to premeditation,
    or was it a last-minute idea?
How can I get Maya to explain herself?

She paused and then added:

Why does this case matter so much to me?

"Hey there." Williams interrupted her concentration. "Ready for lunch?"

"Give me half a second to finish these notes." But when Bernie looked back at the screen, she discovered she had nothing else to add.

Williams drove to a casual place that specialized in New Mexican food—red and green chile, posole, flan, sopaipillas, even tender tortillas made with blue corn. "They do great rellenos with fresh green chile this time of year. I think you'll love their specials, but if not, they have regular American food, too."

Williams asked for a combination plate with a chile relleno on the side. Bernie studied the menu and ordered her usual burger. While they waited, Bernie used Williams as a sounding board to review what she'd learned about the arguments between the scientists and about the relationship between Jones and Joy Peterson.

"If we didn't know the divorce was her idea, I'd picture Maya finding out about his girlfriend and getting jealous. They argued, and that's why Maya killed him." Williams said it as a statement. "But your old friend was done with the man. His having a girlfriend ought to have made him happy to sign those papers."

The waitress brought their drinks and the food. Bernie sipped her tea—wishing it was a Coke—before she spoke. "Maya left him years ago. I remember how surprised I was when I learned Maya and her baby were coming back to the reservation. She told me she was homesick, and never said anything terrible about Jones."

"I thought they were long divorced."

"I checked. Neither party filed either in New Mexico or Hawaii. Jones hadn't signed those papers. That could be motive, but we can't put words in her mouth."

Bernie removed the lettuce, onion, and tomato from her burger and added catsup. "I drove from the spot where you found the car up toward Maya's house in Alamo. The place where Jones died is at least twenty miles from where she lives. A long walk at night in the dark even without the fancy shoes."

"Does that bring Chavez back in the picture? Maybe she called him to pick her up after she'd killed Jones."

"I wondered the same thing. Maya's neighbor told me she saw a black car drive up to Maya's house the night of her date and leave again after a few minutes. Later that evening, she heard a vehicle heading up the road and back down again. I figure that could have been Jones, alive and dropping off the woman who said she killed him after their date. Or it could have been Chavez—or someone he sent to help Maya."

"Can the neighbor identify the car on the return trip?"

"No."

"Too bad." Tara mopped up some chile sauce with a tortilla. "Bernie, you've been like a dog with a bone on Maya's innocence. You should have been a defense attorney."

"I just want to know the truth. I just want justice, that's all." Bernie reached for the bill. "This is on me."

Maya seemed older than just a few days ago. The dark, puffy half-circles above her cheekbones made her eyes look sunken. Instead of the feisty, funny woman Bernie had known, Maya was now someone given over to sadness.

Williams read the Miranda rights, and Maya signed the waiver again. Williams offered her some coffee or a soda, both of which she refused, this time with a "no, thank you."

Bernie opened with small talk. "I hear Junior has applied to New Mexico Tech. You must be proud of him."

"I am. I know he'll get in. He's very smart."

"Now that you've been working in Alamo, I bet you miss him."

"I do miss him, and Leon, and the rest of my relatives, but I love it here. I enjoy my job. I like the landscape. People are friendly." As Maya spoke, a touch of life came into her face. Bernie noticed Williams's slight smile, an acknowledgment that the suspect seemed more agreeable.

"When I can't make it to Shiprock, Junior and Leon come to Alamo to see me. Leon has been so good to my son."

Bernie nodded. "When Jones got the position at the VLA, that meant Junior could see his dad as well as his 'shidá'í.'"

"Yeah. That's right." But she saw Maya stiffen.

"Were Junior and his dad close? I mean, Leon must have seemed like Junior's father."

Maya coughed and coughed again. She turned to Williams. "I would like some water if it's not too much trouble."

"Sure. I'll be right back."

As soon as she left, Maya switched to Navajo. "Bernie, let this be. You have a kind heart. You want to save me from myself. I don't want that."

"I want justice for you and the man who is dead. That is my job as an officer."

"You did your job when you brought me here, and you went beyond that when you helped Leon deliver the project for my class. You've been a good officer and a good friend. Let this go. If you want to help more, tell Leon to take that food at my house. He and Junior can use it. And don't forget about my van."

Bernie spoke before she could stop herself. "Maya, be reasonable and tell the truth. If you are convicted of this murder, you'll miss Junior's graduation from college, his wedding. You won't hug your grand-children. Think about that."

"Be quiet."

"No matter what went on with Steve in that car, I know you loved him once and he loved you. You might have been angry with him, but you're no killer."

"Leave me alone." Anger made her voice louder.

"You are a valuable person. You have to let Detective Williams know what really happened."

"Shut up. You can't fix this. Steve is dead. I wish . . ." She stopped when she heard the door open.

Williams put a bottle of water on the table in front of her. Maya twisted off the lid and took a long sip. She sat a bit straighter and looked away from Bernie as she spoke.

"I can save you ladies some time. Here's what happened. Steve Jones and I were in the car together. We were arguing. He pulled off the road. I shot him dead. That's all I have to say."

"What were you arguing about?"

"It doesn't matter."

"Was it the divorce?"

"He didn't want to sign the papers. He said he wanted to get back together with me after all these years."

Williams smiled. "I understand from your son that you and Jones had a cordial relationship."

Maya kept her eyes lowered and her mouth closed.

Bernie jumped in. "Where did the gun come from?"

"It was his. My fingerprints are on it."

330 · ANNE HILLERMAN

"How did you get home?"

She shrugged. "I hitchhiked."

Williams stepped in. "A man named Bronson Chavez got into a fight with Steve Jones at the school. He says he's your boyfriend. Was he involved in this murder?"

Maya said nothing.

"A surveillance tape shows you doing something on your phone at the restaurant before you got in the car with Jones. Were you contacting Chavez or someone else to come for you after the murder?"

Nothing.

"Did you know Jones had a girlfriend?"

Maya raised her shoulders to her ears, a silent *So what?*

Bernie softened the tone. "Let's go back to something. You said you and Jones were arguing over the divorce. If you killed him in self-defense, it's a different ball game than what we have now—coldhearted murder. If you tell us the circumstances that led to Jones's death, we can help you."

Maya took another sip of water and put the bottle down. "OK, ladies. Let's call it self-defense. That's all I have to say for now."

After the guard escorted Maya back to her cell, Williams plopped down in the chair across from Bernie. "Well, we made a little progress."

Bernie nodded. "We learned that they actually did argue about the divorce and that she had access to his gun. And that something happened to justify self-defense."

"Did you see her stiffen when you asked about Junior and his dad? Maybe Jones abused the kid when he was a boy. That might add to Maya's motivation." Williams tightened her lips. "But the only abuse that's documented is Jones's old restraining order against Maya. She'll have to be more forthcoming."

Bernie sighed. "Someone else shows up. This person gets the gun—that's the third set of prints—and kills Jones and drives away."

"Come on, Bernie. Who is this someone who pulls up, shoots him with his own gun without a struggle, and drives away?" Williams shook her head. "I need coffee. You want some?"

"No thanks." While Tara was gone, Bernie sent a quick text to Leon about the food at Maya's house. A few moments later Bernie's phone buzzed. She saw "Leaphorn" on the caller ID.

"Yá'át'ééh, Lieutenant."

"Yá'át'ééh. Is this a good time to talk?"

"I have a minute, yes, sir. Thanks for sending the photo of that missing woman poster. She doesn't look anything like Bee, the woman I was dealing with."

Leaphorn moved on to the reason for his call. "I've been thinking about the confession you mentioned, and I came up with an idea that might apply to your situation. You told me the person who confessed did so freely, right? I mean, no pressure from the police."

"That's right. She came into the station out of the blue and said, 'Arrest me, I killed him.'"

"No motive?"

"She told me I didn't need to know."

"Consider the possibility that this woman is covering for the real killer, either willingly or because she's under duress. She might be lying to protect someone who holds great power over her. It could be threats to herself or a family member, or it might be love."

"Love?" She'd rarely heard the Lieutenant say that word.

"You could call it love, or honor or a sense of duty."

"You're suggesting that she's lying to save someone, because she's more afraid of whoever it is than of going to prison or she's making the sacrifice out of love." That thought brought back her conversation with Junior.

"I could be mistaken, but I wanted to add these ideas to the discussion."

"My gut says she's not guilty. I'll think about your suggestions."

"Don't let your friendship cloud your judgment." Leaphorn ended the call.

Tara returned. "Unless you can come up with a good reason, I think we'll call this investigation done. Do you have any loose ends?"

"Give me one more day, OK? If I don't have anything new, we'll wrap it up."

"Tell me what you'll do with that time."

She used her fingers to tick off the list. "I want to follow up with Giovanni Bellinger. I'm curious about that unidentified print on the gun and the match for that shoe sole you took a picture of. I'd like to look at your crime scene report again and the official OMI findings. I want to reread my notes from the interviews and see if we missed anything." Bernie sighed. "If I run into dead ends, I'll admit I made a mistake about Maya, pack up, and head home."

Williams raised her eyebrows.

"I mean it."

"I'll tell Chee I need you for another twenty-four hours. This case bothers me, too, but Maya may be ready to talk. We made progress with her today." Williams looked at her. "Twenty-four hours. That's it. I'm happy you're almost ready to move on, too."

Bernie didn't feel happy. She felt the weight of failure.

"Use my desk. I'm taking time off this afternoon and tomorrow. I told Rockfeld I'd help him with Honey."

"Is she any better?"

Tara shook her heard. "The medicine isn't working. Bob thinks this evening may be it. That's why I need be there."

Bernie thought about asking how appropriate it was for Tara to show up at Honey's deathbed with Mr. Squeaky Shoe, but she kept her mouth shut. She didn't want to be as irritating as her mother. The relationship was none of her business.

"If I stay over at Bob's, you remember how to let yourself in?"

"I do."

"Give me a call tonight even if you don't have anything new, OK?"

"I will. Who can I talk to about those unidentified prints on the gun?"

Williams told her and pulled up the reports Bernie had asked about before she left.

Bernie got to work. She followed up with the fingerprint expert and asked him to call her. She found the number Jones had jotted down for Giovanni Bellinger and called it, only to hear a message that it was "no longer in service." She recalled Bellinger's email address from the correspondence Joy showed her and typed him a message with Law enforcement inquiry re: Dr. Steve Jones as the subject line.

> Dr. Bellinger,
>   This is Officer Bernadette Manuelito. I urgently need to talk to you in connection with an ongoing investigation underway by the Socorro New Mexico Sheriff's office. Please call as soon as possible.

Bernie left the number at the Socorro police station.

> If I am not available, ask for Detective Tara Williams.

She did a preliminary background check on Giovanni Bellinger. He was clean—impressively so, in fact. He'd become a US citizen a few years after arriving from the Netherlands in 1990, received his PhD from Massachusetts Institute of Technology, and won several awards for his work.

She reread her report on the email exchange between Bellinger and the dead man, noting the anger but no threats of violence. She began a list of questions for Bellinger and, when she ran short of ideas, decided to take a break to call Darleen.

Her sister answered on the first ring. "Hey there. How's everything?"

"OK, I guess. How's it with you?"

"Great! I'm at work. We're just about to watch one of those old movies, *Singing in a Storm* or something like that. I always thought they were corny, but you know, some of the stories are really sweet, and these elderlies love them." Darleen sounded happy and perkier than usual. "Can I call you when I get a break?"

"Whenever. I'm just checking in. Have you talked to Mama?"

"Sort of. She's grumpy. I wish she was here. This movie would cheer her up."

"Call me later."

"Sure thing."

Bernie thought about checking on her mother, but she wasn't up for an argument, an emotional beatdown, or rolling over and playing dead.

She was reading about Bellinger's impressive contributions to the discovery of black holes and wondering if he checked his email regularly when the phone on her desk rang. It was the man himself.

"Dr. Bellinger, thank you for calling."

"How may I assist you? And please call me Giovanni."

"I understand that you collaborated with an astronomer named Steve Jones."

"That is correct, Officer." His English had an accent she hadn't heard before. "We work in the same field."

"Did you have a dispute with him?"

"So, that is why you are calling?" He didn't wait for her to answer. "Is Jones bringing some sort of charges against me? I do not see why this bickering among scientists about how black holes operate would be a police matter. What havoc is that lunatic wreaking now?"

"Sir, I am investigating Dr. Jones's death."

"Oh." The phone fell silent. "I am truly sorry to hear that. We didn't agree on everything, but he was a brilliant researcher. His passing is a real loss to the world." Bellinger's shock was palpable. "When and how did this tragedy unfold?"

"The investigation is ongoing, sir."

"Please, what happened to the man?"

"I can't discuss the details. I called to speak to you about your disagreements."

Giovanni didn't seem surprised at the question. "Jones and I verbally grappled over the interpretation of results from studies we reviewed together, based on observations over a period of months, all conducted at the VLA. Do you know what that is?"

"Yes, sir. Please continue."

"Sadly, in the process of looking into those results, I discovered that the late Dr. Jones and a colleague of his had taken credit for my research. When I raised the issue, they accused me of plagiarizing him. I do not mean to speak ill of the dead, but the man had a bigger ego than his work warranted. And the third scientist seemed to enjoy stirring trouble between us."

"Dr. Jones received some angry emails from you."

"Yes. I was totally out of order to write such things to him; however, he returned my outburst with an equally adolescent flare. I took great umbrage at Jones's assertion that I would steal his research when, in fact, he and his associate at the VLA appropriated my unpublished findings without giving me credit. They used knowledge we had shared in confidence and made it seem as though they had discovered it themselves. Jones's behavior shocked and disappointed me. As for Peterson, well, she seems like a person with more ambition than talent."

"Peterson. Do you mean Dr. Joy Peterson?"

"Yes. I gather she showed you our correspondence."

"That's correct."

"In those emails, you will see that Dr. Jones continued to vigorously deny appropriating my work even though I had assembled a sizable body of proof. We had collaborated extensively and productively for years. A few days ago, we agreed to disagree out of respect for our long-standing professional relationship. I urged him to speak to Dr. Peterson about the plagiarism, and he and I buried the hatchet, as you New Mexicans might say out there in the desert." Giovanni cleared his throat. "And now he is tragically dead."

"Are you relieved you don't have to sue him?"

Giovanni seemed to be weighing the question. "I would not have followed up on my threat of legal action. I simply wanted to encourage him to admit his wrong-doing. I am old enough to be his father, and I have taught and worked with too many people puffed up on their own assumed importance. I wanted him to act like an adult. I deeply regret that Dr. Jones has passed. His demise is a loss to the astroscience community."

"Where do you live, sir?"

He rattled off the name of a place she had never heard of and added Hawaii at the end. "I work at the IFA, the Institute for Astronomy, helping to coordinate research among the Mauna Kea Observatories. We have thirteen active telescopes near the summit of the Mauna Kea, one of which is for radio astronomy, the type of observa-tion in which the VLA specializes. You may have heard of IFA. We came to world attention for observations that ruled out potential collisions between Earth and a deadly asteroid. Dr. Jones and I met over that research."

She remembered being in Hawaii and on the Big Island, when she and Chee honeymooned there. She recalled the thrill of watching lava flow into the ocean.

But they hadn't taken the tour of the observatory. She'd had other things on her mind that week.

"Do you know if Dr. Jones had enemies?"

"Probably. He cared more about science than human relationships. Dr. Peterson might be better equipped to answer that question."

Bernie sensed that he had more to say. "Can you think of anything else that might be helpful for me to know about Dr. Jones?"

He hesitated. "I hear it is rough country out there in New Mexico—the Wild West with cowboys, Indians, and rattlesnakes. But I would not have expected a fellow stargazer, a man who spent his career thinking about the mysteries of the universe, to lose his life there."

"You're right about the snakes and the cowboys and Indians, but on most days, things are peaceful. We give snakes a healthy respect and people get along."

Dr. Bellinger laughed. "The way Dr. Peterson described it, life there is right out of one of those classic Western movies."

"Really?"

"She told me the coyotes howling at night frightened her, so she asked Dr. Jones to teach her to fire a gun. And she said Jones's ex-wife lived on an Indian reservation near the telescopes. That statement struck me as odd."

"Why?"

"From pictures I have seen, those instruments are beautifully isolated, situated in the midst of a broad and empty desert, surrounded by mountains to block sound wave interference I hadn't imagined people nearby."

"Your imagination is correct. Except for the buildings associated with the VLA, the telescopes stand alone."

"I'm glad to hear that." He cleared his throat. "Officer Manuelito . . ." She heard him take a breath. "You have a lovely day."

"Dr. Bellinger, did you want to tell me something else?"

But he had hung up.

She scowled at the phone, wondering what he'd left unsaid. She jotted down a summary of the conversation and decided that she needed to contact Joy Peterson again. Their stories didn't match. This professional jealousy probably had nothing to do with why Jones was dead, but Bernie didn't like inconsistencies. She sent Peterson a text, telling her she had some follow-up questions about the controversy over Dr. Jones's research and their collaboration with Dr. Bellinger, and asking her to get in touch ASAP.

She was considering what to do next when her cell phone rang. Chee started talking before she could say more than hello. He must have known that she needed a lift because he spoke in Navajo, the language of her heart.

"Bernie, how's it going down there?"

"It's frustrating. A possible suspect just turned into a reasonable scientist. The only thing I know for sure is that Jones is still dead and Maya says she did it. What's new in Shiprock?"

"We've got good news here. Captain Largo will be back the day after tomorrow."

"I'm glad."

She heard Chee take a breath. "I'm sorry about Maya. I had a case once where this old guy confessed to murder. I knocked myself out trying to prove he didn't do it. Turned out, he did it."

"Was that the Archie Pinto case?"

"How did you know?"

"The Lieutenant told me to ask you about it. I think he figured that might make it easier for me to believe Maya is guilty."

"Keep your chin up, Sweetheart. There are more battles to fight out here."

"I'd like to wrap this up and get home."

"I'd like that, too. I miss you."

Bernie felt her heart melt. "I miss you, too."

She called the number Williams had given her to check on fingerprints again and eventually found someone to confirm that the third set of prints on the gun were not Dr. Bellinger's. On a whim, and because Bellinger had mentioned that Jones was teaching her how to shoot, she asked about Dr. Joy Peterson. "Same thing. Not hers."

"Why are they on file?"

"Oh, because of their security clearances."

Bernie went to the break room and made herself a cup of coffee despite the sugary call of a Coke. The warmth and the caffeine stirred a new idea. What if Kristen had picked up Maya and made up the story to protect her friend, not realizing Maya had confessed? That would explain her vagueness about the vehicle that drove up Maya's road later that evening.

She grabbed the phone to call the woman, and then set it down. She could detect a lie better face-to-face. And she'd pay a visit to Bronson Chavez, too, while she was out that way. Perhaps outside the tension of an interrogation room, with himself not in jeopardy, Chavez could offer some clue as to why Maya would change from a laid-back third-grade teacher to a killer. It was worth the drive to Alamo to talk to them both one more time for her own peace of mind.

As she drove, her phone chimed with a text from Kathy, the woman who had given her the awards and pictures for Junior—the items still in her trunk.

She pushed the button to have the mechanical voice read to her.

"Officer Manuelito, I found more things that belonged to Dr. Jones. I can bring them to Socorro after work so you can share them with the family. May I meet you somewhere for dinner?"

Bernie thought of the pub where Maya and Jones had their date. She wanted to see it for herself. She responded with a quick Thumbs up, 6 p.m. and Big River Brew Pub?

Kathy came back: C U THEN.

She turned at the mini-mart and headed up the hill toward Alamo Community School. She drove past the building where she had met the Alamo principal and worried the children, and noticed a lush expanse of green on her left. She watched the boys, strong and spry as colts, practicing tackles. Basketball was the sport that ruled her heart, but she liked football, too. She noticed Coach Chavez on the field with the team.

A few clouds had rolled in, moving slowly with upper-level winds and bringing some autumn chill. She slipped on her jacket. Not only would it keep her warmer, it would make her look like someone's auntie instead of a cop, and perhaps keep gossip to a low roar instead of a siren blast.

She walked to the field, enjoying the fragrance of grass, dust, and cool air with a tantalizing hint of moisture. She observed Chavez encouraging the boys while he made them work. The clear beauty of the day was a gift, too rare and perfect for dark thoughts. The team ran sprints while Chavez studied their speed and endurance, offering a strong, friendly blend of direction and motivation. He and the boys were having fun.

Coach announced a ten-minute water break and jogged toward her.

"Officer?"

"Yá'át'ééh, Mr. Chavez. I'm here because I need your help."

She saw him tense. "What's up?"

"I'm worried about Maya. The detective and I can't get her to cooperate."

"You mean confess?"

She didn't tell him that was a moot point. "I mean to help herself by telling the truth. I've known Maya a long time. We were roommates in college. I like her."

Chavez looked at the grass. "I don't have any idea about her and Jones, what went on between them, but I know she wouldn't kill anybody."

"Did she ever . . ." Her cell phone vibrated in her pocket, momentarily distracting her. She let it be. "Did Maya ever talk to you about the dead guy?"

"Not exactly. She told me she'd been with somebody and that they had some disagreements so she and her son left to come home to Navajo and she went back to school and became a teacher." He glanced out at the boys. "A few months ago, she mentioned that her son's dad landed a job at the VLA and at Tech, and she hoped he'd spend more time with Junior. I asked what she thought of the guy, and she said she didn't think of him very much." Chavez shook his head. "I didn't expect to see them together so cozy."

Bernie watched the clouds scoot along for a moment. "Did she say anything else about Jones?"

"Just that his return would give Leon a chance to make peace with the guy. Her brother sure keeps an eye on her—calls every day. I gather he never cared for her husband." Chavez shifted his weight from heel to toe. "He and Maya did a great job raising Junior. I mean, Junior's still a work in progress, but we all were at his age."

Chavez looked at his watch. "This problem with Maya has Leon on edge. He wanted me to give him a lift to her house, and when I told him I had practice he got belligerent."

"What happened to his wheels?"

"He loaned the truck to Junior to drive out to the college. He hitched a ride to school and figured I would help him." Chavez shrugged. "Then he went off the deep end and wanted to fight me."

Bernie thought about what she needed to ask next, and could find no graceful way to say it. "Did it bother you to date a married woman?"

"I didn't know she was married until you told me. When I saw Jones kissing her, I wondered if he was the one Maya had been with in Hawaii. I wondered how Maya really felt about the guy, and about me." He looked toward the field, and Bernie followed his gaze. The boys sat in the bleachers in small groups or stood stretching or drinking from their water bottles. "One thing I love about that woman is that she's full of life. Her passion makes her a good teacher, but you don't wanna be on her bad side. She and the principal have gone a few rounds over some of the rules here." He laughed, but then turned serious.

"Maya has a temper. You know her, right?"

"I thought I did."

"Something's wrong here." He kicked at the ground with a toe of his boot. "Maya might not be the gal we figured she was, but she wouldn't shoot her only boy's father. No way. Do you believe me?"

"I want to."

Chavez exhaled. "I gotta get back to the field. Good luck."

Bernie watched the team a few minutes more after Chavez restarted the practice, then walked to her unit. She checked her phone and found a missed call from a number she didn't recognize. The person hadn't left a message, but the call came from area code 575—the zone for Socorro and twenty-three New Mexico counties. She dialed.

"Officer, it's Kristen. Remember me?" She didn't wait for an answer. "You asked me to call if I saw anything suspicious at Maya's house. I just tried you at the police station."

"I'm at the Alamo school. What's going on?"

"Well, somebody drove a pickup by here, headed toward Maya's place. I didn't recognize the truck and it hasn't come back. I wonder if someone is stealing stuff from up there. That's not right. Do you want me to check on the house?"

"When was this?"

"About ten minutes ago. I can walk up that way and make sure things are OK."

"No, absolutely not." Bernie used the tone that worked on Darleen when she came up with a bad idea. "You stay put. I'll be there shortly. Did you see the driver?"

"No, too much glare."

"If the truck comes by again, get a good description and the license plate number. Then call me back as quickly as you can."

"I will. I'm glad you'll check it out."

Bernie left the parking lot, with Kristen still on the phone. "Can you tell me how to find Maya's place?"

"It would be better if I went with you. It's confusing. Unless you're from here, it's hard to know which rut is the road."

"Tell me. I'm good with directions." Bernie didn't mention the obvious—she didn't know what she'd discover there, and she couldn't risk endangering a civilian.

"You remember how to get to my place?"

"Yes."

"Well, start there." Kristen sounded disappointed. "I'm thinking about the best way to say the rest."

When they came, the directions had details of landmarks, but not in terms of distance. They meshed on the edges with what Mrs. Rodriguez had told her earlier at the convenience store.

"I haven't seen the truck come back yet. Be careful."

Bernie called the Socorro station and told the dispatchers she was responding to a potential burglary in progress. The directions worked. She found Maya's house and a black pickup parked close to an open front door. The truck seemed familiar, but she knew better than to make an assumption that could have deadly consequences.

Bernie cautiously approached the house and stood outside the doorway a moment, listening. She heard a noise coming from the back of the building. She had already drawn her gun. "Police. Show yourself now. Come out quickly."

The response was immediate. "Don't shoot me. I'm not doing . . . Officer Bernie? Is that you?"

The voice went with the truck. "Junior Jones?"

"Yes, ma'am."

"Are you OK?"

"Sort of."

She holstered her gun and walked inside, moving toward his voice.

The house looked neat with everything in its designated place. She noticed a framed photo of Junior with Leon and another picture of them with Maya, three faces smiling from the entry wall. A table Maya used as a desk had piles of bills, credit card offers, and the like organized into neat stacks. On it was a bouquet. It must be the one Chavez found offensive, a perky-looking arrangement dominated by golden sunflowers with mums and roses in shades of red, yellow, and orange with greenery for additional color. A small white card lay next to the vase. Bernie didn't have to touch it to read the message: "Sweetness, I'm so looking forward to tonight." It was not signed.

Junior sat on the edge of Maya's bed. He glanced up with red-rimmed eyes.

"What are you doing here, Officer?"

Bernie squatted in front of him to talk face-to-face. "A lady down the hill saw the truck and worried that your mom's place had a burglar. She called me to check. How about you?"

"I was at the college looking into student loans and Leon called. He got your message about Mom's food and asked me to pick it up because I had the truck. He said he'd get a ride and meet me here." Junior fell silent and Bernie gave him time. "I saw that picture of us three together and then all of a sudden a wave of sadness just flowed right over me." Junior's voice cracked. "Last week, everything was cool. Dad was back, Mom was happy. Now, now it's all different. Cosmo's gone and Mom's in jail. Uncle Leon ought to be here by now and maybe something happened to him, too. I don't understand."

Bernie sat on the bed next to him. "I don't understand either. My job is to figure out what really happened to your father."

"Cosmo killed himself. He sent me a letter explaining that. You read it."

"I did read it, but the autopsy report doesn't make that conclusion. And I doubt that you really believe that."

"Then someone shot him. But not Mom. She loved him even though they couldn't live together. She liked him, too. Why would she kill him? I can't believe it. It's too awful." Junior shook his head. "You're the cop. Don't you know what happened?"

Bernie let the question sit, thinking of what Leaphorn had said about liars and their motivation. Thinking of what Chavez had said about Leon's protectiveness. "Did you and Cosmo ever argue?"

"Yeah, sometimes. Who doesn't? He could get on my nerves. He was always telling me I should make more of myself, you know?"

Bernie thought of all the advice Mama had for her and Darleen. "Did you argue about anything else?"

"Oh, sure. Like when he told me about the lady at work that he was dating. I got upset because I thought maybe him and Mom, you know . . ." His voice trailed off. "It doesn't matter. Cosmo's dead."

"Were you angry with him about that lady?"

Junior raised his eyes to the ceiling, as if he were searching there for the answer. "It's complicated."

"Why?"

"For instance, one time he asked me to go stargazing with him, and Joy, his date, came, too. I liked her. We got there early and saw some cool petroglyphs that looked like clusters of stars. Dad joked around with us, all happy, and Joy was nice to me. Anyway, later, when Cosmo and I were alone, I asked if Mom knew about his girlfriend. He said that his love life was none of my business and that Mom meant more to him than any other woman ever could. I told him then he should stop flirting with Joy and acting like an idiot." Junior squeezed his hands into fists, and then released them. "I called my own dad an idiot. And now he's dead. Those words . . . I can't take them back."

Bernie gave his sorrow time to settle.

"Later, Cosmo told me he and Joy had cooled it."

"Did he seem sad because she had ended their relationship?"

"No, he dumped her."

"Did he say why?"

"He told me he wanted to get back with Mom. That was the main thing."

She noted how Junior's story of the breakoff differed from Joy's.

"Did your father ever say much about his work?"

"Sometimes. Wow. It was super amazing. A couple weeks ago he told me that he and Joy and another guy were doing a complicated project about gravity and black holes. Then later, he said something kinda screwy had gone down and they were having arguments."

"All three of them?"

"I guess so."

Bernie had a final crucial question. "You said you went shooting with your dad. Do you have a gun?"

"No. I used my his pistol."

And that, she thought, explained the third set of fingerprints. And, perhaps, pointed to Maya as guilty.

Bernie stood. "Before you leave, remember to pack up the food your mom has here. You know she'll feel terrible if it goes to waste."

She saw the hesitation in his face.

"You can restock for her when she's out of jail."

"What if I take stuff in the refrigerator and the apples and bananas. I'll leave the cans. Think that's OK?"

"Sure."

Junior walked into the kitchen. He found a cooler with wheels in one corner, rolled it to the refrigerator, and lifted the lid. He leaned down, and Bernie watched him remove an envelope.

"What's that?"

He looked at it. "It's for my 'shidá'í." He folded it in half and started to shove it in his back pocket.

"Wait. Open it. I need to know what it says."

Junior shrugged. "Mom always leaves instructions for us. Usually for me, but I guess this was my uncle's turn." He handed it to her.

Bernie eased the flap loose and pulled out a single sheet of white paper. Maya had written in black ink. She felt Junior's eyes on her as she read.

"Your mother wrote this to Leon about you and about your dad's death. Do you want to see it?"

He shook his head. "Could you read it to me?"

She swallowed and began:

Dear Leon,

  With Junior's biological father gone, it's up to you to continue as guide and mentor to my son. You know that he is beyond precious to me, and even though he is nearly an adult, he will rely on your guidance for years to come, now more than ever. Despite your differences with my husband, he played an important role in my son's life. Now that he has passed, Junior needs you to be his father as well as his 'shidá'í.

I'm sorry we haven't been able to talk about what happened out there. I did the right thing. Now you have to, too.

I love you dear brother; don't make this more difficult.

Please tell Junior as often as possible that I love him, too.

"Your mom signed with a little heart and the initial *M*."

"That's what she always does." Junior stared at the floor.

"I have to keep this, but I'll make a copy for you."

He looked up. "What does it mean, 'I did the right thing'? Does that mean she killed my dad?" He shook his head. "No, she'd never do that. This is my fault. One time after Cosmo and I argued, I called Mom and told her I wished Cosmo was dead. I was just venting, you know? But maybe Mom thinks I killed him. She's lying to keep me from going to prison."

"If that's what happened, talk to her, set this straight. OK?"

She saw his bottom lip begin to tremble and then he put his head in his hands.

"Junior, can you do that?"

He looked up. "I can't believe she'd think that I would murder my dad. If I'd killed Cosmo, I'd own up to it. I wouldn't let her lie to save me."

Bernie felt his double sorrow. "This situation has so many complications. Remember that your mother really loves you."

Bernie left him to his thoughts and drove back to Socorro with Maya's note. It read like another confession. From the writing style, she doubted that Maya had composed the first letter, the one Junior had received in his mailbox allegedly from Steve Jones. Someone else had faked that, and Leon topped the list. She called him from her unit and left an urgent message.

The drive went quickly. A few cars passed heading in the opposite direction, and then she noticed the man in a van in front of her lower his window and wave his arm to get her attention. He turned on his emergency flashers and pulled to the shoulder. Bernie saw the handicapped license plate as she parked behind him. She approached to learn what the problem was.

"Hey, Officer. Sorry to stop you like that, but I have to talk to the police. I'm Ralph Apacheito."

The name rang a bell. "Oh, right. You're the father of the boy who found the car."

"You're the officer they sent to help with the investigation, aren't you?"

"Yes, I've been working with Detective Williams."

"I thought so."

She introduced herself. She noticed a boy next to him in the front seat. "Yá'át'ééh. Are you Raul?"

The child nodded.

Ralph picked up the conversation. "When Raul was out there, he came across a fancy phone, too. With the shock of everything, he forgot about the phone. He just told me. We were heading home to get it and then to Socorro to give it to Detective Williams. Instead of that, can we give it to you?"

"Yes. And I'd like to talk to Raul a minute."

"If you follow us, we'll take care of all this. We live just a few miles from here."

When they got to the house, she saw the front passenger door fly open. Young Raul ran to her unit.

"Dad asked me to get the phone for you. It takes a while for him to get in and out because of the wheelchair, so he's waiting in the van."

The boy raced up the ramp to the front door and returned moments later with an iPhone. He handed it to her through the open window.

"Where did you find this?"

The boy shrugged. "On the ground."

"Was the phone by the car?"

"No, it was outside in the weeds, kinda near the road."

"Wow. You were a good detective."

Raul smiled. "I saw it when I tied my shoe. And so then I picked it up and put it in my jacket pocket. That was before I saw the car and, you know, the rest of it. I forgot about the phone until today."

"I need to talk to your dad a minute. Come with me."

She introduced herself officially this time, and Apacheito did the same.

"Sir, Detective Williams noticed some shoe tracks near the car Raul discovered." She turned to the boy. "Were you wearing those shoes when you found the car?"

He looked at his feet. "Yep. They're the only ones I got."

"I'd like to take a picture of Raul's sneakers and talk to him a little."

"That's fine."

"Did you happen to walk out that way to check on the boy's story?"

Ralph smiled. "Officer, I don't walk. I roll."

She squatted down to the boy's level. "Would you sit in the van while I get the picture?"

"Could I be in the police car instead?"

She looked at Apacheito and he nodded.

Bernie took the photos of Raul's shoe soles and explained the equipment in her unit to the fascinated child. Then she asked about the dead man's car. He told the story the way Williams had recorded it, and added a few details.

"When I got home, I was crying. Then I threw up. I wished my shima was here. Daddy called Ms. Kelsey to be with me. She said she'd make sure the chindii didn't get me. She's my favorite teacher."

And that, Bernie thought, explained how Maya knew Jones was dead. And how she managed to confess before someone she loved went to jail for the crime.

She took the phone to the sheriff's office as evidence, and asked a technician there to verify that it had belonged to the dead man. If Jones had owned it, she requested a list of all incoming and outgoing calls and texts on the day he died and a couple days before that. She pulled into the Big River Brew Pub parking lot at dusk. She called Leon again, both numbers, and left the same urgent message.

She locked the unit and walked toward the restaurant, giving the building a quick scan to locate the security cameras that had captured Maya and Jones. Inside, she didn't spot Kathy, so she asked the hostess for a table for two where she could see the front door.

While she waited, she called Leon again, got the *leave a message* recording, and hung up.

Kathy hadn't arrived fifteen minutes past the agreed-upon time, so Bernie requested nachos and thought about having a Coke, but stuck with water instead. She was checking her phone for the *I can't make it* text when she saw a message from Joy Peterson: Let's combine business and pleasure. I'm going stargazing tonight. Want to join me?

Bernie texted, Tell me more, and put her phone down as Kathy arrived.

"Sorry I'm late. I'm starving." Kathy scooted into the booth just as the server arrived with the food. She placed the nachos in the center of the table.

"I ordered these to share." Bernie gave the plate a gentle shove toward Kathy. "Please have some."

"I will." She served herself a pile of corn chips with melted cheese, olives, beans, onions, chicken, and jalapeños. Then she took a packet from her purse—white paper around something wrapped with a rubber band—and set it on the table. "I thought you might like to have this for Dr. Jones's family."

Bernie leaned toward her. "What is it?"

"A journal he was keeping, along with more photos. I overlooked it at first."

Kathy ate while Bernie loosened the rubber band and pulled out a spiral notebook and a small envelope with the photographs. She glanced at the picture on top, a shot of a thin white man with his arm around a very young-looking Maya. She held a baby. An older woman in the traditional long skirt, velvet blouse, and much turquoise jewelry looked on.

She held it out to Kathy. "What a lovely photo."

"That's Dr. Jones with his boy. He sure loves, I mean . . ."

"I know."

Bernie again noticed how much Junior resembled his father. She flipped through the rest—photos that focused only on the baby, shots of the baby and Maya with and without the older woman, probably the shimásání, Maya's grandmother. She saw the baby and Jones, and the baby with both parents and Maya's grandma. She stopped when she came to the photo of a younger Leon holding Junior. It tugged at her heart. She'd never seen such a look of pure love on a man's face. She put the image on top of the stack.

"It seems odd that Jones would have had these at the office."

"That's because he was going to create a photo collage to give his son and his son's mom for Thanksgiving. He wanted me and Joy, back when they were a couple, to help him decide how to frame them, which ones to use, you know?"

"That would have been a nice gift." And asking Joy to help with such a project certainly sent an *I'm not that into you* message.

The word *Thanksgiving* launched Kathy into a long, funny story of how she'd gone back to Africa last November to see her family and encountered unexpected adventures. Bernie listened, transferring nachos from the big pile onto her own plate and even taking a few with the diced tomatoes on top. She looked at the photo of Leon with the baby again and smiled. Maya's lie finally made sense.

Kathy reached for more chips. "You look like that story hit a chord with you."

The waitress returned with Kathy's salad and Bernie's onion rings. She refilled Bernie's water and left some iced tea for the other woman.

The golden rings had the right sweetness in the batter, and a good crunch. Bernie added a puddle of thick red catsup to dip them in. She offered one to Kathy and was glad when she declined.

Kathy tried her salad, then put the fork down. "I'd like to ask you something. A big box arrived this afternoon for Dr. Jones. It's a telescope. You know, the backyard kind."

Bernie smiled. "Was that because he didn't get enough of the stars at work?"

"Our telescopes aren't optical, like this one. They listen to space. This is one that the average guy could use to see the stars." She speared a tomato and held it on her fork. "I called about returning it, but the company wouldn't take it back unless someone pays the shipping. Steve told me he ordered it so he and Junior could look at the sky and do some bonding. That endeared Steve to me right away."

"When Dr. Jones came out to do his research, he told me how much he was looking forward to reconnecting with his son. I've heard of dads, lots of them, who ignore their kids after they split from the moms. My father did that."

"Junior mentioned that he'd gone stargazing with his father and Dr. Peterson. Didn't his father have another telescope?"

"They used hers. Joy owns the fanciest backyard scope they make. This one is less powerful, not up to her standards, but I'm sure it's nice." Kathy put the tomato in her mouth. "Anyway, could you get in touch with Junior and ask him if he'd like to have the telescope?"

Bernie grabbed another onion ring. "I'll ask him when I give him the photos. If he doesn't want it, you could offer to donate it to the Alamo school. Maybe they'd like it."

"Good idea."

"I appreciate getting the notebook. It might help with the case."

Kathy's perfect eyebrows rose slightly. "We thought you were done with that. Dr. Peterson told me Junior's mom had been arrested for his murder. Is that true?"

"The death is still under investigation."

While Kathy finished her tea, Bernie looked at the old photographs again before she put them in her backpack. Each person pictured clearly treasured baby Junior. She wondered about Jones's family, Junior's other relatives. Did they embrace this half-Navajo child?

The next time the server came, Bernie asked for the bill, refused Kathy's offer to pay, and thanked her again for her help as she left. Then, she opened the notebook. She skimmed Jones's daily to-do lists, records of his car's gas mileage, notations about diet and sleep, and, occasionally, some mention of Maya, the conflict with Giovanni, and his thoughts about Joy Peterson. Evidently the romance cooled in part because he had lost respect for her as a scientist.

She was halfway through the little book when her phone buzzed. She hoped for Leon but saw Dr. Peterson's name on the screen.

"Hey, Bernie. Got your text. Can we celebrate your wrapping up the case with some stargazing?"

"I wish it was settled. I've been waiting for a person of interest to call me. I was just looking through Jones's notebook to tie up some loose ends. I have some questions for you, too."

"You mentioned that. You know, nothing puts problems in perspective like a look at the stellar universe. Come out stargazing with me while we talk. That will make me feel like I've done a little something to help you find justice for Steve. He was a good, good man. I really miss him."

Bernie thought quiet time under the starlit sky might be just what she needed. How many opportunities would she have for a private star session with a real astronomer?

"When?"

"I'll meet you in an hour, as soon as I finish cooking some chicken and clams for Fur Boy."

"That sounds fancy."

"Yes, he's a picky eater." Joy gave her directions to a rendezvous point. "Don't be late. The clouds are moving in a few hours from now."

Bernie caught the server's eye, got a refill on her water, and asked for a box for the nachos. Then she went back to the notebook, opening it from the back to read Jones's most recent entries for references to Leon or Maya or Junior. Of the three, Junior's name came up most often, not as Junior but as Sherman or Sherm, with notes on how to help him get ready for college. Jones's worry reminded her of the concern Mama still had for her. References to Maya were frequent. Near the end, she found cryptic notes that included Leon's name. She called Williams as soon as she'd finished reading.

24

Joe Leaphorn had never liked unfinished business, and he especially didn't want to leave loose ends he'd have to contend with after a week or so in Washington.

He called Sergeant Chee at the Shiprock station and learned Chee wasn't available from the young officer who answered the phone, a man he had attempted to mentor, Wilson Sam.

"Sir, can I ask you something?"

"Go ahead."

"Did you hear that Captain Largo might be retiring?"

"Yes. The rumor is everywhere. Ask Sergeant Chee to call me."

Chee returned the call an hour later, and they quickly moved through the required pleasantries. "Any news on the dead baby?"

"A little. I got the report on the DNA. The baby's father was among the felons Berke suspected were involved in the case." Leaphorn gave him the name. "He's not familiar to me."

"Me neither. What about the mother?"

"That's a bigger mystery. They're still looking for a maternal match, but the FBI didn't volunteer the same list of likely women as they did with paternity. Berke didn't provide DNA for Bee or Gabriela, and evidently there's nothing on file."

From the silence, he knew Chee was waiting for him to add something more conclusive.

"That's all I've got for now."

"Bee spit at Bernie, and some landed on her boot. I teased her about leaving the boots here in case the Feds needed them for the DNA, and they are at our house. But Bee's in custody, so her DNA swab should be no problem."

"I'll mention the boots to my contact at the lab." Leaphorn paused. "I wonder if Bernie cleaned those boots."

"I doubt it. I've been keeping her busy."

The conversation ended, and instead of making another call to his OMI contact, he sent Agent Johnson a follow-up message about maternal DNA, asking if there was a link between the male felon and Bee. He put urgency and concern in his words and left out the judgment.

As Leaphorn was thinking about what to do next, his phone rang.

"Hey Lieutenant. It's Hancock. Glad I caught you."

"Yá'át'ééh." He waited for Hancock to start the conversation.

"This is kind of a good news/bad news call. What do you want first?"

"Give me da good news." He assumed one of the two concerned cancer.

"So, the good news is I'm not leaving the task force after all, but I talked to the director and we'd really like you to join us. When you say yes to the invitation, I'll be there with you, and we can work together on projects. You can buy me lunch in Gallup before the sessions. I know you told me you're not big on meetings, but this is a good cause and I'd love to work with you again."

"Wad's da bad news?"

Hancock exhaled. "The reason I'm not leaving the task force is because Christina urged me to stay. Her cancer has spread, and it's not operable."

Cancer. The first Navajo word he had heard for it was *lóód doo nádziihii*—meaning "the sore that does not heal." Now, as more patients recovered, the word *cancer* was appropriately translated into words meaning "cells that divide uncontrollably." This scientific description and more hopeful outlook served to encourage a greater number of Navajos to get tested and treated for the disease.

"Christina says she wants me thinking of something besides her in the days ahead, something I enjoy and where I can make a difference. She knows the task force charges my batteries. So of course I told her yes, I'd stay on."

"Send me da info on da meeting. I'll give id a shot. Tell Christina I'm thinkin' of her."

"I'll do it." Hancock paused. "You and Louisa going to Washington?"

"Yes." And then, to his own surprise, he said, "I'm lookin' forward to it."

He stood to stretch before clicking on the "No More Fear of Flying" video. When he glanced at his computer, he noticed a new email. It came from the Closely Watched Foundation.

He sat, took a breath, and opened it, wondering what Ginger Symons had to sell.

Dear Lieutenant Joe Leaphorn,

This note is a long, long time in coming. You may not remember, but many years ago you saved my

life. I never thanked you. I realize at the time you
must have considered me, basically, a spoiled brat.
I've grown up, but I understand if you choose not to
respond to this note and respect that decision.

Not only am I writing to tell you how enormously
grateful I am that you didn't let me die in that cave.
I'm also writing to ask you a favor.

Leaphorn looked out the window for a moment.
Here it comes, he thought, the sales pitch.

I have established a foundation, initially to help
immigrant women and children. I would like to
expand our focus to work with Native Americans,
especially in the areas of missing women and child
welfare, and would appreciate any advice you
might have for me on this topic. I've attached some
information about the foundation.

I am planning a trip to the Navajo Nation later
this fall. Perhaps we could arrange to meet then and
I could express my gratitude in person.

Please thank your assistant for reaching out
to me.

She signed the note "Ginger Symons, a.k.a. Theodora Adams."

He clicked on the attachments, and there was her photo—those blue eyes staring at him with the same look of smug confidence he recalled from so long ago.

Later, as he was getting ready to end work for the day, his computer told him he had a new message. He opened it, and then called Chee.

"I've got some news about the baby. Agent Johnson says it's not Bee's."

"Interesting."

"The mother was arrested in Farmington and left the infant in the care of the father, a known drug dealer." Leaphorn paused, considering what came next. "The child died from brain damage caused by shaking among other things. Agent Johnson said the man confessed to dumping the baby there when he realized it was dying. He's in custody for that and for what happened to Bee."

Leaphorn could practically hear Chee thinking in the silence.

"Johnson said she appreciated your call about it. You got things moving. Thanks for wrapping that up. Send me an invoice for your time."

"No. This one's on me."

25

"Say that again." Bernie heard the disbelief in Detective Williams's voice.

She repeated her revelation: "I believe Maya lied to us because she thinks her brother, Leon, killed Jones."

Williams laughed. "Based on that letter in the cooler? No way. You're making an assumption without enough evidence."

"Listen to me. It's not just on the letter. I'm thinking of conversations with Junior and Coach Chavez, and a note I found about Leon in Jones's journal and what I saw in some old photos."

"Go ahead. Lay it out."

"Leon positioned himself as the protector of Maya and Junior. He's raised that boy as his own son. Jones's return changed the dynamics of their little family and threatened Leon's role as a fill-in father. Jones mentions some rude behavior on Leon's part since he's been back in New Mexico, even a threat that if he ever hurt Maya or Junior, he'd regret it. That sounds like a motive to me."

Bernie opened Jones's notebook.

"Listen to this."

She read:

Need to talk to Leon about Sherm. How can I make peace?

Leon hates me. What did I do to that guy?

Need to get Maya's advice and help to resolve this. That man is seriously angry. I'm nervous around him. He's got a temper.

Williams cleared her throat. "That sounds like a motive for family therapy. Not murder. Where's the hard evidence? Why aren't Leon's prints on the gun?"

"Chew on this. When Maya learned Jones was dead, she assumed Leon killed him because of her brother's long-standing animosity. That's why she lied and why she has nothing else to tell us."

Williams waited a beat. "I don't know. If he's her protector, why would he let her take the rap?"

"Maybe because he didn't expect her to step up and let him get away with murder? We have to talk to him.

Can you set that up? I've left a message, but he hasn't called back."

"Getting the interview will be easy. Leon got arrested. That's why he couldn't call you."

"What happened?"

"He went out to the Alamo school and argued with Chavez. The principal called. Officer Taylor picked Leon up for assault."

"I talked to Chavez. He didn't mention the arrest."

"Leon didn't assault Chavez. When Officer Taylor caught up with him, Leon gave the guy some lip, kicked at him, and threw a punch. He got arrested for assaulting a police officer."

"So, we know Leon has a temper. Maya knows that, too."

"You might be on to something. I'll set up the interview for the morning."

"Tomorrow? I have a couple questions for Leon that can't wait."

"Yeah, they can. Jones will still be dead, and both Kelsey sibs will still be locked up. We've got this. Lighten up, girlfriend."

Williams's bossy tone brought back her conflict with Chee. She felt her throat tighten.

"Tomorrow, Bernie. We'll deal with it. We'll get Leon to talk about Jones, Junior, Maya, the whole mess. If you're right about him wanting to take care of his baby sister, he'll confess rather than see her go to prison."

"How's Honey doing?"

"Don't ask. See you tomorrow."

Bernie felt a wave of relief. She lacked a few crucial details, but the case finally made sense. Leon resented Jones stepping in now—after he'd raised Junior all those years—and acting like a dad. In the notebook, Jones had mentioned his disagreements with Leon, and she'd heard Leon complain about Jones's bad behavior toward his sister.

The fake suicide letter Junior found with the mail fell into place. His 'shidá'í would write it to ease Junior's mind and to try to get Maya out of the trouble she'd invited for his sake. Leon wouldn't know the nicknames Jones and his son had given each other. Bernie remembered her conversation with Leon in the police station parking lot when he so vehemently denied his sister's guilt. Leon had said Maya was "all twisted up inside." The writer of the suicide letter used that same phrase to describe Steve Jones's mental state. And the letter explained why Leon stuck to suicide as the cause of Jones's death.

But how did Leon know where Jones would be the evening he died? Bernie focused on recalling what she had seen on the restaurant's security tape. She remembered Maya doing something on her phone. Was she communicating with Leon? As she remembered the surveillance video, something else tickled her brain. She closed her eyes and saw the truck that drove up behind Jones's Jaguar, waited at the exit, and turned the same direction. It was an old, full-size black Chevy pickup. Leon's truck, sandwiched between the Jaguar and a white SUV that pulled up behind him. Bernie pictured Leon following the car until he realized Jones was taking Maya home, waiting until Jones returned to the lonely highway, and confronting him.

But how did Leon get Jones to pull off the road in that isolated spot? How did he get Jones's gun? Why didn't Jones resist? They were big questions. She let them fester.

Williams was right. Leon wasn't going anywhere tonight. Unlike the botched warrant for Melvin Shorty, this time a suspect had played into her hands. How fortunate that he got himself arrested.

With the promise of his interview tomorrow, she could relax. In the meantime, it would be fun to look at the stars with Joy.

Bernie went back to the notebook and read on. In one place, Jones had printed "JOY PETERSON" and "GIOVANNI BELLINGER" all in capital letters and drawn a box around the names with a design that re-sembled lightning bolts. Beneath it he'd written: "Call G and figure this out!" And below that: "Give Joy the news. Move on." She speculated that the note foreshad-owed the end of the romance.

She found sets of numbers, equations that didn't mean anything to her but reminded her that Joy had mentioned needing Jones's notes. She snapped a picture of the pages with her phone, then put the notebook in her backpack until she could place it in an evidence bag.

The server finally arrived with the boxed nachos and her change. Bernie left a tip and headed to her unit. She eagerly anticipated standing outside in the moonlight, looking up at the heroes and the animals in the sky as they looked down on her and the rest of the five-fingered creatures. Getting away from the claus-trophobia of her own thoughts might help her deal with Leon tomorrow.

Bernie had always found the night sky intriguing and loved telescopes. Even though some elders didn't venture out at night for fear of things unseen and supernatural evil, and advised their children not to look at the moon, the night never frightened her. When she saw the blanket of twinkling stars and planets, she searched for the images the Holy People had left to remind the Diné of their sacred origins.

She strolled to her unit and secured the notebook in the trunk. She put the nachos there, too, to share with Williams later. Then she called Chee at home, hoping his long workday had finally ended. When he didn't answer, she tried the station, disappointed but not surprised to find him still working. Time and physical distance had softened her anger.

"Hey, Sergeant, shouldn't you be heading home?"

"Hey out there. I miss you. Anything new?"

"Maybe I finally have a break in the case." She summarized. "The Lieutenant mentioned that sometimes suspects make false confessions to protect people they love. I think that's what happened here. I wish I had clicked to it sooner."

"Don't be hard on yourself. Every cop, every person in the world, has run into a situation where they get conned by a liar. When do you think you'll be back?"

"Probably tomorrow after the interview with Leon."

"Call me before you head home, OK?"

"Sure. But you don't have to worry about me."

"I can't help it." Chee sounded tired. "I wish you were here right now."

"And I wish *you* were *here* tonight. I'm going to look at the stars with one of the scientists Jones worked with—Joy Peterson."

"She's the one who led you on that wild-goose chase about the other scientist stealing Jones's research?"

"Yeah. I still have a question or two for her about that."

"Stargazing? I thought those VLA telescopes just recorded low frequency soundwaves."

"Joy has her own telescope. Are you about ready to call it a day?"

"I guess, if *about* is a relative term. Have fun, Sweetheart."

After the conversation ended, she thought again about Giovanni and their interview. The niggling inconsistencies between the way Giovanni portrayed the three-cornered collaboration, the use and misuse of research data, and Joy's different account of what happened left her unsettled. Bernie figured she could wrap that up tonight with Joy's explanation.

Joy asked her to call when she left Socorro, so she tapped her number.

"You're about twenty minutes out. I'm in a Range Rover on the shoulder. You'll see my car at the highway junction."

"I'll be there soon."

As she drove, Bernie reconsidered the notations in Jones's notebook. Had she jumped to the wrong conclusion about Leon and let Giovanni off the hook too soon? He might not have told her the whole truth about the situation with Jones, Joy, and the stolen research, but was that really her business? The interview with Leon should provide some clarity. If he confessed, as she expected, she could go home knowing that her intuition about Maya had been correct.

She noticed the SUV where Joy had said it would be. Bernie rolled down her window. "This looks like a good spot."

"I know someplace better. It's another twenty minutes or so, but the road is terrible. You can ride the last stretch in here with me. After the moon comes up, I'll show you the petroglyphs out that way, too. One of them refers to the stars."

"Is this the place you and Jones went with Junior?"

"Yeah, that's the spot. Park and climb in."

"No. I'd feel like a cowgirl without her horse. I'll follow you."

"It's a terrible road. You sure?"

"Let's go."

Joy started her car and pulled onto the road.

As Bernie drove behind her, she tried her radio to let the station know her whereabouts, but she was out of the service area.

They passed Ralph Apacheito's house, the inside lights casting a soft glow into the October darkness. The road quickly morphed from decent gravel to jarring dirt with sandy patches. Then it became ruts, rocks, and potholes difficult to avoid in the dark, until it dwindled to a bone-shaking track. Bernie had traveled roads like this on remote parts of the Navajo Nation. She was impressed that a white woman in a fancy car could forge ahead at a reasonable rate of speed. Bernie hadn't seen a sign of any other humans since they'd passed the Apacheito place.

Joy slowed as the road continued to disappear. In the glow of her headlights, Bernie saw the earthen mounds that she knew could mean the walls of an abandoned pueblo. She preferred to keep her distance from what nature had preserved of the old villages, remembering the elders' admonition: *Leave undisturbed the spirits of the ancestors that cling to these places.*

Joy finally stopped near some cliffs beyond the ruins. Bernie pulled up next to her, grabbed her backpack, zipped up her jacket against the October night, and locked her unit. The cool air seeped through her uniform pants. She wished she'd taken time to change into something warmer. In the distance, a coyote chorus sang to the stars.

Joy lowered her window. "Do you hear that?"

"You mean the coyotes?"

"They give me the willies. I love animals, but not those mangy things."

Bernie appreciated Ma'ii, the being who was both a trickster and a Holy Person, a disreputable character and one who offered guidance. But instead of defending coyotes, she changed the subject. "I'm eager to see the stars tonight. Kathy mentioned that you have a fine telescope."

"We'll do that in a minute. My brain needs to settle after all those potholes. Sit in here with me where it's warm."

Bernie opened the passenger door, noticing that a step emerged to make it easier for someone of her height to climb in. She liked the new-car smell and the elegance of the leather seats. "Nice vehicle."

"I love it. You don't find many like this around here."

"What kind of car is this?"

"It's a Land Rover Velar S. My indulgence. Worth every penny."

"Something about it looks familiar."

"Really? They're hard to come by. You don't see many of them. You wouldn't believe how hard I looked before I found it. I negotiated to get all the features I wanted, like this color, Valloire White Pearl. The salesman didn't seem to realize that I don't like to compromise. And I love all this new technology."

As Joy talked on, Bernie studied the interior. In addition to the view out the windshield, the car had two monitors. One looked like it controlled navigation, phone calls, and maybe music or podcasts. Beneath it, a second screen had settings to control the temperature for heat and air-conditioning in the front and rear compartments, and adjustments for the angle and closeness of the steering wheel. And there were more features Bernie didn't recognize.

"Do you like my ride?"

"It's amazing. All this equipment looks complicated. I don't see a place for a key. How do you start it?"

"I push this button." She motioned to it. "As long as I have the electronic key in my pocket, the car comes to life and the seat automatically adjusts to the preferences I've set."

"Sweet." Bernie switched to business. "Let's talk about Dr. Jones for a minute. I'm still curious about the relationship between him and Dr. Bellinger, and your role in that whole situation."

"What's bugging you?"

"You showed me those emails where they accuse each other of improprieties. But Dr. Bellinger told me he and Jones had worked together without any friction until you joined the team. When I spoke to Giovanni about Jones's claims of plagiarism, he told me the problem started when Jones began to work with you at the VLA.

"Steve considered Giovanni a fraud, and I agree. You can't trust anything the man says."

"How was it for you, the other research partner, to be in the middle of that situation?"

Joy sighed. "Their growing animosity seriously concerned me. I told Steve I wanted our project to succeed no matter what, and their differences hampered our progress. I needed to focus on science, not personalities. It was a relief when Giovanni withdrew."

"So, let me see if I understand. Giovanni backed out of the collaboration because he and Steve couldn't work together. Now Steve's dead. That leaves you with the credit, correct?"

"Sadly, his recognition will be posthumous. I will do everything possible to acknowledge his contributions."

Joy sighed again and tapped her fingers on the steering wheel. "Giovanni, that unscrupulous plagiarist, might have told you I was to blame for his conflict with Steve. He resents losing his place as Steve's research partner to a younger person, and the fact that I'm a woman makes him even more bitter. That man is evil." She shook her head. "Did you get the autopsy report?"

"We have it."

"Did it show that the death was suicide?"

"I can't talk about it. Like I said, the case still has some loose ends."

"You have a suspect in custody, right?"

"Yes, but things are evolving. Speaking of that, I have an interview tomorrow. May I help you set up the telescope?"

"I can do it, thanks." Joy clicked her seat belt free. "I feel bad for Junior. I like that young man. I know he will be glad to have those photos Kathy found. And I'm eager to get the notebook."

"I thought she had forgotten about our meeting because she was so late getting to the brewpub."

"The Big River?" She heard a spark of interest in Joy's voice.

"Big River, that's right."

"Steve liked that place. He and I had some dates there. I'm surprised you met there. Kathy doesn't drink."

"I don't either but it was my idea. I wanted to see their surveillance cameras."

"Was the system actually functioning the night Steve died?"

"Yes, thank goodness." Bernie smiled. "So often the opposite happens at a crime scene."

Joy slipped the seat belt off her shoulder, and it retracted smoothly. "Did you bring the notebook? I need it to add his notes to my ongoing research as a tribute to our partnership."

"I have it, but it's evidence in the investigation. I can't give it to you."

"I have to have it."

"Don't worry. I took a picture of the pages with the computations you asked about."

Bernie pulled her phone from her pocket, noting there was no cell coverage. She called up the gallery and then her photos of the notebook pages, and held it out to Joy.

Joy took the phone, looked at the photos for a moment. "Is this all?"

"All I photographed."

Then the screen went dark and Joy returned the phone. "Thanks. I appreciate your effort, but that wasn't what I wanted. I need the notebook itself."

"Maybe after the case is settled. You'll have to talk to Detective Williams about that."

They walked to the back of the car. "We'll have the best night-sky view for another hour, then the rising moon will begin to interfere. I'll set up the scope."

Bernie watched the rear door smoothly rise with a move of Joy's foot under the bumper. Inside, she noticed a long zippered gray case, a white jacket, and some gloves on top of a blanket that covered whatever else Joy stored in the rear compartment. Joy picked up the jacket and slipped it on. Beneath it, Bernie saw some paper targets peppered with ragged bullet holes.

Joy noticed her noticing. "Not bad, eh? Steve taught me how to use a rifle when I told him I was worried about hungry coyotes getting my precious Fur Boy. He was a good teacher. That's another thing I'll miss about him."

She grabbed the large case and carried it to a level piece of ground near the vehicle. She unzipped it.

Bernie observed her efficiency in erecting the telescope. "I'm surprised you enjoy this after spending your time at work thinking about the galaxies."

"My job has a lot to do with calculations and theories. Standing here in the dark reminds me of why astronomy captured my heart. What a gift to be outside now beneath these magnificent stars."

Bernie looked in awe at Yadilhil, the never-ending dome of dark sky. She remembered the summer nights she'd spent as a girl with her auntie's sheep, watching the stars, searching for meteors, falling asleep and awakening to find the constellations, the Star People, in a different spot. She learned where to search for Náhookòs Bi'kà', the Male Revolving One, also known as the Big Dipper. Tonight, she spotted Náhookòs Bi'ááá, the Female Revolving One, or Cassiopeia. And she found Náhookòs Bikò', Central Fire, also named Polaris or the North Star. These three, like the entire universe and life itself, swirled in constant motion. The arrangement of these Star People spoke of the importance of family relationships, the need for cooperation between male and female, and the central role of the home, the hogan, with its crucial warming fire.

Joy focused the scope on a specific area of the sky and motioned to Bernie to step closer. "This is where we've been doing our work on gravity. Far beyond what we can see with this instrument is a black hole."

"Are there many black holes?"

"Countless. Oh, maybe somewhere between a hundred million and a billion of them, and that's just in the Milky Way alone."

Bernie looked through the eyepiece, amazed and humbled at the magnificence of the universe.

Joy adjusted the telescope to bring the rings of Saturn into view and then the large sphere of Jupiter. "I consider everything in the sky as reflective of the ongoing dynamic balance between expansion and contraction, or an illustration of the tension between gravity and dark energy, the force in opposition to it. Astronomy reminds me what the book of Genesis says about the force of creation to bringing light into the darkness."

Bernie moved her eyes away from the telescope. "Like our Diné origin stories."

"Yes, your people trekking over the ice bridge through the dim light of the Arctic autumn looking for a more temperate home and finally arriving in our bright Southwest. I like that image."

"I do, too, but I meant the ancestral stories, the People's emergence from the dark First World and ultimately ascending to the Glittering World where we live now."

Joy made a telescope adjustment. "Do the stories mention stars?"

"Yes." Bernie gave a brief version of the way First Man carefully designed constellations to add to the light from the moon; how he placed a fragment of mica in the North as a fixed point that would never move and three more bright pieces of mica in the South, East, and West; and how he built several constellations before Ma'ii, the Coyote Trickster, grabbed the blanket on which the stars sat and tossed them all into the sky.

"Interesting. Another reason to justify my hatred of coyotes. I enjoy watching them die." She motioned Bernie to the scope, now focused on the half-moon, Haniibaazii Alnii Nabiiska.

Bernie studied the moon, shoving her cold hands into her pockets. "Joy, I need to go. I have a big day tomorrow. Let's find a time for you to come in and talk more formally, get our conversation about Jones's research on the record. I think it could have a bearing on his death."

Joy raised an eyebrow. "Of course. I'm glad to do whatever I can to help figure out what happened to Steve. But you can't leave yet. You have to see the star ceiling."

"I really should—"

Joy interrupted. "When will you have this chance again? You *really* should see that. It's not far, and the moonlight will help you on the trail. I'll take the scope down and load the car. We can leave together."

"Where does the trail begin?"

Joy pointed the way. "After about ten minutes you'll see a rock face to the right. Stay close to it. When you get to the top, the moon should be high enough to illuminate the left side of the cliff. You'll see the overhang, and you ought to be able to catch the petroglyphs with the moonglow."

Bernie found the trail and climbed, focusing on her footsteps. It warmed her to move, and she appreciated the moonlight as she picked her way around the boulders and narrow places. After some time, she noticed a panel of images chipped into the sandstone. Curious and excited, she continued moving toward the symbols the ancient ones had left on the rock.

At the trail's end she stopped and breathed in the beauty of the night, listening to the sounds of the evening. She was grateful to live in a landscape where the traces of those who had come before were visible to their grand-children. Grateful, but eager to get home, she turned to leave. Then she saw the overhang Joy had mentioned.

Star ceilings get their name from the clusters of stars painted or stamped in natural rock shelters. The stars are similar in shape, each an equal-armed cross, but may vary in size and color, black, red, or white, occasionally orange, yellow, or green. Some cave ceilings have a single star; some have a hundred imprints or more. The stars are concentrated in the Canyon de Chelly area, but have been discovered throughout the Navajo heartland and the Four Corners area. Bernie hadn't heard of any near Alamo, but here it was. The very place she'd admired in the photograph on Jones's desk.

The moonlight enabled her to see the cluster of black stars against the pale rock. She stood beneath the decorated overhang and closed her eyes a moment. The place reverberated with the power of the ancestors and the prayers and ceremonies that helped them stay strong.

She filled her lungs with the velvet night air and exhaled, letting go of some of the worry that had come up the trail with her. She would talk to Leon and Maya tomorrow and call Giovanni. The disconnect between Joy's story and Giovanni's bothered her. Joy knew that Steve Jones had been at the brewpub the night he died, but if that was where they had gone on their dates, it made sense. The scientific squabble involved prestige and money as well as large egos, but it seemed unrelated to Jones's death and Maya's confession, the lie that had drawn her into the case.

Tomorrow, she could leave the final details to Williams. Maybe Mama would be in a better mood. Maybe someone else had served the warrant she botched. Maybe Largo would return and she and Chee could focus on how much they loved each other. Maybe she'd figure out what to do about the detective application.

She looked at the star ceiling once more. This time she saw a pattern of stars arranged with obvious care: a diagonal line of three and four larger images in the place where the warrior's feet and head would be. She marveled at the ancient ones' representation of the main components of Átsé Ets'ózí, the First Slender One, whom the stargazers like Joy called Orion. The warrior carried a bow drawn with an arrow made of stars to protect his people.

She decided to try taking a picture of the petroglyph for Chee and pulled out her phone. She snapped a few shots, wondering if they could do the cave's art justice. She would bring Chee here someday. She went to her picture file to adjust the image and noticed that Joy had deleted the notebook pages. It couldn't have been accidental—the woman prided herself on her familiarity with technology. She wondered if the professional jealousy ran deeper than Joy had said.

Bernie headed down the trail. She looked for Joy but didn't see her even though the Range Rover's pearly finish seemed to absorb the moon's glow. Something about the vehicle was familiar, she thought again, and she felt her heart beat faster. She stopped walking as her memory flashed to the surveillance video and the car behind Leon's truck as he followed Jones's Jaguar out of the parking lot. Of the thousands of SUVs in the Socorro area, Joy's seemed a perfect match. She recalled her interest in the surveillance tape. What if Leon hadn't killed Jones? What if Joy had set up the stargazing trip to find out what she knew? Had she revealed too much?

She resumed her descent, eyes on the trail, all senses alert. When she reached a steep spot near the end of the route, she realized how exposed she would be with the next few steps. A few rocks rolled down in front of her, bouncing off other stones with a percussive sound.

The rifle blast hit the tall piñon just off the trail in front of her, and Bernie felt the sting of bark and debris on her face. She flattened onto the trail, her weapon drawn, and waited for Joy's next shot. Because the bullet meant for her hadn't struck rock or dirt, Joy might conclude she had succeeded in getting off a hit. Assuming Joy's ears were ringing, Bernie quickly scooted to the shadows at the edge of the trail and stayed still.

The woman and the rifle moved into her line of sight. Joy stood at the base of the path, scanning the darkness, pointing the weapon in her general direction. Bernie took a deep breath.

She remembered her firearms training, especially the lessons about low-light conditions, shooting at night, and the tritium sights with their three green dots to guide her aim. She had the right gun and the right attitude. Bernie fired two shots without hesitation.

Joy struggled to remain standing, then reeled and staggered into the night.

Bernie sprinted toward the vehicles, keeping to the shadows. She moved as quickly as she could without losing her balance, watching the area of sagebrush where Joy had disappeared. When she reached the bottom, she sheltered behind the white car, listening for her adversary as she caught her breath.

The coyote chorus had fallen silent. The wind was still, too, the darkness growing less intense as the moon emerged from behind the clouds. Bernie heard a soft noise and then saw an owl. It swooped, beautiful long white wings extended, and rose again with the doomed body of a small rodent squirming in its talons. The bird soared away, disappearing into the night. Although owls had spied for the monsters against the Hero Twins, they had their place in the Glittering World, keeping the population of mice and squirrels in check. They were powerful omens, precursors of bad news and death, or perhaps of resolution. She told herself it was an omen of Joy's fate, not her own.

She expected Joy to return to her car and attempt to drive away, explaining the bullet wound as self-inflicted and quickly leaving the country before she could be charged with Jones's murder. Bernie considered disabling the SUV and waiting, limiting her own risk. No, she thought—like the owl, she would hunt. The minutes that passed gave Joy's wound time to bleed, time to ache, perhaps become painful enough to convince her that she faced a formidable opponent.

Bernie raised her head just enough to see over the vehicle out into the mesa land. No movement. She watched and waited. In the silent starlight, the coyote pack began to call to each other again. Time passed.

Then, from somewhere in the darkness, she heard a thud—like the sound of someone falling—and a groan. She looked toward the sound and at first saw nothing. After a few long minutes, she noticed Joy's head and shoulders. The woman pushed herself to standing and began limping in the direction of the cars. The moonlight captured the shape of the rifle she held.

Bernie carefully left the SUV's protective shield and moved to intercept Joy, keeping low as she negotiated the uneven terrain. She had almost reached a thicker stand of brush when her foot encountered a discarded can hidden by the sand. She winced as the night air amplified the sound, and flattened herself onto the dirt.

"Bernie? I heard you fall. How badly are you bleeding?"

"I don't know." She moaned loudly. If Joy thought she was seriously wounded, she'd feel empowered to move closer. "Why did you shoot me?"

Joy laughed. "Don't play dumb. You said enough to let me know you are dangerous. I could leave you here to die a slow painful death. Or I could put you out of your misery if you tell me where you put Steve's note-book. Your call. It's too bad you were clever enough to figure this out. But then again, that's why I liked you."

Bernie raised herself a fraction of an inch, followed the voice, and saw a dark figure too far away to risk a shot. She had to bring Joy closer. "I knew that's what you wanted, so I hid it." She faked a cough and lowered her voice. "Put your gun down and we'll make a deal, the notebook and you let me live. I forget everything and Maya takes the rap."

"Did you recognize my car on the surveillance tape? Is that how you figured out I followed Steve?"

Bernie made an unintelligible mumbling sound.

"I can't hear you."

She coughed again and spoke slightly louder, adding hesitation to her words. "You want . . . notebook?"

The coyotes resumed their high-pitched symphony, closer now. The animals seldom attacked people, but Joy's bleeding might attract them. Bernie used their music to muffle the sound of her movement. She crept behind a rock and some low junipers, then tossed a stone in the opposite direction, close to where she'd been hiding. Barely risking a breath, she stayed as still as náshdóí, a bobcat, with its prey in sight.

The air smelled of sage, dust, and the end of summer as she listened and waited.

"Bernie?"

Her muscles stiffened in the cold. She willed the woman to come closer. Finally, she heard the crunch of hesitant steps.

The clouds drifted to hide the moon and Bernie rose quietly, just enough to see over the sagebrush. The woman with the rifle stood out clearly in her light jacket, facing where the rock had made a noise.

Bernie stood and anchored herself, her weapon pointing at the woman's torso.

"Joy. It's over."

As Joy turned to aim the rifle. Bernie lined up the night sights and fired twice. Joy staggered backward, her own shot going wild, and collapsed into the dirt. In the brief moments of moonlight before the cloud curtain closed again, Bernie saw the start of a dark blossom of blood against the white of the jacket.

The coyotes once again grew silent.

26

B ernie sprinted to the fallen woman and squatted next to her.

"Joy?"

She grunted, either in response to her name or as a reaction to the situation.

Bernie looked at the dark stain on the woman's coat and the blood on her pant leg that had dripped onto her shoe. Bernie saw the little circles that formed a pattern on the sole. She took the handcuffs from her belt and reached for Joy's wrists as gently as she could. Even with that, Joy groaned in pain. The shoulder wound bled profusely, but the bullet to the thigh also needed attention before she could get Joy to her unit and begin the drive to the hospital.

"If you stay still, the bleeding will slow down. I'll be right back."

Joy spit out an obscenity.

Bernie picked up Joy's rifle, which had landed close to where she lay. She quickly unloaded it and took it with her as she ran to her unit. She knew that the Socorro and Alamo police stations were out of radio-contact distance.

She put what she needed from the first aid kit into her backpack along with a bottle of water. As she placed Joy's rifle in the trunk, Bernie noticed that it had plain iron sights compared to the more useful tritium night sights on her own gun. If she hadn't had the better weapon and firearms training in low-light conditions, Bernie thought, she could have been the person lying wounded.

She raced back to tend to Joy, thinking of the irony in rushing to save a woman who would have gladly killed her.

Joy had attempted to drag herself away, but only managed to go a few yards. Bernie noticed the blood trail in the dirt, but didn't waste time scolding.

"I'm going to work on your shoulder first, then your leg, and then we'll get to my unit." She slipped on the gloves as she spoke. "I'll have to press hard to try to stop the bleeding. It will hurt."

Joy glared.

Bernie used all the gauze from the first aid kit. Her hands felt cold in contrast to the woman's warm chest. As she increased the pressure, she added a silent prayer for herself and Joy.

The woman moaned loudly and tried to pull away from the pain.

Bernie kept pushing to pack the wound. "Stop moving. Do you want to die?"

"I wanted you to. You should have."

Bernie's flare of anger let her press harder.

Joy groaned out an obscenity. "None of this would have gone wrong except for crazy Maya. You wouldn't be here if she hadn't lied, would you?"

"Don't blame Maya. This is all on you."

"Stop. You're hurting me. Don't push so hard. Leave me alone."

Bernie reduced the pressure and felt the bleeding increase. She knew that once the adrenaline that coursed through her own veins began to ebb, a Grand Canyon of bone-numbing fatigue lay on the other side. She had to act now.

"You heard Ma'ii singing out there. That coyote is a famous trickster. He wants you to think you can rest here, that things will be OK. They won't be. You'll go into shock and die. He wants to feast on your body."

As if on cue, the coyotes began yipping again.

"I could leave you to bleed to death and to feed them. Or you can help save your own life."

"So I can die here, under the night sky I love, or I die in prison. What would you pick? We both know the answer to that."

Bernie looked at the panorama of shimmering stars, planets, and unseen mysteries, all in dramatic motion her eyes couldn't detect. The moon added its own light to the dark dome. She recognized the constellations of Thunderbird, Mountain Sheep, Big Snake, Bear, and Horse Who Carries the Sun and Moon. The starry animals gave her the gift of an idea.

"What about Fur Boy? Who will care for that precious little one if you die here? Think of him locked up in a filthy little cage in a public shelter. Or given an injection to stop his heart by someone he's never seen before. Do you want that for your beautiful sweet baby?"

She felt the woman take in a halting breath.

"Joy, you showed me Fur Boy's handsome picture. He's very special. You don't want him locked up in some awful place. It would break his heart. He would probably starve to death, terrified and alone, before he got the drug to kill him."

They sat in silence, and she wondered if Joy was thinking about the option she hadn't mentioned: Fur

Boy's future when she went to prison. Bernie felt the sharp cold moving from the ground through the material of her pants, into her skin and her bones. She wondered if the other woman noticed it.

Joy broke the silence. "OK. Help me."

Bernie applied stronger pressure until the blood flow from the shoulder wound slowed to a seep. She saw fresh blood on Joy's jeans at the thigh from her first gunshot. She pulled the tourniquet strap from her backpack. "I'm going to use this on your injured leg. It will hurt, too."

Joy didn't resist this time and didn't make a sound when Bernie applied the tourniquet.

Bernie helped her to sitting.

Joy winced. "Give me a minute."

"No, we have to go while you can still walk." Bernie stood and moved to Joy's left, undamaged shoulder. With her help, Joy pushed up to wobbly standing.

"I need to call my sister about Fur Boy in case I don't make it."

"We'll call her, but you're tough, remember? You'll survive this."

"I am tough." Joy stood a bit straighter. "That's what Steve used to say."

After a few solid steps, Joy began to lean on her more heavily. The blood loss, along with pain from her leg wound and the shattered shoulder were taking their toll.

"By the way, just to make it official, you're under arrest." Bernie recited the Miranda rights from memory.

"You'll never prove I killed Jones. And I was obviously impaired and under duress just now when I waived my rights." Joy took a breath and then another. "You said I made a mistake. What was it?"

"You shot Jones in the left side of the head."

"That was no mistake. He was left-handed. I put the gun in that hand. I knew what I was doing."

"But you forgot to close the window. Jones wouldn't have opened it unless he was talking to someone outside. That someone was you."

Joy uttered an obscenity. "You'll never substantiate that."

"Save your energy for walking." Bernie felt her lips rise to a half smile. It was hard to imagine another situation where she would tell a person who had confessed to murder—and tried to kill her—to be quiet.

She focused on ordering the muscles in her quads and back to keep working, bribing them to support more of Joy's weight with the promise of warmth and rest when they reached her unit. She gave herself credit for staying in shape as her legs stuck to the job without much complaining. Bernie wondered if the alluring smell of Joy's fresh blood had emboldened the coyotes to follow. And, she wondered, when Joy couldn't take another step, would she have enough strength to carry her the rest of the way?

Bernie stopped, adjusting the woman's position to make the walking easier.

"Where's my car?" Joy's voice sounded weaker.

"We're not there yet."

"I need to lie down."

"Not now. We have to keep moving. Think of Fur Boy."

They weren't close enough to see the vehicles, but Bernie's eye caught a ribbon of light ahead in the distance. She watched it bounce along for a few moments and then heard a faint rumbling. The noise grew subtly louder and the light came closer.

"Did you ask someone to join us out here?"

"No."

She kept Joy moving, step by slow step, thinking about the approaching vehicle and wondering if Joy was lying. Who would be out this time of night? This wasn't the spot or the time for random travelers.

Most law-abiding souls didn't drive to the boondocks in the dark. She remembered the Lieutenant's mantra: there were no coincidences.

Instead of continuing on the main road, the vehicle slowed as it approached the turnoff she and Joy had taken. It took that route and stopped where they had parked. Bernie's unease grew. This visit was no accident.

They made their way forward, Bernie supporting most of Joy's weight. The vehicle lights went off; now all she heard was the engine noise. The women moved closer until Bernie could see Joy's car and, beyond it, the new vehicle that had just arrived. She helped Joy slip to the ground as gently as possible and drew her gun. Then she shouted. "Police. Step out so I can see you. Now."

No answer. The motor was running. Whoever sat inside might have the heater turned up, making a racket, or music blaring through headphones. She moved a few cautious steps closer and shone her flashlight at the van. She shouted as loudly as she could.

"Police. Out of the vehicle. Now."

The overhead light snapped on as the door opened. Only one person in the front seat. From her distance, it looked like a man.

"Don't shoot."

"Out. Now. With your hands up." The strength of her voice surprised her.

"Officer Manuelito? Is that you there in the dark? It's Ralph Apacheito, Raul's daddy, remember? It takes me a while to get into the wheelchair."

She recognized the voice and lowered her gun.

"Ralph. Stay put. What are you doing out here?"

"I saw you come by earlier, but I never saw you or the car you were following drive out. It didn't sit right. I have trouble sleeping anyway, so I figured I'd come out here and see if you'd broken down. Is everything OK?"

"No. The person with me is badly hurt. I need to get her to the hospital."

"I could drive you, but there's no back seat."

"Get home as quick as you can. Call 911 and tell them a police officer is bringing in a gunshot victim who has lost a lot of blood. Let them know I'm heading out from this location and to send an ambulance to meet me."

"Shot? Are you serious? Are you—"

Bernie spoke over him. "I'm fine. Tell the dispatcher to contact Detective Tara Williams and have her meet us at the hospital. Have you got all that?"

"Tara Williams. An ambulance."

"Go. Make the call."

"OK. Good luck."

The conversation energized her. She lifted Joy from the ground more easily and partly carried, partly dragged her to her police unit as she watched Apacheito drive off. She leaned Joy against the car before she noticed that both rear tires were flat. She shrugged off her anger.

"Joy, we're taking your car."

"No. I'm bloody."

"You should have thought of that before you slashed my tires. Is your car locked?"

Joy hesitated. "Probably. I lock it out of habit."

"Where's the key?"

"In my right front pants pocket."

Bernie reached in for the key, noticing that Joy's skin felt icy even to her cold hand.

"I can't get it."

"You can open the door as long as I'm close to you with the key."

She maneuvered the woman into the rear seat, noticing that Joy had stopped resisting. She remembered the blanket in the back of the SUV and the way Joy had opened the door with a move of her leg.

She grabbed two bottles of water and the blanket, which she used with the seat belt to stabilize the shoulder wound. Bernie then climbed in behind the steering wheel. She couldn't reach the gas pedal or the brake.

"Joy?" Using the mirror, she realized the woman's chin had fallen toward her chest. Bernie spoke louder. "Joy, wake up. I have to move the seat forward."

The woman remained unresponsive.

"Joy. Listen." She was yelling now. "Tell me how to adjust the seat. Remember Fur Boy."

She saw Joy open her eyes and wave a hand toward the bottom screen. "Tap it."

Bernie did, and the screen lit up. She found an icon that looked like a car seat, pressed it and the arrow that pointed toward the windshield. The seat moved forward. She touched a green button and the engine started to purr. She turned on the headlights and shifted into drive. The heat came on automatically.

She opened the other water bottle and headed away from her disabled unit, finding the route by instinct. The warmth of the car felt good. Bernie liked its smooth power. Her old Tercel would be jealous. The jostling stirred Joy to alertness. "What else gave me away?"

"Your shoes. They left tracks at the murder site."

"So?"

"I noticed them when I checked your leg wound. I saw that same round shoe prints outside Jones's car. I knew they weren't Maya's. So tell me, how did you kill Jones without a struggle?"

"What do you think?"

"I figure you knew about the date with Maya and you assumed Maya would reject him. You contacted Steve at the restaurant, suggested the meet-up on that dark road after he took her home, and sent him some follow-up texts. Maybe even told him how much you missed him. You were brilliant to do that."

"I was."

"How did you persuade Jones to let you shoot him?"

"When he rolled down the window so we could talk, I brought up the Giovanni stuff first, and how much trouble that man caused. I said I was worried that he'd kill himself because his career was over and Maya had rejected him. I explained that I was there as a concerned friend. It was cool so I put on my gloves. I asked him to give me the gun he had in the car so I could keep it safe until he felt better. After that I told him to close his eyes and relax. Bang."

Bernie preserved every word in her memory. When they reached the junction she saw the flashing lights of the ambulance. The attendants had expected a police car, not the ivory SUV, but they reacted appropriately at the sight of her uniform. She followed them to the hospital in Joy's plush mobile.

After Joy was taken care of, she found a seat in the emergency room waiting area and closed her eyes. Just for a minute.

She startled awake when she felt a hand on her arm and saw Williams, worry in her face. "What happened? You don't look so good."

"Long story, but the blood isn't mine. Joy Peterson is in surgery. They told me her chances for survival are good. I arrested her for the murder of Steve Jones. And I took a picture of the soles of her shoes. They've got little circles. They'll match your crime scene photos."

Tara smiled. "I thought you were just going stargazing."

"We did some of that before she took a shot at me."

"I didn't see your unit outside."

"No." Bernie smiled. "I'm driving that pearly white Range Rover. It's a sweet ride except for the blood in the back seat."

They cleared up the details in the morning, including getting Bernie's tires replaced. Williams quickly arranged an exit interview with Maya, and while they waited for her to arrive, Bernie phoned Giovanni Bellinger. She wanted to call from the station so he'd see the ID and pick up. She told him what had happened.

"Officer, I wasn't entirely truthful when we spoke earlier. When you informed me of Dr. Jones's death, I feared for my own life."

"Why was that?"

"Dr. Peterson had threatened me. She strongly suggested that I withdraw from the project so my own research would not be suspect. She said Jones was talking about suicide because of the mistakes he'd made. She told me I should be careful not to make those same errors. I began recording the conversation when we started to argue about the quality of her research compared to the work Jones and I did. She grew more and more belligerent and defensive. She told me I should withdraw from the project or watch my back."

"I'd like that recording."

"It's yours. I have the emails you talked about, too."

"Would you send all of this to Detective Tara Williams? She will be following up with you."

"I'm glad to know that woman is in custody. She has a bright mind but a ruthless heart."

"One more question, sir. Did you make an anonymous call to Detective Williams?"

"I did. I've never done that in my life but I feared for Dr. Jones's well-being. I mentioned my concerns to him, but he laughed at me. Dr. Peterson's rage made me think she could be dangerous. I'm glad you have arrested her. The man I knew was not one to take his own life."

She typed up her notes on the conversation. Then, Bernie treated herself to a celebratory Coke and headed to the interrogation room for a final session with Maya Kelsey.

Williams opened by informing Maya that she was to be released and that someone else had confessed to the crime.

"Leon? No. Don't believe him. That's garbage. He didn't do it."

"You're right. Dr. Joy Peterson has been arrested for the murder of Steve Jones."

"Who? What?"

Williams turned to Bernie. "You want to explain it?"

"Joy Peterson worked with Steve Jones. She killed him because he threatened to expose her for stealing his research."

"Is this some sort of trick?"

"No."

Maya smiled and then, in the next moment, Bernie saw the tears.

Williams took charge. "So tell us what happened and why you wasted our time."

"Oh, gosh. Where to start?"

"Start the evening he was killed."

"Well, after Steve wouldn't let me buy my own dinner, I went outside to calm down, and Leon texted and asked me what happened. I told him it was none of his business. He offered me a ride home. I told him to quit spying on me. He said it made him mad to see me so upset and that he would protect me, no matter what I thought." She swallowed. "I watched his truck following us when Steve took me home."

"How did you find out Jones was dead?"

Bernie knew the answer, but she wondered what Maya would say.

"Ralph Apacheito asked if I could come and talk to Raul because he'd seen a dead guy and asked if I knew someone for a ceremony. I drove over and when I saw the Jaguar parked on the shoulder, I realized the dead guy was Steve." Maya glanced at Bernie and then at Williams. "I knew my brother was angry and I made an assumption. Leon really didn't do it?"

Bernie nodded. "That's right. Can you tell us anything else about the night Jones died?"

"Someone called while we were at the restaurant. Steve said it was a person from work and I went to the ladies' room while they talked. When I got back, he told me that he'd been dating a colleague, but he'd broken it off. She wanted to see him but he told her no, he was on a date with me at the brewpub."

And, Bernie thought, Jones had given Joy what she needed to ambush him.

"Maya, my husband knows a lot of singers. I'm sure he'd be glad to find someone to help with Raul's ceremony."

"Ahéhee'. That's very kind."

Williams looked baffled.

"It's a gathering of family and friends to support a person, to ask for healing. That's how we traditionally deal with a trauma like this." She turned to Maya. "I have a couple more questions."

Williams stood. "Hold on. I have some, too, and also some questions for Leon. I'd like him to join us. He's waiting outside."

When she left, Maya leaned in toward Bernie. "I am embarrassed that I gave you so much trouble. You knew I was lying. I wish I could undo all this."

Before Bernie could respond, the door opened and Leon entered. He went to his sister and embraced her.

Maya started to cry. "I'm sorry for all the worry I caused you."

"Why did you lie?"

"I thought *you* shot Steve, and after all you did for us, I wanted to do something good for you. You helped Junior all those years I was drinking. You were his good, caring 'shidá'í, his little father."

"You don't owe me anything. I love that boy."

Maya sat down. "I couldn't stand the thought of you in prison. And I knew that Junior would rely on you more than ever with Steve gone."

"Sister, why didn't you ask me if I'd shot him? We could have avoided all this." He sat next to Maya.

"I never liked Jones, but I wouldn't kill my son's father."

Williams straightened in her chair across from him. "So, why did you follow Maya and Jones from the restaurant?"

"I wanted to make sure she got home OK. When I heard Jones was dead, I couldn't believe it. I figured it must have been suicide." He looked at Bernie. "And then, when I learned that my sister had confessed, I thought maybe they'd had an argument and, well, maybe she'd had to defend herself."

"Why did you write the fake suicide letter?"

Leon pursed his lips and exhaled. "Even though I couldn't stand him, I knew Jones loved Junior. I thought the letter might help our son deal with the loss."

"And help your sister get out of jail." Williams phrased it as a statement, not a question.

"That's right."

Williams stood. "Maya, if it hadn't been for Bernie, I would have taken you at your word and ended the investigation. You need to thank her for not giving up on the case."

"No." Bernie swallowed and sat a bit straighter. "I just did my job. And speaking of that, Detective Williams, if you can finish up here, I have an important call to make."

When Sandra—and not Mrs. Slim—answered the phone at the station Bernie smiled. She heard fresh energy in Sandra's voice.

"Hello there. I'm glad you're back at work. Sounds like you're having a good day."

"I'm happy to be here. I missed this crazy place."

"Is everything OK?"

"No, but it's better. I can't talk about it now. I bet you want the sergeant."

"That's right. But first just tell me—"

"I'll transfer you."

As she waited, Bernie realized Sandra was entitled to her privacy. Next time they were alone, she'd ask if everything was as it should be and see if her friend wanted to share whatever problem she'd faced. When Chee came on the line, Bernie offered an update on the case, including a recap of last night's adventure.

"No wonder you sound tired, Sweetheart. I have a million questions but the most important one is when can you come home?"

"As soon as my tires get replaced. I'll call you from the road."

"Big news here. The captain's retirement is on hold."

"Good. What's the status of the two cases I worked before the Maya stuff? That Shorty warrant still bothers me."

"Well, believe it or not, Mr. Shorty came here and asked for Officer Bernie. Turned himself in."

"I'm glad. And Bee?"

"Agent Johnson told me they'd traced the evidence in the house to sex traffickers as well as a drug operation. They've got some strong leads on the people who hurt her."

"What about the baby?"

"Bee told the truth when she said she wasn't the mother. The baby's father is a known drug dealer. He's already in custody, but that can't undo what he did." She heard sadness and the anger in his voice.

"That helpless baby deserved better."

"You've been thinking about that baby as much as I have."

The phone was silent, and when he spoke again, she heard the emotion behind his words. "I think about babies a lot, ever since Officer Bigman told me he and his wife were expecting. I'd like a baby someday. Someday with you."

Williams gave her a ride to pick up her unit at the garage.

"I really appreciate your help. It was good working with you."

"You, too. I'm glad I could fill in while Rockfeld was out. Is Honey any better?"

"No. She finally died yesterday."

Bernie noticed Williams's lack of sympathy. "Tell Rockfeld I'm sorry."

"I will."

"When's the funeral?"

"A funeral? You're funny. He'll be out the rest of the day. He had to a borrow a bulldozer to bury her."

"You're kidding!" The words flew out before she could stop them.

"Bob's got plenty of room on the ranch, and she loved it there. They'd been together since high school. Honey had been declining all summer. Most of her teeth were gone."

"Wow. What happened?"

"Just old age."

"How old was she?"

"Almost thirty."

"*What?*"

"I know. The vet said she'd had a great healthy life."

"The vet? I thought Honey was his wife."

"Wife?" Tara laughed. "No. His palomino."

Bernie couldn't recall a day when she'd been happier to head for home. She stopped for gas in Grants, got a green chile cheeseburger at Blake's Lotaburger, and checked her messages.

Agent Johnson had texted: She asked me to make sure you got this. I'll send you the hard copy.

She had attached a photograph of a letter printed on lined paper.

> *Officer Bernie, back in that house you asked about the baby. I lied. I knew it was there. I heard it crying and I couldn't go to help. I was glad and sad when the crying stopped. You were kind to me when I didn't deserve it. I'm sorry I spit on you.*

It was signed Gabriela Beatrice Hernandez.

27

Leaphorn and Louisa left Window Rock long before sunrise for the three-hour drive to the Sunport. They watched the cool morning light reveal the rocky blue bulk of the Sandia Mountains as they drew closer to Albuquerque. It was rare that Louisa had nothing to say, especially when he drove her car, but she sat quietly staring out the window.

Leaphorn mentioned this.

"I'm anxious about getting to the airport on time, finding a parking spot, waiting for the little van, checking the luggage, going through security. So many things can go wrong, and we could miss the flight. I relax when I'm at the gate." She squeezed his hand. "I couldn't sleep last night. I kept going over my talk, wondering if it's what the people at the conference want to hear. How about you?"

"Not berry well." Anticipatory anxiety, that's what the experts called it. "Restless . . ." He saw no reason to mention the nightmare.

"Maybe we'll nap on the plane."

He had never fallen asleep on a plane in his life. If the airplane crashed, he wanted to see it coming. He didn't struggle to stay awake; anxiety served as a stimulant.

He took I-25 south to the airport and parked where the woman at the entrance gate directed. Louisa glanced at her watch, but the van to the terminal arrived even before Leaphorn could remove their suitcases. They shared the shuttle with a young woman and two men in cowboy boots, all flying different airlines. Louisa grew more nervous; their stop came last.

"Even if we hab to wait, we still hab plenty time." He tried to sound reassuring. Their flight wouldn't start boarding for ninety minutes. But as he said it he knew facts did nothing to soothe rampant airport panic.

They made it through TSA screening and walked to the gate listed on their boarding passes. He noticed that Louisa had begun to relax and that his palms had started to sweat.

"We made it. Thank goodness that's over and we still have an hour before the plane boards. What about breakfast?"

He took a deep breath and exhaled through his mouth. "I'll bring ya somethin'."

"Great."

She found two seats together with a view of the runway and smiled at him for the first time that morning. "I'd like a large latte with skim milk. And something to eat. Surprise me."

He walked down the corridor and looked at the monitor. Fifty-five minutes until boarding began. Through the window he caught a glimpse of the plane glistening in the sun. The idea of eating anything made his stomach lurch.

The familiar aroma led him to the coffee stand. He waited to order, silently grumbling that for the price of Louisa's special coffee he could have purchased a pound at Bashas'. Usually he had consumed two cups by this time of the morning, but coffee worsened his anxiety. His phone buzzed just as he reached the counter, and he ignored it.

He rejoined Louisa with the latte, a chocolate croissant, and a napkin.

"Sinful." She grinned at him. "Where's yours?"

"Na hungry."

She patted the seat next to her.

"In a mint."

He walked from the last A gate to the last B gate twice, keeping an eye on the time. He sat next to Louisa just as the announcement came that boarding for their flight would soon begin. He felt his throat constrict. No reason to be afraid. More people die in traffic accidents than in plane crashes.

She patted his hand. "You sure are quiet."

He nodded. "I doan like flying."

"I know. I love you for doing this."

The attendant called their group, and he followed Louisa into the tunnel that led to the plane, his heart pounding. Deep breath, he told himself. You can do this.

When he stepped from the boarding tunnel onto the tighter space of the plane itself, he felt the blood pulsing in his jaw and a surge of queasiness. The flight attendant said hello and he managed a nod. Louisa paused before an empty row about three-fourths of the way back. "Here we are. You've got the window."

"Go 'head."

He sat in the middle seat and closed his eyes. Breathing calm in, he told himself. Breathing peace out.

He'd noticed that the plane had three attendants, each trained to stop bleeding, deal with a heart attack, or handle childbirth. Somewhere on the flight might be an air marshal, assigned at random after the 9/11 tragedy. Breathing calm in, he told himself. Breathing peace out.

Someone stopped at the empty seat next to him. He opened his eyes to see a male flight attendant and a boy with curly brown hair and a little green backpack.

"This is your place, buddy."

"You can't sit with me?" Leaphorn heard the quiver in the child's voice.

"No. The people working on this plane will help if you need anything. Slip off your pack, and I'll put it under the seat in front of you."

The child started to remove the pack, then hesitated. "How far is it?"

"About three hours."

The attendant watched as the boy stowed the pack under the seat. "Joel, when the plane lands, do you know what to do?"

He nodded.

"Can you tell me?"

"Stay here until another flight attendant comes to get me and asks if my name is Joel Delisa." The tremor in the voice made the words hard to understand.

"You got it. Enjoy the flight."

The child sat silently, as still as death, his hands glued to his lap.

The announcement that the door to the outside world had closed came over the loudspeaker. They were captives now. No, Leaphorn told himself, they were resting safely in the hands of skilled professionals.

He noticed sweat glistening at the boy's temples, and he felt sweaty, too. He reached overhead and adjusted the vent to release more cool air.

The voice instructed them to watch the safety video. Louisa kept reading, but he complied and Joel focused on it intently, too. When the program urged passengers to read the crucial information on the card in the seatback pocket, the boy reached for it, but his arms were too short. Leaphorn handed it to him.

"Thank you. Could, ah . . . could I ask you a favor?"

"Go ahead."

"If the oxygen mask comes down, will you help me put it on?"

He nodded.

"And that yellow thing that you have to put on and blow into?"

"Da life vest. Sure."

"Do you think that will happen?"

"No." But he felt his chest tighten.

"But it could. Otherwise they wouldn't tell us about it."

"Right. Remember, da more knowledge ya hab, da better prepared ya are ta stay safe."

The boy pressed the information card tightly against his chest as the plane began to move.

Leaphorn felt the same bone-chilling dread. The plane lurched as it rolled and the boy cringed. He saw the boy squeeze the arm rest between them.

"I get nervous, too, even though I used ta be a policeman."

"Really?"

"Yes."

"Did you ever get shot?"

"Yes." Leaphorn glanced at the arid landscape. The plane came to a halt.

"Why did we stop? Is something wrong?"

"Da pilot has to make sure dat all da planes are out of da way. Den we can go again. Doan worry."

The child pushed himself back farther in the seat. "Then everything shakes and there's pressure and the noise gets loud. I—"

A male voice flooded the cabin. "A slight delay, folks. We're fifth in line for takeoff."

Breathe in calm, Leaphorn told himself. Breathe out peace.

"Were you really a policeman?"

"Yes. Now, I'm a detective. Joe Leaphorn. Whad's your name?"

"Joel. People call me Joe sometimes, too. They get my name wrong."

He extended a hand to the boy as if he were a grown-up. Joel shook and, instead of releasing, grasped it tightly.

"I never talked to a policeman before. The next part is what really makes me scared."

"Me, too."

"I didn't think policemen got scared."

"Part of our training is ta learn about dings dat might be scary or dangerous and how ta deal with dem."

"Why?"

"In case we have a chance to hep somebody."

The plane began to roll, then shake as it picked up speed. It tilted slightly as it rose from the runway. Leaphorn's ears sensed the change in pressure as the plane headed skyward.

He and Joel looked out the window as the plane climbed. The shaking stopped and the noise quieted. The roads and houses below them gradually grew smaller.

"What if the plane catches on fire or runs out of gas or crashes into another plane or something else bad happens?"

"Doan worry. Da pilot and attendants will tell us whad da do. I'll help you if you need id. We're here togeder. We will be fine."

"If something happens, will my parents know where to find me?"

He noticed the boy's lower lip trembling. "Absolutely. I would stay wid you until dey came."

They held hands until the plane reached cruising altitude and a flight attendant came by with the drink cart and cookies. Then he fell asleep with crumbs on his chin.

To his left, Louisa slept, too, and beyond her was the vast sky at thirty-two thousand feet. The higher clouds were smears of crystal on the flat blue background. Below them, the stratocumulus reminded him of a castle made from cotton balls.

Beauty all around him.

For some reason, he remembered the missed phone call and took the phone—which he had placed on airplane mode earlier—from his pocket. He clicked to hear the recorded message.

"My goodness, Lieutenant Joe Leaphorn, this is the woman you knew as Theodora Adams." She laughed, and he remembered how that sound had charmed the priest. "It pleased me so to get your email. I'm sorry my name change caused you distress. I married another person whose life you saved that day, Thomas Symons. Dear Tom died last year. One of his final wishes was that I reach out to thank you. I'd love to do so in person and to talk to you about how our foundation could help women and girls on the Navajo Nation. Please call or email me at your convenience."

Leaphorn saved the message. When they got to the hotel in Washington, he would call her back. He would open himself to the possibility that a vain, manipulative, unprincipled female had grown into a good woman. Perhaps she, too, now walked in beauty.

He closed his eyes and let the sounds of ninety-five tons of people, luggage, glass, aluminum, and wiring moving through the atmosphere lull him to sleep.

28

J oe Leaphorn took a freshly grilled hamburger patty from the plate, gently set it on a warm toasted bun. Well equipped with his favorite lunch, he continued the story. He spoke in Navajo, having reassured Louisa that she had already heard what he had to say. Chee and Bernie sat across from their two friends and kept to English for Louisa's sake. The cottonwood leaves rustled in the light breeze adding their notes to the smooth melody of Sá bito', the San Juan River.

"Well, my friend here"—he moved his chin in Louisa's direction—"she persuaded me to meet with the woman who said I had saved her life. She had grown to be a good person. I liked her."

"Her father, a doctor, died about a year after the kidnapping incident. She went back to school, got a nursing degree to honor his memory, and eventually became a hospital manager." Leaphorn added mustard to his burger.

"She looked older, of course, but I would have recognized those blue eyes anywhere."

Bernie selected a hamburger for herself. "Lieutenant, why did she call to thank you after so many years?"

"I think I came to mind because of her foundation. She'd like to expand it to help with missing indigenous women. We discussed that. She's planning a trip out here and we'll keep talking."

"Will her husband join her?" Chee asked the question. "You saved his life, too."

Leaphorn shook his head. "Mr. Symons died last year. That's another reason she's coming. He asked her to go back to the cave where they met and say a prayer for him. I told her I'd let her know if that was possible. I was hoping you could guide her."

Chee looked surprised. "I've never been to that cave. Couldn't you do it?"

Leaphorn shook his head. "Have you heard of the place?"

"Yes. My hataÃi friends have stories."

Leaphorn placed a large envelope he'd brought with him on the table near Chee's plate. "This is the important matter I wanted to talk to you about. I marked the map where the cave could be, based on my memory. Go before the lady comes to make sure you can find it and that it will be appropriate to take her to that place. There could still be something sacred, something important to our people."

"Something holy. That's what I've been told."

Leaphorn nodded ever so slightly.

Chee put his hand on the envelope. "Now that Largo's back, Bernie encouraged me to take some time off, quietly, by myself. This would be the perfect place to do that."

Leaphorn turned to Bernie. "What about your future?"

"When I asked for advice, my husband told me to follow my heart, to do what I thought best. I wanted him to make it easier, maybe so I'd have someone to blame if I made the wrong choice."

She took a breath. "The stargazer case showed me a lot about love and love gone wrong. As I drove home after that, I realized that he meant it, really meant it, when he said he'd love me no matter what. I know he'd like to start a family. I want to, too, but not yet."

She smiled. "I applied to become a criminal investigator, a detective. We'll see what comes next."

Author's Note

As a fiction writer, I enjoy inventing characters and situations, but I didn't have to invent the settings for *Stargazer*, including the Alamo community and the VLA.

The VLA, officially known as the Karl G. Jansky Very Large Array, is an actual, real-life radio astronomy observatory located in central New Mexico on the beautiful, mountain-rimmed Plains of San Agustin. The facility sits between the little towns of Magdalena and Datil, a two-hour drive from Albuquerque and fifty miles west of Socorro.

Scientists use radio astronomy to research astronomical phenomena invisible to the optical telescopes with which most people are more familiar. One of the VLA's newest projects is listening for signals that could be communications from other life forms in our vast and complicated universe.

The VLA has twenty-seven dish antennas pointed to the heavens, each of which weighs 230 tons and is eighty-two feet across. The huge discs work as a single instrument, retrieving data not only from our own solar system but also from galaxies millions and billions of light-years away. The telescopes are mounted on rails and arranged in a Y shape, which the scientists adjust four times a year. The unique design offers three long arms of nine discs each. The rails allow the telescopes to move farther apart, so they can zoom in for more details, or closer together, to see a larger slice of the universe. A specially designed machine called a transporter picks up telescopes and hauls them one at a time farther down their track and then, when the time is right, brings them back. Over the course of a year, the VLA extends each of its arms from two-thirds of a mile to twenty-three miles long.

The array of saucers forms an intriguing site as they sit at a 7,030-foot elevation and observe radiation from our sun and the planets as well as stars, comets, distant galaxies, black holes, and more. Discoveries made here include the surprise of ice on the planet Mercury, which orbits closest to the sun; a new species of celestial object called a microquasar; phenomena that show early stages of planet formation; and the first observation and photographs of an Einstein ring, a gravitational lens around a black hole.

Before the pandemic, the VLA hosted free guided tours for the public on the first and third Saturday of each month. The tours last about fifty minutes and take visitors to behind-the-scenes areas at the observatory. Staff and volunteers eagerly answer questions. (Who knows what will happen to the tours in our post-COVID-19 world.)

The New Mexico outpost is part of the National Radio Astronomy Observatory, a facility of the National Science Foundation. Another major array of radio telescopes sits in the Atacama Desert of northern Chile. Here, the National Radio Astronomy Observatory, along with its international partners, worked to construct ALMA, the world's most complex astronomical telescope.

Unlike these scientists, the Navajo ancestors observed the vast night sky with their sharp eyes alone. Diné star stories are rich and wonderful. Authors Nancy C. Maryboy and David Begay do an outstanding job of explaining this cultural heritage in their book, *Sharing the Skies: Navajo Astronomy*. In addition to insights into the unique way in which Navajo people view the cosmos and their place within it, the book offers interesting comparisons to the stories of the stars that originated in ancient Greece.

In traditional Navajo families, young people would learn about So' Dine'e, the Star People or constellations, from the most knowledgeable elder through winter stories told in a hogan. They would probably hear about the eight main star groupings, beginning with the North Star (Náhookòs Bikò') and ending with the Milky Way (Łees'áán yílzhódí). Most Navajo constellations include a feather, which signifies its spiritual essence. The storyteller would use action, tone, pitch, and volume of voice to enhance and convey meanings and importance beyond the words themselves. The stories set the listeners inside a complex, holistic, and well-ordered universe where all parts interrelate and in which every piece also contains the entire universe. This crucial network of cosmic relationships exists in a state of constant change—paralleling the conclusion of modern astronomy!

But, as Maryboy and Begay write: "Unlike western astronomy, traditional Navajo astronomy is highly spiritual in accordance with a world view where everything is considered living and sacred. The entire universe is considered to be a living organism, a sacred organism existing in a non-static and constantly regenerating process."

I took some liberties with New Mexico geography and archaeology in this book, adding a road for a murder here, a star ceiling petroglyph there, and tightening up some distances. However, the Alamo and To'Hajiilee Navajo Reservations, the New Mexico Institute of Mining and Technology, and the historic towns of Datil, Socorro, and Magdalena, New Mexico, are all real. The landscape is more beautiful than I have attempted to describe. You don't have to take my word for it; come and see for yourself.

The women's shelter in Shiprock, New Mexico, is a composite with a made-up name. I would never reveal the location of an actual shelter because that could threaten the safety of the staff or the guests. I have tremendous admiration for those who do this difficult and important work.

Acknowledgments

First of all, sincere appreciation to the real Navajo Nation law enforcement staff, from officers on patrol to the detectives, supervisors, trainers, and support staff. The Navajo Nation Police operation consists of slightly more than two hundred sworn police officers and civilian support workers for the department responsible for the 27,413-square-mile reservation occupying portions of Arizona, Utah, and New Mexico—the largest land area retained by an indigenous tribe in the United States. (The Navajo and the Oglala Lakota are the only Indian nations with police forces of more than a hundred officers.) A lone officer often patrols seventy square miles of reservation land. I admire your courage and your dedication to keeping your constituents safe. You are the real-life inspiration behind these stories.

Writing a book is both a solitary exercise and a team project. For the solitary time, I am grateful to the helpers who made sure my husband was safe while I worked and he struggled through the thickets of vascular dementia. A shout-out to my husband's "girl friends," Pam Ulibarri, Maria Velasquez, Tanya Stephenson, and the other openhearted helpers. Dorothy Fitch became a midwife to this book, generously providing a quiet space for me to finish a draft of *Stargazer* as Don moved into hospice care at home. The hospice workers, including Angela Menendez and nurses Lindsey Hacker-McNew and Kati Schwartz, provided clear, kind insights when the view ahead grew tearstained. This book would not exist without the support of family and generosity of friends who stepped in when I needed to step away, take a deep breath, and quietly focus on my writing.

In terms of professional community and collaboration, any mistakes readers will notice rest on my shoulders. My colleagues did their best to steer me straight. I am grateful to Ann and Edward Bradley for the insights they offered into the life of an astronomer and an astronomer's spouse. Lieutenant Michele Williams, recently retired from the Santa Fe, New Mexico, police department, shared her advice and wisdom based on firsthand experience. Allison Colborne, library director at the New Mexico Museum of Indian Arts and Culture and Laboratory of Anthropology, provided me with wonderful maps and research material about the Alamo Navajo. I am deeply indebted to Nancy C. Maryboy and David Begay for their wonderful and interesting book about the Diné view of the stars, *Sharing the Skies: Navajo Astronomy*. Beautifully illustrated with original Navajo paintings and NASA photography, this cross-cultural look at astronomy would be a worthy addition to any reader's library. A tip of the hat to the folks at the Very Large Array for the tour and for answering my questions.

Insightful readers and volunteer editors Rebecca Carrier, Charmaine Coimbra, David and Gail Greenberg, Lucy Moore, and my agent Elizabeth Trupin-Pulli all generously shared comments and suggestions. I appreciate you more than I can say. Big thanks to my fellow writers in the Croak and Dagger chapter of Sisters in Crime and to David and Donna Morrell, Jean Schaumberg, and James McGrath-Morris for your encouragement.

My colleagues at HarperCollins Publishers are spectacular: Sarah Stein, my editor; Alicia Tan, her assistant; Nikki Baldauf, senior production editor; copy editor supreme, Mary Beth Constant; and Jarrod Taylor, who designs the beautiful covers. And a special shout-out to Rachel Elinsky and Tom Hopke Jr. for helping with promotion and public relations for this book and the others in the series.

Thank you to my friends on the Navajo Nation for their help and support and affection for these stories. I deeply appreciate the bookstores, historical societies, book clubs, writers' conferences, Rotary and Kiwanis groups, public libraries, and other venues that have offered me an opportunity to meet with readers and talk about my books and the writing process.

The mention of the Placitas (NM) Community Library and the character named Joel Delisa are both the results of the kindness of strangers. The real-life Dr. Joel Delisa made a donation to the New Mexico Children's Foundation and in exchange allowed me to use his name for a character. Dr. Delisa has been a longtime fan of Joe Leaphorn beginning with my dear dad's novels. Through his avatar, he gets to sit next to Joe in *Stargazer*. The Placitas Community Library has welcomed me as a speaker numerous times and hosted a photography exhibit for Don Strel, my husband. Our relationship began with the debut of *Tony Hillerman's Landscape* ten years ago. I deeply appreciate donor Catherine Harris for her generosity in support of the library's building fund and her request that I mention the library in this book.

And finally, thank you to my father, Tony Hillerman, for bringing Joe Leaphorn to life. March 11, 2020, marked the fiftieth anniversary of the publication of Dad's first mystery, *The Blessing Way*. That novel introduced a young Navajo officer to the reading public. I am enormously grateful to longtime fans of my father who overcame their skepticism and approached my continuation and reenvisioning of the Leaphorn and Chee series with open minds. You gave Bernadette Manuelito a thumbs-up. We both value your continued support more than I can say.

Glossary

A FEW NAVAJO WORDS

ahéhee': Thank you

atsáeelchii: Red-tailed hawk

bilagáana: A white person

chindii: Spirit of a dead person

Diné: Navajo people's word for themselves

Dinétah: Navajo homeland

Ghaaji': October, the month of the "Separation of Seasons" and in Diné culture the beginning of the New Year

hastiin: Term of respect for an elderly man

hatałii: A person who knows the sacred healing ceremonies, a "medicine man"

hogan: A traditional six-sided Navajo home used for ceremonies

hózhó: Loosely translated as peace, balance, beauty, and harmony

Hwéeldi: The time of sorrow or the Long Walk, a reference to the Navajos' forced removal from their traditional homelands and imprisonment at Bosque Redondo in southeastern New Mexico from 1863 to 1868

Ma'ii: Coyote, the mythical trickster and Holy Person whose descendants still sing to the moon

náshdóí: Bobcat

Sá bito': San Juan River

'shidá'í: Maternal uncle or "little father," a term that reflects the special kinship relation between a mother's brother and his nephews and nieces

shima: Mother

shimásání: Maternal grandmother; this can also mean a mother's mother's sister or a mother's father's sister (great-aunts), as well as other older female clan relatives

t'áá dzígaidi: In the middle of nowhere

To'Hajiilee: Navajo community, formerly known as Cañoncito, not adjoining the larger Navajo Nation, about thirty miles west of Albuquerque; the Navajo phrase roughly translates in English as "dipping water"

Tsé Bit'a'í: Ship Rock

Tsoodził: Mount Taylor

yá'át'ééh: Hello; "it is good"

STAR TERMS

Átsé Ets'ózí: The First Slender One, or Orion

Haniibaazii Alnii Nabiiska: Half-moon

Łees'áán yílzhódí: The Cake (baked in ash) That Is Dragged Along (leaving crumbs), or the Milky Way

Náhookòs Bi'áád: Female Revolving One, or Cassiopeia

Náhookòs Bi'kà': Male Revolving One, or the Big Dipper

Náhookòs Bikò': Central Fire, or Polaris, the North Star

So' Dine'e: Constellations, the Star People

Tł'éé'honaa'éí: October moon

Yadilhil: Dome of night sky

About the Author

ANNE HILLERMAN began her career as a journalist and writer of nonfiction books. The daughter of the *New York Times* bestselling author Tony Hillerman, she lives in Santa Fe, New Mexico. This is her sixth novel and the twenty-fourth in the Leaphorn, Chee & Manuelito series, begun by her late father.